STARFIGHTER DOWN

RELICS OF THE ANCIENTS BOOK 1

M.G. HERRON

NEXT IN THE SERIES

You're reading: ***Starfighter Down***
Up next: ***Hidden Relics***
Then: ***Rogue Swarm***

ONE

Captain Elya Nevers exhaled, shook out the bone-deep ache in his hands, and tilted his Sabre into the canyon.

Sheer rock walls rushed by as he plunged into shadow. He inhaled, gripped the stick in a sweaty palm and pulled back to level the starfighter, guiding it smoothly forward, testing its pitch and roll as he settled in. He was aware of the weight of his helmet, the sound of his breath, the way the spinal port at the base of his skull rubbed against the stimchem injector. By now he'd flown dozens of missions on as many worlds and though the landscapes blurred together sometimes, he never got bored of being in the cockpit—as if it were possible for him to grow tired of being a starfighter pilot in the Solaran Defense Forces. How could he? He was living his boyhood dream.

A Kryl drone tore around the corner ahead and beamed toward him, its wing-tip cannons held open on full auto. Elya banked hard right, dodging the projectiles and passing the ship with less than a meter to spare between his canopy and unforgiving stone. As he came around to give chase, his wing scraped a scree-covered ledge along the canyon wall.

Although the Sabre's forcefield saved him from serious damage, the impact caused a rockslide, forcing him to dodge falling boulders and fly with reduced visibility as he followed the drone's blurred form.

He gained on it until the teardrop-shaped ship was only a few hundred meters in front of him. Engines screamed as two more bogeys dropped in on his six. Elya opened his throttles and blasted forward, separating himself from his pursuers only to see the one ahead had dropped a floating mine in his path at a chokepoint where the canyon walls tapered inward. He hauled back on the stick, narrowly dodging the explosive. The control column shook so hard his fingers went numb. Elya gritted his teeth and held tight.

His Sabre shot out of the canyon at a near vertical trajectory. He pointed the ship at the deep orange sun so that the two enemy ships still dogging him would have a difficult time spotting him in the glare. The drones, being both organism and ship in one, had faster reaction times than Solaran pilots, but even their ability to see was affected by the light of a star.

A blast to his left wing rocked the Sabre and took out an engine. "Lucky shot," he muttered. Reaching for a switch, Elya cut the engine's power, swung back around and mashed his trigger, blowing one drone into a cloud of carapace and guts. He banked and rolled, keeping his flight erratic to prevent any heat-seeking torpedoes from getting a lock on him. His detection and ranging systems, a combination of radar and lidar, bleeped loudly as he maneuvered, helping him out of danger.

He adjusted his course to lead him back down into the canyon. A yellow flash in his peripheral vision drew his awareness into the cockpit. For a split second, he was hyper-aware of the harness strapped tight around his chest, the array of digital and haptic controls curving around him.

With an effort of will, he set aside the distraction and returned to the hunt, banking, twisting and turning at top speed.

One of the two remaining drones dropped into view ahead of him. His weapons system chimed for lock and Elya shot its left wing off, grinning as the drone bounced off the wall and exploded.

"That leaves one."

Another alert pinged in at the top right of his visor. With an irritated growl and a flick of his eyes, he swiped it away, annoyed he had forgotten to mute notifications.

He led the final enemy, who had dropped in behind him, on a meandering chase through the canyon, bringing his starfighter so low at one point the Sabre's belly skimmed the surface of a river cutting through the canyon floor.

Then he climbed high and fast, intending to loop back over the top of the drone and force it into the rocks. He crested the ridge, pulling up, feeling a heaviness on his chest and shoulders. Stim chemicals flooded into his spinal port, making him momentarily more resistant to the G-forces, and decreasing his reaction time. An orangish-red light flashed, then went blue, distracting him again and causing him to miss the moment.

Instead of a successful kill, Elya ended up a smudge of grease against the canyon wall.

The sim went dark. Red letters appeared superimposed over the front window: *Mission Failed*.

"Damn it!" Elya snatched his helmet off, careful to detach the stimchem injector, and dropped it to the floor. He jammed the heels of his hands into his eyes so hard red spots swam in his vision.

"Extreme canyon run?"

The woman's voice sounded wry, amused, mocking. Elya only knew one person who snarked at him like that. He stepped out of the simulator, hopped to the ground, and glared at the muscled blonde leaning against the small room's curved door frame.

Captain Casey Osprey held her hands together, supporting a small bot shaped like a hedgehog in her cupped palms. Hedgebot circled three times and curled up, comfortable as could be. No wonder his bot wasn't by the cockpit, where it normally sat, during the last part of that canyon run. True to form, the danger detection bot had sensed movement on the sim deck and gone to scope it out.

"How could you tell?" Elya asked. From the outside, the sim itself was transparent so instructors could observe the pilots they were coaching. However, she wouldn't have been able to see the landscape he'd been immersed in unless she had been here when he set the parameters.

"You tried to do that loop maneuver again. I told you, it'll never work. It takes too long."

"You don't know that for sure."

"Have you managed it yet, Fancypants?" She used his call sign like a prod. Most of the time he didn't think twice about the nickname his style and record-breaking training runs earned him in flight school, but when she used it like *that* it rankled.

"It's just a matter of time," he said.

He didn't use her call sign, since "Raptor" was too cool to be a taunt. It was a play on the captain's family name and matched tattoos of the mythological Earth hawks adorning the inside of her forearms. He'd gotten Naab back for sticking him with "Fancypants," but Elya's chance for a cool call sign was as out of reach now as owning property on overpopulated Ariadne.

"Mmhmm. Speaking of time," Osprey said, "you spend an awful lot of yours on that sim, especially with this being our first deployment to the outer rim. Why don't you live a little? Come hang out with us. See the galaxy."

She had only been appointed flight lead right before this deployment, and already she was giving him orders? "I'm busy training. Besides, there's nothing to see right now. The evac is going smoothly."

"We'll see action soon enough. What are you trying to prove?"

"I want to be ready."

Osprey moved into the room and hitched her hip against the steps leading up to the sim. "Listen, Nevers, I'm not busting your chops for fun. It's my job to make us a cohesive unit, and I can't do that when you won't act like part of the team. This isn't just about being a good pilot. It's about knowing we have each other's backs."

He frowned. "Have I ever given you a reason not to trust me?"

"No. You always take your assignment without whining. You never leave your wingman. You're never late to drill. But you aren't always *present*. Captain Elya Nevers is there. Yes-sir-reporting-for-duty-sir. Thing is, the squad needs Elya the friend, too. The guy who's good with bot mods and completely insufferable after he beats you at a game of aleacc."

"Hey! I'm not insuf—"

She rolled her eyes and chuckled softly. "I'm just giving you a hard time, Nevers. I want you to be you... come on, whaddya say? I'll even offer to relieve you of a month's pay in a game of handles."

"Oh, how generous of you."

Elya fought down a smile. He'd always liked Osprey's competitive streak. Something in him loved to rise to the challenge. At the same time, he didn't like the censure, and hated knowing deep down that she was right. He wanted to be part of the team. He'd *always* wanted to be part of something where he felt connected to other people. But he didn't always know how, and he wasn't going to give Osprey any more ammunition.

He whistled, calling Hedgebot back to him. The little hedgehog-shaped machine—finely bristled, with sensing mechanisms running along its back and feet, and a whole lot of personality crammed into the color-shifting lights in its belly—hopped from Osprey's hands to the floor and scampered up his arm to perch on his shoulder. It felt natural to have Hedgebot rest its weight there. The bot was clever and had no trouble balancing. It'd been given to Elya as a gift when he first became a refugee, long before he joined the Solaran Defense Forces. He'd been ordered to make several modifications to the bot's programming and mechanics to meet Fleet requirements, but he'd been allowed to keep it, and for that he was grateful.

"Look, I appreciate the pep talk, but I need to take care of a few things. I'm good doing what I'm doing, all right?"

Elya dug his tablet out of his pocket and was trying to locate the notification that had distracted him during the sim when Osprey's muffled snort caught his attention. She had picked up his helmet and was peering through it at the viewscreen.

"What's so funny?" Elya snatched the helmet out of her hands. Hedgebot beeped at her, a dissonant sequence with a rising inflection.

"You actually used Captain Ruidiaz as your avatar?"

"Mind your own business, Raptor."

"Hey, I didn't mean it like that. Ruidiaz was a war hero and an incredibly talented pilot. Wish he were still around to teach us a few tricks." She paused, lifting her chin and narrowing her eyes. "I bet you were the kind of kid that had a holovid of him in your bedroom, didn't you?"

"Nah. I would have had one if I'd learned about Ruidiaz back on Yuzosix. Once we became refugees, we couldn't afford luxuries like having our own bedrooms."

Elya's family relocated to a settler's moon after the Kryl invasion of Yuzosix and spent the next several years skirting the edges of abject poverty. There had been months-long stretches where it was a good day if he got two meals and a roof over his head. Not having a holovid of the legendary pilot who was his hero—or a bedroom to put it in—was something his brother Rojer would have whined and moaned endlessly about. Not Elya. Instead of complaining, he invested every ounce of energy into getting off that rock and learning to fly Sabres.

Osprey put her hand on his shoulder. "You know, now that I think about it, you do kind of fly like him."

"I guess that's what happens when you study countless hours of footage in the library archives."

One thing the refugee colony did have was a library. He was able to spend as much time as he wanted watching holovids of Ruidiaz's Kryl encounters. That footage was the main reason he'd decided to join up. At least as an Imperial pilot, he could count on being able to send a few credits home each month. That was more than most could say.

Osprey snorted. "That's some way for a kid to entertain himself. When I was a kid, I got so sick of my dad and granddad telling war stories and talking about how being in the Fleet was such a noble calling that watching old footage was the last thing I wanted to do."

"So why'd you join up?"

She shrugged. "Didn't want to let him down, I guess. Plus, I'm good at it. I can outfly your butt any day."

He grinned. "That's the best you got? And you became flight lead, how?"

The thought of settler's moons and sending money home

made something click in his mind. The notification had been a bank alert. A quick review with his tab confirmed that his paycheck, measly though it may be, had been deposited into his account.

"One nice thing about working for the Solaran Empire," he said. "The money always shows up on time."

He swung around Osprey and ducked into the hallway. Soon he was making his way out of the living quarters and into the communal spaces at the center of the Imperial destroyer.

"Hey, wait up," Osprey called. "I'm not done with you yet."

Elya didn't slow his pace. She may be flight lead, but they were technically the same rank and he wasn't about to let her boss him around on his personal time. If she wanted to talk, he wasn't going to stop her. But he wasn't about to wait up for her, either.

Her footsteps quickened. Osprey jogged until she came alongside him, giving him an irritated look.

"Look, the last thing I want to do is order you to rec."

"You can't order me to spend my free time with anyone I don't want to." He usually had a better hold on his temper but screwing up the sim and getting lectured by his flight lead drilled on his last nerve. "I know we both wanted to see more action on this mission, but since we haven't seen any Kryl yet, I don't see why spending a little extra time in the sim is a bad thing."

Plus, the rec wasn't exactly his idea of restful. It held ball courts, game tables, pleasure sims—all sorts of mindless crap designed to keep soldiers entertained. There was a bar, too, although they closed at 2200 Galactic Standard Time to prevent the crew from getting too rowdy.

Her smile was strained. "All the more reason for you to be well rested and ready to go."

"To be fair, I was there yesterday. We played aleacc,

remember?"

"Yeah, you showed up," Osprey said. "But like I said, you weren't really *there*, you know? The rest of the squad thinks you're kind of standoffish."

He was careful not to let it show how much that remark stung. He'd never had problems with any of his squadmates. But would they have told him if they did?

Of all the other pilots, it was Osprey he knew best. She hated broccoli and liked to workout first thing in the morning. She sweated over other people's approval, and it was no wonder, since her father had packed her off to a military academy without so much as a warning when she was still a girl. It taught her to adapt quickly to awkward social situations and strive to fit in. She was also a damn good pilot. In flight training, which they had gone through together, they'd always been neck and neck in the rankings, with instructors pitting them against each other in maneuvering and shooting drills.

This forced competition had one huge advantage: It made *both* of them better pilots. When they began to fly real Sabres in mock combat missions, they separated from the pack. This shared history was probably the reason why Osprey had come to talk to him. No one else would have bothered. He grudgingly gave her credit for caring at least that much.

"Look, Captain, I like playing aleacc, but I don't like spending the whole day killing time. Plus, I'm not much of a drinker. And you know most of those guys, if they don't have to fly that day, they don't want to be walking straight, either."

"Yorra rarely drinks and yet she always hangs out with us. You could do the same."

"I maintain my starfighter and keep my blaster clean. I help the others repair their bots when they can't do it themselves. I'm never late to a briefing. I'm a good pilot. What more do you want from me?"

Osprey sighed and ran her hand over her face. She stared up and away. He studied her out of the corner of his eye, tracing the strong line of her jaw, the slightly crooked cut of her nose from where it had been broken in a fight. She looked like a hologram of an Old Earth statue. Not his type, exactly, but attractive in a patrician sort of way.

"You don't have to like it. But you could at least make an effort."

By now they had taken three or four turns down nearly identical hallways. Every so often, a supporting frame jutted out a bit into the hall so that he got the feeling that he was walking through the ribbed belly of a whale, or some other ancient creature out of Old Earth mythology.

"The others have to know they can count on you when it matters most," Osprey said. "If you don't build that connection with them now, when it comes to a firefight, they're not going to know that *you* have *their* back either. Training is important. Believe me, I love how hard you work. I always have. No one pushes me to be a better pilot than you do. But you've got to make an effort to be friends with the rest of the squad, and the time for that is at the rec."

The whole conversation annoyed him. He was doing his best. He knew Lieutenant Park was the only boy in a family of six. He knew Lieutenant Yorra had lost her parents in a raid during the Kryl War. He knew their birthdays, home planets, religions. He had made all the requisite inquiries. He wanted to fit in, but they had been on missions for the past six months, and though they hadn't seen much action *yet*, they would soon. In his mind, this was the time to get serious about training. He'd be damned if his career ended early because he made an amateurish mistake. It had happened to better pilots than him.

"We're not out here evacuating a rim world colony to make pals. We're here to kill Kryl." *And to take vengeance against the xeno scum who stole my homeworld*, he added silently.

Osprey stepped in front of him and forced him to stop walking. She reached out and gripped his shoulder, squaring herself up. She hesitated a moment before saying, "You're not a refugee anymore. All I'm saying is, you don't have to do this alone."

He stiffened against her touch but didn't jerk away. He didn't like to talk about his past with anyone, not even Osprey. "It's not about that. I just want to be ready when the time comes."

She dropped her hands. He pushed past her and picked up the pace. Several more turns through the halls of the destroyer led him to the library and the computers that could transmit data back to the settler's moon. It was the only place on the ship with a secure ansible connection, which he needed to transfer credits to his mom's bank account back home.

And the place was jam-packed with people.

"Oh, Earth," he muttered, scanning for an opening.

"How about the colonel over there?" Osprey said. "Looks like he's getting up to leave."

A hungover balding man in his mid-fifties with a colonel's sunburst on his shoulder pushed up from his seat at a console in the far corner of the room. Elya made his way through the crowded library, past the rows of immersion holodecks until he reached a relatively private row of functional monitors with screens much larger than the tab in his pocket. He let a servant bot sanitize the workstation, impatient at the delay, then groaned when he tried to log on.

There was a queue for ansible access, too.

A lanky man with sloped shoulders sitting two seats down, who Elya recognized as a line cook, chuckled and said, "Me too, man. Imperial technology!"

He stewed in silence while he waited, studying the crowded library. More people than usual filled the place, but with fifty thousand personnel stationed on the *Paladin of Abniss*, there was no such thing as quiet in here. Everyone came to the library to get their news, talk to their families, check their mail, and more. Most people seemed to be in good spirits. Perhaps, like him, they were pleased they'd been sent out here to the galaxy's edge to evacuate a colony because it meant a chance to see action. After a twelve-year stalemate in the war against the Kryl, most soldiers—especially Sabre pilots—were itching for a fight.

When his turn finally came, he logged on to his bank account, put half the money in savings, set aside some for spending, and sent the remainder home to his mom. It wasn't much, but the money assuaged a little of his guilt at leaving them in a place with little chance for employment and ration cards that barely put food on the table.

He tabbed over to a news aggregator and checked if there was any word from the system where his family was located. After scouring the feeds for a while, he blew out his breath. No news was good news.

Stretching, he relinquished the seat to the next person in line and headed for the exit. Thankfully, Osprey was nowhere to be found, and no one else took it upon themselves to yank his chain about his social ineptitude.

Hedgebot beeped. Elya reached up and touched the sensor on the tip of the bot's nose. "What's that, bud? You want to fly another sim? Great idea. Let's swing by the mess for a bite to eat and a charge, and then we can get back to work."

He pushed away thoughts of Osprey's advice, of his mom, of the hellhole his family couldn't escape. His only job was to train. Get better. Be ready.

It was only a matter of time.

TWO

Casey scrolled through the library terminal, opening files at random and hoping she might get lucky. You'd think that with access to centuries' worth of leadership content, at least one book or holovid would be able to reveal the key to getting through to that idiot, so intent on staying walled off from anyone and anything except a training sim. But no such luck.

The next time she looked up, the terminal Nevers had been using was occupied by someone else. Casey logged out and hurried to the doorway in time to see him turn down the next corridor and out of sight. That damnably cute little robot of his pulsed blue and scurried along the curved wall after him, as if it moved on an invisible leash. She'd never seen a bot more devoted, and while usually this fact made Nevers seem endearing, today it made him seem like an aloof jerk.

She fumed at his stubbornness the whole walk back to the rec. When Lt. Colonel Walcott first told her she'd made flight lead, the news had filled her with pride and excitement. She knew it was a big responsibility, but it was also her first step on the leadership path—the path she'd been groomed her whole life to take. She just never realized the most difficult part of the job would be dealing with other people. Casey was usually great with people.

What am I missing? she wondered.

The portal to the rec where the rest of her flight was killing time irised open as she approached, belching out a cloud of acrid tabac smoke. She caught a whiff of ganja mixed into the scent and knew that Lieutenant Innovesh Park must have been digging into his stash again. Cannabis was sold in most base exchanges, right alongside the loose tabac and cigars. Casey felt a hankering to light up a smoke of her own right now but resisted the urge while she hunted Park out of the crowd. True to form he was puffing on a rolly as he slouched in a chair at a card table in the corner.

He bent the hexagonal cards in a fan toward himself and gazed around the table, then pushed all his chips into the pot. He flipped a card over, tapped a symbol on the table, and the hologram of a saber-toothed tiger sauntered forward and ripped out the guts of a dragon guarding Lieutenant Olara Yorra's position.

"Oh, no fair, Naab!" Yorra said, throwing down her cards. "I had you cornered."

Park shrugged, a boyish grin lighting his brown eyes. He was descended from the colonists of Taj Su and shared the canted eyes, sharp cheekbones, and short, stocky frame common on his planet. A jokester at heart, Naab was a head shorter than most women on the ship, but broad in the chest and handsome. And he always had a big smile for a pretty girl.

Spotting Casey, Park turned that smile on her and waved. She wove through the crowd. As she reached the table and stood over him, she plucked the rolly from his mouth and took a big drag. "See you've been having fun." She exhaled the sweet smoke. A hint of mango and cannabis coated her tongue.

"Told him we were still technically on call, but this flyboy didn't listen."

"Does he ever?"

Always the jokester, Naab had earned his call sign when he went streaking through the mess hall and ended up getting locked outside on a cold winter morning, naked as a baby. Hence, Naab. She always suspected Fancypants was the one who locked him out, but Nevers refused to admit it.

"What's the big deal? Tiny dose of stim and I'm right as rain." He tapped the port on the back of his neck. Casey felt her own tingle. All starfighter pilots had them installed when they joined, and most days she forgot it was there.

Casey shrugged and collapsed into the free chair. She may have been flight lead, but she wasn't the squadron commander. They were still on call, but as long as they weren't flying, Casey wasn't about to police their consumption. If the Fleet didn't want pilots smoking ganja, they shouldn't sell it in the exchange. Besides, Casey had tested it herself and Park was right. Even if you were half drunk *and* stoned out of your gourd, those stim chemicals sobered you right up.

Park eyeballed Casey as he reshuffled the deck of cards and dealt them out between himself and Yorra. "Where've you been, Raptor?"

She scratched at an imperfection in the table.

"You were checking in on Nevers, weren't you?" Gears sat up straighter, catching a card as it came sliding across the table. "Yeah, I can see it in your face."

Casey crossed her arms and frowned. Olara Yorra wasn't the most experienced pilot in their flight, but she was whip smart and always scored top marks on written exams. She had jet black hair, big green eyes, enviably smooth skin, and saw more than she let on. Casey had long ago learned to listen when Yorra spoke.

"Why are you always after him like that?" Naab asked.

"Because, I need him to know we've got each other's backs."

"'Course he knows." Yorra stuck her tongue in her cheek and cocked her head as she reordered the cards in her hand. "I think it just bothers you that he's happy spending time alone. What was he doing? Running sims?"

Casey huffed air out through her nose and nodded reluctantly.

"He's always training," Park took back the rolly Casey had commandeered, inhaling one more time and then carefully stamping it out and storing the joint in his jacket for later. "Kid doesn't know how to relax."

She let her arms fall to her side and slouched lower in her chair. She signaled to one of the servobots. It rolled over, and she tapped an order into the tab mounted, into its round head. It spit out a glass of ginger beer; sipping, she enjoyed the slight bite and the bubbles on her tongue. "It's more than that," Casey insisted. "He barely spends any rec time with us."

"Hah!" Gears barked a laugh. "Don't you think we spend enough time together, Raptor? We train together, we sleep in the same room, we spend hours running drills. We practically live in each other's heads. He probably just needs a break."

She frowned. That idea was foreign to her. Being around her friends on her off hours was revivifying. She took energy from a gathering like this, where they were sitting with each other playing cards and shooting the breeze. It never even occurred to her that somebody could *enjoy* spending time alone, running extra sims by himself. How was that fun?

But then, Nevers had always been internally motivated. Even when they were in pilot training together, he only sought help when he needed a second in the cockpit. Casey, on the other hand, had picked out individual people who excelled in one thing—navigation, or the physics of flying in zero grav—and leaned on each of them from the get-go, absorbing their knowledge like a sponge. Nevers had been content to figure things out on his own. Oh sure, he helped her when she asked. His specialty was the mechanics of the Sabre and working with the astrobots. (He had modified Hedgebot to be his personal astrobot, after all, and never relied on a bot machinist when he could do the repairs himself.)

Casey's rumination was interrupted when every screen and tab in the place began to flash midnight blue and crimson. A klaxon alarm followed on a half-second delay, echoing through the rec and reverberating in her chest.

"All starfighters," said a voice over the intercom, "report to battle stations. Repeat, all starfighters report to battle stations immediately."

THREE

Admiral Kira Miyaru gazed through the main window of the bridge, over the fleet of Mammoth-class long-haulers and the lush forest moon in the distance. All around her, the crew worked, monitoring systems on dozens of bright holoscreens, relaying updates on the status of the evacuation and watching surrounding space in all directions for any sign of Kryl. Everything was going according to plan —which was exactly what had her worried. Even with a whole wing of starfighters on patrol, two dozen civilian transports were a lot for one destroyer and a handful of support craft to protect. And that wasn't accounting for what was happening on the ground.

Robichar was one of a dozen expansion colonies authorized since the end of the Kryl War. Irritatingly, the feeling among the Colonization Board continued to be that Solaran space was secure enough to continue approving new charters, even *after* verified reports of a rogue Kryl hive had precipitated the prudent evacuation of this one. For the past year, the civilian population had been reporting Kryl attacks with alarming frequency. The sudden movement of the hive had finally forced the Board to pull out of Robichar.

"Despite this minor setback, we have a moral imperative to expand," the chairman of the Colonization Board had declared the last time Kira stood before the balding bureaucrat. Not even the Empire's most advanced AI programs had been able to fix male pattern baldness, and for some reason this insight brought her joy while his words raked at her nerves. "If the Solaran Empire isn't growing, it's dying. The Emperor refuses to give the Kryl the satisfaction."

The Emperor, indeed, she thought bitterly. The Emperor and his harem were no doubt sequestered in his pleasure palace orbiting Ariadne, blissfully unaware of the Kryl's latest movements, as he had been for the past decade. Kira would be shocked to learn he was even aware of the so-called "moral imperative" espoused by the flunkies operating in his absence.

So here she was, following orders to evacuate Robichar with minimal support. Kira had requested additional firepower—an extra destroyer or five, and several heavy cruisers —but her requests were denied.

Fools.

With an effort of will forged in the fire of twelve years of calculated patience, Kira forced her fury back down. She ran her fingers through the carefully cropped mohawk that was her preferred hairstyle—a style that had faded from jet black to silver around the time of her last promotion. She was here to do a job, and no amount of bellyaching over Imperial policy would save the people of Robichar from being ravaged by a Kryl hive.

Only soldiers could do that. *Her* soldiers.

The sphere of Robichar was mottled green and brown, kissed by wispy clouds and dotted with a round ocean that took up a third of the moon's surface. As the *Paladin of Abniss* orbited the moon, the moon in turn danced around a gas giant, the fifth rock from the sun of this system.

"Admiral, the shuttles have reached escape velocity." The resonant voice seemed to come from every speaker, from the room itself. The voice belonged to the ship—or rather, to Harmony, a branch of the artificial intelligence program that piloted every starship in the Solaran Defense Forces. The program was installed in the neural network of the ship itself, and controlled by a nanochip embedded in Kira's neck, right above her spinal port. Technically, no one else needed to see Harmony or hear her voice, but since Kira preferred to have a face to talk to—and not look like a lunatic talking to herself on the bridge, in full view of her officers—a pattern of vibrant bluish nodes and purple clusters arranged themselves into a face-like shape floating next to the command couch.

"Show me," she ordered.

"Visual on shuttles in three, two..."

As Harmony counted down, the main viewscreen, configured to show relevant space outside the ship, refocused. A group of ten transport shuttles appeared on a backdrop of cloud-streaked forest. Engines burned red as they followed a vector toward the group of two dozen Mammoth long-haulers. At a capacity of a hundred thousand persons each, the Mammoths could hold 2.4 million people—enough to fit the entire population of Robichar with plenty of room to spare.

"Any sign of the Kryl?"

"No, Admiral," Harmony said. "The Overmind is still working her way through the asteroid field."

"And if she changes her mind, how long would it take her to reach us?"

Harmony's face moved aside and a series of calculations scrolled across the holoscreen without displacing the multiwindow readout from the stealth tracking beacons. Though no one objected, Kira could tell by over-the-shoulder glances and stiff postures that referring to the Overmind as a "she" made the rest of her crew uncomfortable. *Good.*

It had been over a decade since any Solaran Defense Forces engaged a Kryl hive directly. Her people needed to understand who their enemy really was—not merely the thousands of Kryl spawn and their venomous talons, but the consciousness that controlled them. This knowledge was imperative to winning any battle they found themselves in.

"If the hive continues its normal feeding patterns," Harmony said, "there is an eighty-three percent probability they will arrive in-system twenty-eight hours from now."

A galactic standard day, or close enough. And the Kryl prediction models, though vastly improved since the days of the Kryl War, had been wrong before. "Thank you, Harmony."

Kira stepped off the small pedestal holding the command couch and clasped her hands behind her back. She wanted to pace, but forced herself to stand with her shoulders back and locked. The group docked with the Mammoth fleet and began to unload passengers. *Another hundred thousand people to safety,* she thought.

By her estimation, it would take another twelve hours to evacuate the rest of the population. So why, when all signs pointed to a successful operation, did she still feel so high strung?

The bridge door irised open and a tall, balding man in his fifties strode into the room. She recognized the sound of Colonel Volk's measured steps before she saw him; her executive officer usually projected an air of quiet competence, but today he was suffering. Sweat at his temples made his waxen skin glisten under the glare of the holoscreens at his duty station. Despite his hangover, Volk was fifteen minutes early for his shift.

"Morning, Colonel."

"Good morning, sir." Volk winced slightly at the sound of his own voice.

"Up late?"

"No later than usual, sir. You know I never sleep well during an operation." His attention flickered over the tactical displays, surreptitiously confirming the status of the evacuation, the capacity of the Mammoth fleet, the location of the Kryl hive and a hundred other details.

The two of them had been working together for fifteen years. The number stunned her for a moment. Fifteen years was a long time—not to a Kryl Overmind like the Queen Mother, mind you. To *her*, a decade or two was the blink of an eye. A restful night's sleep. Kira set her shock gently aside, wary of underestimating her enemy.

"Any news from our automaton friends?" Volk asked.

Though it wasn't Kira's favorite description, the Kryl were often referred to as automatons because they seemed to mindlessly obey the Overmind they served, often without thought or care for their own personal safety. It was one way soldiers distanced themselves mentally from the Kryl—if the bugs were mindless insects, no one had to feel bad about blowing them to a million slimy, invertebrate pieces.

Kira sniffed. "Nothing significant. Still eating their way through the asteroid field. They've raided three different planetary bodies for ice, by our reports, but none we need to be worried about." Meaning: None occupied by Solarans or of interest to the Colonization Board.

"You still think it's this colony they're after?"

"I have no reason to think it's *not* this colony. Of course, I'd be happy to be proven wrong."

The colonel cleared his throat. "You and me both, sir. And

yet, as you have pointed out countless times, this is the only planet in this volume of space that makes a viable target."

"Even if it is lacking in useful radioactive isotopes."

"And heavy metals."

A weighted silence fell between them. This was a familiar debate, one they had rehearsed many times on the journey to Robichar. Neither of them had been able to come up with a better explanation for the Kryl's movements. Twelve years they kept to their own territory... why were they on the move now? It was a mystery to the Executive Council of the Solaran Defense Forces, and even to the galaxy's preeminent xenobiologists. Unfortunately, they didn't have time to study the hive's movements further. They had to act. The lives of millions were at stake, and evacuating the colony was the only sure way to save them.

Volk finally grunted, then crossed the bridge to retrieve a bottle of water from the refreshment dispenser. "Impressive sight."

Kira followed his gaze to the fleet of twenty-four Mammoths and the two hundred starfighters patrolling the region of space around the moon itself. She had about five hundred starfighters on this ship. They rotated out several squadrons at a time, taking shifts, remaining vigilant. She was sure to give her pilots plenty of time off to rest. As somber as the occasion was, evacuating a planet had become a routine operation, something the Empire had done many times in its century-long conflict with the Kryl. There were systems and SOPs to follow. So far, they had encountered no hiccups.

Maybe that's why Kira was so jumpy. What mission ever went off without a hitch?

No one knew what the Kryl were looking for when they invaded a planet, but no one wanted to be there when it happened. Some people believed the Kryl came simply to devour. Others believed—rightly so, perhaps, as they had to build their ships out of something—that the Kryl invaded a planet primarily for the resources the world had to offer: radioactive isotopes to power their mountainous lairs, and the heavy metals they favored for growing drones, weapons and, of course, starships.

Kira had always been skeptical of these theories. It didn't help that they were put forward by xenobiologists who'd never seen the frontlines of the war, never looked into the eyes of a Kryl as it tried to introduce your intestines to the open air. For another, if it was simply a matter of resources, why did the Kryl seem to have such a voracious desire to expand? Critics of this line of thinking would point out they hadn't expanded in the last twelve years. They'd retreated back into the core of their volume of space, to the planet the Queen Mother occupied and which was thought to be the species' home world.

Kira always found this rather suspicious. They had retreated, yes, after the Queen Mother's hive was assaulted, and roughly a quarter of her species annihilated by anti-matter bombs. They hadn't *disappeared*. The Kryl species still thrived, and Kira didn't think their memories were so short.

"The evacuation is proceeding on schedule," Kira told her XO. "We're up to the equivalent of eighteen craft at capacity."

"I heard there were some holdouts among the population planetside."

Kira winced. "There are always a few."

"Do we know why?"

"I've had some people ask around on the Mammoths. Rumor is it's mostly religious fanatics."

Volk sneered, taking a swig of his water. "The Spirit of Old Earth won't save you from being eviscerated by a Kryl talon."

Kira understood how he felt. He'd lost a brother in the

war. She had lost someone she'd loved, too. She understood how long grief could burn, how a wound caused by the loss of a loved one never truly healed. Grief never vanishes. You just learn how to live with it.

"How's the crew holding up?" She'd been hearing increased reports of minor fights and scuffles onboard, indicators of jagged nerves. It may have seemed like a large ask to inquire after the well-being of thousands of people, for the *Paladin of Abniss* was one of the largest vessels in the Fleet, and fully manned, but Volk had always been able to assess the mood of a ship with striking accuracy.

"A bit too eager, sir. Most of these pilots have never seen real action, except for the few squads who put down the rebellion on Ezekiel. And that wasn't much of a fight."

"Our starfighter pilots are the best in the galaxy."

"That's not under dispute. We do train brilliant pilots. But that doesn't mean they can earn their wings by flying sim programs and peaceful recon missions."

Kira nodded and let the conversation lapse into silence. She kept her eyes on the screen, squinting, trying to suss out exactly what had her nerves on edge, but all she saw was the darkness of surrounding space pierced by pinprick stars.

Volk recycled the water bottle and returned to stand at her side. He studied the next set of shuttles crossing the gulf between the planet and the longhaulers.

They had been speaking loud enough for the officers to hear—she had wanted the officers on the bridge to know what the XO had to say. It was one thing to give her own opinions and quite another to elicit them from her trusted senior officers and be seen doing so. Now, however, Volk took half a step closer and lowered his voice so that the two of them could converse alone.

"Admiral, do you still think the Kryl are up to something?"

"I always think they're up to something. The question is... what?"

"You don't think, after twelve years, this movement is merely necessary survival?"

"I think we should wait and see what happens."

"Yet you suspect something."

"Don't you?"

"After a decade-plus of keeping to themselves, a rear-guard hive detaches itself from the bulk of the horde and begins to raid planets out on the edge of the galaxy. If it was a human fleet, I'd say there were two options. One, they're pirates, deserters... they left the horde to rape and pillage."

Kira snorted. "And two?"

"This rogue Overmind is headed here on orders from the Queen Mother herself. What I don't understand is, what are they after?"

"That's always been the question, ever since we made first contact. What are the Kryl after?"

"A warlike species who devours all they touch... The obvious answer is resources—radioactive isotopes, metals, water."

"But why this hive? Why would the Queen Mother not move from the center like she always has before?"

"Maybe it's a hive of rebels."

"Let's hope we're so lucky. I don't want to be right about this, but I've got a feeling something else is going on. We may have cowed the Kryl and forced them to retreat. Over the last twelve years, however, as you have rightly pointed out before, the Solaran Empire has grown soft. We've continued to expand. The Fleet is larger than ever, but we have more colonies to protect and our forces are spread too thin."

Volk shrugged. "Maybe the Kryl are just annoyed we're expanding and they're not."

"It was stupid." Kira felt the heat of her fury rising like

lava from the crater of a volcano. "I told the Executive Council we needed to be cautious."

"They waited seven years before they started writing new charters."

"They should have waited longer. Do you think the Queen Mother thinks seven years, or twelve or twenty, is a long time? If you believe our xenobiologists, the Mother Queen has lived for over two thousand years. Each Queen Mother that rises to prominence lasts a couple millennia."

Volk just grunted and ran a hand over his face.

An urgent chime rang across the bridge.

"Report," Kira said.

"Kryl ships spotted in system, Admiral." Harmony's pleasant, androgynous voice sent a chill down her spine.

"Where?"

"On the far side of the moon."

"The whole hive? How'd they get here so blasted fast?"

"It's not the whole hive." Volk raced over to a tactical display and parsed through a stream of information with focused intensity. "It seems to be some kind of advanced scouting party. Sixty to eighty fighter drones and one Mantis-class refueler."

She locked eyes with Volk. Their orders were to evacuate the planet and get out of the system before the Overmind realized what was happening.

So much for that idea.

"Time to give your fresh-faced young starfighters a taste of Kryl blood. Give the order, Colonel."

A flash of worry creased Volk's forehead, but it was quickly hidden beneath a veneer of experienced focus. He straightened up and planted his feet. "Sound the alarm! Activate battle shields. Charge the fore and aft laser defense arrays. Scramble all available starfighter squadrons. I want those drones to be sucking vacuum before they catch sight of a single Mammoth. Patch squadron commanders through to the bridge so I can brief them on their way out. Let's go, let's go, let's go!"

Kira sank into her command couch and practiced stillness while sitting at the nexus of this flurry of action. Screens flashed as senior officers hurried around her, running checklists and performing the necessary duties to deploy additional starfighter squadrons and ready the destroyer's defenses. She inhaled deeply, trying to control the way her heart thundered in her chest.

No matter how old she got, the rush of battle still made her feel more alive than anything ever had.

Come on, you bug-faced bitch, she thought furiously. *Show me why you're here.*

FOUR

Mechanics raced down the columns of Sabres parked on Deck One, unsealing cockpits and priming engines while the concave threshold protecting the hangar yawned wide.

The serrated metal mouth was six hundred meters high and twice as long. It petaled open like a steel flower to reveal a star-studded midnight expanse. Soon the only thing separating the hangar's atmosphere from the vacuum was a breathtakingly thin energy shield through which the battalion of starfighters would be launched.

Elya rushed into the hangar with a stream of pilots called from his part of the ship. Hundreds more came through the other two entrances, but he didn't see anyone from his squad yet. No matter. Everyone knew exactly what to do when they heard the klaxon.

Elya's sharp eyes picked out the flag for the Furies—a winged sword over the number "137th". He ran toward the green banner, weaving through the parked starfighters and hundreds of other pilots all clambering toward their craft. The dampened roar that rose from the chaos of rushing mechanics, pilots and bots was swallowed in the vast space, through air criss-crossed by the support craft taking off from Decks Two and Three, overhead and behind them.

Elya finally reached his Sabre. He double checked the tail number, took a slow lap around the ship to inspect the exterior, then scurried up an angled wing and dove feet first into the seat. These were the best starfighter models the Fleet had ever designed, equally capable of flying in vacuum as in air, with adjustable fins and wing configurations to handle any kind of atmosphere.

Boo BE doo, Hedgebot hailed as he hopped into the cockpit behind Elya. The bot's magnetic toes plucked at the hull and then clacked across the instrument panel in front of him while Elya fitted on his oxygen mask, buckled the safety harness across his chest, and pressed the button that would lower the transparent canopy, sealing the pair inside.

Through the window, Elya shot a thumbs-up at Petty Officer Mick Perry as the Fleet's friendliest mechanic worked his way down Elya's row, unhooking cables tying each jet into power and diagnostics, and lashing them down to avoid damage if they encountered unexpected turbulence. Perry jerked his chin and returned the thumbs-up, flashing grease-stained knuckles while counting under his breath. He ducked under the wing of Elya's Sabre and moved on to the next ship.

Osprey ran in from his right and vaulted into a starfighter ahead of him, followed by Park, Yorra, Lieutenant Colonel Walcott and the rest of their squad. The jets had been preflighted, so it took the whole squad less than ninety seconds to complete their checklist and get situated on comms. Elya'd rehearsed this routine until his eyes swam, but with his nerves shooting off like jury-rigged fireworks, he'd never been so glad for the muscle memory his relentless training had instilled in him.

As they waited to be cleared for takeoff, they taxied toward the tinted blue barricade separating the hangar's atmosphere from the life-threatening vacuum on the other side. Elya double checked his oxygen to make sure it was flowing. Usually, he enjoyed watching the other starfighters get catapulted from the deck and then arc out of sight around the hull of the destroyer. This time, his mind wandered off in a dozen different directions of its own—had the money he sent home made it there yet? Should he have sent his mom a longer message? Or a video? There was real danger on the other side of that energy shield. Did he have time to make up with Captain Osprey? He liked her, in spite of her unique ability to goad him.

Captain Osprey short circuited his train of thought before it skittered too far off track. "Furies one-eight, check?"

"Two," said Elya.

"Three," said Naab.

"Four," said Gears.

Osprey relayed their readiness to the squadron commander, Lieutenant Colonel Walcott, a somber veteran pilot and steady leader who had fought in the Kryl War and was never caught smiling.

When they got clearance, they rolled into the catapult one by one, fired up their engines, and rocketed out of the *Paladin* like avenging angels.

Three minutes from preflight to take-off.

Though he'd performed these maneuvers countless times, only a handful of those had been in actual combat situations. As Elya crossed the energy shield and burned toward the flotilla of longhaulers, he found his hands trembling against the controls. Hedgebot circled the cockpit three times before pausing directly overhead and pulsing a nervous pale-yellow.

"I know, little buddy," Elya said. "I've got butterflies in my stomach, too."

Hedgebot's light flickered questioningly.

"I don't know. I've only ever seen pictures of butterflies. It's just something my grandmother used to say when she got nervous."

Hedgebot puffed its whole body up and then deflated as if giving a big shrug. It continued to pulse in anticipation, cycling through a series of colors.

Hedgebot had no trouble withstanding the G-forces that Elya's own body underwent during the course of a hard flight. The bot was also helpful to have with him, as it was designed to warn planetary colonists of incoming danger in hostile environments. Elya had programmed it to perform the other typical duties of an astrobot as well, such as calculating coordinates for navigation, implementing minor repairs, and operating some non-critical controls. It made him a particularly useful flying partner.

"Captain Nevers," Lieutenant Colonel Walcott said over squad-wide comms. "Is that your bot flashing like a lighthouse? Knock it off. We don't want to broadcast our position to the Kryl."

"Yes, sir," Elya said, chagrined. He muted his mic and looked up. "You heard the man." Hedgebot purred in a minor key, but did as instructed, dimming its light so that only Elya could see it. "I know, you didn't mean anything by it."

"All right, squad," the commander's voice continued. "Flight paths have been relayed to your nav. Our job is to protect the Mammoths while other squads engage the Kryl drones directly. We'll act as support and swap in if needed."

The squad's collective groan was only stifled by the need to maintain comms discipline. A few moments passed in silence as they all realized how unlikely it was that anyone would be killing any drones today. Another unit had drawn that honor. Instead, their job was to protect the civilians—and sit with their thumbs up their butts.

"I don't want to hear it," Lieutenant Colonel Walcott said. "You have your orders. Over."

A yellow path appeared, superimposed on the transparent aluminite shell of the cockpit. Elya banked right, in sync with the rest of the squad, Osprey at the vanguard and himself bringing up the rear. Soon they were soaring toward the fleet of twenty-four longhaulers, orbiting above and behind the fleet in the controlled sequence mapped out by the AI.

Although his fingers were itching for action, Elya didn't mind taking a defensive position as much as the others seemed to. Being assigned to protect the refugees lit a deep, warm glow of pride in his chest. Every person he served with, down to a man, had endured some kind of personal loss during the Kryl War. But as far as he knew, among his immediate comrades, only Elya had been a refugee himself.

The bulky Mammoths floated in a loose cluster, like a pack of giant blimps. His flight path curved around them in a clockwise direction from his position. These enormous transport vessels were heavy on armor and defensive turrets, but severely lacking on maneuverability. They took a full fifteen minutes to come about and, to an offensive segment of the fleet, were nothing more than dead weight. It was no wonder the admiral had dispatched her starfighters to defend these fat sitting ducks, loaded as they were with nearly a million civilians.

Elya tuned into the flight frequency. He was dropped into the middle of a conversation between Park and Osprey.

"Do you think they've engaged by now?" Park asked.

"Black Lightning and Viking squads went around the moon to flank them."

A new voice crackled over the command channel. "Kryl drones positively identified. Permission to engage?"

"Granted," Admiral Miyaru's hard voice responded, flat and cold. It was one of the things Elya had always admired about the admiral. Every story he'd heard about her during the Kryl War spoke to her calm under pressure and her ability to think rationally in the heat of battle. However, the admiral was safe in the *Paladin*, not exposed in the cockpit of a Sabre. She had started as a pilot, but now it was up to people like them to put their necks on the line.

Elya wouldn't have had it any other way. His unblinking eyes fixed on the little dots representing the offensive squadrons on his lidar. He readjusted his sweaty grip on the stick.

The speed of their orbital patrol increased as the pilots' trigger fingers sought an outlet for their aggression. But they encountered no threats. They couldn't even see the exchange since the moon blocked their view of the Kryl.

Elya's wing had been involved, a couple years back, in putting down the Ezekiel rebellion. The class that Elya and Osprey belonged to had graduated after that incident, so at least half of the pilots he flew with now had never seen a Kryl drone except for those preserved in military labs and archival footage, himself included. If he didn't get to see one today, who knew when he'd get the chance again?

"This is Viking squad. We have a man down."

Elya's whole body tensed. He gripped the stick with both hands. The action remained on the opposite side of the moon. He could sense its closeness.

"Black Lightning, engage."

Elya referred to his tactical displays. Black Lightning had flown the opposite way around the moon, and now the Kryl force would be caught between the two squads.

"Stick to your flight pattern," Osprey barked over their comms.

Elya lifted his eyes, saw that he had veered from his path.

A gentle nudge put him back onto the line. Yorra, ahead of him, had also veered and quickly corrected.

"Back on track," Yorra said in a shaky voice after she reoriented her fighter.

"Same here," Elya said. He hoped the others didn't hear his voice shaking.

Maybe Osprey had been right. Maybe he shouldn't have been training so hard today. By this point, he was either ready or he wasn't. There was nothing he could do to prepare further, no matter how much he wished it were otherwise.

He refocused, letting his eyes slide along the bulbous side of the nearest Mammoth's silver hull, and the slight reflection that vanished when he tried to focus on it. Focusing on his surroundings kept his mind busy. He tried to ignore the panicked shouting now coming over the command comms from the battle.

The screams and curses coming from the two squads dried his mouth out and set his heart to racing. Adrenaline rushed through his veins. This was something no sim could train you for.

"Whoa! Did you see that?"

Elya's attention snapped back to his comms. He thought that was the voice of the leader of Black Lightning. A raspy male voice came from Fleet Command.

"Black Lightning, report!"

Elya thought that was Colonel Volk, but he couldn't be sure.

"We just lost a group of Kryl drones."

"Do you have visual?"

"Negative, Colonel. A whole pack of 'em just up and vanished."

"Where the void did they go? I've never—"

"Whoa! Coming in hot." The comm system crackled as

some kind of electromagnetic interference disturbed the channel.

Colonel Volk's voice came back a beat after the interference subsided. "—on course. Stick to the plan."

"Loud and clear, sir. We see another pack up ahead."

The interference returned a moment later. And then, as Elya came over the nose of a Mammoth and banked left to make another circuit, he came face-to-face with a Kryl drone. The shape of the teardrop ship had become so familiar in his training, yet he almost didn't believe it was there in front of him. Like the others, this drone had an organic build to it, sleek metal panels fused together by seams of thick carapace, with tentacles trailing from its body. This one was freshly grown, without a scar on it, and seemed more aerodynamic and modern than the one from the sim database—slightly elongated, with more cutouts and curves than the older models stored in his sim. Looking down at his lidar readout, Elya saw that it wasn't the only drone. His squad was suddenly surrounded by a dozen of them.

"Contact!" Elya cried out.

"Permission to engage? I've got eyes on two," Osprey said. "Command?"

"Fire at will."

Osprey opened up her blasters. A stream of bolts skipped off the carapace of the first drone and were absorbed harmlessly by the shield of the Mammoth Elya had been circling. It was good someone had the foresight to activate those shields; he certainly hadn't expected that the drones would actually make it this far. He didn't think anyone else on his squad had, either.

"How the devil did they get here so fast?" Park asked. "Weren't they just on the other side of the moon?"

There was no time to think about it. Elya took aim at the same drone that Osprey had just shot at and fired in tight bursts. The drone banked and weaved. When the blasters overloaded its shields, they flickered and died, and the drone cracked in half the moment before a bright explosion as its engines burst. The light momentarily blinded him.

"Got one!" Elya and Osprey cried out at the same time.

"No way you're getting credit for that, Fancypants."

"I took out the shields."

"My shot destroyed it."

"Would you two quit bickering?" Park said.

Yorra sucked air in through her teeth. "Torpedoes at three o'clock!"

Hedgebot's excited green light, which had been pulsing constantly while he and Osprey engaged the Kryl drone, darkened to a burnt orange color. The bot squawked several electronic tones in a sequence and scurried around to his right.

Turning to look in the direction Hedgebot indicated, Elya spotted the torpedoes. The drone he and Osprey destroyed managed to drop three torpedoes before it was obliterated— typical bait and switch tactics from expendable, unmanned Kryl drones. Elya cursed as the torpedoes blasted straight for the underbelly of the nearest Mammoth.

Elya switched to projectiles. They were more effective against torpedoes, whose shields were designed to deflect blaster fire but were less effective than projectile rounds. Elya split the shell of the nearest torpedo and it exploded harmlessly a hundred klicks from the Mammoth.

"One down, two left," Elya reported.

"I'm on it," Osprey shouted.

"Right behind you, Raptor," Park said.

"Fancypants, with me on the other one," Yorra called out.

Their flight split as a pair of starfighters dove after each torpedo.

Gears was a good pilot, but her maneuvering wasn't as

tight as Osprey's. Elya soon pulled ahead of her. He had the torpedo in his sights but it, too, had gained momentum and was now outspeeding him. The torpedo was a small, nimble missile with a powerful engine designed to outrun starfighters and cut through defense arrays. The only chance he had now was to intercept it before it could hit the Mammoth.

"Come on, come on!" Elya rocketed forward, opening his engines to maximum. The G-forces flattened his body into his seat. He sucked oxygen through his mask as his cheeks were pressed back and his head felt heavy like an oversized bowling ball. As he came within range to shoot it down, another Kryl drone came up from below the Mammoth and twisted into his path. Unlike the torpedo, the drone's shields *were* designed to handle projectiles. His shots bounced harmlessly off the drone.

Yorra swerved around the Kryl, but she had been too far back to catch up. And though she fired at the torpedo, her shots went wide. Elya saw, out of the corner of his eye, the little flashes where her bullets hit the shields of the Mammoth and plinked harmlessly off. The torpedo, however, was not nearly so ineffective. It impacted the shell of the transport vessel and ruptured the Mammoth's underside. The machine's capably equipped shields soon contained the atmospheric leak, but not before a store of water had evacuated the body of the ship, crystallized into ice, and sent a cloud of sharp crystals drifting into the path of Elya and his squadmates. He banked away to avoid sustaining damage to the Sabre.

Furious, Elya pulled his starfighter around and angled back to chase after the drone that had foiled his attempts to take the torpedo down.

Fortunately, Osprey and Park caught the other projectile, so the torpedo that hit the Mammoth on his watch was the only one to cause damage. The chatter that followed coming from Command and from the rest of the squad became too chaotic to follow, but he picked out the admiral's voice.

"Protect the Mammoths!" she snapped.

The destroyer's laser defense array took out a handful of drones before the pack moved out of range. Only three had survived the surprise attack.

Elya took stock of the distance and decided he could catch up to them. His eyes had followed the drone that had distracted him.

"Fancypants," Osprey's voice snapped over the squad, cutting through the rest of the squabble and chatter. "Do not pursue. I repeat, do not pursue."

"I can catch him."

The Kryl drone looped around and began to make zigzags between the Mammoth longhaulers. The ships rose like canyon walls on either side of him as he pursued.

"By the Spirit of Old Earth," Osprey growled. "You're gonna get us in trouble, Nevers!"

"I'm not losing him," Elya replied. *Besides*, he thought, *isn't this what I've been training for?*

Elya hurtled after the Kryl, curving along the hull of a Mammoth at the edge of the cluster. Bursts of blaster fire alternating with the occasional missile kept the Kryl spinning and dodging, preventing it from getting a smooth heading on which to release another torpedo. Elya need not have worried, however, for after a dozen of these tight turns, looping over and under, it quickly became clear that the Kryl drone was merely playing with him. It didn't seem intent on launching another torpedo attack at all.

"What's your endgame?" Elya wondered aloud. *Earth!* The drone was quick. Park and Yorra took out the other two remaining drones, leaving only the one Elya was after. Debris from the shattered craft caused both Elya and the drone he was chasing to spin and dodge to avoid taking damage. And though this time Elya gained on the lone drone, he got the sense that the ship seemed to be enjoying the chase as much as he was.

It flew better than any of the other drones had...

Osprey had ceased barking at him. She drifted off his left wing.

"You're gonna be in deep for this, Fancypants. You should have stayed with the rest of the squad."

"I'm not letting him get away," Elya insisted. But he heard the undertone of her criticism. *You're not being a team player,* she seemed to be saying. *Your actions are selfish. And even if you do catch this drone, the rest of the squad will resent the way you flew.* But it was too late now. A tenacious stubbornness wouldn't let Elya give up the chase.

"It's two-on-one. We've got it outnumbered."

Presently, the drone veered away from the Mammoth fleet and accelerated toward Robichar. Seeing his opportunity, Elya opened his thrusters to full burn. Osprey tailed him, the two of them flying neck and neck like they had back at the academy. The next few minutes passed in tense silence. When they were a hundred klicks out from the fleet, the Kryl drone flipped around and shot backward at them without losing its momentum. It was even able to maneuver in reverse to avoid their shots when they returned fire, dipping and dodging. *Impressive.* That was the kind of flying Elya got criticized for. Osprey would have called it pretty but ineffective flying.

Kryl didn't think like people. They were controlled by a remote Overmind that gave them abilities that human pilots could never hope to match. It was one of the reasons starfighters weren't piloted remotely; starfighters needed every edge they could get.

Elya stayed close, keeping up the steady stream of attack

and refusing to back down. Hedgebot scurried back and forth along the window over his head, keeping him on track with the Kryl's erratic flight pattern. At some point, the starfighter's internal AI determined that the G-forces were too much for Elya's body to handle on its own, and a pinch at the back of his neck, followed by a relaxing of his muscles, told him he'd been injected with the dose of targeted chemicals that would sharpen his senses and make the G-forces easier to handle.

Hopped up on the cocktail of stimulants and stabilizers, Elya managed to close the distance between himself and the drone to within half a kilometer. At this point, the Kryl drone flipped back around and arced up overhead in a loop —the same maneuver that Osprey had cautioned him against earlier that day.

As it came around, Elya cut his thrust, repositioning himself and waiting for his weapons system to lock onto the drone. As he expected, the craft came down in front of him, and when it did he mashed on his trigger, only to watch his blaster bolts soar right through the craft.

"Impossible," Elya whispered.

"Nevers, pull up! *Pull up!*"

The drone braked and though Hedgebot flashed a bright red warning, Elya was too slow and too close to do anything except brace himself. To his complete and utter astonishment, the Kryl drone phased *through his ship*. His starfighter should have cut that drone in half, killing them both; instead, it passed through him, unharmed.

For a frozen moment, Elya's Sabre occupied the same physical space as the Kryl drone. The craft was twice as large as his Sabre... and though he had expected it to be unmanned, it wasn't. A vicious and deformed-looking Kryl with a midnight-black carapace and six arms terminating in skeletal claws, veered past him clacking its mandibles.

Above the mandibles, Elya met a pair of eyes set deep into a face that seemed far too human. He blinked and it was gone, the pilot once again hidden behind the hull of the Kryl drone.

"Nevers!" Osprey shouted, forgetting to use his call sign in her concern for him. "Nevers, are you okay?"

His starfighter beeped a warning as the drone's weapons system locked onto him from behind.

"Oh no." A cold spark of fear shivered through him, and his skin burst out in tingling gooseflesh. Elya's body rocked violently as the drone's weapons landed a direct hit on the rear left wing of his Sabre, taking out one of his two main engines. Warning systems blared, his control panel lit up, the filaments along Hedgebot's back flashed red. Another targeted salvo from the Kryl took out two of his maneuvering thrusters. Elya's Sabre went into an uncontrollable tailspin, pulled in by the gravity of the moon.

The blinking white of an explosion behind him told him that Osprey had landed a hit on the drone and damaged it. Elya didn't think it had been taken out of commission completely, though, as it veered away from them.

Captain Osprey wavered between pursuing the damaged drone and sticking with him, but eventually she stuck with him.

"Nevers!" Osprey called. "Hang on! I'm coming after you."

Elya did his best. He fought to regain control of the starfighter, but it had been lost to him. Caught in the gravitational pull of Robichar, Elya spiraled down toward the colony moon. As his starfighter spun, the movement overwhelmed even the cocktail of stimulants in his system, and he lost consciousness.

FIVE

W hen the Kryl drone disappeared from the lidar and then reappeared a moment later, Admiral Kira Miyaru sat bolt upright.

Did that Kryl drone just drop off the scanners? Drones shouldn't be able to do that. *No* spacecraft should.

Her fingernails dug into the underside of the command couch's padded arms. Every officer on the bridge inhaled and tensed with her. She'd let Colonel Volk give most of the orders during the engagement—she preferred to remain silent as much as possible, projecting an air of calm and letting her officers focus on their work. They knew their jobs and didn't need their commander barking at them; that was Colonel Volk's job.

"Starfighter down!" Colonel Volk turned and raised a salt-and-pepper eyebrow in her direction. "He's gonna have a rough landing on Robichar."

Kira drew a deep, measured breath. Several officers pulled their caps off their heads in a sign of respect.

"He's not dead yet," Kira snarled, a gust of emotion momentarily lifting the lid she'd been keeping on top of her fury. She released the chair's arms and the foam expanded, filling the crescent-shaped indents her nails had left behind. "Dispatch a Search and Rescue team."

"Aye, sir."

She wouldn't even think of leaving a starfighter pilot on an abandoned moon to fend for himself during a Kryl invasion, and she wanted everyone to know it.

But there was something else, too—whatever trick that Kryl drone had pulled was pregnant with potential strategic significance. The brief disappearance of a Kryl drone from a lidar monitor could be explained away as a glitch in the tech; Earth knew none of their equipment worked perfectly, and it was a running joke that every destroyer spent twice as much time under repair as other ships in the fleet. Video footage from the cockpit of Captain Nevers' Sabre was another story. That footage could be the evidence she needed to finally convince the Colonization Board—even the Emperor, if he ever came out of his endless orgy—to finally listen to her. This was evidence that the Kryl were not merely keeping to their volume of space out of fear of the Empire. The twelve-year peace the galaxy had enjoyed had been a temporary reprieve. Instead of minding their own business, the Kryl had been biding their time, gathering their strength. They were on the move again and apparently they had come back armed with new tricks.

In the meantime, she needed to make sure that lidar data got saved. "Harmony, send the last five minutes of the lidar stream to my console."

"Already sent, Admiral," the AI responded.

"Show-off," she muttered.

The holoscreen brightened softly as the packet arrived. Her heartbeat quickened as she called it up. Kira was reviewing the path the Kryl drone had led Captain Nevers on when another pilot's voice cut in over the comms.

"He's not responding. I'm going after him."

"Harmony, who is that?" Kira demanded.

"Captain Casey Osprey."

Kira opened her personal communications device. "You will do no such thing, Captain. Return to your assigned patrol path and protect the Mammoth fleet."

"I can't leave him behind, sir," Captain Osprey said. "Permission to go after him? I have eyes on his Sabre."

"So do we, Captain Osprey. Stand down."

"Sir!" Osprey said. "As the flight lead, his safety is my responsibility."

"You have your orders, Captain Osprey."

The captain ignored her, however and Kira saw on the lidar that she had begun to angle down toward the moon, entering the moon's gravity well in the same direction the downed starfighter had fallen.

"Captain Osprey, this is your last chance. Turn around or I will take over your starfighter and bring you back myself."

A ringing silence filled the bridge. All officers had frozen at their stations. Kira didn't need to see the face of the hotheaded young pilot to know that Captain Osprey was fighting an internal battle with her conscience—obey orders and abandon her squadmate, someone she was obviously close to, or disobey orders and go after him like the hero she imagined herself to be.

This silent struggle was one Kira was intimately familiar with. It was never easy to watch someone you loved face danger on their own... but that was a burden soldiers of the Solaran Empire had to bear. Sometimes, for the greater good, you had to let your friends fight their own battles.

Captain Osprey couldn't know that Kira had no intention of leaving one of her pilots behind. The pilot hadn't heard Kira give the order to dispatch a SAR team. Assuming Captain Nevers survived the crash—and he had about a fifty percent chance of doing so, if the skies were clear and he stayed conscious after entering the moon's atmosphere—and followed protocol, the Search and Rescue team would pick him up in a matter of hours.

Captain Osprey's starfighter continued on its vector toward the moon.

"Captain Osprey," Kira repeated. "This is your last warning. I will RemOp your starfighter and bring you in if you do not stand down immediately."

"Ahhh!" Osprey yelled. "Damn you!" There was the sound of a fist against metal as she punched the control panel. The path of her starfighter continued its pursuit of the injured drone.

"Harmony, bring Captain Osprey back to the *Paladin*."

"Yes, Admiral." The path of Osprey's Sabre veered around as the AI took control of the craft.

Kira closed the comm link. Better if she didn't hear the string of insults the captain would undoubtedly hurl in her direction. That pilot just did one of the hardest things any flight lead had to do—leave her squadmate to fend for himself in enemy-occupied territory—and she needed space to vent. "Colonel Volk, I want the video footage from Captain Osprey's cube as well."

"Yes, sir."

"And she's to report to me as soon as she lands." Kira didn't care that three generations of Ospreys had fought the Kryl. Not even the daughter of a retired Inquisitor got special treatment under her command.

"Yes, sir," Colonel Volk said.

A flurry of activity resumed on the bridge as her officers returned their attention to their stations.

Short work was made of the remaining pack of Kryl drones on the other side of the moon. Those that got away descended to the moon's surface. Her starfighters were ordered not to pursue. It was the responsibility of the Robichar ground forces overseeing evacuation to defend the civilians planetside. Except for the Search and Rescue team who would retrieve Captain Nevers, she needed the rest of her forces in orbit around the planet, ready to protect their retreat upon arrival of the bulk of the Kryl hive, still headed in their direction.

Kira took advantage of the pause to return to the lidar readout on her personal holoscreen. She played the relevant section through several times. Captain Nevers' quick reactions and tight flying had allowed him to gain on the Kryl drone, little by little, as it maneuvered through the Mammoth fleet. Though he had abandoned his patrol path, she felt a grudging admiration grow for the young pilot's dogged pursuit. His flying and his stubbornness reminded her of someone she had once known very well: the now-legendary Captain Ruidiaz. The two seemed to have similar flying styles, as well as similar hardheaded personalities which made ignoring orders to pursue Kryl craft seem like a sensible decision in the heat of battle.

These were fleeting thoughts, however. Her attention was occupied by the teardrop icon representing the unusual Kryl drone. Her eyes hadn't deceived her; the ship dropped off the lidar for half a second before reappearing behind Captain Nevers. If it hadn't skipped over such a short distance—and if drones were outfitted with the right kind of drive, which they weren't—she might have thought it had entered hyperspace.

As she played it back again, her breath caught in her throat and her heartbeat danced in her chest. She had never seen such a thing before and it confirmed her deepest fears: the Kryl were evolving. She didn't know how, but here was the proof. They hadn't been licking their wounds over the past dozen years of intergalactic peace—they'd been developing new technologies that made them more dangerous than ever.

She would review the video footage of Captain Osprey and Captain Nevers to corroborate her theory. But first, she had to secure the civilian fleet. Kira forced her eyes away from the holoscreen.

"How's that Mammoth doing?"

"They're patching it up now, sir. It won't be fit to enter hyperspace for another few hours. And even then we'll have to be careful it's properly shielded."

She nodded. The Mammoth that got hit with a torpedo was a risk, but the repair techs manning it were among the Empire's finest. The repairs would be completed before the rest of the Kryl hive arrived. She would make sure of it.

"Dispatch additional repair units. They need all the extra hands they can get right now," Kira said. "I want that Mammoth ready to go in three hours."

"Yes, sir."

"In the meantime, check in on the shuttle schedule. See if we can do anything to speed up the evacuation."

Kira returned to the lidar recap, then checked on the status of Captain Osprey. The pilot had just landed in the hangar of the destroyer. The rest of Nevers' squad had been recalled as well.

Kira returned to the command couch and drummed her fingers on the armrest as she thought through the implications of this discovery. She had already pointed out to Imperial Command and the Colonization Board that the Kryl hive's sudden activity couldn't be without an explanation. At the time, they had demanded to know the reason for the hive splintering from the bulk of the horde, and she had been unable to supply a satisfactory explanation. In the end, they had grudgingly agreed to evacuate Robichar, the only colony that happened to be in the path of the hive's apparent movement. And getting them to agree to *that* had been like pulling teeth from the mouth of a madman.

Evacuating this colony was only a minor setback to the board. In the time that the evacuation had been approved, charters for two new colonies had been signed. Those colonization efforts were already underway.

If she could figure out what this meant, she would have evidence to present to the board that would force them to call a halt to their aggressive colonization efforts. The last thing they wanted, if the Kryl were indeed on the move again, was to continue colonial expansion—especially if the hive had been developing new technologies during their hibernation. It was impossible for the Fleet to effectively defend all the new colonies; that's what had Kira so worried. But of course, she needed proof to convince the board of anything. Especially without direct involvement from the cloistered Emperor.

She was working through how to approach the board with this evidence when a tremor shook through the floor of the bridge.

"What was that?"

Harmony turned her glowing face toward Kira. "There has been an explosion in the hangar, Admiral. I've managed to contain the atmosphere. Currently assessing the damage and preparing a report."

A pit formed in the bottom of Kira's stomach. "Earth's last lights. Colonel Volk, you have the bridge."

A security team fell in behind her as she marched into the halls of the *Paladin* to deal with the next emergency.

SIX

Elya was flung back into consciousness while the world spun around him. His head rattled and, for a terrifying moment, he thought he was a child again, fleeing Yuzosix. Elya, his mother, and his two older brothers had fought their way onto a shuttle in order to escape the planet during a Kryl invasion. He remembered the ship shaking so hard during launch it felt like his brains would rattle right out of his skull.

The same feeling now consumed him as his body was thrown against his safety harness. His helmet rebounded off the cockpit's frame, splashing black and red smudges across his vision. It was only thanks to thousands of hours in the cockpit and the deep grooves of muscle memory that Elya reached out blindly and found the controls by feel. He kicked the rudder in the opposite direction of the spin and held it there, then shoved the stick fully forward to lower the nose. The jet didn't respond. His flight controls were unresponsive.

Hedgebot blinked bright red. The little guy was jammed into a corner by the centrifugal force of the spinning craft. Elya tried the thrusters and found that all of his engines were dead. That's when he remembered what had happened: Kryl drones dropping in among the Mammoth fleet and attacking, then drawing him away before phasing through his ship in an impossible maneuver and shooting out his engines.

The other ship! He craned his neck, looking around, but didn't spot it. Maybe it had burned up in the heat of atmospheric reentry.

Did the Kryl drone really phase through my ship? Or had I imagined that?

His mind recoiled when he remembered the even more unsettling part of that experience—that the drone he'd been chasing had been piloted by a monstrous Kryl. Not a living Kryl spawn shaped like a ship, as he'd been taught in his xenos class at the academy. Had the pilot's face been partially human? Or had he imagined that? Elya knew only that he'd passed within inches of the arachnoid alien.

That drone had been *manned*.

There was no time to consider these questions, no matter how wild their implications were or how scared he might be. He was too busy to be scared. His first order of business was to land the Sabre safely. Though the world outside of his cockpit continued to whirl about him, he began to make out landmarks—a cloudy blue sky, green and red treetops, a dark jagged scar of a mountain range in the distance. He was plummeting to the surface of the forest moon and would soon be turned into paste if he didn't get this thing under control.

Hedgebot scurried around his seat and busied itself behind him, motors whining as it struggled to move. The sound of soldering filled the cockpit as it operated a set of repair tools Elya had installed into its machinery, an aftermarket improvement that had been required to clear it for military use as an astrobot. There was a racket of noise, a burning smell, and then the control column in his hands rose to life as power returned. Hedgebot scurried back in front of him, its warning lights fading from a deep red to a burning orange.

"Hang on, little buddy," Elya mumbled. "We're not out of the woods yet."

The creature beeped erratically in an irritated tone, letting Elya know that, *Yes, any bot with danger sensors could detect that, you idiot.*

In spite of the very real danger, Elya grinned.

With neck muscles straining from the effort, he pushed down on the rudder pedal and shoved the stick forward again. He didn't have full control, but the Sabre began to respond. After a concerted effort that felt like he was manhandling a SecBot on elimination mode, he exited the spin and the plane entered a glide. He struggled to keep the nose straight with one hand while, with the other, he adjusted the attitude flaps on the wings. The engines may have been dead, but with limited electrics he could now control the pitch of the plane.

His elevation continued to drop precipitously, from ten thousand meters, to nine, to eight... Keeping the mountain range on his left side, Elya angled toward the only open space visible amongst the tree cover. There was a long track of pavement that might have been a runway. It sprung out of a crowd of buildings that may have been a small town, or perhaps just the outbuildings of a spaceport.

He directed the starfighter toward the clearing and the strip of pavement visible there.

As he dove through a layer of cumulus clouds, and the items on the ground began to enlarge in his vision, he picked out columns of smoke. A roaring sound filled the cockpit even through the sound-dampening seal of the starfighter, followed by a flash of light as an explosive hit the largest building next to the runway—presumably the spaceport.

More smoke billowed up. A Kryl drone arced into the sky, away from where the bomb had been dropped.

Those not immediately incinerated in the blast scattered in every direction as hundreds of people and dozens of vehicles fled for their lives.

Elya veered away from the spaceport. He needed to get there so he could contact the *Paladin*, but he couldn't guarantee a safe landing in all that chaos. It would do no good to survive this landing only to walk into a firefight.

He kept the wings of the starfighter level and pulled the nose gently up, still fighting against gravity, watching his airspeed and taking care not to stall his craft. With feeling returned to his controls, he managed to direct the plane out over the forest, looking for another safe place to land where he wouldn't get himself impaled by one of the thin trees that spread like a carpet of reddish-orange and green nails over the ground.

The Sabre gave small shakes each time it touched the edge of a stall, and each time he had to drop the nose a fraction to maintain the glide. He picked out a small clearing. It would have to do. He had just enough time to take a deep breath as the ground rushed up to meet him.

An explosion of dirt rushed over the canopy, blocking his view with rich red soil. Hedgebot tumbled over his shoulder and struck the metal frame with a sickening crunch.

The Sabre skidded forward for a long time. He hit something hard, maybe a boulder, that sent the ship bouncing and spinning again. There was a loud crack as he plowed into something else—a tree?—and Elya's helmet smashed against the side of the cockpit, darkness crowding the edge of his vision.

And then there was stillness cut only by the sound of his own ragged breathing.

The darkness receded. In its place rose a keen, gurgling

nausea. Smoke filled the cockpit, making him cough. He tried to discern his surroundings. There were thin patches of blue sky visible through the soil-covered canopy, trees in the distance, and dirt piled high against the windows. He tried to open the canopy, but it was stuck.

Beep-boop, Hedgebot beeped from the floor. Elya sighed in relief. They'd made it down alive, both of them. And he'd like to keep it that way.

A panel of safety glass at his right protected a standard-issue SB-44 Imperial Blaster and a multi-use hatchet combo tool. Somehow it hadn't been broken in the crash. He flipped open the protective lid and pressed a button that caused spiderweb cracks to shoot through the glass. Cracks were then pumped full of a clear liquid which, in turn, dissolved the glass into a pile of sand.

Elya swept the silicate grains aside with a shaking, gloved hand. He removed the hatchet, spun it around, and used the handle to pry the canopy loose until he'd formed a crack big enough for Hedgebot to pass through.

Hedgebot slipped out and limped crookedly away from the Sabre, pulsing yellow-orange. Elya gave it a moment to do its thing while he tried to calm himself. Hedgebot was measuring the atmospheric pressure and gravity, checking the air for toxic elements, and reporting the results back to Elya's tab. He didn't know where his tab was, though. A lot of good that did. He rooted around until he located it under his seat.

The tab was dead, its screen cracked. He dropped it back to the floor.

Hedgebot glowed blue, indicating that their surroundings were safe, at least for the moment. Elya felt his whole body sag in relief. He wouldn't be able to see the specific results of the bot's measurements, but he'd long ago come to trust his little hedgehog-shaped companion. The blue light was good enough for him.

Elya used the hatchet's butt to pry open the crack in the lid of the starfighter, releasing the rest of the canopy. Its powered hinges finally activated and did some of the lifting for him. Then, holding the blaster in one hand and the combo tool in the other, he stuck his own helmeted head through the opening.

Elya's starfighter seemed to be alone in a clearing, or rather, buried in the treeline at the edge of it. There was some screaming and yelling in the distance, but it wasn't close enough to locate its source. He pulled his head back inside. There was one more thing he needed to do first.

The Kryl drones which must have followed him to the moon's surface and bombed the spaceport would continue their search, eventually finding his Sabre and coming for it. Standard operating procedure was clear. Elya's task now was to scuttle the Sabre so that the enemy couldn't use it, either for its weapons or any intelligence they could glean from it.

Hideous, savage, and poisonous they might be, but stupid the Kryl were certainly not. Enough ground had been lost in the Kryl War when humanity underestimated them that these sorts of procedures had been developed in the first place.

Elya had read his manuals front to back, more than once. He'd been in the same SERE—Survival, Evasion, Resistance and Escape—training as every Imperial pilot. He knew exactly what to do. But the hull of the starfighter had warped upon impact and, try as he might, Elya couldn't reach the area behind his seat where the flight data cube was located. He'd have to climb out and go around to get it.

Shedding his helmet and oxygen mask, Elya climbed outside. He inhaled smoke and coughed. Apart from the smoke, the air was heavy and thick with moisture, something he wasn't used to breathing on the destroyer. Onboard, the dry air was filtered and recycled. Down here, it took extra labor from his lungs just to draw a normal breath.

Tucking his blaster into his waistband and hefting the hatchet, Elya made his way quickly around the back of the starfighter.

Once again using the butt end of the hatchet, he began to work his way around the edge of a rectangular panel designed for just such a situation. The panel had been crushed inward like the thumb of a giant had pressed down on the hull.

After a few minutes attacking the mangled metal, he managed to pry enough of it up to fit his arm inside. He disconnected the metal cube and hauled it out. Hedgebot stood on its hind legs and sniffed at it, then turned away, disinterested.

The black box was small enough to fit in his palm. Not only did this encrypted little computer contain the video footage of his last flight, the coordinates of his crash landing, and any information the AI had picked up from his fight with the unusual Kryl drone… but the shipboard AI was even now analyzing it for additional insight. It was supposed to activate automatically, but for some reason it hadn't. Elya found the button to activate the emergency tightbeam manually on one side of the cube, pressed it in and held it, then waited for the telltale blinking. The indicator was supposed to go solid when it had made contact with the *Paladin of Abniss*, but it was taking its sweet time. He had no doubt that once the connection was established the Search and Rescue team would be able to find him, if they hadn't located him already. Now, he could evade the enemy and go into hiding until they came for him.

He clipped the hatchet onto his belt on the opposite side of his blaster and knelt on the ground. Before he could move on, there was one more thing he had to do. He reached back into the compartment where he'd found the cube and located the timed charge. After activating it, he'd only have ten minutes to get clear. Elya paused, took a deep breath, and activated it.

Hedgebot scurried up to his feet and beeped sadly. Picking up the bot, Elya examined it and noticed that one of its feet had come clean off in the crash. Fortunately, it could walk on three feet for the time being, until he found parts to repair it.

Actually, he remembered he had put some spare parts in the medkit for this very possibility. Reaching back into the starfighter, he located the medkit, which he'd never had to use before. Lifting the medkit out, he turned back and saw a flash of red from Hedgebot. Before he had a chance to register the danger, something heavy and hard struck Elya broadside and slammed him against the Sabre's hull. Vicious claws tore at his left leg. Elya kicked away and struggled to free himself. A nauseous gust of breath blew over him as a wild animal roared in his face.

Elya inhaled sharply, eyes widening in fear—this was no wild animal, it was a Kryl groundling. Hunched back, scaly sides, long double-jointed forelimbs and knife-sharp talons. It must have been dropped by the Kryl drones he'd seen attack the spaceport. No wonder there were people screaming in the distance. These creatures were savage as rabid wolves and twice as fast, with claws that could eviscerate a person with a single swipe.

He went for his hatchet at the same moment the groundling launched itself into the air, stretched out its fore-limbs, and came down on top of Elya, pinning him to the ground. His flight suit was reinforced nanofiber and doubled as body armor, so while the Kryl's talons ripped away some of the cloth around his belly, they didn't penetrate the material. He grabbed the creature by the neck with both hands and, twisting, slammed its head into the hull of the starfighter, dazing it. He held its face hard against the hot metal until it whined. The groundling wriggled free and backed several paces away along the body of the Sabre, growling and dripping saliva.

Elya took advantage of the distance and drew his blaster. He put a hole in the creature's head, leaving a black plasma scar along the Sabre's length as the groundling's brains splattered across the hull and the trunks of broken trees behind it. The creature shivered violently and, even in death, swung its talons out at Elya. He leaned out of range and shot two more blasts into the xeno's torso.

That did the trick. The xeno collapsed in a smoking heap, with laser burns in its head and its side, its ribcage partially exposed. Soft greenish-yellow guts oozed out the holes his blaster had made. It bubbled and sizzled where it came into contact with the red dirt.

"Ugh," Elya said, holding his nose. "Disgusting. They never said anything about the smell in training." He took a couple shaky steps, gorge rising in his throat, and then retched into the torn earth. Afterward, he straightened again, wiped his mouth, and kicked some soil over the puke.

Hedgebot beeped and ran about in circles. Its warning sensors were still flashing red, reminding Elya that he'd set the scuttling charge. The fight with the groundling had taken place in less than thirty seconds, so he still had time to get clear.

Elya took a deep drag of the heavy air and looked around, for the first time focusing clearly on his surroundings. He was, indeed, in a small clearing, but up against the treeline, where several broken tree trunks had halted the starfighter's skid across the ground. He saw now how the Kryl had managed to sneak up on him, using the tangle of wood and the starfighter itself as cover.

Through the forest, at the farthest edge of his vision, Elya could see the outbuildings of a small village. People were sprinting between them. That's where the screaming he'd heard earlier was coming from. The groundling must have approached from that direction.

He quickly stuffed the medkit back into his backpack, along with the cube, and began to make his way toward the village. Hedgebot ran ahead of him.

He hadn't taken a dozen steps when a woman's high-pitched scream pierced through the forest. He broke into a run, weaving between the tall, thin trees. A handful of strange birds with four wings flitted through the canopy above him.

Ratatatat. Gunfire cut through the screaming as somebody fought back against the snarling pack of groundlings.

Thirst parched his throat, his whole whole body ached, but Elya managed to make it through the strip of woods to the edge of the village unmolested.

Smoke was whipped away on the wind as it rose from simple log cabins, constructed of the same trees that made up the forest he'd just run through. Dozens of bodies lay strewn haphazardly between the houses—women, men, children, some of them still writhing, their stomachs opened with jagged slashes, eyes blank and staring, blood soaking into the rich red dirt. It was surreal, like he'd crash landed in the kind of xeno slasher film that had become popular on Ariadne after the end of the Kryl War. For a moment his mind couldn't process it, throwing him once again back to his childhood.

His family had managed to get out of Yuzosix in time, but he'd always imagined that the people who got left behind in the chaos of that evacuation must have suffered a similar fate. He heaved at the sight of the carnage but, in a small stroke of good luck, his stomach was empty and nothing came up.

A deafening *BOOOOM* shook him from his paralysis. The scuttling charge had slagged his Sabre. A plume of greasy black smoke rose from the crash site.

Another round of gunfire drew his attention back to his immediate surroundings. It came from the other side of a small cabin to his left. He ran twenty meters, drew his blaster and peeked around the corner. He saw three groundlings circling a trio of men.

Before he could react, one of the groundlings leaped forward, sneaking under the gunfire coming from the rifle of a man facing in its direction. The groundling took out the man's leg, severing his hamstring behind his right kneecap, and then reached deftly around and cut his throat. The two surviving defenders gunned that groundling down, turning their backs long enough for the other groundlings to leap forward and knock them over.

As the remaining two men fought the two groundlings, their rifles caught uselessly between them, and their arms getting sliced by groundling talons, one of the men spotted Elya and cried out. "Save the woman and the boy! Get them out of here!"

Elya was confused. *What woman? What boy?* Then he remembered the screams and realized it was probably the woman's voice he'd heard. While these thoughts passed through his head, the talon of one of the groundlings emerged from the mouth of the man who had shouted the instructions. The groundling jerked its leg back, removing its talon from the man's mouth and leaving a hole the size of a fist in his skull.

The groundling spotted Elya then and, with the three men finished, began to advance on him.

"No, no!" came a woman's voice from Elya's left.

Stepping in front of the cabin, he saw the woman and a young boy who must have been ten, maybe eleven years old, clutching each other and cowering against the wall of the cabin. The door of the cabin had been torn off its hinges, and they had propped it up, using it like a feeble shield. The woman held a kitchen knife in front of her while the boy clung to her dress.

They won't last two minutes against those groundlings.

Drawing his blaster, he shot at the scuttling aliens. They dodged and sprinted at him. He continued to fire at them as rapidly as he could, but they were too quick. He was trained as a starfighter pilot, not an infantry soldier or sharpshooter. His aim just wasn't good enough.

The groundlings split, drawing his aim in two different directions. One came straight at him, while the other went for the woman and the boy.

Rising to her knees and coming to a crouch behind the door, the woman left the boy and stepped out with the big kitchen knife outstretched, determined to meet the groundling head on.

Though he saw the one coming straight for him, Elya took a deep breath, steadied both hands on the gun, and waited until the other groundling leaped at the woman, aiming just in front of it. His blaster caught the groundling in a back leg, sending it spinning straight onto the blade of the woman's knife.

He nearly whooped in triumph—and then the other groundling smashed into him, knocking Elya backwards. His gun went clattering to the ground behind him. The groundling's talons swept at his face, slicing his cheek. Another of the knife-like blades cut at his gloved hands, shredding the leather.

Hedgebot scurried around, flashing and beeping to

distract the Kryl. The xeno turned from Elya and went after Hedgebot, stabbing several times into the ground in quick succession as it tried to impale the bot. But Hedgebot was quick, could change directions on a dime, and the groundling missed each strike by centimeters. Frustrated, the groundling stabbed hard into the soft, red earth, getting its claw stuck in the wet soil.

Elya took advantage of the momentary distraction to draw his hatchet. He brought it down on top of the Kryl, breaching its exoskeleton.

"Eat aluminite, you ugly bug!" Elya shouted as he drew the hatchet back and slammed it into the creature's neck a second time.

The xeno separated its double rows of fangs and bellowed in pain. Lifting its body backwards, it shook to dislodge the hatchet from between two sections of its chitinous armor. The hatchet flew back and landed at the foot of the woman, who was covered in yellow blood. She kicked the groundling, causing the injured creature to rush after her with a show of death-defying strength and speed. Elya scrabbled back on his hands and knees, found his blaster and raised it in front of him.

He lined up the shot. Three red bolts buried themselves in the Kryl. It collapsed atop the woman.

Had he killed it? Had he killed *her*?

Elya hurried forward and hauled the groundling's body off her. The woman groaned. Elya sighed in relief. She was scratched and bloody, covered in stinking Kryl guts, but did not seem to be mortally wounded.

"Are you okay?"

"I—" she gagged. Elya could relate. "Ugh, ah, I think so." She spoke in heavily accented galactic standard. He didn't know what language they spoke primarily on Robichar, but most people spoke a little bit of galactic standard.

"The boy?" Elya asked.

Her eyes widened as she stumbled to her feet and rushed around the corner of the cabin, hauling the door aside with the superhuman strength only a threatened mama bear could muster. She found the boy cowering, holding his arms over his head. He bared his teeth when the woman tried to pick him up and she had to spend a couple minutes calming him down and reassuring him that the threat had passed.

Elya looked around him. His eyes passed over the three men tangled up together, dead, with the corpses of half a dozen Kryl groundlings surrounding them.

"Is that all of them?" Elya asked. "The groundlings, are there more? They travel in packs. Did you see any others come through here?"

"I don't know," the woman said. "There were so many. We killed two before they got any of us, but they were too fast… we…" She trailed off.

"How many people were in the village when they got here?"

"Maybe a dozen? Most had already left. We were on our way to the spaceport when a drone flew overhead and dropped them on us." She pointed at a slimy pad, like six fleshy tongues stitched together, that lay on the ground between the log cabins, about thirty meters from where they stood. It was open like a giant flower on the ground—the Kryl delivery system for the pack of groundlings.

"Come on," Elya said, "we've gotta get out of here before another pack of them finds us. We should head to the spaceport." If his cube wouldn't transmit, his best bet for making contact with the *Paladin* would be there. He hoped the comms equipment had survived the attack.

"No! That's the direction the drone went."

"It's our best bet. If another pack of groundlings find us

alone, we're done for. I only have a little bit of power left in my blaster, and you don't have a weapon at all."

"Take the rifles," the woman said.

Of course. What was he thinking? That crash landing and the subsequent fighting had shaken him.

"Good idea. We'll try the spaceport first, it's our best bet," Elya said, hauling the woman to her feet. "Which direction?" She pointed. "Come on."

Holstering his blaster, Elya picked up one of the rifles for himself and handed another to her. Together, with the dazed boy between them, they began to make their way toward the spaceport. They found a skimmer abandoned at the edge of the village and climbed into it. The vehicle, a topless four-seater with maglev thrusters instead of wheels, hummed to life when he pushed the power button.

Elya began to drive overground along a path through the woods. "How far away is the spaceport?"

"Just a few kilometers in that direction," she said. "Follow the road."

Some road, Elya thought. *Amazing they even have a spaceport nearby.* Most colonies started like this: a scattering of small villages connected by dirt trails. This one wasn't very far along in terms of infrastructure development.

They crossed over a small field of tilled soil, an acreage that had just been planted, and drove through another couple sections of thick woods before they came out at the top of a hill.

The ground rolled down toward the spaceport and the runway he'd wanted to land on before. Smoke rose from the outbuildings in great, thick columns. The half-dozen vehicles they saw were all moving *away* from the spaceport, and a few hundred people milled about on the opposite end by a shuttle that was tilting upward, prepping for takeoff.

Elya directed the skimmer down the slope at the same

time that the shuttle lifted on rocket boosters from the pad. Its engine roared and its body surged skyward as the crowd of people at the end of the spaceport jumped and hollered, raising their hands in the air in desperation.

A cold dread settled in his stomach. He'd seen that sort of thing before. It had been years, but he knew with an uncanny certainty that those people had been fighting to board the shuttle. It was amazing they had even managed to get the people to step back far enough not to hurt anyone in the blast of the takeoff.

The spaceport where he'd escaped Yuzosix as a child had been similar. People panicking, desperate to get off planet. A shuttle that couldn't fit them all. The shuttle would come back, he thought, but now that the Kryl had landed in force, sending everybody into a panic, there was more urgency to the evacuation.

They should have listened to the Empire's orders to evacuate.

Some part of him, perhaps drilled into him from Imperial training, caused him to shake his head, irritated at the thought. These people knew they had to evacuate. Why hadn't they done it sooner? The other half of him, the part that came from his childhood and had been raised as a refugee, felt nothing but empathy. His heart ached for these people. Uprooting their whole lives, running to the spaceport, flying out to a fleet of Mammoths in orbit, where they would spend the next weeks or months of their lives as they were taken to a new colony where they could start over. Not an appealing idea. These people had invested everything to come to Robichar, and now they had to leave it all behind. These thoughts rolled up and lodged themselves in his throat. He was so angry he saw nothing but the curve of the dirt road as the skimmer sped over the field toward the spaceport.

A screaming noise ripped the air as three Kryl drones

dove into view. The woman beside him gasped as a torpedo dropped out of the belly of the leading craft and shot toward the launching shuttle, which ruptured and exploded upon impact.

Elya leaned on the brakes and pulled the skimmer up short. "No…" he said. *All those poor, innocent people.* "No!" He smashed a fist against the dashboard.

The woman grabbed the control wheel of the skimmer. "Go the other way! Head for the mountain range."

Elya forced himself to take a deep breath. "What's in the mountain range?"

"I don't know, but it's got to be better than going down there."

"The Kryl are going to invade this planet. They're going to destroy this place. If you stay on Robichhar, you're as good as dead."

"Do you have a better idea? They just shot the shuttle out of the sky! I'd rather we take our chances in the mountains."

Elya shook his head and pressed his tongue into the back of his teeth as he forced himself to think it through. She had a good point. And he still had the cube in his pack. "I have an Imperial tightbeam. The Fleet will find us wherever we are, once it connects. You know somewhere we can hide out? Somewhere safe from the groundlings?"

She thought about it. "Safer than here."

"Tell me where to go."

"That way." The woman pointed at a place where the foothills of two soaring mountains met.

Glancing down at the dashboard of the skimmer he saw that the battery was close to empty. "We don't have much power left. Let's hope we can make it."

Pulling the skimmer around, Elya put the wreckage of the shuttle and the spaceport, with its pack of panicked refugees, at his back. Overhead, the Kryl drones continued to strafe across the sky, searching for new targets. He prayed they wouldn't follow the skimmer as he found a trail that seemed to lead toward the foothills and guided it back into the forest. He didn't see any Imperial jets in the sky yet. While he drove, Elya used his free hand to take the cube, with its embedded tightbeam, out of his backpack. He spun it around until he found the light—still blinking. Not connected.

His heart sank into his stomach.

SEVEN

evers better survive that crash, Casey thought furiously. *He better survive because when I see him, I'm going to kill him.*

She bit the inside of her cheek and bowed her head, fighting back the tears of anger that threatened to overwhelm her, as they often did.

No, she corrected herself, *as they often* used *to*. She hadn't angry-cried in years. And she wasn't about to start now.

But damn it, it was her fault. She should have flown faster. She should have flown harder. If Nevers wasn't such a damn good pilot, she would have caught him, but by the time he'd begun to chase that Kryl out toward the moon, he was already too far ahead of her.

She wanted that drone dead as badly as he did, but he never should have disobeyed orders. She was his flight lead and it was a stupid thing he did, a stupid brave stupid thing. But still. If she'd been more careful, if she'd trained a little harder, if she was paying better attention… she would have been there with him. Instead, as she emerged from the Mammoth fleet and spotted them ahead of her, twirling and swerving and spinning through space on the backdrop of Robichar's green-blue surface, she tried to get a lock on the Kryl, but Nevers had been in the way. She couldn't get a good angle—at least not fast enough to make a difference.

The Kryl had been in front of Nevers, then behind him, and then Nevers' engines blew out in a bright flash. His smoking craft was pulled into the moon's gravity well. She shot at the Kryl drone then, and even hit it, but it got clear and she chose to follow Nevers instead of giving pursuit.

If the crash didn't kill him, that drone had a damn good chance. She could only hope Nevers was fast enough and smart enough to evade capture—or worse. This thought spurred her imagination to take several gruesome liberties that made her even more sad and angry.

Casey bashed her hands against the useless control column in her starfighter. Admiral Miyaru had taken over her craft and she'd been left to fume in silence, her comms cut off from the rest of her squad while autopilot carried her back into the destroyer.

Controlling jerk, Casey thought. All because she tried to save her own squadmate. Who punishes a pilot for trying to rescue one of her own? She forced herself to take several deep breaths, attempting to quell the fury that rose within her like a writhing snake in her gut.

The starfighters of the other pilots on her squad fell in behind and in front of her auto-piloted craft, and soon they were queuing up to dock in the hangar.

Park and Yorra went ahead, with Lieutenant Colonel Walcott and the rest of the squad bringing up the rear.

As she floated toward the open mouth of the hangar, tinged a soft blue from the energy shield containing the atmosphere, she wondered what kind of punishment Admiral Miyaru had in store for her, and if the admiral would let her lead a search and rescue mission to bring Nevers home.

No doubt Nevers would scuttle his Sabre like he was supposed to and activate the tightbeam with his location. They'd be able to find him in a matter of hours, assuming he'd...

She couldn't finish the thought. Until today, she held great respect for Admiral Miyaru. Perhaps a search and rescue mission was already underway. Casey would have dispatched one already if she were in charge.

The nose of her Sabre passed through the energy shield. The artificial gravity pulled her down into her seat as her normal weight returned. She ripped off her oxygen mask and helmet and threw them to the floor.

A few seconds later, she had docked safely and Petty Officer Mick Perry was there to plug in her refueling and diagnostic cables. Once he was done, he popped the lid of her starfighter from the outside.

The aluminite canopy lifted up and Casey jumped out, not even bothering with the angled wing that doubled as a ramp. She landed in a crouch, then stood, the tight sleeves of her nanofiber suit flexing as she straightened her arms.

"You okay, Raptor?" Mick asked.

"Fine," Casey said.

Mick sniffed, shook his head and then sneezed into the elbow of his grease-stained Imperial uniform.

"Hoo! Excuse me," he said. "Well, you don't sound fine." He blinked several times. "Glad you're okay, though. I heard Nevers..." He trailed off.

Casey gritted her teeth, squared her shoulders and marched by Mick before he could finish the sentence.

Park and Yorra knew better than to try to talk to her right now. They'd seen her angry before. She couldn't talk to anybody when anger consumed her like this, as if the whole world was wrapped in red cellophane and her voice was bursting to be let out.

"Captain Osprey," a familiar baritone voice called out from behind her. "Wait."

She kept walking.

"Captain Osprey," he said, more emphasis this time on her last name, as if it was a leash he could whip around her neck and use to haul her back to him. She ducked under the wing of a starfighter, snaked around a group of mechanics conferring over a shared tablet, and increased the length of her stride as she marched away.

"If you don't stop, I'll have you court-martialed."

That put a stutter in her step.

What would her father think of his oldest daughter, the tomboy turned headstrong Sabre pilot, getting court-martialed?

Casey spun and glared daggers at Lieutenant Colonel Walcott. "You wouldn't dare."

"Wanna bet?"

Everyone around them froze and turned to watch the spectacle—the mechanics, the pilots... it seemed like the whole hangar hung their eyes on her flight suit. Lieutenant Colonel Walcott had moved faster than she thought he would. He was only a few feet away from her. Everybody else had fallen silent. The crowd watched with bated breath for the two tigers to attack each other.

Walcott was a head taller than her, and he outweighed her by fifty pounds, but she could take him. He may have been bigger than her, the more experienced commander, but he wasn't a scrapper. She was. Casey balled her fists. If he took another step, he would regret it.

"You shouldn't have gone after him," Walcott said.

"I had to."

"You didn't," he said in a gentle voice. "You shouldn't have.

Now, whatever punishment the admiral metes out to him, it will be appropriate to give you as well."

"And you would rather me have just let him go? Let the xenos have him?"

"He was gunned down by that drone anyway. He got outflown. But that's beside the point. Admiral Miyaru wants to see you."

The fire rushing through her veins went out in a gust of chill wind. The admiral wanted to see her? Right now?

"Colonel Volk told me to tell you to bring the black box from your starfighter, too. Go get it."

Lieutenant Colonel Walcott pointed back toward her Sabre, which waited where she had left it, on the opposite side of the hangar from where they stood.

Though her fury mounted at being embarrassed by her superior officer in front of all these other people, Captain Osprey tossed back the blonde bangs that had fallen into her eyes, pulled her shoulders back like her father had taught her, and walked calmly back across the hangar to her starfighter.

As she approached, Petty Officer Perry was busy taking diagnostic readouts on his tab. Unaware of her approach, he tapped a few buttons on the screen, winced and put his head into both hands as he bit down on a surprised cry of pain, like a small animal being struck by a steel-toed boot.

"Perry," Casey said, redirecting her path to check on the mechanic. "Are you okay?"

He gritted his teeth loud enough that she could hear his molars chipping as they ground together.

"Mick!" She reached down and when she brushed her fingers across his right shoulder he struck upward with a blocking forearm and backpedaled several paces.

Casey rocked back on her heels. That was strange. Mick

was normally such a calm, even-keeled guy. Young, sure, and always chuckling with an amused, infectious laugh.

It seemed like every time Casey tried to help, her allies spit in her face. Casey felt her anger rise up again. "What's your problem? I was just checking to see if you were okay."

"Xeno!" Mick yelled. He pointed at her. *"Xeno!"* Mick raised his voice and bellowed, "There's a Kryl in the hangar!"

"What—" she began to ask, but bit off the question. The sclera of his eyes had gone an orangish yellow color, and was shot through with red like fissures filled with lava. "Mick, what happened to your eyes?"

"Xeno!" he called. "Xeno, back!"

He fled, falling onto his hands and knees twice as he raced toward the closest wall of the hangar. Supplies the mechanics used to repair ships were stored along this wall, behind steel doors, on shelves and hanging from magnetic strips that would keep them battened down in case of an attack.

Mick knew these shelves very well.

Casey was surprised to see him reach not for a blaster, which she expected—after all, if she saw a killer "xeno" she'd want to shoot it in the face, too. Instead, he rushed to grip a plasma welding torch, the industrial strength kind that would be used to cut open the cockpit of a starfighter if it had been melted shut during a flawed atmospheric reentry.

With two quick motions, Mick sparked the torch to life and pointed it in her direction. Casey had been running after him, her body moving on instinct, but she stopped just short of the range of the flame, thinking that she might be able to talk him down off the ledge.

Instead, he took a swing at her, and she had to pivot her hips to avoid taking a blue flame to the neck. The torch passed within inches of her face, hissing hotly. As he stumbled past her, she kicked his right leg out from under him.

But he was fast. Mick got his leg back under him and twisted up, coming around and shoving her into the grate of one of the mechanic's tool cages. A metal edge jabbed hard into her ribs and the wind gushed from her lungs.

Mick came at her again, this time pushing the torch in front of him instead of swinging it overhead. She leaned to the side. Sparks jumped as the flame skated across the metal grate by her left ear.

She popped him once in the nose and he reeled back as blood flowed down over his lips. She punched him a second time in the right temple. He staggered back and landed with his right hand braced on a metal canister.

Breathing hard, he closed his fist and lifted the canister, about the size of a small backpack, and turned to face her, holding both the torch and the canister up in front of him.

Park, Yorra, Lieutenant Colonel Walcott and several others had run over by this point. Mick must have realized he was surrounded.

"Cosmic hellspawn," Mick cried, "from out of the darkest depths of space. If I can't escape you, at least I'll take you with me."

He began to bring the flame to the canister. She gasped. In a moment of breathless, clawing panic, Casey realized that the canister was full of highly explosive, compressed gas.

The canister of gas was used to operate certain kinds of power tools; sometimes, on extended starfighter missions, they would carry these same canisters in the plane to use on the ground as fuel once they landed. It wasn't as combustible as the type of solid-state fuel needed to power the antimatter engines on the Sabres and destroyers but it was, nonetheless, *highly* explosive.

The last time she had tried to talk him down, Mick had swung a torch at her. Casey looked around, meeting Walcott's eyes and recognizing, even if she didn't think these words consciously, that a calm personality like the commander's might be better suited to negotiating with the panicked terrorist Mick had turned into.

"Now, Mick," Walcott said, picking up Casey's unspoken cue, "I understand you're upset. I'd be upset, too, if I were in your shoes, but listen, man. It's not worth it. This is all just a misunderstanding. You're gonna be okay. Just put the torch down and let me take you to the sick bay. All right?"

Mick paused with the torch flame inches from the canister, but didn't lower it.

"Yeah," Yorra said. "See, Mick? We're friends. It's all good, man. Remember me? You helped me get into that Sabre earlier? You recognize me, don't you?"

Mick contorted his face in a series of confused expressions, shaking his head as if to deny what his eyes were showing him.

Casey reached out, her fingers brushing the wall on her left, searching for a weapon without taking her eyes off the threat.

Her hands found a metal pry bar, a workbench... what might have been a toolbox... A couple extra tablets. Where was the case for those damned blasters? If she could get the gun, one quick shot at his knee would disarm Petty Officer Perry. He'd drop the torch, probably. If this negotiation failed, she couldn't be sure there was another option.

"Mick," Park said. "'Member me? We had a couple drinks together last night. Come on, man. You rolled a straight in aleacc to win the last hand."

"You're... you're lying," Mick said.

"Come on, Perry," Yorra said. "Put it down. Do it for Talia."

Casey had seen the photo. Perry had been shoving it in anybody's face who would look last night. His wife and little daughter, just three years old.

"Buddy," Park said. "Put the torch down, man."

"We're just trying to help," Walcott said.

"No. You're lying. You can't make me." Mick's eyes widened. "For the Empire!" He shoved the flame into the side of the canister. A coin-sized circle of heat rapidly changed from silver to orange to red to white.

Park stepped forward and grabbed the canister, trying to yank it away. But Mick pulled and Park's grip carried him onto Mick's back. Together, they fell toward a group of spare gas canisters stacked together in the corner. There was a bright light and then a concussion. Captain Casey Osprey, and every person within a five meter radius, was flung backward. The back of her knees struck the wing of a starfighter and flipped her, heels over head. She landed beneath the plane as a second explosion erupted in a blinding flash, followed by another series of deafening concussions as several more canisters were set off by the first one.

That parked starfighter saved Casey's life. It was the last one that Mick had secured before losing his mind, the one that he'd been reading the diagnostics on his tab for. As explosions forced her back, she clung to the diagnostic cable. Desperately, Casey managed to grab onto one of the wheel wells as the explosions ruptured the force field separating the hangar from the dead vacuum of space. The pressure differential began to rip objects out of the hangar and cast them into the black void. Casey held on to the plane even while the physics of the rupture tried, with all its might, to space her.

She was certain that her fingers were going to give out when the ship's automated defenses sealed the hangar once more. Atmospheric pressure and standard gravity returned in a rush. She gulped air as oxygen trickled back into the room.

With shaking arms and legs, she pressed herself to her

feet and straightened, taking in the carnage. Several starfighters had been sucked out of the opening, hers included. There was debris and scattered flames for a hundred yards around the breach. Yorra bent over Park's unconscious body. He had a deep gash in the side of his forehead that bled into his left ear. Yorra clutched her left arm.

Casey ran to them and helped Yorra haul the unconscious pilot away from the wreckage and the charred area where the explosion had been centered.

"You're hurt," Yorra said, eyes wide, as she reached up to touch the side of Casey's face.

Casey twisted away from her. "Speak for yourself." But she lifted a hand to her neck where Yorra had indicated. Her fingers came away red, wet and sticky. It seemed like a superficial cut for all that. Her back and torso hurt far more where they'd struck the wing of the starfighter.

"Where's Walcott?" she asked, looking around.

Yorra swallowed and shook her head.

Casey covered her mouth with both hands as she swallowed a cry. The tears threatened again, but she refused to give them the satisfaction of flowing. She had to be strong—for Yorra, for Park, for Nevers.

"Captain Casey Osprey," a voice whip-cracked across the hangar.

A dozen Imperial troopers in crimson body armor, and the tall, leanly muscular form of Admiral Miyaru, stood just inside the hangar's closest entrance. The commander's sharp chin was lifted, her broad flat nose upraised. A platinum mohawk crowned the commander's head—her famous marker, the thing that Admiral Miyaru was known for in all the stories Casey had heard of her escapades during the Kryl War. That platinum mohawk was her one allowance, the one exception to her extraordinary discipline.

Admiral Miyaru cut an imposing figure, just like any Fleet

leader should. The starburst on her shoulders signified her rank, and the crimson and midnight blue uniform had been tailored to her form and crisply pressed.

Casey swallowed against the lump in her dry throat, which was raw and sore. First she lost a pilot, now she lost her superior officer and squadron commander. The hits just kept coming.

Admiral Miyaru made a single curt gesture. *Come with me*, it said plainly. Casey let her chin drop to her chest as she trudged slowly after the admiral.

EIGHT

As he guided the skimmer through the forest, Elya kept the cube on the seat between his legs. The light's slow blinking distracted him as he drove; it still hadn't connected. Something was blocking the tightbeam signal.

The woman directed him to... where, exactly? Down a packed dirt path that resembled more of a game trail than a road. They climbed gently into the mountain range, winding back and forth for some twenty kilometers before the skimmer beeped a warning at him.

"Well, I have good news and I have bad news," Elya said. "Which do you want first?"

The woman kept her eyes on the trail ahead. "It's not much farther."

"I'm not sure we're gonna make it much farther. The battery light just came on. That's the bad news."

She turned to check the curled form of her sleeping son. "I was hoping I wouldn't have to wake him again so soon." She turned back to the road. "What's the good news?"

"The good news is, I don't think those groundlings are following us anymore."

She froze. Elya could almost smell the rank scent of fear creeping back into the cab of the skimmer. "They were following us?"

"A new pack. They dogged us for a couple klicks before they ran out of stamina and fell back."

"Why didn't you say anything?"

Elya glanced at the boy, whose eyes shot open perhaps as a subconscious reaction to his mother's fear. The child stared raptly up at Elya, eyes wide and hands clenched in the blanket his mother had laid over him—the emergency blanket from Elya's pack.

Elya supposed he couldn't blame the colonists for being frightened. He would have been too if he had fled his home by climbing into a skimmer with a Fleet pilot whose uniform was spattered with yellow Kryl blood. Elya may have saved them from certain death, but that made him *more* dangerous, not less.

If he was being honest, Elya was just as scared as they were and bad at hiding it. As a former refugee, this situation was not unfamiliar. The only difference was that Elya had had years to process what he'd gone through. To find himself back in this situation was surreal—and heavy. He felt the weight of responsibility to get this woman and her son to safety, just as his own mother had done for him and his two brothers. He found himself thinking about the money he'd sent home only a handful of hours ago—had it really been just this morning? What was his mother doing at this moment? He found himself sympathizing with her plight as a younger woman who'd had to escort three boys on an inter-stellar pilgrimage.

Feeling the woman's eyes studying him, Elya wrenched himself away from his memories and cleared his throat. "Anyway, I don't think the skimmer's got much juice left."

"Here's the turnoff," she said, pointing to the side of the road.

"Where are you taking us?" She knew this country better than he did, and after that shuttle got shot out of the sky he didn't have many options left. He was hoping that gaining some altitude would resolve whatever interference was preventing his cube from connecting to the *Paladin*. It hadn't happened yet, and until it did he couldn't hope for rescue. Maybe he needed to go higher still.

Elya planned out his next moves—get these two refugees somewhere safe and take a closer look at the cube. Even if he couldn't fix it, he'd still have time to find somewhere conspicuous to send up a smoke signal for the Search and Rescue team to home in on his location.

It wasn't lost on him, however, that the fleet didn't intend to be here twenty-four hours from now. They might delay a few hours, given the situation... but Elya was only one man. He couldn't count on them changing plans just for him. Admiral Miyaru had built a reputation during the Kryl War as a fearless leader. Unflinching at the helm of a destroyer. She wouldn't wait long.

Sighing out his frustration, Elya guided the skimmer carefully onto the turnoff that the woman indicated. They bumped up a steeper, rocky incline into the foothills.

At this elevation, the forest thinned out. It was still a wooded area, but it wasn't the thick jungle of the valley bottom. Up here, the trees were stocky and sparse, gathered in clumps among the foothills.

"So," Elya said, "are you going to tell me where we're going?"

"Somewhere safe."

"Yeah, you said that before."

"There was a priest," she said. "A priest of Animus. He comes to our village twice a year to make Solstice offerings."

"Local Solstice?"

"Old Earth calendar."

Followers of Animus celebrated the Summer Solstice once every three hundred and sixty-five days—and a quarter if the priest was a stickler for details. According to tradition, this ritual was the single unbroken thread tying humanity back to Old Earth. He'd once heard a priest claim their religion originated during the Great Migration when our ancestors left their dying homeworld behind, but no one knew for sure. The history from that era was jumbled and incomplete.

Modern practice had long ago switched the Solstice celebrations to match the summer and winter solstice on each colony which observed the holiday—so that each planet celebrated their local Summer Solstice during the time in which their planet's axial tilt was positioned to give them the maximum amount of light and warmth from their sun. In other words, on the actual solstice as the residents of that planet experienced it.

Only the most fanatical sects kept to the Old Earth calendar. His mother had come from such a family. Elya remembered how she kept a separate calendar to track the holiday, which was staggered from the local rotation of Yuzosix (a two hundred and twenty-day orbit). It was confusing, but to a kid it had seemed magical. When he was very young, Elya had been ecstatic to learn that the Summer Solstice fell on different days, in different seasons, each year. It was through this offset rhythm that he first came to realize that planets orbited their suns at different speeds and cadences, dancing to the beat of their own individual gravity. Once the door to that knowledge opened, each time the Solstice came, Elya felt like he was witnessing a wild spirit manifest itself in reality. From there, the whole universe opened up for him. Though she never let go of the Solstice traditions, his mother had left that sect when she was sixteen. She ran away with his father, they were granted a homestead charter on Yuzosix and the rest, as they say, is history.

The woman next to him must have mistaken his silent musings for hesitation. Into the pause, she spoke again. "The priest showed up last week, after Robichar received the Emperor's evacuation order, and told us that we had another option. Instead of fleeing, we could join him in the mountains. He promised to keep us safe."

Elya stared at her with bugged-out eyes and his mouth hanging slightly open. His foot came off the accelerator and the skimmer slowed to a stop. "Safe? Here? That's insane."

"That's what he said."

"And you believe him?"

She shrugged. "I don't disbelieve him. Besides, what choice do we have now? You saw what happened to the shuttle!"

It was difficult to argue that point. Elya took a slow, deep breath in and blew it out. It sounded grumpier than he intended.

"Listen. Do you know about Yuzosix?"

When she shook her head, Elya cringed inwardly. Almost everyone he had ever met in the Fleet knew the story of his home planet. It was such common knowledge that Elya avoided the topic just so he didn't get pity stares from those who knew his history.

This woman, though, was from the middle-of-nowhere. "The Kryl invaded my homeworld when I was a boy," Elya explained. "Ten years it's been. There's nothing human left there now. The entire planet is a honeycombed Kryl hive and everyone who insisted on staying behind was slaughtered. So, no, you can't stay here. It's not safe. Not in that village, not in the mountains, not anywhere. When the Fleet comes to pick me up—and they will—you and the boy can come with me. I'll take you to the *Paladin*, and you can rejoin the rest of the refugees later."

The woman grimaced. She glanced down at the cube between his legs. "And that thing's going to get us there?"

Elya felt the blood rush to his face. He was momentarily glad that the sun had disappeared behind the mountaintops and the fading light masked his features.

"I'll get it working. It got busted up when I landed. Once we find somewhere to hunker down for the night, I'll be able to take a closer look at it."

She looked at him out of the corner of her eye. Elya wasn't interested in arguing with her any more than he already had. He knew his own skill with bots and electronics. Whether he had the time and tools to fix it was another question.

Why was he trying so hard to help her? Elya turned around to look at the boy. Shame squeezed its hand around his throat. "I'm sorry. I'm glad you know somewhere safe we can hunker down for the night."

"Thank you."

"I'll go with you to where you think this priest is hiding. But I'm not going to stick around. And you shouldn't either."

She shrugged. "Maybe. Maybe not."

He sighed. "If we're gonna travel together, we should know each other's names, don't you think? I'm Elya." He cleared his throat. "I'm a starfighter pilot with the Solaran Defense Forces."

The woman rolled her eyes. "Really? I couldn't tell." Her sweeping gesture took in the cube and his Imperial uniform.

Elya opened his mouth to defend himself, then let out a bark of laughter. People on fringe colonies had a reputation for not always being kind to Imperial soldiers... but he definitely deserved that one. "Fair enough. It's been a rough day." A pinching feeling in the small of his back was a testament to his words. Those groundlings had done a number on him.

Elya broke eye contact with the woman and turned fully around in the seat to gaze at the boy, who took a panicked breath and widened his eyes even further. His eyes were already like saucers, big white rings around turquoise irises that shone in the fading pink light, just like his mother's but sharper somehow. In addition to his striking eyes, the boy had a round chin, hair the color of Robichar's brownish-red soil and sun-kissed skin.

The boy was deeply tanned from spending so much time outdoors. Rural life had been good to him. Elya had lost some of his own pigment since he'd become a starfighter. He spent so much time on space stations and destroyers and in the shielded cockpit of his Sabre that he didn't actually get much sun these days. Vitamin D supplements didn't cut it. They had tanning decks on most space stations, but while the rest of his squadmates were there, Elya typically stayed behind, choosing to use the extra time to do additional training, or perhaps drafting and discarding long messages to his mom and his brothers, Arn and Rojer, rather than join his squad gabbing and gambling.

You don't have to do this alone. He felt his face redden when he realized he was parroting Casey Osprey's words in his mind. *You're not a refugee anymore.*

The boy cocked his head, watching him warily. Elya smiled affably and held up his hands, trying to show the boy that he was no threat. Perhaps the kid was still in shock from the Kryl encounter. He would have been. In fact, Elya had realized in recent years that the fear he'd experienced during the evacuation from Yuzosix, and during the subsequent dark flight on the Mammoth longhauler, had lingered for years. He had suffered a combination of habitual fidgeting paired with a low-key yet persistent distrusting paranoia. He hadn't known it at the time. He'd been angry and scared and isolated, and it had taken years for the chop to settle.

This boy must have been experiencing something very much like what Elya went through. The difference was, Elya could help him. Or at least try.

Elya crossed his arms on the back of the seat. "Now you know my name. What's yours?"

"His name is Hedrick," the woman said. "I'm Heidi."

"It's nice to meet you both." He kept his eyes on the boy. "I'm really sorry about what those Kryl did to your village, but I'm glad I found you when I did. I'm glad I was able to help."

The boy sniffed and nodded reluctantly. Tears filled his eyes, making them shimmer and swim like the ocean they resembled. The combination of dark hair and turquoise eyes was unusual. Elya's own eyes were a rich brown like his mother's.

"Me too," the boy said, his voice barely above a whisper. He cast his eyes into his lap. Hedrick had let the blanket slip down and Elya saw that he was not kneading the blanket, but rather a tiny bot in his hand. It was the kind that they gave to children when they were old enough not to try to eat them; they often resembled Old Earth animals.

His was a turtle.

The shell on its back was carved with sun symbols from the religious sect of Animus. Chips of silver paint showed that the coloring of the symbols had been worn away over time. The turtle's head popped out, and it crawled around on the boy's lap before settling down and retracting its head.

"Nice bot," Elya said. "Did you see mine?"

Elya snapped his fingers and Hedgebot crawled up from the floor to perch on the headrest at eye level. It chittered in digital tones at the turtle in the boy's lap.

Hedrick smiled. "What's he do?"

Hedgebot gave off a soft blue nimbus. "He helps keep me safe. And he'll help keep you safe, too, while you're with me."

"How does he do that?" the boy asked.

"When he detects danger nearby, he turns red. See how he's blue now?" Hedrick nodded. "He's also a pretty good pilot. Saved my life up there today." Elya pointed at the sky.

Something about this twist of the conversation turned the boy off. He wouldn't say anything else, though Elya tried to coax more out of him.

"He's had a rough day," Heidi said.

"Totally understandable. Now, let's see if we can find that priest of yours."

The skimmer's battery died four kilometers later. Though the sun had stepped behind the mountain peaks, there was light enough to last for two or three hours of hiking. They climbed out of the skimmer and Elya hiked his ruck onto his back.

Neither Heidi nor the boy had time to pick up supplies of their own, so there wasn't that much to carry. Elya's pack held a couple liters of water, a dozen pre-packaged rations, the insulated blanket, flares, and a few other necessary items. He had his hatchet and his blaster as well, so even if they had to camp for the night, their chances looked good.

He told Heidi so.

"We won't need to camp," she said. "It's not much farther."

They followed the game trail into increasingly rocky terrain. They had climbed more than two or three thousand meters in elevation since leaving the valley, and by this point, trees had been replaced by sparse shrubs and the grass had all but thinned to dirt.

They followed the trail as it wound ever upward. Even

had the skimmer's battery lasted longer, they wouldn't have been able to use it to navigate this terrain, with the narrow trail and the ever-larger boulders. He was relying entirely on Heidi's ability to lead them to wherever this priest had holed himself up. Elya fretted silently, yet Heidi hurried onward, sure-footed and solid. And the boy, though he tended to drag his feet and kick small rocks and roots, did not complain and was careful to keep close. Hedgebot, glowing a soft blue, lit the boy's way while Hedrick made a game of trying to catch him.

They hiked, stopping occasionally to rest and take sips of the water in Elya's pack. He was careful to conserve it, even showing the boy how to project how long the water would last by counting the ticks on the side of each bottle.

Heidi stopped at the next fork. The trail to the right wound up along an exposed slope, its scree-covered incline angling down into darkness. The other way meandered left and then cut into a ravine.

He couldn't quite tell from here, but Elya thought the ravine walked down into a canyon and was reminded of the flight simulation he'd run just that morning. Had the AI somehow known that he would have to navigate a canyon later that day? He shook his head. Those training runs that morning seemed so long ago. There was no way the shipboard AI could have known he would come here. An uncanny coincidence, that was all. Still, it unnerved him.

Heidi hadn't moved.

"Which way?" he asked.

She muttered under her breath, glancing back and forth until she settled on the left-hand path. "This way."

"Are you sure?"

"Sort of."

"How sure is sort of sure?"

"I followed his directions…"

"You've never been here?"

"Well, no, but it seemed so simple…"

Elya groaned. Heidi had no clue where she was going. She was going to take them up into the mountains and get them all lost. The water and rations in his pack suddenly seemed much more precious. They only had enough light for maybe an hour before they would have to make camp. He itched to take the cube out of his pack and try it again but fought down the urge as well as his mounting frustration. He took three full breaths as they taught him to do in pilot training to maintain calm and focus. He tried to detach himself from the situation, to assess it logically. He reviewed the standard operating procedures for a downed starfighter pilot.

One: Survive.

Two: Evade.

Three: Resist.

Four: Escape.

These were his orders. Survive the crash, evade capture, resist if necessary, and escape if possible. He didn't intend to let any Kryl take him hostage, but there was always the chance. That's why every pilot went through the SERE class. But he may have taken the evade *too* far by following Heidi up here. If he evaded too well, he'd also evade being rescued and that would be a disaster. The kind you didn't come back from. They had wall-mounted brass plaques in the halls of the *Paladin* for soldiers like that.

"What?" Heidi snapped.

Elya forced himself to remain calm. Hedgebot circled him and came to rest between his feet. He was working up a response when there was a groan and a rumble from the scree-covered slope to their right.

The boy leaped behind him, wrapping his arms around Elya's leg. Heidi staggered back while gravel and stone skittered down the slope in a rush.

"Probably just an animal," Elya said as the cacophony receded, echoing in the night. Hedgebot darted forward and raised itself up, poised and sensing... but it remained soft blue. There was no danger—at least none it could sense yet.

"There are mountain goats up here," Heidi said. "The governor had them imported once the charter was approved."

"Mountain goats? What the hell'd they bring mountain goats all the way out here for?"

She glared at him. "To balance the ecology."

Elya snorted. "Well, I guess if they need creatures to crop the grass, mountain goats are probably pretty useful."

Heidi's glare softened. Her eyes glittered in the fading light as a sly smirk formed on her lips. "You're funny."

The echo of the rock slide faded and the whispering silence of nature returned. The sound of birds chirping in the distance, bright stars twinkling overhead, a fresh crisp smell like it might rain overnight. If Elya wasn't so worried about reconnecting with the *Paladin* and getting this woman and her young son to safety, he might have enjoyed being outdoors; after being stuck on the ship for weeks, the fresh air in his lungs felt glorious.

Heidi seemed to come to a decision. "This way." She took the left fork, marching toward the ravine.

The trail descended as the walls climbed and the ravine turned into a canyon. The trail narrowed and widened and narrowed again. They climbed over two-meter-wide boulders, using handholds in the craggy red rock walls to haul themselves up and over. Hedrick tripped and fell, once. Then again. On the third time, he scraped his palms raw against the gravel.

"Maybe we should stop for the night," Elya suggested.

There was a wide area on a ledge in front of them. If they climbed up, he thought he might be able to find a cave or an overhang sheltered from the wind. They'd passed many such outcroppings, and any one of them would do. They would be high enough, away from the trail, sheltered from any rain that might blow in overnight. They might even be able to start a fire if they managed to find enough wood. Regardless, the blanket in his pack would keep them warm for the night. Sleep seemed very appealing.

"It's just the end of this ravine," Heidi insisted.

But Elya no longer believed she knew where she was going. She didn't know where this priest of Animus and his followers were hiding. She had been told to follow this trail, but had never been here herself, didn't know any of the specifics, had no clue—

Hedgebot darted forward, raised its bristles and shimmered ruby red, revealing malformed shadow shapes.

Whatever argument Elya was preparing to make trickled out of his mind. He heard the scuffle of rocks and the crunch of gravel ahead. Heidi, breathing heavily, turned toward it. Two eyes glowed out of the darkness. "Oh, Animus protect us," she whispered.

"Behind me," Elya said, drawing his blaster and flicking off the safety.

The creature stepped down the slope, swaying as it sauntered toward them. How much Elya would have given for it to be a goat... or even a native beast, something hairy with claws and teeth that evolved on the moon of Robichar or had been brought here by the colonists to "balance the ecology." But there was no mistaking it. That humped back, the way the light glistened off its scales, the creature's eyes glowing a contaminated, sickly yellow-orange, like a demon possessed. It was another Kryl groundling. The pack *had* managed to follow them. And now it had them cornered.

Elya had been trained on the vicious, strategic intelligence of these creatures—not to mention years of stories he'd heard passed down from refugees, from survivors. The groundlings had no doubt waited until the three travelers entered the canyon to make their appearance.

Two more revealed themselves, padding softly up from the other direction. Their jaws hung open, saliva dripping from their double rows of savage teeth as they leered at the travelers they had cornered.

Elya lifted his blaster and fired at the pair of groundlings behind them, then twisted and shot at the lone one coming from the front. The bolts ricocheted off the stone, throwing shards of rock and sand into the face of the groundlings when the shots fell short.

The creatures bounded toward them as Heidi unhooked the hatchet from Elya's belt and swung. The first groundling to reach them saw the blade coming and put on the brakes, hissing, growling.

The boy, trapped between them, began to wail. Hedgebot scurried up a rock behind them and uttered a series of high-pitched, pleading tones, trying to get the boy to follow him to safety. Hedrick was too panicked to recognize what the bot was trying to get him to do.

They backed up against the canyon wall as the trio of groundlings converged.

Elya let loose with his blaster, firing five more shots before the trigger lost pressure, the weapon's charge depleted.

He reached down with his free hand, making sure the kid was fully protected behind him, feeling his shaking hands clutching his uniform.

"You'll have to go through me first, you xeno scum," Elya growled.

The groundlings had slowed. Several of his shots had burned or sent them reeling, but their slimy carapace was tough. None of the wild shots had hit a vulnerable spot.

Somehow recognizing that Elya's blaster was out of power and that, as brave a face as Heidi put on with a hatchet in her hand, she was not trained to hack anything to pieces, the Kryl beasts slowly stepped forward...

And froze.

The three groundlings, as if they were the same organism, glanced up the trail in the direction the trio of travelers had been heading. A dark figure swathed in flowing robes stood at the top of the incline, silhouetted against the starry sky.

"Begone!" the man yelled. "In the name of Animus, I command you. Begone, creatures of darkness!"

The man held up an object that flared bright green in his hand. It warped Elya's vision and made him feel like he was staring into a shimmering heatwave.

In unison, the groundlings backed away from Elya, Heidi, and Hedrick. They bared their teeth in the direction of the cloaked figure, then broke and loped off into the darkness, moving away in the direction the travelers had come.

The green light winked out and the man descended the opposite slope, staggering downward with his right leg forward, as if the back one couldn't be trusted, and using a gnarled wooden walking stick for balance. "Are you all right?" the man asked. His voice was breathless and thin. Elya immediately had a picture of a fragile, older man, though he couldn't make out the face hooded in the robe's cowl. As he drew closer, Elya looked for the glowing green object. He thought the object had been rounder, more like a lantern. Instead, the man held a normal flashlight. Maybe it had some kind of filter mechanism that could change the light's color? He wasn't sure. He'd only glanced at it for a moment. Mostly, he'd been focused on the groundlings and his own terror.

Hedrick clutched Elya's uniform tighter. Heidi, eyes wide, stared at the old man, slowly cocking her head to one side.

As he approached, recognition softened her features. "It's you."

"Do I know you?"

Heidi took a step toward the man. Hedrick leaped from Elya and hauled back on his mother's arm. "Mom, no!"

"It's okay, sweetheart. It's safe."

She gently detached the boy's hands and went to meet the robed man.

"Ahh, yes, I remember you now. From the village near the spaceport. I'm glad you came. Though I must say, you have terrible timing. You're lucky we set a watch tonight."

He turned the flashlight back on—now a softer, more natural whitish-yellow beam of light—upward. Elya's eyes followed it to the rim of the canyon where he found a stationary SecBot's cylindrical torso and multi-hinged camera arm pointed downward.

He didn't know where the green filter went, but by the beam of the flashlight, Elya was finally able to make out the man's features. He did, indeed, wear the robes of a priest of Animus, earth brown with rich green trim that would have been considered understated yet luxurious once, and now simply looked worn.

"How did you do that?" Elya asked. "How did you scare off the groundlings?"

The behavior of the Kryl was the opposite of what he had been taught to expect in such a situation. The footage he'd seen showed groundlings giving no quarter, fighting tooth and claw even as they were ripped to pieces by larger, more powerful mechs and infantry grenadiers. He had been told they didn't understand human concepts like fear or mercy. Yet this priest had somehow managed to scare them off without lifting a hand. Had it been the green filter on the flashlight? Some way to send subconscious signals to their brains, to scare them into fleeing? Or perhaps the SecBot had been modded, equipped with psionic tech that would imitate the psychic connection of an Overmind and order them to retreat? Elya had heard rumors of such innovations coming out of the Fleet's experimental divisions. If this priest had developed something on his own, the admiral would want to hear about it.

He expected a more detailed explanation, but all the priest said was, "Animus protects the faithful."

Elya blinked dumbly, taken aback at the man's unwavering certainty, his audacious arrogance.

Elya's mother had been a believer in the "One True God." He remembered the long nights in the Mammoth longhauler, after they fled Yuzosix, when she clutched her beads and prayed for Animus to deliver them to safety. When he had asked her why she prayed, she said, "So Animus protects us like he protected the million souls who embarked on the Great Migration."

Elya had always believed that the crew of the Mammoth had saved them from being devoured by the Kryl horde that destroyed Yuzosix... but his mother had attributed their deliverance to her god. Elya had a much harder time believing that a divine spirit was watching over them. The Spirit of Old Earth hadn't filled his belly with food; the crew of the Mammoth had done that. And, of course, the Empire was not a religious institution. Their galactic government served to protect humanity from an invasive alien species. Religion had nothing to do with it.

Oh, the Empire tolerated religion well enough. Pagan rituals in the Outer Rim, holy days observed by followers of Animus, they were all the same to the Empire.

Heidi must have sensed the animosity building between the priest and Elya. She stepped forward and put herself in between them.

"We came, as you suggested," Heidi said. "Is your offer still open?"

The priest looked them over. "For you and the boy, of course. For the Imperial soldier...? I am not so sure."

"My mother still makes offerings to the Spirit of Old Earth," Elya said. "I may not have her unwavering faith in Animus, but I can follow orders."

"Please," Heidi added. "He saved our lives. We wouldn't be here at all were it not for him. My friends…"

"I'm sorry for your loss." The priest squeezed Heidi's shoulder with his free hand. Once again his eyes skipped over the three of them—boring into Elya, resting for a beat on Hedrick. This made the boy edge several inches back behind Elya, skittish after their close encounter. Elya rested his hand on the boy's head as he felt something swell in his chest—an inkling of what his mother must have felt when she prayed so fervently, responsible for shepherding not one but three young charges to safety.

"If the boy has taken a liking to you," the priest said, "I suppose I can house you for the night."

Elya felt his body droop as tension was released. He was exhausted by this point and wanted only to rest a moment, to look at his cube to see if he could fix whatever was wrong with it.

A quiet part of him, the part who had pledged fealty to the Emperor when he signed on to the Solaran Defense Forces, thought it might prove useful to know the location of the enclave of this priest and his cult of followers. So that when he *was* rescued, he could tell Admiral Miyaru where these people were hiding and get them escorted to safety before the inevitable tragedy struck. The priest might have been able to scare off a few groundlings, but no way could he intimidate an Overmind and her entire murderous, devouring hive with a simple light show.

Elya shot the priest his best, most cooperative smile, the same one he'd given Osprey earlier that day. The priest spun, his robes fanning out, and struck the walking stick firmly into the earth. He handed the flashlight to Heidi, who shone the beam of light up the ravine.

"It's not far. Follow me."

NINE

When Kira entered the war room, Captain Casey Osprey had her hands planted on the octagonal table, head bowed, greasy blonde locks hanging over her face like a curtain. A hologram of the forest moon of Robichar hung in the air over the table, slowly spinning between them.

Osprey straightened and gave a sharp salute.

"At ease, Captain."

Osprey relaxed, but only slightly. Her cheeks were red, like she was embarrassed to have been caught sulking. The captain stared right at her and yet somehow managed to avoid meeting Kira's eyes. Her father must have been a brute when it came to discipline. Osprey looked like she was steeling herself to take thirty lashes.

"I'll not defend my actions."

"I'm not asking you to."

Osprey blinked and did her best to contain a relieved sigh. She looked everywhere in the war room except at her commander's face.

Kira supposed this was only natural. Most of her junior

officers had trouble meeting her eyes. Not just because of her imposing two-meter height, but because they couldn't separate the person standing in front of them from the infamous Kryl War hero they had heard about in stories.

Of course, those who were the subject of such stories knew the way people told them rarely reflected the reality of the situation. Kira never bothered to correct anyone's mistellings. Not the ones where they left her out and made Captain Ruidiaz into the sole hero. And not the ones that portrayed her as brave and glorious when she had been nothing of the sort, either. The stories did a great job building her reputation—she had risen to the rank of admiral on their power—and it wasn't her responsibility to litigate history. She had more pressing duties.

Kira set a black cube on the table. "You know what this is?"

Captain Osprey peered at the object through slitted eyes. "Looks like a cube from a Sabre."

"Not just any Sabre," Kira said. "*Your* Sabre. I had to send two starfighters and an astrobot out to retrieve it." Osprey's jaw muscles bulged. "This is not meant to be a criticism, Captain."

"Why else do you have my cube but to examine my flight patterns and point out my mistakes?" She scowled, then added, "Sir."

Kira chose to ignore the slight. "Because what your starfighter captured may be vital to our mission here on Robichar. And, potentially, critical to the continued survival of all humanity."

"Sir, I'll be honest, I thought you brought me here to talk about what happened in the hangar."

"First, I'd like to know what you saw before Captain Nevers' Sabre got shot down by that drone."

Kira placed the cube in the middle of the table next to the holoprojector. A cone of light shimmered forth, replacing the 3D model of Robichar with a first-person view from the nose of Osprey's Sabre. The surface of the moon, the brown curve of the gas giant beyond, and the stars arrayed above jerked and spun as the captain dogged her pilot and the Kryl drone.

A string of curses emanated from the speakers. Osprey reddened at the sound of her own voice.

Kira hadn't meant to make the girl uncomfortable—at least not yet. But she did not offer any words of comfort, either. She'd heard and said much worse things in her time in the cockpit. Besides, she wanted to see how the captain would react.

"I couldn't catch them," Casey blurted out. "The drone was flying erratically and he was pushing his limits just to keep up."

"Captain Nevers is a good pilot."

Osprey's eyes snapped up and locked on her face, truly seeing the admiral for the first time since she entered the room. Kira watched her squirm. She tossed back her short blonde hair with a shake of her head. "Fancypants can fly, that's for sure. Didn't keep him from getting shot down though."

"Did you see him get out-maneuvered?"

Their eyes both returned to the footage as it played out. Osprey's starfighter arced over the last Mammoth and shot towards Robichar in the direction the Kryl drone had gone, sticking close to Nevers' tail. The teardrop-shaped enemy ship bobbed and weaved, trying to shake them, but Captain Nevers stayed true, matching each hairpin turn with precision as he tried to get a lock on the Kryl. The few shots he did fire went wide or skipped off the drone's shields. The two ships came together, then drifted apart. The drone pulled up and looped back to its original trajectory. Suddenly the Kryl drone was behind Captain Nevers. Captain Osprey's voice came through thin and frantic: "Nevers, pull up! *Pull up!*" His engines exploded, first the left and then the right, in bright flashes followed by an ominous absence of light. Antimatter engines shone white-hot from the rear and, though it had been years since she'd sat in the cockpit of a Sabre, to see them darken made Kira's stomach turn.

The drone peeled off and Osprey laid into her own blasters, cutting through the Kryl's shields and raking across its underbelly. The shots must have ruptured fuel sacs there, for the alien craft vented a cloud of translucent, viscous liquid that her Sabre cut right through. As the drone fell toward Robichar—hamstrung but not destroyed—Osprey pulled off its trail and went after Nevers.

"Nevers! Hang on!" Casey's recorded voice cried out. "I'm coming after you."

Kira reached out and paused the playback by resting her open hand in the hologram.

"Did you see that?" Kira asked.

Osprey's eyes narrowed. Her face was red again. "See what, sir?"

"How the Kryl drone got behind your pilot."

"He was out-maneuvered, sir."

"Yes, but how?"

Kira waved her hand. The hologram footage rewound, the Kryl drone piecing itself back together and Captain Nevers flying backwards, until he was behind the Kryl drone again.

"Watch carefully."

Again, the footage played forward, the Kryl drone swerving and bobbing. Elya followed, shadowing its movements. And then suddenly the Kryl drone was behind Captain Nevers. Kira paused the footage once more.

"Blink and you'll miss it."

"It must have fired up its reverse thrusters and pulled in behind him. A human pilot would suffer from those G-forces but a Kryl drone is unmanned and can take more force than we can."

"A textbook explanation. But if that were true, why did the Kryl drone fall off the lidar when it performed the maneuver?" With her other hand, Kira brought up the telemetry. These readings were nothing more than miniaturized visual representations of the ships in a particular volume of space. It showed none of the detail of the footage from Captain Osprey's Sabre—no stars, no sleek xeno curve of the Kryl craft. What it did show, however, was whether a given ship was present in real space or not.

As far as tools go, the lidar readings were essential ones for the Fleet. Kryl ships could drop out of hyperspace at any time, and without continual monitoring using lidar—Light Detection and Ranging, a remote sensing method utilizing pulsed lasers—they might not know when or where enemy forces appeared.

Captain Osprey easily read the volumes, picking out the Kryl drone. When the teardrop ship disappeared and then reappeared a moment later, Osprey's nostrils widened and she inhaled sharply.

This is what Kira had been looking for. When she entered the room, Captain Osprey had been distracted by the contents of her mind. Now she was riveted upon the lidar scans and the ship's movements, fully intent and focused.

"Admiral, can you play it back again?" she asked, leaning forward, fists on the table, now intent on the footage. Kira rewound the video from the Sabre and played it forward at half speed. It happened so fast that if you didn't slow down the playback you might miss it, like Osprey had the first time.

"There." The captain paused the footage with her own hand this time, cycling back a few frames and then forward, zooming in and then repeating the process.

"It just... appears behind him. I was too far back to see in person, but... how is that possible?"

"I trust what is seen and said in this room will remain between us."

"Yes, sir. Of course."

"The Kryl drone appears to have phased out of real space. Maybe it flickered into hyperspace for half a second to outmaneuver Captain Nevers."

"No ship can phase in and out of hyperspace like that without tearing itself apart." Osprey gave a small gasp. "Is that how they suddenly appeared in our flight path earlier, too?"

"I don't know. Seems likely," Kira said. "Maybe it's a new technology the Kryl grew in their radioactive scum ponds. But to be clear, it doesn't matter *how*."

"Sir! Respectfully, I disagree. It matters a whole hell of a lot for my pilots. If—"

Kira's upheld hand dammed the flow of Osprey's reactive tongue. *Protective, this one.* When Kira's lips tried to curl up into a smile she forced it down. It wouldn't do any good to have Osprey think she was pleased with her outburst. She had a reputation to uphold, after all.

"It matters *that* it happened—ours is not to wonder how. I saw a great deal I didn't understand during the Kryl War."

"And you never questioned it?"

Kira scoffed. "Please, Captain. Of course I did. What I saw drove people mad—men and women I respected, soldiers I fought beside. But we had to keep moving, keep fighting. Once the Kryl retreated, what I had seen was of no consequence." Kira added in her thoughts: *And who knows which half of what I saw was real and which half was a grief-induced hallucination.* A decade later, that harrowing period of her life was nothing but a confused blur.

Captain Osprey's eyes made their way back to the holo-screen. Kira forced her memories away with a practiced shove. Now was neither the time nor the place to hash it all out again.

"With the Kryl on the move," Kira said, "this is the evidence we need to convince the Emperor and the Colonization Board that the Kryl threat has truly returned—and that they're more dangerous than ever."

"What about Nevers?" Osprey asked. "If this is so important, don't you want the footage from his Sabre?"

"A Search and Rescue team has been dispatched to find and bring him back."

"Let me go look for him," Osprey said leaning forward, eyes intent. "He's my responsibility. Please."

"The SAR team has already been dispatched," she repeated, her voice flat.

Osprey shook her hair out of her eyes. Those jaw muscles bulged again.

"We'll find him, Captain."

"It's my fault," she said. "I should have gone after him when I had the chance."

"You were ordered not to."

"Nonetheless, sir, *I'm* the flight lead. He got shot down under my watch. I should have caught up to the drone. I should have—"

"Enough," Kira said. "You can't change what happened. You can only move forward. Besides, I need you here. Not only are you the only other person who witnessed what that

Kryl ship did, but with Lieutenant Colonel Walcott gone, and half of your squad injured, the Furies need leadership."

Osprey huffed a heavy breath through her nose, opened her mouth, closed it, opened it again. She wanted to say something, but she obviously didn't want to speak out of turn. Kira could see how difficult it was for Captain Osprey *not* to speak her mind. She could relate.

Finally Captain Osprey said, "Permission to speak freely, sir."

"Of course, Captain. Keep in mind, speaking freely doesn't mean there are no consequences for the words you choose, so choose wisely."

Captain Osprey rolled her bottom lip between her teeth and bit down on it. She shuffled her feet and, after a moment, threw her shoulders back and came to attention. "Yes, sir. What am I going to do here, sir? Sit on my hands, sir?"

Kira fought down another smirk. This girl had spirit, she'd give her that. "You think Walcott would have just sat on his hands?"

Osprey cast her eyes to the ground. Nothing chastised a soldier like invoking the name of a fallen comrade, especially one so recently departed. They had retrieved Walcott's frozen body—what was left of it after the explosion, anyway. Kira had ordered the lead medic to prepare his body for the journey home, where he would receive a proper send-off.

Osprey straightened again. Her eyes went up to the ceiling, as if something had just occurred to her. "Speaking of Lieutenant Colonel Walcott, sir... what happened—"

"What happened was a tragedy, and not your fault."

"No, sir, I know that. Only... what happened makes about as much sense as what you just showed me here." She gestured at the hologram, which was frozen on Elya's Sabre, with the Kryl drone blazing behind him. "Less, even. If I'm not allowed to go after Elya, I'd like to look into Petty Officer Mick Perry's strange behavior in the hangar."

Perhaps some commanders would have ordered Captain Osprey to her berth and told her to stay put and shut up. With most soldiers, that would be a fine option. But Kira could see the type of person Captain Osprey was. If she didn't have something to occupy her mind and her hands while she was forced to stay put on the *Paladin*, she would undoubtedly stir up trouble. No. It would be far better to make use of her.

And while what she had seen the Kryl drone do was evolutionary in terms of the Kryl's currently known and documented abilities, that was not her only concern at the moment. Kira still had a fleet to command, a Mammoth to repair, an evacuation to complete—not to mention the bulk of the incoming Kryl hive to mitigate against. The situation in the hangar was done and over with—untangling what happened was, unfortunately, fairly low on her list of priorities.

What would Fleet brass think of the captain investigating the death of her commanding officer? She couldn't imagine they would be thrilled. "Technically, we should call for an Imperial Inquisitor so that an objective third party can investigate the situation."

"Yes, sir, technically. But we're out on the edge of the galaxy to evacuate this colony, and there's no way we can get one sent here in a timely manner."

Her father, the Inquisitor, had taught Captain Osprey well indeed. Besides, Kira had seen the security film of the hangar. What happened was certainly unusual and warranted investigation, if for no other reason than to put her crew's mind at ease.

"Sir, what if…" Captain Osprey said, her voice pitched low. Kira took a step closer to her to hear the words she practically whispered. "I always thought these were just war stories my dad and his friends told, but... what if it was the space madness?"

Kira spun away and paced the width of the room, her memory casting back over a decade to the last time she'd seen the space madness for herself, during that confused and tragic period of her life. "Those weren't just war stories."

It wasn't uncommon for a fleet on a long deployment to have a few crew members go stir crazy. In this case, however, they had only been deployed a few weeks, not years. And she had seen the videos—the mechanic's cries of *Xeno! Xeno!* had been rather unsettling. She'd seen the space madness overtake soldiers before, but this was a novel kind of hysteria. It would be good for morale to try to pinpoint a root cause, or at least come up with a logical explanation that proved Petty Officer Perry's behavior had been an isolated occurrence.

"Very well," Kira said. "In all likelihood, the arrival of the Kryl caused the young mechanic to panic. I've already given orders to remove the gas canisters to a more secure location in order to avoid an accident like this in the future. But to reassure the crew, you have my permission to look into it. Review the security footage from the hangar. Talk to those he worked with and, if you can, find out what caused him to snap like that. I've seen space madness take people before. But rarely does it result in the deaths of three soldiers and a giant gaping hole in my hangar, so your point is well taken. Report directly to me with your findings—no one else."

"Yes, sir. Thank you, sir." Osprey's relief was palpable. She finally spread her feet and stood truly at ease.

The captain was right, this *was* an unusual request. But few people had seen the mechanic's behavior up close. Captain Osprey was a good fit for this special assignment. At least the girl had some self-awareness—and, apparently, a chip on her shoulder.

"I'll make sure you get access to the security system. Remember, not a word of the other thing we discussed here outside of this room. At least not until we have time to make a full report to the Executive Council."

"Yes, sir. I won't let you down."

"See that you don't."

TEN

When the door to the war room irised closed behind the admiral, Casey blew out her breath and braced her hands on her knees as she fought down the urge to vomit that had been present through most of her meeting with Admiral Miyaru. Thankfully, she'd been left alone in the war room and no other officer would see her lose her composure.

A head and a half taller than her, lean, mean and muscular, Admiral Miyaru intimidated the hell out of Casey. It had taken all of her energy not to show it during that conversation. With that close-cropped blaze of white hair and a gaze that cut to the soul, the admiral was perhaps the most impressive woman she had ever met, a feeling amplified by the war stories about how she killed a Kryl duralisk with a boot knife—then, not two weeks later, watched a comrade sacrifice his life to take out half a dozen Kryl overminds, injure the Mother Queen, and end the war in a nuclear explosion. There were rumors that Captain Ruidiaz and Admiral Miyaru had been lovers, but Casey hadn't met anyone who knew for sure. Not even her father had been willing to talk about it.

She was certain of one thing, however: Casey longed for Admiral Miyaru's respect. While her heartbeat settled back into a normal rhythm, she paced in circles around the war room and reflected on what the admiral had just shown her.

A Kryl drone with the ability to phase through another ship without engaging a hyperdrive? The fact that Admiral Miyaru needed this evidence to prove to the Emperor and the Colonization Board that the Kryl presented a greater threat than humanity currently believed spoke to how far their leaders had drawn the wool down over their own eyes —and over the eyes of the Solaran people. Seven hub systems and no one except border-patrol and a few units on an evacuation mission seemed to be the wiser. Dozens of colonies had been chartered since the end of the Kryl War. How were they to defend them all if this exercise turned out to be the vanguard of a new conflagration?

It slowly dawned on Casey that the admiral had probably recalled her starfighter *not merely* because she had disobeyed orders to go after Nevers, but also because the admiral needed the footage from her ship. In a way, that was comforting. This wasn't only about her or Nevers; something bigger was at stake.

Something that looked like the fate of humanity.

Casey heard her father's voice clearly in her mind: "The soldiers of the SDF are the protectors of humanity." He had explained this to her many times, starting when she was about five years old. So many times that she could recite it in her sleep. "We serve the greater good. We sacrifice, and sometimes give our lives, so that others across the galaxy may live in peace."

It had been years since she'd heard that speech. She supposed he no longer felt the need to give it once Casey had entered the academy. But never had it seemed as true as it did right now.

Admiral Miyaru was the closest thing to the embodiment of the sacrificial soldier's spirit that Casey had ever encountered. Unlike her father, whom she had let down many times —when she'd been caught drinking and smoking in secondary school, when her father had walked in on her and her first boyfriend having sex, when Nevers, damn him, had graduated as the top pilot in their class, knocking Casey out of the leading spot—Casey resolved never to let Admiral Miyaru down. She would turn over a new leaf.

"But am I even cut out for this?" she asked aloud.

The empty room didn't answer. She continued pacing.

What right did Casey have to investigate the explosion in the hangar? That was a job for an Imperial Inquisitor. The Empire's favored hands traveled throughout occupied space to investigate court-martial claims for validity, interrogate people suspected of crimes, and pass sentences. They were the galaxy's traveling judges and executioners. Who was she to serve in that capacity?

She must have been momentarily out of her mind. Her father had served as an Inquisitor for several years. After he retired from the military, the Emperor brought him back out of retirement personally for the job. Admiral Eben Osprey had a law degree and had commanded a starship, all the experience necessary to be a good Inquisitor. Casey had no such experience, only the knowledge of the toll it took on her father in the five years he served.

Inquisitors were typically chosen from the ranks of the most experienced men and women. The only kind of investigation Casey ever had to perform was trying to figure out how Park managed to sneak alcohol into the rec without her knowing. Or why her bold aleacc strategy had lost her the game.

What did she know about investigating? Now that she'd been given the requested assignment, she couldn't admit her inexperience to anybody. Worse, Admiral Miyaru had put her in a position where she couldn't even ask for help except from the admiral herself. Who would she go to if she did? Lieutenant Colonel Walcott had given his life to save her. Yorra had gone with Park to the hospital wing to treat their injuries. And Nevers was stuck on the moon itself... assuming he had survived that landing.

And once she started investigating the explosion, questioning mechanics and talking to the crew who had been at the scene when Mick lost his mind, her colleagues would immediately begin to distrust her. She may not have been an official Inquisitor, but she had been appointed by the admiral. That meant that she had, at least nominally, some of the Inquisitor's power—to arrest, to interrogate, to imprison... if not to pass judgment.

Good thing this wasn't that kind of crime. Reflecting on what had happened in the hangar with Mick, she supposed there was really only one guilty party. If Casey was careful and didn't ruffle any feathers, there would be no reason for any of the crew to get upset with her. The one person who had committed a crime was Mick, and he was dead, having shredded himself to a thousand fleshy pieces when he set the torch to that canister of gas.

Casey Osprey stopped her endless pacing and gazed around the empty war room. There was the Imperial insignia, the tristar logo, emblazoned large against one wall. The octagonal table at which she sat held seven more empty seats. The hologram floating over the table still showed the paused footage from her Sabre, half of the forest moon looming in the background.

Casey called up the holocontrol menus and logged herself in. Normally, a captain wouldn't have access to the video footage of the hangar. That was reserved for the commanding officers and security personnel—with built-in overrides for Inquisitors. Sure enough, once Casey logged in with her password and biometrics, she found she had access to all sorts of information she hadn't been able to acquire before. Personnel records. Security footage. Access logs. The names of the two officers currently in the brig for disorderly conduct.

She opened up a feed of the sick bay and cycled through a number of different cameras until she located the rest of her squad. Park lay in bed covered in sweat, his skin glistening and his eyes closed. He had one arm in a cast already and had been stripped out of his flight suit, down to a black t-shirt and boxer shorts. His identi-ring hung on a chain around his neck. Yorra had a gash to her head that was currently being treated by a nurse, who sprayed an aerosol over the wound, sealing it and coating it with a healing gel.

Casey was glad to see that they were both in recovery. She'd have to talk to them once they had been treated and make sure their stories matched, or see what they remembered differently. Not because they were trying to put one over on anybody. Simply because, as Casey well knew, your vision narrowed to a tunnel in the heat of action. It was likely that they had seen something she hadn't.

Casey pushed that feed back and opened another in the foreground. In this window, she loaded the current feed from the hangar. A timestamp showed in the bottom right corner. Repairs were well underway. A dozen mechanics were hard at work rebuilding the hangar floor so that no one would accidentally fall through the hole and tumble into space.

She cycled back through the footage until a bright orange blast turned the whole screen into a lens flare. She cycled back farther until she spotted her own starfighter entering the hangar. She watched herself find her dock and set the Sabre down. After coming across the row from another starfighter, Mick began to hook up hoses and cables to her Sabre and set chocks under the wheels before hurrying to the next ship that came in behind her.

Casey blinked and knitted her eyebrows together. After Admiral Miyaru showed her what happened with Nevers and the drone, Casey was suspicious of everything, especially her own perceptions. She rewound the footage to watch that again, this time keeping a closer eye on Mick.

This time she spotted clearly what she had seen in passing just a moment ago. Mick ran towards Casey's Sabre, picked up the power cable and plugged it in; picked up the diagnostic cable, opened a panel under the left wing of her starfighter and plugged that in as well. And as he connected the second cable, Mick shook his head and lifted one hand to his ear as if he felt a pain there. He stuck one finger in his ear and twisted it around; dropped his hand, shook his head one more time and then set the wheel chocks before running to the next Sabre.

He had been affected by something; that much was clear in the footage.

Casey thought back to how she'd seen Mick behave before he freaked out. He had done a similar sort of thing, shaking his head and acting like something was bothering him. Casey got migraines herself, sometimes, so she understood the reaction. And perhaps that's why she hadn't given it a second thought when she saw him do it in person.

But the logical part of her brain, the part that liked technical instructions when she was able to sit still long enough to read them, knew that whatever had caused Mick's madness must have a source, a cause.

Mick didn't just have a psychotic break for no reason. Not when he had been acting normal up to that point.

But Casey couldn't very well go back to Admiral Miyaru and say, "Hey, Admiral, I think I found it. Mick had a migraine and then he tried to kill all of his friends." If his strange behavior on camera here had anything to do with what had happened, Casey needed proof.

She fast-forwarded through the rest of the footage. She watched herself march across the hangar, angrily confront Walcott when he caught up to her, then walk all the way back to retrieve the cube from her starfighter, only to get waylaid by Mick. She saw the others come running to help her. She saw them corner Mick, and try to talk him down. She saw Mick light the torch and set it to the canister.

The gas canister ruptured, set off several others, and exploded, sucking equipment and people across the room as atmosphere evacuated into space.

But nothing there gave her any more clues as to what had caused Mick's unusual behavior.

By this point, Casey was getting restless. She was still kind of shaken from her confrontation with Admiral Miyaru, so she determined that while she let her mind work on that puzzle, she would go down to the hospital wing and visit Park and Yorra to make sure they were doing okay. The admiral had been right: the Furies needed her.

Casey closed all the windows, logged out, and powered off the computer. She strode into the corridor of the destroyer. She was near the bridge right now, and people were hurrying back and forth, absorbed in their own assignments. Almost no one paid her any attention except to glance down at her dirty uniform, and then away.

Looking down at herself, Casey realized she was covered in soot marks from the explosion, grease from hanging onto the Sabre's strut, and that her flight suit was ripped in several places. She hadn't had any opportunity to clean up yet. Admiral Miyaru had ushered her straight into the war room and made her wait while they retrieved her black box.

Casey had managed to escape relatively uninjured. She

only had a couple small abrasions, a cut on her forehead that had since stopped bleeding, a few bruises and a sore wrist. There wasn't much to clean up. But as the flight lead, Casey knew how important it was to keep up appearances.

Her father's voice drifted into her head again. "A good leader looks the part," he had once told Casey. "Especially when she doesn't want to."

If it were up to her and her alone, Casey would have gone straight to the hospital wing. It was the kind of thing a good friend did, dismiss their own appearance in order to support each other. *But I'm not merely their friend*, Casey thought. *I'm also supposed to be their leader.*

So Casey turned down the hall that would lead her to the bunk their flight shared. When the door hissed open, she was surprised to find Yorra holding a tiny glass to her lips with her head thrown back. She choked and coughed when she saw Casey, swallowed the liquor and made an unhappy sound in her throat.

"This is the swill Park keeps in his footlocker. Smells like socks and tastes even worse."

Casey snorted, crossed the room and fell on the bed next to Yorra, leaning back and tossing her arms out. Flight leader she may have been, but right now it looked like Yorra needed a friend.

"How're you holding up, Gears?" Casey asked.

"How's it look like I'm holding up?"

Casey unbuttoned the collar of her torn, stained flight suit. "Let me get a swig of that."

Yorra grunted and passed the bottle over. Casey took a small swallow and winced. It was grain alcohol, the kind a bored loadmaster brewed on ship with vat-grown potatoes. Park loved this stuff and saved it for special occasions.

"But you're right," Casey said. "Smells like socks. Not clean ones either."

In spite of this observation, they each took another couple sips. It wasn't enough to make her drunk, but it was enough to quell Casey's frayed nerves and allow her to think straight for a second. She stood up, slipped the ripped and dirty flight suit off and found a new one in her own footlocker.

She pulled on the stretchy suit without bothering to take her boots off, and tidied up her appearance in a mirrored hololens that she summoned with the swipe of a hand.

"How's Park doing?" Casey asked.

"He's still out. Hit his head pretty hard."

Casey grunted.

"I'm gonna go back to stay with him in a minute," Yorra said. "The doc says he should wake up soon. I just needed a… minute to…gather my thoughts."

As Yorra smoothed her hair back, Casey saw that her hands were quaking with a constant tremor. Gently, Casey helped Yorra out of her dirty flight suit—also torn and battered from the explosion—and picked out a fresh change of clothes for her. When she'd changed, they went to the lav together and washed their hands and faces.

Doing something mundane helped calm her, and by the time they were done Yorra's hands had steadied somewhat. Though the lieutenant was obviously just as shaken up as Casey felt, she hadn't been sure up until this point if she was going to tell her friends what she had convinced Admiral Miyaru to let her do.

But now she felt the need to confide in someone. To keep an open, honest line of communication between the two of them, no matter what. Casey hoped that talking to Yorra about everything would get her friend's mind off what had happened. And it worked. As Casey recounted her conversation with Admiral Miyaru—the assignment to investigate Mick's behavior, *not* what the Kryl drone had done—Yorra's eyes went from distant and unfocused to sharp and alert.

"So she just gave you access to the security system?"

Casey nodded. "I already reviewed the hangar incident a few times."

"Damn," Yorra said. "That's intense. Did you figure out what made him go crazy?"

"Not yet. I'll interrogate every single mechanic on that hangar floor if I have to."

Yorra gave her a judgy look.

"What?" Casey asked.

"Don't take this the wrong way, Captain, but you tend to come off a little strong. Maybe try something a little more subtle first."

"Okay, maybe interrogate was the wrong word..."

"You think?"

After this was all over, Casey would have to return to her normal duties as flight lead and starfighter pilot. The last thing she wanted to do was piss off the people she'd have to work with every day. Mechanics, in particular, were in a position to make her life a living hell. From something as simple as putting her repairs at the back of the queue to a more sinister sabotage, like filling her starfighter with itching mites or ship rats.

Yorra was right. She needed to be more thoughtful. Delicate. "That's a good point. How would you approach it?"

"Well, I'd talk to them, sure, but don't *interrogate* anyone. Don't isolate them. Speak to them together. Show them you're on their side. Charm them."

"Okay. I'll try that. Thanks." She got up to go but hesitated.

"What is it?" Yorra asked.

"Nothing."

"No, you just thought of something. Tell me."

"You promise to keep this between us?"

She nodded.

"You ever heard of something called space madness?"

"A legend from the Kryl War," Yorra said. "It happened to pilots who flew too close to a star, or who were exposed to excess radiation when their ship's shielding broke. Or so I've heard."

"You know of anyone who caught it?"

"Not personally. My uncle was a Fleet mechanic back during the Kryl War. He told me a story once. They were on the front, fighting around the planet Fila before the Kryl invaded. A squadron of starfighters had been sent to do recon of a Kryl encampment near the planet's north pole. The squadron flew the mission, took photos of the encampment—later used to plan an attack—but on their way back, the starfighter pilots were ambushed by Kryl drones. Only one pilot survived. My uncle was on duty when the guy barreled into the hangar. His Sabre was all busted up, so his landing was rather clumsy, but he hadn't said three words when he got out of the cockpit before he went mad. It took ten people to detain him."

"Hmm," Casey said. "Sounds similar. Only, Mick isn't a pilot. I don't know how he would have been exposed to the same thing the pilot in your uncle's story was exposed to—excess radiation or whatever."

"Yeah," Yorra said, "I don't know. But while Mick was losing it, calling you a xeno, staring around with those bloodshot eyes and grabbing that torch off the wall, all I could think about was my uncle. Even years later, he got this haunted look in his eyes telling us that story. I tried to ask him more about it but my mom said, 'Chacho, stop it, you're scaring the kids!' And that was the end of it."

"What happened to that pilot?"

Yorra's tongue darted out, wetting her lips. "When I

joined the Fleet I looked him up. Took a while, had to make friends with someone who had clearance to view the archives. Records say they were able to detain the pilot, like my uncle told us. They threw him in the brig. Sadly, while an Imperial Inquisitor was en route to the station to determine what to do with him, the pilot committed suicide."

"No way."

It was no secret that they left you nothing but a pair of athletic shorts and a t-shirt in the brig. Service members causing self-harm in isolation was a frequent enough occurrence early in the war that Fleet security personnel took no risks.

"How did he do it?" Casey said.

"The records didn't say. You hear all sorts of things, though. One rumor is the pilot clawed his own throat out. They found him with a piece of his esophagus clutched in his hand."

"Ugh," Casey said. "Are you serious?"

"That's what I heard. My friend in the archives couldn't confirm it, though. If they do keep those kind of records, it's above our pay grade."

Casey's mind recoiled. She didn't want to believe what Yorra was telling her. She didn't want to believe that it had anything to do with what had happened to Mick. There were too many differences between the stories. Yorra's uncle hadn't said anything about this pilot calling people xenos. That pilot had probably just gone mad from seeing his whole squadron killed by the Kryl. Plenty of soldiers lost their minds in the war. Surely, there was some rational explanation.

"I heard another rumor," Yorra said. "This is probably nonsense, but since you asked... I heard once that a group of explorers found a Telos artifact on a colony world and got the space madness that way."

"But the Telos are just a legend. They died millennia ago, before Ariadne was founded."

"And left shrines and ruins scattered across the galaxy. If you believe the legends, the tech they had makes the Solaran Empire look like a bunch of monkeys banging rocks together."

Casey chuckled. She'd heard similar stories, but nothing credible. For instance, it was common knowledge that the Great Migration ended when Solarans invented the hyperspace drive. They settled on Ariadne shortly afterward. Some people, however, still believed that Solarans didn't invent the hyperspace drive at all, but reverse engineered it from a Telos artifact they discovered on their journey.

All that was ancient history, though. No one had ever seen a Telos before or any of their tech. They'd been extinct for millennia.

"Anyway," Yorra said, "The important thing is, don't go in hot when you're talking to people. Act normal. Keep your cool. Listen more than you talk."

"Thanks for the advice."

"Sure. I'm gonna go check on Naab again."

"I'll swing by in a little bit. Remember, not a word of this to anyone." Casey had kept her promise to Admiral Miyaru, not saying a word about the drone that shot Nevers down or the strange ability the drone used to outmaneuver him. But she didn't want any rumors about her wagging tongue making their way back to the admiral through back channels.

"Of course not, Raptor." Yorra drew her thumb and forefinger across her mouth. "My lips are sealed."

Yorra stood and opened the door. Her confident swagger had returned. You wouldn't know that just a few minutes ago, Casey had found her hiding in here, drinking by herself and trying to control her shaking hands.

Yorra was right. It had been a rough day for everybody. Before visiting Park, she'd go talk to a few of those mechanics in the hangar, but she'd play it cool. Just a captain asking questions, not a sanctioned Inquisitor.

Not her father.

As she walked with Yorra through the halls, Casey organized in her mind the other stories she'd heard about people who caught the space madness—the plausible ones, not the myths about Telos artifacts.

Those were just rumors, right? Exaggerated war stories? Misunderstandings? They couldn't be real.

Could they?

ELEVEN

The old priest limped out of the ravine. He turned up a game trail that was barely visible in the evening halflight, despite the pinprick stars overhead and the orange gas giant cresting the horizon through a haze.

At a snap of Elya's fingers, Hedgebot scurried ahead of them and helped light the way, so his own tired feet, and those of Hedrick, wouldn't trip on the rubble littering the path. The priest, despite his limping, had no trouble navigating the familiar terrain in the dark.

Even with the light from his bot and the flashlight Heidi shone forward, Hedrick struck his foot on a rock, stubbed his toe and fell. He lay in the dirt for a while, sobbing into the darkness. Elya recognized it wasn't because of the pain alone, but rather from the combined weight of everything that had happened to him today. Heidi tried to pick the boy up, but she was too tired and Hedrick didn't want to get up, so Elya lifted the boy in his arms. Hedrick clasped his wrists around Elya's neck and buried his wet face into the shoulder of his flight suit, soaking the slick fabric through in an instant. But he stopped struggling and let Elya carry him.

They rose out of the canyon, took another path, and soon reached a rock wall at a dead end. The priest tapped on the rock in a pattern of raps and pauses. When he stopped, there was a rustling and then a section of stone slid aside, revealing the mouth of a cave lit by warm orange firelight.

The priests gestured the three of them inside. "Here we are."

Elya didn't know what to expect, but it wasn't this. Inside the cave was a semi-permanent camp with twenty to thirty people. Tents of different sizes and shapes, held up with sturdy metal poles, or makeshift wooden ones, had been set around the edge of the cave to create a sense of privacy. The cave arched up high overhead, where stalactites hung from the ceiling, and extended far back beyond the tents, where the shadows deepened.

A low fireplace had been dug into the middle of the dirt floor and lined with large stones. Red-hot embers burned in it, illuminating several people and a few servant bots moving among them. One of the bots swept the dirt floor in front of a tent. Another was stationed on a battery-powered charging station, arms akimbo, supporting wet laundry hung on him to dry while he recharged.

The priest exchanged warm greetings with several of the men and women who came out of their tents upon his arrival. The people were all older, ranging from their early thirties to mid-sixties. They were dressed simply, not in robes like the priest, but in brown, black or tan homespun pants and white cotton shirts, with sandals or sturdy work boots on their feet. Typical dress for faithful adherents of Animus, at least the more conservative kind. Elya couldn't help but think that his mother would feel quite at home here. She always had simple tastes; Elya wondered how much of that came from her religious upbringing, and how much came from her own fashion preferences.

Despite the dirt, the people's faces were clean, their eyes sharp and suspicious as they studied Heidi and Elya and the boy in his arms.

While the priest and a couple of the people exchanged words in a low tone that he couldn't make out, his bot circled the cave, searching and pulsing blue light as it greeted each of the servant bots. Hedgebot moved past the tents and explored the shadows at the back of the cave, its blue light warming with pink overtones. However, it didn't seem to find anything it considered dangerous, and faded back to blue as it completed its circuit and returned to Elya's side.

The priest finally broke away from the men and came to stand in front of them.

"My name is Father Pohl," he said. The old priest clasped his hands behind his back. In the light of the cave, Elya could finally see the kind, lined face of the priest clearly. Deep wrinkles formed near his eyes when he smiled. He was either bald or shaved his hair close to the scalp. His prominent nose, which hooked at the end, had the crooked look that comes from being broken many times.

The group of men and women the priest had been speaking to remained stern and stood apart, their faces guarded and suspicious. The priest seemed the gracious host by comparison.

"Charlie has agreed to give up his tent for the night." Father Pohl pointed to one of the tents that was square and tall and white. "He'll sleep in mine so the three of you can have some privacy."

Heidi sighed deeply. Elya could almost hear the tension leak out of her.

"Thank you," she said. "Oh, thank you, Father." She threw her arms around the priest.

The boy squirmed in Elya's arms so he set Hedrick down. The tears on his face had dried, and though his mother obviously felt warmly toward the priest, the boy gazed around cautiously at the unfamiliar surroundings and strange people. There was no one else his age here.

"What is this place?" Elya asked. "And why are you all hiding out here? The Kryl are coming to invade Robichar. Didn't you get the Imperial order to evacuate?" As soon as he said it, he regretted the words. It was the wrong thing to say. He'd already promised the priest he wouldn't cause trouble, yet the first thing he said openly questioned their decisions.

Father Pohl stood up a little straighter. Behind him, the broad-shouldered, sandy-haired man he'd identified as Charlie lifted his chin in Elya's direction. Several others crossed their arms and looked down their noses at him as if he was a simpleton.

"We are followers of the one true God," Father Pohl said. "Animus, the Spirit of Old Earth, who will keep us from harm."

Elya took a deep breath and blew it out. This language was familiar to him, but that didn't mean it wasn't delusional. Elya had seen how the Kryl could ravage a planet. People's beliefs played no part in it. You could believe what you wanted to believe and the Kryl would still rip your throat out. Elya had relearned this hard truth today in Heidi's village.

Then Elya thought back to what he'd seen in the ravine, how the groundlings had spotted the priest and the flashlight in his hands and beat a hasty retreat, leaving the travelers unmolested.

As if they could follow his thoughts, the man that the priest had referred to as Charlie and one of his comrades walked over to the mouth of the cave and rolled the giant stone that had been blocking the entrance back across it, sealing them inside.

Elya couldn't help himself. He tried to keep any animosity

out of his voice when he said, "If Animus will protect you, why take these kinds of precautions?"

The priest didn't even hesitate. "Animus protects those who protect themselves. Just because we believe in God doesn't mean that we are fools."

Somehow, this reassured him. "I can see that."

Father Pohl gave him an icy smile. "Please, make yourselves comfortable. Warm your hands by the fire. There's water to wash with in your tent. We'll have supper ready soon."

With that, the priest turned his back and walked among his people. He started by going over near the fire where a middle-aged, redheaded woman lifted stew out of a pot with a wooden spoon and allowed him to taste it. He made a happy sound, rubbed his stomach and gripped her shoulder genially. She glowed and sat up a little straighter in response. Father Pohl moved on, as if he was a doctor of the soul making rounds among his ailing patients.

Heidi grabbed Hedrick's hand and led the boy to the tent the priest had indicated. She was pulling the flap of white cloth aside when a faint roaring resounded in the cavern, penetrating even through the thick stone walls.

Hedrick reacted, flinging himself to his knees and covering his head. Charlie and several of the younger men and women leaped for heaps of blankets behind a tent, which, when cast aside, revealed a pile of arms—rifles, blasters, extra magazines, boxes of ammunition, and a handful of remote-operated charges.

The roaring noise faded as fast as it had come, passing in the space of a breath except for a faint echo and leaving a taut silence in its wake. The speed with which it passed, and the pitch, triggered a memory from pilot training in Elya's mind.

The whole squadron had been dropped into a remote

jungle with nothing but their sidearms and backpacks. A pair of Sabres had streaked overhead, letting them know that the exercise was about to begin—it was that sound which Elya recognized.

He raised two empty hands and took a few steps toward the men and women, who were now lifting up their rifles and checking the power levels of their blasters.

"It's okay," Elya said. "I think those were Imperial starfighters."

Suspicion drew down their faces. Half hidden in shadows at the back of the cavern, Elya felt the priest's eyes light upon him.

"They're looking for you," Father Pohl said.

He didn't want to admit it, but Elya didn't see another option. The men still held their weapons and he didn't think it would be wise to lie to them. "They are," Elya said. "My tightbeam hasn't been able to connect, so I expect they're flying a search pattern."

Charle slammed the butt of a rifle to his shoulder and aimed it at Elya, finger on the trigger.

"You led them right to us!" he shouted.

"N-No! That wasn't my intention! I didn't even know they were out there." He hadn't known, but he'd hoped, and was happy to learn they were looking for him. Elya needed to figure out how to signal them before one of these paranoid, trigger-happy maniacs accidentally gave him a new breathing hole.

As the man marched forward, it took all of Elya's willpower not to draw his own sidearm. *De-escalate. Stay calm!*

"We're not leaving this place." The man forced the words through gritted teeth.

"Charlie!" the priest barked. "Lower your weapon. You will not threaten our guests in this holy place."

Sheepishly, Charlie lowered the rifle until its barrel pointed at the ground. Elya sighed. The priest approached him from across the cavern and lowered his voice, immediately defusing the situation with his presence.

"It's okay, son," Father Pohl said when he turned back to Elya. "I know it was not your intent. But understand that we have made up our minds to stay here."

Elya's blood pounded in his ears. He found that he had one hand on his SB-44 blaster in spite of his own intentions. He relaxed his arms.

Charlie grumbled something under his breath, then turned and stashed the rifle back under the pile of blankets.

Elya felt his body sag, the adrenaline rush making his hands shake. He thrust them into his pockets to hide the tremors, and then was nearly knocked over as the boy, Hedrick, tackled Elya with a bear hug around his waist.

Elya found his balance and gently disengaged the boy's arms. He knelt down so he could look into his eyes. "It's okay. Everything's going to be fine."

"I don't want you to get hurt." The boy's eyes shimmered with tears.

"It's not going to happen. He didn't mean anything by it."

"Come on, you two," Heidi said. She lifted Elya to his feet, both hands under one arm. "Let's go get cleaned up." Her eyes darted around and Elya realized that everybody in the cave was staring at them. Elya had barely noticed. Or maybe he had gotten used to living under the watchful eye of his fellow soldiers, senior officers, and ever-present ship security cameras on the *Paladin*. It seemed like he hardly had a chance to be alone since he joined the Fleet. Though he hadn't said so to Osprey when she brought it up, that was certainly one of the reasons he liked spending the little recreational time he was given alone. It wasn't *just* to get extra training hours. It was also to get a breather from being around other people all the time.

Nonetheless, Heidi made a compelling case. The looks from these people weren't the same as the healthy appraisals of his comrades in arms. They were the suspicious looks people give to outsiders who don't belong. He was glad to follow Heidi into the tent.

Elya brought his pack with him and when they were inside, he quickly located the cube from his Sabre. The metal was cool to his touch as he drew it out of the bag. The indicator light continued to blink. Elya sighed.

"Still nothing?"

"I thought it would connect by now..." He glanced up, as if he could see the search and rescue jets criss-crossing the air in a grid pattern above him. But they were long gone by now. They couldn't see anything in the dark, and they were mostly looking for an active tightbeam broadcast. If he couldn't get the cube to connect or send up a visible signal, there was a good chance they wouldn't find him at all.

"One thing at a time," Heidi said, her voice soft in his ear. She gripped his shoulders from behind and pressed her thumbs into his neck.

Elya groaned. "Oh, that feels good."

"Clean up. Get some rest. You can tackle it again in the morning."

Heidi smiled at him then took Hedrick over to a wash basin in the corner. She poured water from a jug into the basin, found a clean cloth and gave it to the boy. "Scrub up," she said. "Use the soap." The boy put up a bit of a fight, probably out of habit, but quickly relented.

Heidi returned to Elya's side when she was done. He'd settled onto the floor while she gave instructions to the boy. He didn't feel right sitting on Charlie's bed, so he laid down with his feet flat on the ground and his knees up.

Heidi came to sit beside him. She put her back to the bed, pulled her legs to her chest and wrapped her arms around her knees.

"How are you so calm?" Elya asked.

She gave him a lopsided smile. He could see now that she may have been calm, but she wasn't really okay. Maybe she was still processing what had happened to her friends in the village earlier. Bruising had begun to show on her upper arms and around her eyes. This woman had put up the fight of her life today.

"I don't feel calm," she said. "I feel like I'm living a nightmare. There were Kryl attacks when I was a kid. Not in my city, but in a nearby town. Scared the piss out of me as a teenager, but then the war ended and I thought, well, thank Animus *that's* over." She snorted.

"I'm so sorry," Elya said.

"What do you have to be sorry for?"

"That I didn't get there faster. That you and your son aren't safe here." Elya shook his head.

Heidi rolled her eyes. "Who do you think you are? You can't control everything."

"The Fleet could have gotten here sooner."

"But they didn't. And that wasn't your call."

Elya rolled his head to the side and gazed at the white tent wall. She was right. "I still feel responsible."

"You saved our lives today," she said. "I want you to know how much we appreciate that."

She glanced over at the boy, who was scrubbing dirt off his arms with a grimace on his face that made Elya smile. He'd hated washing as a boy, too, but not as much as his brother Rojer. Rojer would go weeks without taking a shower, and Elya realized with some surprise that this was a fond memory—though Rojer had always irritated him as a kid. He wondered how his family was doing. How his mother, and his eldest brother, Arn, were holding up. He wondered if Rojer had finally landed a job. If Arn and his girlfriend had gotten engaged yet.

He wondered if he'd ever seen any of them again.

"The Kryl invaded my homeworld," Elya said, "when I was about Hedrick's age. We barely got out in time. Fled our home in the middle of the night with what we could carry on our backs. The idea of going up in the shuttle terrified me, but we made it and transferred to a Mammoth longhauler, like the ones waiting in orbit for the evacuation right now. And then the Kryl horde was spotted in the region, so we were forced to hide. Floated in space without power for three weeks until the Fleet found us."

"Thank the stars they did." Heidi's face was flushed, her voice thin and breathless. He could see how much the idea terrified her. "That's unbelievable."

"It was a miracle the Kryl didn't find us first."

"What happened then?"

"They worked us into the system. We transferred to a space station for a little while and, from there, made our way to a new colony."

"Is that where your parents are now?"

"Just my mom and my two brothers. My dad died when I was very little."

"Your brothers didn't want to join the Empire's finest?"

Elya snorted. "Arn's made a life for himself there, and Rojer... well, he's always struggled but he'll figure things out eventually. He's a smart guy and a talented programmer. He'll find something."

"Your mom must be very proud of you," Heidi said.

His mother had cried when he first told her that he had signed on to join the Fleet. Sobbed, actually. He'd never seen anything like it. He should have worked her up to the big news, rather than dropping it on her all at once like a bombshell. Elya regretted that. He'd thought he had all the answers, but there were things he would have done differently had he been given a second chance.

A sing-song pattern of electronic tones heralded the entrance of Hedgebot, who had finished his exploration of the cave and returned by nudging aside a corner of the cloth curtain that served as the tent's doorway. The bot climbed onto Elya's chest and bleeped down at him, bringing a smile to his face.

Elya had always been good with machines. He'd first acquired Hedgebot on the flight from Yuzosix. A bot machinist named Core had given it to him, an enormous gift of kindness to a terrified refugee child.

Elya's heart ached. He wished he had something valuable he could give to Hedrick, some way to let the boy know that there was a future for him—*when* they made it through this incident, *when* Heidi and Hedrick were safe aboard their own Mammoth. Elya supposed he could give the boy the hatchet from his Sabre, but that didn't seem very meaningful.

He pushed the thought to the back of his mind, stashed away for later. He could probably find something. He'd get Heidi and her son rescued by making contact with the *Paladin*. Then he could give the boy a gift. Maybe something from his bunk—one of his old computers, a spare part of his own…

Elya took a deep breath as a renewed determination infused his will. He picked up the cube, tossed it into the air and caught it. "I'm going to see if someone has the tools I need to fix this thing. Thanks for the chat."

Elya stifled a yawn as he stood and pushed through the tent flap. The fire had been built up higher. It cast a soft yellow glow over the robes of the priest, the plain homespun of the others, and the dented and scratched metal shells of servant bots waiting or charging around the edge of the irregular cavern.

Anywhere there were bots, there were tools with which to fix them. Hedgebot had some tools, but he wasn't big enough to carry the hardware for sophisticated tightbeam diagnostics. Since these people had obviously been wealthy enough to afford servant bots in their previous lives, he hoped one of them had the right equipment. You couldn't expect the bots to last more than a couple years around this much dirt and dust without maintaining them.

The priest's followers gave Elya guarded looks and tight smiles that weren't smiles at all as he walked among them, peering surreptitiously into their tents. Toward the back of the cavern, in the light of an electric lamp, he found a wiry man cleaning out the base of a gyroscope with a brush.

"Mind if I borrow some of your tools?" Elya asked.

The man glanced stiffly up, his eyes skipping over the black cube in Elya's hands, and then to Hedgebot, who dogged Elya's heels and was now inspecting the man's open toolbox, climbing over wrenches, drills, screwdrivers, a rubber mallet.

"No harm, I suppose," the man said. He held out a hand. After a cursory sniff, Hedgebot crawled into his palm.

"Hmm," he said, "I don't think I have an extra foot for your little fella."

Oh, right, Elya thought. He'd intended to fix Hedgebot with the spare parts in his medkit before the groundling had attacked them near the crash site. In the chaos that ensued, it had slipped his mind completely. "That's okay. He can get around fine on three for now."

The man held up one finger, then dug around in a bag and pulled out a round, peg-like piece that, while clearly not a foot, ended in the standard round joint which could be attached to where Hedgebot's missing limb would go.

At the sight of it, Hedgebot did donuts, pulsing blue and green and purple in rapid succession.

"Seems like it meets his approval."

"Guess so." Elya sat on the ground, joining the man in a cross-legged position. It only took a few seconds to snap the foot into place and secure it by engaging and syncing the internal magnets. Hedgebot jumped in the air a few times off his back legs, testing the new foot—or peg. Then he scurried happily around the cavern, causing even the most suspicious of the priest's followers to grin at the bot's antics.

"'Fraid I can't help you with that," the man said, nodding at the cube.

Elya set it face up so that the irritating blinking light illuminated the distant stalactites.

"I'm Elya. What's your name?"

The man's calloused hand took Elya's in a firm grip. His knuckles were like knots on a tree, telling Elya that the man worked with his hands and, perhaps in a former life, was a machinist or botsmith of some kind. He had an open face and green eyes crowned with thick eyebrows like caterpillars that knit together in the middle. "Thom."

"Nice to meet you, Thom. Thanks for your help with Hedgebot, he really appreciates it."

"I can see that."

"Now, about this cube... I'm not sure I can fix it, but I need to try."

"Even if you could get one of those cubes open, I don't think you're likely to get it to connect."

Elya looked up sharply. "Why not?"

The man reached back and picked up an old-fashioned communicator that used radio waves to broadcast over long distances—the ancestor from which the tightbeam technology in his cube descended. Thom cycled through a range of frequencies. All he found was a uniform static.

"Because that cube isn't the problem," the man said. "All of our communicators stopped working about six hours ago."

A chill washed over Elya's body. He cast his memory back. Had he really crash-landed on the planet six hours ago? It seemed to fit. He had been so busy trying to survive, and then run from the Kryl, and then the hike took ages and he lost track of time but... Night fell and, yeah, he supposed it could have been about six hours.

"Earth," Elya swore. "What's causing it?" *And why did it start at the same time as I crash landed on Robichar?*

"That, I can't tell you."

Elya wondered if those Kryl drones could have dropped some kind of signal jamming device either before or after they shot down that shuttle. His mind scrambled back over all the training he'd received, recalling some intel about the Kryl that was taught to him in one of his groundschool classes.

The major difference that separated Kryl technology from that invented by humanity was that Kryl tech was grown from organic parts. The Kryl, for instance, didn't need space suits to survive the vacuum. They planted and grew their spawn using specific types of radiation and heavy metals to produce a creature whose exoskeleton happened to be vacuum-resistant. The drones were one such example.

He supposed that if the Kryl were able to do that, they could certainly grow an organism capable of jamming radio signals and other communication devices. Such a thing would be difficult to use in a space battle because the distances were so great. But on the ground, something like that would give them a tactical advantage.

"What did you just think about?" Thom asked.

Elya shook his head. It wasn't that what he learned from his training was top secret. But he knew from his time as a refugee that people didn't like to talk about the Kryl, so he was hesitant to speak of it.

"It's the Kryl, ain't it?" Thom asked.

No fooling him. Elya dipped his chin.

"Yeah. We figured it was them. I was keeping in touch with a couple different villages with this radio. We got news that a few Kryl ships had landed right before the signal cut out. Then, nothing but static."

"Do you think they have some kind of jamming device?"

"Seems logical. Only, I wouldn't know what to look for. But," Thom said, reaching around behind him. He came up with a device that looked like a Geiger counter, designed to read radiation levels. Its meters didn't seem to be counting in curie's or becquerel's, but some other unit. "This might help you locate the source."

Elya took the device with a nod right as Father Pohl limped up beside them and lowered himself clumsily to the ground, massaging his bum leg with his long, thin fingers.

"That what's gonna take you home?" the priest asked, pointing to the black cube and its blinking light.

"Not unless I can disable whatever's jamming the signal."

"Hmm," the priest said. Elya could tell that the idea of getting him out of their hair appealed to him.

"You know I don't mean you or any of your people harm, right?" Elya said. "I just want to get back to the Fleet."

"I know," Father Pohl said, glancing over his shoulder at Charlie, who sat warming his hands by the fire. "But, still, you make some of them nervous. We're disobeying direct orders from the Emperor to evacuate Robichar, so we're outlaws."

"The Fleet is trying to save your lives, priest."

"I already told you, we don't need to be saved. Regardless, you're one of them, and if we continue down this path, it won't be good to have you around."

"What are you saying?"

"Don't worry," Father Pohl said, holding up a hand and making a placating gesture. "You can stay the night, like I promised. I'm a man of my word and Animus will protect us here." The priest seemed so sure of this. Elya swallowed a sarcastic retort. "But the sooner you're gone, the better."

Thom was suddenly very busy looking for a tool in his kit. Not sure what to say, Elya merely bobbed his head. He'd been planning to leave in the morning anyway, but now it looked like he would be forced to.

But the priest looked so kind and sympathetic as he said it. Elya tried to put himself in the priest's shoes. He supposed, if he was hell bent on staying put, Elya wouldn't want some Imperial flunky hanging around either. There was wisdom in what the old man was saying, even if Elya and his Imperial uniform happened to attract the brunt of the anger.

So he was surprised when Father Pohl said, "I'll go with you, in the morning. Help you find this jamming device. We'd like it gone, too, so our interests are aligned there. Besides, there are bound to be more Kryl out there and I'm worried you won't make it if you go on your own."

"That's kind of you, but you don't have to do that."

"We do. Besides, I suspect I know where the Kryl are keeping this jamming device. There's only one strategically defensible place nearby that an occupying force would find attractive. You better get some rest. We leave at first light."

TWELVE

"The last Kryl drone has been eliminated, Admiral," Harmony reported. Her face-shaped cluster of star-burst neurons smiled serenely and blossomed the body of a woman, drawn in light, who gripped her fist and pumped her elbow at her side as if celebrating victory.

The shipmind liked to form shapes when she was pleased with herself, and sometimes also when she was bored. Often, these shapes mimicked living things. Only rarely did she imitate people.

It amused Kira that the shape Harmony had chosen to take this time was the exact height and build of Captain Osprey. Harmony must have taken a liking to the captain after the conversation in the war room. The shipmind hadn't made herself known during the conversation, but Kira knew she'd been present throughout. Rarely did anything happen on this ship that escaped the AI's notice.

"Good," Kira replied.

When she sat down, the officers manning their stations on the bridge seemed to sag. They'd been chasing Kryl drones around the moon for the past six hours and they were all tired. Colonel Volk, who had been leading them while she dealt with Captain Osprey, fell heavily into his chair. He spun around to face a screen and counted under his breath. "Admiral, twelve packages made it through our patrols and landed on Robichar. I'm having the Search and Rescue pilots flag their landing sites. Some forty more were eliminated en route to Robichar."

In response to the colonel's report, Harmony zoomed into the forest moon on the bridge's main viewscreen. The twelve packages were clustered around the area where Captain Nevers' Sabre had gone down.

What are they up to? Kira thought furiously.

She had seen such tactics before. Kryl drones liked to drop groundlings on planet as scouts or diversions. Ultimately, the groundlings weren't tactically effective against a well-prepared infantry—and back during the Kryl War, this tactic was so common she got the impression they frequently did it just for fun. In this case, with only a handful of people left on the surface, none of whom had seen real battle before, she feared to imagine the havoc they'd cause. Not to mention she was still pissed about the shuttle their drones destroyed. Harmony estimated the casualties at three hundred and fifty. How many more had been caught in the pathway of the carnage, injured... or worse.

"Have Search and Rescue managed to locate our missing pilot yet?"

Colonel Volk frowned and shook his head. "No, sir. The SAR leader reported that they found his scuttled starfighter, slagged by a thermal charge."

"Then we have to assume he's alive. We have roughly twelve hours left before the evacuation is complete. I want that pilot found."

"Yes, sir." Colonel Volk spoke to the comms officer and dispatched a second Search and Rescue team to widen the range of the first. After a short conversation, he turned back to Kira. "They're still trying to home in on Captain Nevers' tightbeam. They're also reporting trouble with their own comms, so it's likely the Kryl are interfering with the signal somehow."

Night had fallen on the portion of Robichar facing the *Paladin*. If the captain's tightbeam broadcast hadn't been located, they likely wouldn't find him until they had better visibility.

"Harmony, how are the repairs to the damaged Mammoth coming?"

Harmony opened one of the private channels. Data streamed back and forth. "They'll be ready to go in just a few hours, Admiral."

"Good. I want the longhaulers to be ready to jump at a moment's notice."

"Why not send some ahead?" Volk asked.

"I would if we had a full armada and could spare a security escort. But it takes multiple jumps to get back to Ariadne and I don't want them floating out there without any firepower."

Volk chewed on the inside of his cheek, which made his mouth twist in distaste. He knew she was right. "Send a few squadrons of starfighters?"

"Only if we have to. I'm not risking splitting the group up until I have no other choice."

He grunted. "They're safe for now. I'll prep a backup plan."

"Thank you, Volk."

She just had to hope that Captain Nevers made contact before they jumped. If not, she'd be forced to leave him behind. She wouldn't like it, but the safety of a million civilians was far more important than a single starfighter pilot. She hated the idea, but steeled herself to make the decision anyway. She'd been forced to leave a man behind once. A decade later, the memory still burned like salt in an open wound. She pushed the foul thought aside.

"Admiral, bad news." Harmony turned Captain Osprey's body-shape toward her and came to attention. The shipmind mirrored the captain's body language perfectly.

"Stop that."

Harmony's lights flew apart and reformed as a bodiless face, looking once more like the AI Kira was used to. "Is that better, Admiral?"

"Yes. Now, spit it out."

"The Kryl hive is no longer in the asteroid field."

"Where are they?"

"Attempting to locate them, Admiral."

"They must have jumped to hyperspace," Colonel Volk said.

"Nothing's ever easy," Kira muttered under her breath. Then, louder, "Contact Fleet Command and ask for reinforcements."

Colonel Volk raised an eyebrow and caught her gaze.

She didn't have to exchange a word with him to know what he was thinking. They were out here on the galaxy's edge, at the far end of an outer spiral arm beyond which there was nothing but vacuum for hundreds of light years. Reinforcements, should the Empire deign to send them, would come from Ariadne at the core of the Empire's strength, and take several days to reach them—if they left immediately and jumped the maximum distance on each leg. And that didn't count the time it took to muster troops and gather starfighters. At the earliest, those reinforcements wouldn't make it here until long after their timetable to evacuate Robichar had expired.

They were on their own. The only reason reinforcements would be needed would be as witnesses to the *Paladin of*

Abniss' failure to complete this mission. To verify that the Kryl had taken Robichar, and sweep up any survivors.

Kira kept her face impassive. After a moment spent looking into her eyes, Volk drew up and saluted sharply. "Yes, sir!"

Her eyelid twitched. Kira shoved down the phantom memory that threatened to foam over each time someone brought up the topic. The days she spent isolated in her room after Ruidiaz died... there had been rumors. It still smarted, over a decade later, despite how she'd moved past that time in her life. When her nightmares startled her awake to the salty smell and sticky feel of sweat-soaked sheets, Kira would calm herself by reciting the symptoms of space madness. To remind herself that the fugue state into which she'd fallen after the man she loved killed himself in a nuclear blast had been a different kind of psychosis.

A high-pitched warning signal emanated from the surround sound speakers embedded into the walls of the bridge.

"Enemy detected," Harmony reported. "The Kryl hive is back in-system, moving at maximum sub-light speed in the direction of Robichar."

"Colonel Volk!" Kira barked over her shoulder.

"Charge the defensive array to full power!" Colonel Volk shouted. "Prepare the torpedoes! Scramble the starfighters and order them to make a blockade and cut off *any* attempt on the Mammoths."

"How many ships have they got?"

Harmony's nodes exploded and re-formed themselves in a diagram beside her command couch. It showed the entire Kryl hive in three dimensions, measured by the lidar system and rendered in detail by the AI. At the center of the Kryl hive was the bulging, top-heavy mothership. Grotesquely shaped, these massive warships always looked like they were about to topple over but never did. The mothership contained the Overmind directing this hive. Several warships with knife-edge noses, the equivalent to her destroyer, fanned out behind it. And all around them, a thousand tiny gnats buzzed—drones. There were easily a hundred times as many drones as they had destroyed in the advance party.

"Protect the Mammoth fleet at all costs," Kira said. "I don't want that mothership to come within a hundred thousand klicks of Robichar."

As if reading her mind, Colonel Volk reported from across the bridge. "Admiral Miyaru, Fleet Command recognizes your request for reinforcements," he said "they're sending a dozen more destroyers to us. They say they're three days out."

Better than she expected, but still not close enough to make a difference.

"Dispatch an extra repair crew to fix that Mammoth. *Now*. I want it hyperspace-ready within the next thirty minutes."

"Yes, sir."

A communications officer pulled headphones down around his neck and glanced furtively in her direction. The whites of his eyes were wide.

"What is it, man?"

"The hospital wing, sir. There's a situation."

"What *kind* of situation?" Kira demanded. Like she didn't have enough to deal with right now?

"I… I can't tell, sir. The nurse who called was panicked. She said one of the pilots woke up. He started going crazy, throwing chairs at the nurses and calling them 'voidborn hellspawn.'"

"Harmony, get me Captain Osprey."

Harmony immediately established a connection. The young captain's face appeared on a viewscreen. She seemed to be in the hangar, talking to a group of mechanics. She'd stepped away from them to take the call on her tab, but Kira could see them in the background with worried looks on their faces.

"There's a problem in the sick bay. I think it's related to your investigation."

Captain Osprey inhaled sharply. "Is it—"

She didn't even finish the words before Kira barked out, "I don't know, but you'd better hurry, Captain."

Osprey turned and sprinted out of the hangar, disconnecting the call as she careened around a corner at full speed.

"Colonel Volk," Kira said. "Meet her there. I can't afford to fight battles on both fronts. I'll deal with the Kryl. You make sure to keep the peace on the ship. We don't need another incident like what happened before."

"Yes, sir!" Colonel Volk sprinted out the door. He wasn't in the same shape as the young captain and would be hurting by the time he got to the sick bay.

Kira then turned her attention back to the holograms of the Kryl hive. "Come on, you ugly bugs. Just a little further…"

On the hologram, a knife-like vessel flanking the mothership rocked sideways as it triggered one of the floating stealth mines her starfighter pilots had scattered around that side of the moon's gravity well, in the region where the advance squadron of Kryl drones had appeared previously.

A whooping cry went up around the bridge. Even Harmony materialized a hologram fist and attached arm to raise in celebration.

"Gotcha. Now, tell me all your dirty little secrets."

THIRTEEN

Elya's eyelids shot open and he inhaled himself out of a dead sleep. His heart battered the inside of his chest. Hedgebot warmed to a burnished copper tone and darted a few feet from where Elya lay, pausing, alert, in the corner of the tent.

Moments later there were footsteps and a man with his face draped in shadows shone a flashlight into Elya's eyes. "Dawn," the gruff voice said. "Get up."

"Already?" Elya asked. The shadow snorted and walked out of the tent without another word.

"Be right there," Elya called softly after the man, his own voice husky. He rolled over onto his knees, feeling every ache and pain in his body. There was a big bruise under his left rib cage that stabbed at his torso when he breathed. His legs protested as he stood. Elya checked the straps on the backpack he'd packed and secured the night before. All his scant supplies seemed to be there—the cube, his hatchet, his SB-44 blaster. He felt around on the thin cloth floor to make sure he had everything.

Heidi and Hedrick had fallen asleep in the narrow bed,

tucked into each other like spoons. Heidi wore a borrowed t-shirt which was much too large for her. She had her arms draped over her son, who stirred restlessly and groaned, muttering in his dreams.

With a pang of guilt, Elya slipped out of the tent without saying goodbye.

He arched his back and groaned. The fire had been banked during the night so there was only the dim glow of coals beneath a layer of fine ash. Two men with rifles slung over their shoulders walked out of a tent across the cavern and stepped outside. The stone door rested against the wall, pale sunlight shining through the opening. Elya must have slept through a lot of movement. He squinted as he walked into the sunlight and licked his chapped lips.

Though he had stood here last night, it had been too dark to appreciate the view. Now he could see the cave mouth looked out over a vast wooded slope that angled down to the lowland forest. Elya drew his finger along the horizon, tracing the meandering path of the ravine they had climbed through last night. The place where the groundlings cornered them could be no more than two klicks away, and it was plainly visible. No wonder the priest had found them when he had. The wind roared in his ears and numbed his cheekbones. Elya zipped his jacket up to his chin. Hedgebot scampered up his left leg, crawled along his back and came to sit on top of the strap on his right shoulder.

Elya counted six men, including the priest, waiting for him. Thom was among them, sporting a crooked smile, as was the dour Charlie and three of his comrades, a man and two grim-faced women. Every person except the priest held a rifle. One of the women who had pointed a gun at Elya last night wore a shoulder bag slung diagonally across her body. Thom passed Elya a new water bottle, which he took gratefully, squeezing a stream into his mouth.

"Careful," Thom said.

Looking down, Elya realized he'd already drained a quarter of the bottle in one go. He still had another bottle in his pack, but it wasn't full. He'd have to be more conscious of his supplies. He nodded sheepishly and capped the bottle, letting it hang at his side by the attached strap.

"Thank you all for offering to help me," Elya said.

They averted their eyes, except for Thom, who gave him a thin smile, and the priest, who looked like he was presiding over a funeral.

"Last thing we need is Imperials interfering in our business," Charlie muttered.

"It is in everyone's best interest that you find your way back to the Fleet." Father Pohl's face showed strain around his eyes. "If we can help you do that, then we're glad to be your guides."

"Let's get me out of your hair, then." Elya glanced back at the crescent-shaped mouth of the cave, partially blocked by the stone. Though he thought the priest was crazy to stay here during the Kryl invasion, he obviously had some skill at deterring the xeno menace's lesser forms. Maybe Elya had been wrong. Maybe the priest knew something about how to keep safe among the Kryl that he didn't. If this mission to stop the jamming signal failed, Heidi and Hedrick would be safer with the priest and his followers than with Elya.

If he did get rescued, he planned to keep his promise and send a team to pick up the woman and the boy, the priest's wishes be damned. So this really did seem like the best possible outcome from a bad situation.

Focus on one problem at a time, he reminded himself. First, he had to un-jam the cube. Then, make contact with the *Paladin*. Then he would be in a position to help Heidi and Hedrick. As he'd done so many times throughout his life as a refugee, Elya forced himself to focus on just what was in front of him. Block out everything else.

Or at least, he prepared to do so, when arguing voices drifted out of the cave. At first, Elya thought it was two women bickering, but then the boy came bursting into the sunlight and pulled up short in front of Elya, gazing up at him with tear-filled eyes.

Elya adjusted the blaster at his hip and knelt down in front of Hedrick. He gripped the boy's shoulders and tried to ignore the way his heart ached. "What's wrong?"

"It isn't fair," Hedrick said. "I want to go with you."

"I'm sorry, kid. Life isn't fair sometimes."

The boy blinked, as if no one had ever shared this difficult truth with him before now. "We should be allowed to go with you!" Hedrick insisted. "I don't want to be stuck in this cave. It's *boring.*"

"I don't want you to be stuck in the cave either." *And I certainly don't want you to be here when the Kryl hive arrives in force.* Elya had to hold back a small laugh that bubbled up. Oh, to be a boy and be worried, most of all, about avoiding boredom.

Heidi had come outside and crossed her arms, baring three angry red marks across her forearm. The boy must have scratched her in his haste to get to Elya. Her mouth was set in a hard line and her eyes gleamed—until she saw Elya gripping the boy's shoulders. She came up short and sagged back against the red stone wall, putting her hand over her mouth.

Hedrick didn't see her. He had his back to his mother, whose eyes Elya met her eyes when he said, "If you come with me," —he tilted his chin in Heidi's direction— "who will watch after your mom?"

The boy inhaled sharply, glanced back at her. "She'll come, too. She'd have to!"

Elya shook his head, looked back at the men with the guns arrayed behind him. "She can't. We could get into a firefight. Your mom isn't trained to use a blaster or a rifle, and doesn't have a weapon of her own."

"So, give her one! She's got good aim, believe me." He rubbed the back of his head.

Elya smiled. "They're all out." He had no idea if that was true. "I've got my sidearm." He patted the SB-44 on his hip. "They took all the weapons they could spare. The rest are being left behind to protect the rest of these people—including you."

"Then just take me. I'm small. I won't complain. I'll take care of Hedgebot!"

"Your mom would be worried sick without you. Have you ever been worried sick about somebody? So sick you couldn't eat or sleep or do anything except think about them?"

The boy swallowed, his rebellious courage wavering. Elya didn't know what Hedrick thought about at that moment, but something made the boy's bottom lip tremble and his eyes brim full. Exhaling a heavy breath, he finally nodded.

The priest stepped forward, looking down at the boy. "You and your mother will be safer here, lad. Our cavern is defensible and filled with supplies."

Heidi took one step forward and stopped. Elya dropped his hands from the boy's shoulders.

"Father Pohl," he said. "Can you give us a minute?"

The priest smiled kindly and nodded. Elya took Hedrick by the hand and walked him back over to his mother. In a low voice that only she and the boy could hear, he whispered, "I'll find out where you can catch a ride off planet and make sure you get there."

More likely, once Elya made contact, the Fleet would send a Sabre squadron directly to the cave. But in case the priest and followers were able to hear what Elya was saying, he didn't want them to get any ideas that he was about to violate their autonomy, so he kept it vague as he locked eyes with Heidi. "I won't leave you here. I'll eliminate whatever is jamming the signal on my cube and then come back for you, or send someone back in my stead."

A double sonic boom echoed in the sky. Elya recognized it as a spacecraft breaking the sound barrier as it entered the moon's atmosphere. Heidi, the boy, and Elya all turned their faces up and watched as an egg-shaped object arced to the left, falling beyond the ravine into the valley adjacent to where his starfighter had been scuttled.

"Slocum's in that direction," Elya heard one of the men say to his comrade. "Wh—"

At a minute shake of the priest's head, the man swallowed his words.

"All right," Elya said. "Hedrick, you think you can do this for me? Stay here and protect your mother?"

Tears streaked down Hedrick's face, but he sniffed, nodded and allowed his mother to lead him back toward the cave.

Brave kid, Elya thought, *I won't leave you here. I promise.*

He turned around, humped his pack back onto his shoulders and went to join the group.

"We follow this ridgeline," Charlie said "to the lookout point. You can see the whole valley from there, including where that egg just dropped."

"There's a Kryl encampment in the valley," Father Pohl said. "The overnight watch saw two more of those drop in and land within ten kilometers of each other."

"More groundlings," Elya said. "I can guarantee you that. The trick will be avoiding them."

The men nodded as one, somehow agreeing with Elya without acknowledging him. *Talkative bunch,* he thought. *At least they'll take me where I need to go.* Only Thom seemed worried at the mention of groundlings, which confirmed for Elya that Charlie and his three heavily armed comrades must be former SDF, and used to seeing action.

If he succeeded, he'd get a ride and come back for Heidi and Hedrick. If not, and he died out there... well, soldiers have died in war before, and still the Empire held the front against the Kryl. The war effort would go on without him. Protected in the cave, at least Heidi and Hedrick would have a fighting chance. It wasn't satisfactory, but it would have to be good enough for now.

The group walked in the direction Charlie had indicated, taking their first step down the trail as the local sun broke over the horizon.

FOURTEEN

Casey heard the screaming several turns before she saw the sterile white walls of the hospital corridor. There was one male voice, hoarse and high pitched, yelling at top volume the way Mick had done in the hangar. There were other voices, too, by turns placating, pleading, angry or scared.

The *Paladin* tilted to maneuver itself fast enough that the artificial gravity systems took a beat to catch up. Casey caught herself as she slid into another wall.

She stared down the final corridor that would lead her to the hospital. She started forward again, slowing her pace just slightly so she could catch her breath. Another body slammed into the wall behind her, panting heavily. Turning, she spotted the slightly plump and balding figure of Colonel Volk. He grabbed her flight jacket at the shoulder, pulled a blaster from a holster at his hip, and gestured with his free hand, pressing down towards the ground as if to say, *Go slow.*

Casey saw the sense in this and slowed her pace. She met the XO's alert, darting eyes, lids puffy like he hadn't gotten much sleep lately. The smoky scent of whisky on his breath explained why he was breathing so hard—maybe the old colonel had paused to take a sip from a flask he secreted somewhere on his person. Perhaps he'd done it to steel his nerves for the dangerous situation they were about to walk into. Regardless, the smell annoyed her. She bit her tongue, however, knowing that even if she wasn't on thin ice with the admiral already, she couldn't very well chastise a superior officer. She settled with growling in her throat and pushing in front of the colonel as the two of them made their way, together, towards the hospital wing.

"Get back, voidspawn!"

That's when she recognized the voice. The one that had been screaming. She'd initially pegged the one yelling the loudest as the source of the conflict—Mick's sudden downturn had primed her for that. But now she also knew the person that voice belonged to, and it chilled her blood.

She broke into a run again.

She flipped through possible scenarios in her mind. As far as she knew, there were no welding torches or gas canisters kept in the hospital. But there were surgical instruments capable of being used as weapons, and heavy objects with which to bludgeon people.

"Let me go in first," Casey said. "I don't want the sight of that blaster to cause him to panic."

"Don't do anything rash."

Casey shot Colonel Volk a frown, noticed how the hand holding his blaster shook and said, "Why don't you worry about yourself, *sir*." He scowled at her.

Stepping into the hospital wing, Casey was surprised to find nobody in the front waiting room. The chairs were arranged in neat and orderly rows, bolted to the floor, as most furniture in the Destroyer was. She moved quickly beyond the front desk and through a pair of sliding doors.

That's when the yelling shot up ten decibels and transformed into a blood-curdling screech.

A small knot of people were gathered in the next room. One nurse was leaning against the wall clutching her right ear. Blood trickled down her neck and a doctor was pressing gauze to the wound. The other people in this room must have been patients. They wore thin, papery hospital gowns. An older man, who must have been injured in the hangar incident, dragged an IV along with him as he huddled miserably in the corner, eyes darting back and forth.

"Which way?" Casey asked. A doctor and three patients all pointed in the same direction.

Casey hurried forward. She'd caught her breath by now. Colonel Volk wheezed raggedly as he fought to pull air into his lungs. While Admiral Miyaru stayed almost annoyingly fit, despite being nearly sixty, Colonel Volk, ten years younger, had let himself go. This sprint across the Destroyer had taken a toll on him.

It annoyed her that the First Officer had been sent to babysit her. Why else would Admiral Miyaru order him from the bridge right after the Kryl hive had shown up, other than to make sure that she didn't screw something up?

A loud crash and the sound of glass breaking rattled down the hall.

"No, don't!" a woman's voice shouted.

"Yorra?" Casey called her friend's name as she stepped forward into the next segment of the hospital. A door slid aside to reveal a series of beds separated by curtains. A short, wiry man with wild dark hair and bloodshot eyes held Yorra's neck in the crook of his elbow.

"Park!" Casey shouted. "What are you doing? Let her go!"

He held a jet injector gun to Yorra's neck. She had several cuts along her forearms and one on her cheekbone. Shallow, but obviously painful and each was bleeding. Maybe from a scalpel? Casey marked several bladed instruments among splotches of blood dotting the floor. Yorra gripped Park's arm and leaned away from the injector's barrel.

Park recovered his wits from whatever distraction hearing his name from Casey's mouth had caused, and jammed the gun harder against Yorra's throat.

"This is filled with morphine. If you come any closer, this xeno spawn is dead."

"She's not a xeno! That's Yorra, your squadmate and friend." He jammed the gun against Yorra's throat. "Lieutenant Innovesh Park! You let her go right now. That's an order, Naab."

"You Kryl bastards don't get to give orders," Park snarled. "You want to see one of your own die?"

"No!" Casey shouted, her eyes going wide as she lunged forward.

She was too slow. A blaster bolt sizzled by her ear a fraction of a second after Colonel Volk took the shot. It struck the injector gun, sending it flying backwards to shatter against the wall. Park released Yorra as he clutched his shaking hand in pain.

"My finger!" he shouted.

Casey's eyes darted from the pieces of the gun to Park's bloody hand, to Yorra. One of the pieces that she thought belonged to the injector twitched and she realized it was his severed finger.

Casey lunged forward, grabbed Yorra and hauled her backward, putting herself between the woman and their crazed squadmate.

"Gears, get out of here," Casey ordered. "We've got this under control."

"I'm not leaving him," Yorra said.

Casey glanced over her shoulder, met the eyes of Colonel Volk and jerked her head.

"I don't take orders from you, Captain." He still held the sidearm outstretched. His hands were surprisingly steady. She wondered how long the adrenaline would overcome the flaws engendered by his drinking habit.

"Now is not the time to argue about rank, Colonel!"

After a moment, he saw the sense of what she was suggesting, and hurried the other patients—who had been there trying to calm down Park when they burst into the room—out through the doors behind her.

"We're not here to harm you," Casey said, showing her hands to Park, or whatever was possessing him. Space madness did not mess around. "We're just trying to help."

Park chuckled and for a second, Casey saw his old personality shining through whatever this was.

"Oh, that's rich," Park said. "An Overmind herself offering to help. I've heard these stories before. I won't be one of your experiments!"

Suddenly, the shouts of "xeno, xeno!" that she'd first heard from Mick, and the specific insult of "voidborn hellspawn" from Park, clicked in her brain. The space madness had a specific and surprisingly consistent point of view for possessing two very different people. She didn't know what it meant, but it meant *something*.

"Wait," Casey said. "You honestly think I'm *one* of them? Park, it's me, Raptor. Your squadmate. We've flown together, we've gambled together, we've told each other embarrassing childhood stories. We're friends, man."

"You may look like her, but you're not her. There's nothing coming out of your mouth but lies. Give me a shuttle and let me off this mothership, or I'll jump into the vacuum and die instead of giving you any information that could hurt my friends. I won't do it. I won't betray them. I won't be y—"

His voice climbed to higher pitches of earnestness as he rambled. And then suddenly his mouth opened wide and he clutched his head the way Mick had done, reinforcing her theory that *something* had caused the strange behavior in both men.

What if the space madness wasn't random, as the legend supposed? What if it wasn't caused by toxic radiation, but something else?

What if it was contagious?

What if Mick and Park had both caught it, like a virus?

Casey heard the soft footsteps of Colonel Volk behind her, returning after evacuating the other patients. "What's wrong with him?" he said, aiming his blaster at Park again.

Casey's hand shot out and pushed the gun down. "Don't."

"I'll just shoot him in the leg. It's treatable."

"No. There's another way."

Suddenly Park snapped up and narrowed his eyes. He gritted his teeth, then bent down and swept up a bloody scalpel from the floor, which he held in front of him like a dagger.

Colonel Volk snorted with disdain. "What are you gonna do with that, Lieutenant?"

Casey gasped when Park turned the scalpel against his own throat this time. The blade glimmered dully in the harsh fluorescent light of the hospital wing. "Don't come any closer. I'll do it!"

Casey raised her hands. "Okay. All right."

"What are you doing?" Colonel Volk asked.

"Just give him what he wants. I have an idea," Casey whispered. She looked back at Park. "All right. We'll let you go free. Just—just calm down."

She began to back up.

"This is a bad idea," Colonel Volk whispered.

"Just go with it."

She forced the colonel to back out of the room. They fetched up against a wall in the hallway and she began to slide along it towards where Yorra and a few of the other patients were huddling fearfully, bracing themselves against each other and one medical bot shaped like a cone, colored white with red stripes.

Park followed them out of the room, saw the pack of people blocking the way, and turned and went in the other direction, glancing down each hallway, trying to find another way out.

That's odd, Casey thought. Park would know his way around the hospital wing. But, for some reason, he was acting like this was the first time he'd ever been here.

Maybe he'd never been in the hospital wing in the *Paladin*, but all the hospital wings on every ship in the Solaran Fleet were designed exactly the same way. Not identical, but close enough that she could find her way around any one of them easily.

Instead of heading out towards the rest of the destroyer, Park staggered into the surgical unit.

Just as she'd hoped.

"Come on," Casey whispered.

They followed Park at a discreet distance while he poked into hallways and shook his head. He gripped the scalpel in his good hand. The other hand, the one with the missing finger, he held close to his uniform. Yorra had found a metal cane that would serve as a good club and Colonel Volk still had his blaster. Casey remained empty-handed. She didn't want Park to see all three of them holding weapons and panic.

Leaning back, Casey conferred with Colonel Volk, who she knew had fairly good aim based on his earlier success hitting the injector gun and taking off Park's finger. She didn't want him to lose any more fingers, but they needed a contingency plan. Colonel Volk agreed and they continued dogging Park, deeper and deeper into the hospital wing. He passed one recovery room, and then another before he made it to the ORs.

As Lieutenant Park turned to go into one of the recovery rooms, a blaster bolt from Colonel Volk sent him reeling into the opposite wall. He stumbled away, moaning and dripping blood from his severed finger.

"Good," Casey whispered, "get him into that OR."

Park snarled, shaking his head as if to clear cobwebs or banish a headache. His injured hand kept clawing at his right ear.

Colonel Volk fired at the wall again. Naab stumbled away from the blaster and into one of the automated ORs.

"Perfect. Now let's go," Casey said. She rushed through the door and came under the arcing slash of a bloodied scalpel. Casey ducked and rolled along the floor, slamming her elbow and sending tingles down her arm. She used the other arm to push herself to her feet and leaned against the control console of the operating bot, which looked like a cockpit filled with a thousand spidery metal arms, each bearing sharp implements. The arms were folded up against the top of the shell so that when she pressed the open button, they all slid aside to reveal a lounge chair contoured to the human shape. It looked, she thought, almost like the tanning bed she used to use in the sauna back home.

Turning back, she saw Park caught between herself, the operating robot, and Yorra and Colonel Volk, who blocked the doorway, each bearing their own weapons. Colonel Volk fired his blaster at the floor in front of Park, turning the metal white hot where the bolt struck.

Park hissed at Volk—actually hissed—then slashed out at Yorra. Unlike before, when she had been unprepared and hoping that her friend wouldn't hurt her, this time she was ready. Yorra slapped the metal bar down on Park's wrist. He dropped the scalpel, and his hand curled inward into a claw.

Casey leaped out, grabbed his shoulders and yanked Park into the open bed.

Despite his injuries, the strong and stocky pilot braced himself against the half open shell, like a many-legged insect that refused to be pushed down the drain. He thrashed and squirmed, shoving Casey back with a power she'd never felt from him, even during their sparring sessions—a power fueled by fear of xenos. It took all three of them—Yorra, the colonel, and Casey—to force him down into the bed, but not before Park bit Colonel Volk's bicep between his teeth. The colonel bashed Park in the head with the butt of his blaster, which seemed to daze the pilot long enough to get him strapped in. Casey slapped the button that would close the surgical shell and keyed in the command for an automated diagnostic (all while sending up a prayer to Lt. Colonel Walcott, may he rest in peace, for making sure all his pilots completed their basic first-aid training).

The hologram of the AI's face came up at the foot of the egg casing. Casey blinked dumbly as, for a moment, she thought she saw herself in Harmony's pulsing light-face. She was pulled back to the moment when Park punched the inside of the glass, but she knew this glass was both shatter-proof and durable, actually made out of transparent alumi-nite, and that his hand would break long before the shell would give.

"What kind of operation would you like to perform today?" Harmony asked.

"Diagnostic," Casey huffed. "Diagnostic."

"Certainly," the AI said in a cheerful tone.

Park's straps tightened down, as if pulled by an invisible winch. He struggled so hard against his lashes the veins in his forehead and neck popped out. But though he fought, he couldn't escape.

"No! I won't be one of your experiments!" He spit against

the glass. "Let me go, you voidspawn creeps. The Fleet will find you. They'll wipe you out!"

Behind her, Yorra choked back a sob and slapped both hands over her mouth. She turned away and buried her head into the colonel's shoulder. The XO held her as he, too, put as much distance between himself and the operating robot as he could without leaving the room.

In the chair, beneath the shell, blue lasers swept up and down Park's thrashing body.

"Error," Harmony reported. "Patient must remain still. Applying tranquilizer."

One of the surgical arms, which had been folded up against the shell, shot down and embedded a needle in Park's neck. His eyes went wide as a clear liquid was pushed into his veins. His thrashing slowed, but didn't stop. Any normal person would have been knocked out cold by that quantity of tranqs, even a starfighter pilot accustomed to taking chemicals into their system. Park continued to struggle. Gradually, the fight left his limbs, retreating to his face and vein-riddled neck. Foam drooled out of his mouth.

He looked like a rabid animal. Casey placed a hand against the transparent shell. "I'm sorry."

A blue scanner traced Park again, eliciting a warm chime from the operating bot. "Foreign body detected. Preparing for extraction."

The AI's face blinked out. In its place, a subcutaneous image revealed a xeno form, almost certainly Kryl. The alien resembled a worm, its thin segmented body sprouting eight legs, each terminating in multi-pronged, hair-thin talons. Casey shivered violently. Though every fiber of her being conspired to send her fleeing from the surgical machine, she forced herself to face her fear and remain at Park's side. She had no idea if he'd survive this procedure. Casey hadn't been able to be there for Nevers. Or for Walcott. So she stood her ground here, now, for Park.

Is this loyalty? Casey wondered. *Stubbornness? Or do I just want to prove that I'm not a coward?*

"Hang on, Park," she said.

His face went slack. The drugs had finally taken hold. Several of the operating arms unfolded. Casey flinched when the pilot began to thrash again. She didn't know how he had any strength left, but there it was.

Two of the operating arms clamped down on Park's shoulders with angled grabbers and held him flat against the table. A strap shot out of the bed's tapered edge and lashed down over his forehead. Another extended to restrain his feet. At the same time, a surgical arm lowered and held a mask over Park's mouth that reminded Casey of nothing more than the oxygen mask they each wore in the cockpit of their Sabres. The egg's interior filled with a thin gray gas.

Another of the surgical arms extended and formed scissors that cut away part of Park's uniform, exposing his muscled chest and abs. Suddenly, the gas evacuated and a suction cup fastened down over the top of his sternum, sealing against his skin.

Inside the suction cap, the creature she'd seen in the hologram appeared in outline against Park's flesh. The creature seemed to know it was being tracked. It squirmed forward, disappearing again under Park's left pectoral muscle. The suction cup followed, hurrying after the creature as it burrowed into muscle and tendons. The worm fled down toward his waist, then up along his ribcage until the machine trapped it against Park's neck.

The surgical apparatus applied continuous force, pulling the creature up to the skin until every segment of the xeno— no longer than her pinky, its extremities whip-thin—was outlined clearly against Park's clammy skin. It looked like his flesh had been branded with the xeno's form.

Casey heard somebody gag behind her and turned to see Colonel Volk covering his mouth with one hand. Yorra had her face buried into his shoulder. While Casey was looking at the bewildered pair, a piercing cry of pain erupted from Park.

"AAAAGH!" The pilot's body arched up as his skin split. The worm-like xeno came crawling out, its skin pale and mottled with veins. The worm pulsed with Park's blood. It opened its petal-like mouth and gave off a tiny scream of its own before it was pulled through a tube attached to the suction cup. The operating machine spat the xeno into an aluminite jar, which was immediately sealed.

Park sagged back against the table, his head lolling to one side, and went truly and finally still. The operating bot sealed the wound with staples, then treated and wrapped the blaster-burned stump of his missing finger. The surgical arms retracted. The straps that had been holding him down loosened and slithered away. Pressure released with a hiss. The aluminite shell of the surgical table cracked and levered open.

With her heart hammering in her chest and her breath coming quick, Casey hesitantly approached Park, who was deathly still. Had he survived? He wasn't moving…

She reached out. A low rush of hot breath tickled the hair on the back of her hand. Casey sagged in relief. Park had a raging fever and his skin was clammy, but his chest slowly lifted as his lungs filled with air.

"He's alive," Casey reported. "I think he's gonna make it."

Yorra and Colonel Volk separated sheepishly and studied the situation warily from across the room before slowly approaching.

Seeing Park breathing on his own, Yorra exhaled a

tremulous sigh. Colonel Volk holstered his blaster and dug a flask out of his officer's jacket. He took a swig, then offered it to Yorra, who took a sip and passed the flask to Casey.

Casey's anger at the XO flared. But after what they'd just been through? "Hell, why not," she said and took a shot.

After wiping her mouth, Casey picked up the clear jar containing the Kryl worm. She held it at arm's length. Her skin crawled. The tumescent xeno convulsed and vomited up a surprising amount of blood. She wished the surgical machine had killed the creature, but she'd be damned if she was going to risk opening the jar to finish the job. "The admiral said she needed evidence. Do you two think this little parasite counts as evidence?"

FIFTEEN

E lya crouched atop the ridgeline and gazed down on the compound they called Slocum.

It had the look of a military encampment: six identical rectangular prefab buildings had been placed in a column along one side, evenly spaced like neat little soldiers. The other half of the property featured a "parade ground"—really just a grass field—encircled by a paved track, several small sheds likely used for storage, and a communications array powered by a bank of solar cells feeding into a large battery. The whole thing was encompassed by an electrified chain-link fence. Not the best defensive system, but sturdy enough to keep out large predators in the early days of a new colony. The Empire must have provided the patterns for the buildings, and probably the 3D-printers, too. As usual, they offered the bare necessities and not much more.

Now, however, several details made the structure look distinctly *not* Imperial. For instance, one corner of the fence had been torn open, then patched back together with what looked like a yellowish-gray spider's webbing, but which Elya knew to be Kryl excretions. The ground in front of the security gate was torn and pitted, as if it had been the site of a great brawl, and patterns of soot—blaster marks—told the story of a tragic, last-ditch defense. Packs of groundlings roved the perimeter, occasionally stopping to pick at one of several ravaged human corpses. The bodies had been out so long that they had almost no meat left on their bleach-white bones, which could be seen poking up through the remaining shreds of clothing. Trails of dried blood stained the untrimmed grass leading to the largest pile of bodies in the middle of the parade ground.

"So this is what raised the flag to the Empire," Elya said. "The first packs of groundlings were discovered... what, a year ago?"

"Two years." Thom, the machinist, snorted and glanced sidelong at Elya. "Took a while for the Colonization Board to take us seriously. The Kryl infestation was under control up until about six weeks ago. Once preparations for the evacuation ramped up, the Kryl started to organize themselves. They only raided Slocum recently."

Elya spat into the grass. "At least they didn't make themselves hard to find."

Father Pohl smiled grimly. Charlie and his three soldiers stood apart and held their silence.

"How do you know the jamming signal is coming from here?" Elya asked.

Thom handed his binoculars to Elya. "Check out the communications array."

The satellites were half-covered in what looked, at first, like fungus. Planted on the ground among the panels, a bulbous sac laced with veins slowly expanded, as if breathing. With each contraction, it excreted a small amount of yellow pus onto the ground, and it was this pus that crawled up onto the panels and over the communications antennas, turning into a hard chitin as it spread over the electronics equipment. It took him a moment, but Elya finally picked out the antennas and dishes that broadcasted radio waves and tightbeam signals. The equipment was covered in organic matter.

"Destroy the creature producing the jamming signal," Charlie said, "and your cube should connect."

Elya handed Thom the binoculars and glanced back at the soldier. The facile nature with which Charlie handled his gauss rifle, and the way he un-self-consciously used hand signals to halt the hiking party for water breaks over the past few hours told Elya much about the man. He led the group like he was in command but deferred with shaded glances to Father Pohl.

Thom had chatted amicably with Elya for most of the morning, quizzing him about Hedgebot, the mechanics of his Sabre, and the requirements for qualifying to fly starfighters with the Fleet. He'd also told Elya the names and stories of the three soldiers humping rifles and following Charlie's orders. The tall woman with grey hair was known as Postiss. The younger blond guy with bulging biceps and pecs you could set a teacup on was her son, Brill. And the other woman, with a thick brow, jet-black hair tied back in a pony-tail, and a dimpled chin, was called Taylix. All of them were ex-infantry who had done stints as mercenaries after the Kryl War before retiring to Robichar.

"How do you suggest we get in?" Elya asked. "The place is crawling with Kryl." He stepped back from the ridgeline and widened his gaze to take in the forest, which had grown thicker as they descended toward the encampment. Hedgebot, on his shoulder, stood up to mimic his pose. The last thing they needed was for one of the groundlings roving the perimeter to spot them and sound an alarm. The Kryl's psychic connection meant that they could respond to outside threats faster and with more accuracy than any human security force, and the two larger, uglier creatures—the kind Solarans called sentinels—standing guard near the door of one of the prefab buildings would be a whole hell of a lot harder to kill than the groundlings. This particular brand of xeno could rise to three meters tall and was covered in overlapping plates of purple-black carapace twenty centimeters thick in places. They had two alert, unblinking eyes lodged too far apart in their head, which was crowned with a single horn of dark bone. It made them look kind of goofy, especially when they were just standing there staring at nothing, but Elya wasn't fooled.

Neither was Charlie, who unclipped a remote-activated charge from his belt and said, "We'll need a diversion."

Everyone looked at the priest. Father Pohl nodded solemnly. He'd obviously expected this, and Elya wondered if they'd had time to plan this last night, or while he'd been chatting with Thom on the hike.

The priest took the charge from Charlie. "I'll set it off there." He pointed at the forest beyond the compound. "That should draw them away, give you enough time to get in and out again."

"What if the groundlings find you?" Elya asked.

"Animus will protect me."

Elya looked at the man, biting back a reply. *Same old story.* But as long as they helped him make contact with the Fleet, they could take whatever risks they pleased. It was no skin off his back.

"Just in case, Brill and Taylix will go with you," Charlie added, his voice making it clear that though he deferred to Father Pohl, this point was not up for discussion. "Set the charge on a tree two klicks west of the encampment—no farther than that. They need to be able to see and hear it. When they do, the groundlings *should* go to investigate."

"And how are we supposed to get through the fence?" Elya asked.

Thom waved a U-shaped steel handle with a battery pack attached to it. "I'll use this laser cutter to slice through it."

Elya bowed his head and felt Hedgebot scamper nervously to his other shoulder. They had *clearly* planned this already—without him. His first reaction was annoyance. If this were his squad… but it wasn't. He didn't have to work with these people long term. He only had to get through this mission alive. Elya shoved his irritation away. "That just leaves the two sentinels."

"With luck, they'll be drawn to the explosion as well," Charlie said. "Regardless, we'll enter in their blind spot at the northeast corner, behind the prefab buildings. Set charges on the comms array close enough to kill the creature causing the jamming, then run before they notice we're even there."

That would destroy Slocum's comms array, too, but as long as the equipment was in Kryl possession it posed too great a risk to leave it operational. Otherwise they'd have to come back and do it again.

"And if luck isn't on our side?" Lady luck hadn't exactly been friendly to him lately, Elya knew.

"You've got charge on your blaster, haven't you?"

Elya inhaled through his nose and blew the breath out as he checked the power, then nodded reluctantly. During the hike, he'd used a portable battery pack of Thom's to partially recharge the weapon. His heart fluttered in his chest.

Next to him, Thom bounced his leg and licked his lips nervously. Elya could relate. He didn't want to do this. It was risky. It was dangerous. And there would almost certainly be a fight. But he didn't see another choice.

Plus, the evacuation deadline was drawing close. Elya had only a handful of hours left. Even now, he knew, they were likely ferrying the last shuttle of civilians to the Mammoths.

If Elya didn't signal the Fleet that he was still alive, and soon, they would certainly leave him behind.

"Well, what are we waiting for?"

Elya held his breath as a large groundling crept into view and lifted its nose into the air, sniffing, sensing.

Beside him, Thom sweated buckets, wiping his palms on his jeans every so often. Charlie pressed his back against another tree trunk a few meters from the one Elya and Thom hid behind. Postiss, maintaining her stoic silence, had signaled to Charlie then climbed up into a tree and rested the barrel of her gun on the crotch of a sturdy branch, a makeshift sniper's nest.

The groundling pawed at the ground, picking something up in its mouth and forcing it down its gullet with three leaping gulps. It paused, turned toward them—

Just as Elya was about to draw his blaster, a great explosion erupted in the distance, scattering birds from the canopy. The groundling's hide rippled as it shivered. Then it let rip a great keening howl before bounding off toward the noise.

Thom heaved a shaky sigh.

"Finally," Elya said. They'd been waiting a damn sight longer than he'd wanted, and the groundling's sniffing explorations, coming closer with each pass, had been making him nervous.

"Shh!" Charlie hissed.

Half a dozen more groundlings suddenly thundered out of the thick forest, loping by at a distance. None of them noticed the four Solarans hiding a hundred meters away.

Charlie held up his fist. The group waited until the pounding of dozens of clawed feet faded to a soft thudding, then disappeared from hearing range. Still, Charlie waited. When the birds began to settle back in the branches above them and coo nervously into the humid air, he pushed himself to his feet. "Let's move."

Elya found himself following Charlie's lead, set at ease by the man's focus and composure under pressure. Whatever disagreement had set them at odds the day before had been left behind, which Elya considered a good thing since this was the most clandestine operation he'd ever been a part of. Being so far outside of his comfort zone, he was leaning entirely on the veteran soldier's experience and guidance.

They had agreed that it would be Elya who set the charge and ultimately detonated it, destroying the xeno who had commandeered the comms array. Right now, all he had to do was stay down, keep moving, and not get blindsided by a Kryl. His legs ached and he was winded when they reached the northeast corner of the compound, where the fence had been ripped apart and then re-stitched with Kryl webbing.

"Eye in the sky," Postiss said, the first words Elya heard her speak. She tossed out a hand and a drone soared silently upward, floating out over the rooftops of the prefabs.

Thom approached the fence hesitantly, testing it with a stick and then with a finger. The chain-link itself wasn't wired to shock, just the lattice near the top, which popped with a soft *sszzttt* when Thom tossed up a clod of dirt. Any intruder or animal who tried to climb over would be cooked medium well.

Good thing they weren't going over.

The fencing was sturdy and thick, like the kind used on farms for livestock. Thom got to work, taking the U-shaped wire cutter to the bars of the fence. He started by the ragged edge where the sticky yellow-white webbing terminated. A hissing sound filled the air, like water hitting a hot pan, as the laser began to cut through the metal.

Elya laid his trigger finger along the barrel of his SB-44 and brought it up next to his head as he scanned the woods. He wished he had his bot, but they made him leave it at the rendezvous point for fear it would give away their position with its glowing and uncontrollable scampering. Hedgebot would warn them of danger, sure, but it was no good at sneaking around enemy camps unnoticed, and Elya had readily agreed to leave the bot behind.

"Sentinels?" Charlie whispered.

"One at the western fence looking into the woods like he's got X-ray vision. The other's stationed at the front door of a prefab, second from the end." Postiss pointed to the building without lifting her eyes from the screen attached to her rifle, the one that showed the video feed from the drone.

"Do they know we're here?"

"Negative. Leastwise, not yet."

No pressure, Elya thought. Thom wiped his wrist across his sweaty forehead. He'd managed to cut through a horizontal section of chain-link about three feet across, plenty wide enough for them to slip through one at a time.

Elya grabbed the loose section of chain-link and held it firm so it wouldn't rattle while Tom brought the cutter down the left side and then across the bottom. They switched places as Thom brought the laser back up to meet the original cut, completing the rectangle.

Elya hauled the section of fence out while melted bits of metal dripped, singeing holes in his flight suit and burning his skin beneath. The pain made him squint and tear up, but the molten metal cooled quickly and the pain passed.

With Thom's help, he managed to set the fence gently on the ground with barely a rustle of grass. Thom slipped through the opening, then Charlie, Elya and finally Postiss.

Turning right, the group snuck single-file along the fenceline towards the communications array—and away from where the sentinels were positioned. It struck Elya as odd that one of them had stayed put at the prefab building's entrance. It meant that whatever was inside that building was valuable enough to keep a guard stationed there even in the face of danger.

His train of thought was interrupted when something sticky, gum-like, stuck to the sole of his boot.

"Ugh—" he began to say when Charlie swiped a hand sideways across his neck, silencing him. Elya swallowed whatever words had been about to come out of his mouth, embarrassed. He carefully set his foot back down in the sticky crap.

"The one at the fence is moving this way," Postiss whispered.

Elya glanced down at the sticky substance, then up at the solar panels in front of him. There were six rows of six panels split by a cluster of antennas and dishes, a unit of batteries that hummed noisily and, between him and all of this equipment, the bulbous sac laced with veins that he'd seen from the ridgeline. Up close it was vaguely purplish-red fading to translucent as it expanded. A tangled ball of red and white strings sat inside, visible through its skin, like intestines. The sac itself must have been three feet tall and twice as wide, and seemed to be twisting in his direction, like a plant toward a light source. He glanced between the sac and his foot. He lifted his boot up and stepped backward off the sticky substance.

"It stopped," Postiss reported. "Going back to the fence."

"Don't step on the pus," Elya whispered. "I think they can tell, like some kind of early warning system."

Postiss' nostrils flared. Charlie cursed under his breath and Thom gulped loud enough to hear.

"The antennas are surrounded. How do we get in there to set the charge without them noticing?" Now he sorely missed his astrobot. Hedgebot could have carried the charge and placed it for him.

Elya shoved this thought aside and studied the way intently. The pus leaking out of the sac wasn't coming out evenly. Some of the panels had been covered over completely by the hairy fungus, while others were only partially coated in the stuff. Where it had lost its yellow color and dulled, the pus had also hardened. Whereas out here on the edge, it was still soft and sticky. Elya picked out a line, starting at the corner. If he climbed along a solar panel, he thought he might be able to get behind the sac and close enough to the comms equipment to set the charges without alerting the Kryl by stepping on the excretions.

He moved to the corner and climbed onto a solar panel— without getting his boots dirty this time.

"What the flip are you doing?" Charlie hissed.

Elya waved him off then put his hand over his mouth as the rancid smell of rotting meat drifted to his nose. From his vantage point atop the solar panel, Elya turned and saw the pile of corpses he had noticed on the lawn beyond the circular track.

He turned his focus inward, imagining that he was not here perched atop a thin solar panel, but rather in the sim with his helmet on. He pretended that the bodies were auto-generated by the AI, the smell coming through his spinal port as a simulation, and forced his disgust aside. Breathing through his mouth, Elya moved forward, gingerly stepping from one solar panel to the next and watching carefully to avoid landing on the goop.

He reached the third row, close to the antennas, and paused, looking back at the others. Postiss kept her eye glued to the screen attached to her rifle. Charlie watched in the direction the sentinels were positioned, while Thom watched the direction they had come, still dripping sweat and wringing his hands together. He saw Elya looking and urged him onward with a jerk of his head.

Looking down at his feet, Elya watched as the yellow pus inched forward from the corner of the panel he stood on and nearly annexed the toe of his boot. He managed to shift positions in time to avoid touching it, but as he did so his weight shifted back and his other foot slipped off the edge, tangling up in a wire. He gasped, kicked the wire loose, and barely caught himself before falling backward.

Thom took in a sharp breath behind him and when he looked back, Charlie's eyes were wide as two moons.

Postiss glanced up from the screen, mouthing, "Incoming!" without saying the word.

Charlie ran toward the wall of the prefab nearest them, the one at the end of the row, and raised his gauss rifle to his shoulder. Elya heard the coils in the gun ratchet back as he switched off the safety.

Frantic gestures from Thom caught Elya's eye and reminded him of his purpose. Like he did when he was flying or training in the sim, Elya shut out everything around him and tapped into that well of hyperfocus that was always there for him when he needed it. His vision narrowed to his immediate surroundings.

Removing the first charge from his belt, Elya searched the equipment in front of him and found a dish that had a bald spot of metal the pus hadn't reached. Elya ripped the paper off the back of the charge and stretched, sticking it onto the dish. With quick motions, he stuck another charge onto the panel at his feet, and managed to place a third on a small opening at the base of an antenna, facing the pulsing sac of Kryl fluid. This close to the xeno growth, he could hear a warbling noise that seemed to be coming from the creature itself. That noise was the jamming signal it was broadcasting through the comms array. He stuck another charge on the opposite side, just to be sure the thing would be destroyed. He had to lean way out and down to position the charge correctly, and he nearly fell on his face when a great *wah-JEEOHM* noise made him jump.

He yanked his hand back, fearing he'd accidentally triggered one of the explosives, and it took him a second to realize it was the report of Charlie's rifle. Blood hammered in his ears, drowning out even the roar that erupted from the sentinel as it absorbed the huge round from the coilgun. When Elya glanced up, he saw a cloud of carapace fragments and snot-colored gore spraying backwards. The sentinel's armored hulk spun halfway around—and caught its balance. It pawed at the patchy grass with a foot and jerked its great, horned head.

Then it charged.

"Come on!" Thom shouted, all attempts to keep his volume down forgotten, as he waved the remote in the air.

Elya quickly re-checked the charges, sent a silent prayer consisting of a single desperate thought—*Work!*—into the ether, and dashed back across the panels, where he jumped to the ground and spun toward the fence, sprinting after Thom, who had already begun to retreat.

Postiss recalled her drone and swiped it out of the air. Red blaster bolts fired from her rifle in bursts of three, sizzling against the Kryl's carapace. Though the shots knocked it off balance, they seemed to enrage it more than harm it. The sentinel rocked back, staggered, then came about.

Elya didn't stick around to see what happened next. His line of sight to the sentinel was cut off by the prefabs as he ran along the fenceline behind them. Each time he passed one of the buildings, he glanced through the alley between them, searching for additional threats. In the first alley, nothing. The second, nada. The third, a giant screaming maw. He wondered how the sentinel Postiss had been shooting at got there so quickly, but realized it was the second, the one that had been left behind to guard the building.

"Hurry!" Thom shouted from the breach in the fence. As Elya passed through the ragged opening, the machinist produced another remote-activated charge.

Postiss pumped her arms and sprinted toward them, diving through the breach just a few strides ahead of the sentinel, who came roaring and loping forward, its massive armored body shaking the ground with each step. Thom tossed the charge inside the fence, then Postiss turned and pelted the sentinel with more blaster fire.

Charlie had taken up a position at the treeline. Elya heard the whine of his gauss rifle and staggered clear of his line of fire.

As the sentinel tore through the fence, a projectile from the coilgun struck it square in the chest, the impact shoving it back. Another hail of fire from Postiss pushed it back another meter. Elya remembered—belatedly—about his little SB-44. He yanked the blaster pistol out of its holster and hurled a few bolts at the sentinel.

Combined, the barrage was enough to slow the sentinel down. Thom jammed his finger down on the remote. There was a soft *beep-beep-beep* followed by a hollow *WHUUUMFF* as all the charges they'd set exploded at the same time.

The sentinel transformed into an enormous fountain of dirt, gore, chain-link and carapace. Behind it, the communications array ruptured as the charges went off, sending a cloud of debris into the air. They didn't stand around to gawk. A cloud of dust chased them back into the forest.

Though he'd expected Kryl groundlings to come leaping at them out of every gully and from under each log, they encountered none on their hasty withdrawal.

By the time they made it back to the rendezvous point—a clearing in the woods six or seven klicks from Slocum—Elya's legs were shaking so hard he barely had any control over his steps. He noted the priest conferring with Taylix and Brill, spotted his rucksack at their feet exactly where he'd left it, and collapsed against a tree trunk nearby.

"How'd it go?" Brill asked, approaching as Elya drained his water bottle. As soon as he caught his breath, he'd get the other bottle out—and check the tightbeam connection on his cube.

"Ran into sentinels," Charlie said. "Thom blew one back into orbit."

Brill nodded. "Niiice."

The two conferred while Elya rested his head against the trunk and closed his eyes.

"Heard you set the charges yourself."

When Elya opened his eyes, Taylix was standing over him, arms crossed. Her hair was still slicked back and held in a neat ponytail. She had barely broken a sweat.

"Yeah, guess I did."

Nearby, Thom rubbed his hands over his face. His eyes darted around the woods. Elya could understand how he felt. They weren't all that far from the Kryl encampment and it wasn't unlikely that some of the groundlings had followed their trail here.

"Father Pohl wants to talk to you," Taylix said.

Elya glanced around. "Where is he?"

"Right over there."

Elya lumbered to his feet and, while his knees didn't knock together quite so badly, they felt weak, like wet noodles, barely able to hold him up. He grabbed his rucksack from Brill's feet. The man stood like a door himself, sturdy and wide, pretending to pay no attention to Elya.

A pressure valve released in his chest when Elya's felt inside his pack and his fingers ran over the plastic and metal bristles on Hedgebot's back. He found the power switch and turned on the little bot. He'd climb out when he was ready. Elya's hand then rested on the cold, hard edges of his cube.

He pulled it out, but the light was hard to see in the daylight. He gave a great sigh when, shaded, he saw that the LED light had gone a solid white.

Finally. His face lifted skyward, instinctively searching for a squad of Sabres to come screaming down toward him. But this was no animated feature cast on broadbeam. A tractor beam wouldn't just magically appear and beam him skyward.

If they got the signal in time, they'd be coming for him. If not…

"Did it work?" Thom asked, rubbing his hands together, though it was hot and sticky, and following Elya's gaze upward.

"Yeah, it did. Does your radio work?"

"Yeah, yeah, it should. I left it up at the cave, though."

Elya found it odd that he wouldn't bring the device with him, but shrugged and followed Taylix a little ways out of the clearing. She walked fifteen or twenty meters to where Charlie was standing, then paused and waited for Elya to catch up.

"Where's the priest?" Elya asked.

He looked around, didn't find him, then gazed up at the blue sky, searching for planes again. There was a shuffle of leaves, then the sky and the leaf-strewn ground traded places. The pain came next, slowly, throbbing at the back of his head.

The cube was pried from his fingers as Elya struggled to reorient himself.

"Throw him in."

Elya reached up to take the cube back from whoever had stolen it. To his dismay, Thom pulled it back out of his reach. Elya caught a glimpse of the machinist's sad eyes before Brill and Taylix stepped in front of him. As Elya struggled weakly, the larger, stronger soldiers lifted him bodily and dumped him, like a sack of soy paste, onto the ground.

Only he fell *through* the ground and landed with a thud several feet below. The impact knocked the breath from his lungs. He grabbed at the floor, which was made of packed dirt, cold and damp to the touch.

With panic gripping his chest, Elya rolled onto his knees and gulped air. An object plinked into the dirt beside him, then a metal grate fell, clanging, across the opening above him. Charlie knelt down and bolted a chain onto it with a rattle.

"Hey, wait! Charlie. Thom! Hey. Hey!!!"

Thom appeared with a long face, glancing down at Elya, then away, ashamed.

"Sorry, kid," Charlie said, "but we can't risk the Imperials finding our hideout. And we both know that if they come to pick you up, you won't be able to keep your mouth shut."

"No! Don't leave me here. Don't walk away. Hey, I'm talking to you! It's suicide to stay on Robichar! The Kryl will eat you alive. I don't know what the priest did to scare off those groundlings, but he can't protect you! Once the rest of the hive arrives, you'll all be ground Kryl meat! You hear me? I'm your last chance off this rock. Hey! HEY!!!"

The faint whine of a skimmer drifted into his dirt prison. *They had skimmers this whole time? And they made me hike down here on foot?* Only now did he realize it had been done to tire him out, make him drop his guard. They had used him like the tool that he was.

Elya deflated. With shaking hands, he pulled the object

out of the dirt—it was Hedgebot. The little bot had never turned back on. Turning it over, Elya saw that its battery had been forcibly removed and dropped in the dirt a few feet away. Scratches and grooves from a metal prying tool, maybe a screwdriver, had been made in the bot's belly. The contact plates and mounting brackets were mangled beyond belief, so the battery couldn't be reattached. Hedgebot remained dead in Elya's hands, devoid of power.

"Earth save us," he croaked.

Exhausted, helpless, and sick to his stomach, Elya lowered himself to the ground and lay the lifeless bot in his lap. He gazed up through the grate at the open sky above, his ship and crewmates now farther away than ever.

SIXTEEN

Long after the men with their rucksacks and their guns disappeared from sight, Hedrick waited at the lookout point, watching in the direction they had gone, studying the crease in the landscape the big man they called Charlie had pointed. The others who had stayed behind, including his mother, waited with him for some time but they soon grew bored looking at nothing and wandered back to their chores.

He sat there a while longer, until only his mother was left with him, chewing on her lower lip and watching the others go about their work preparing food and hauling water from a spring nearby. Hedrick watched out of the corner of his eye while one man carried two giant plastic cans by straps, making three separate trips.

Eventually, even his mother got bored.

"Wouldn't you rather be helping folks with the chores?" she asked. "Or maybe napping in the tent?"

In Charlie's tent? Hedrick jerked his head from side to side. He didn't want to be in that man's tent anymore. He hadn't wanted to be in it last night and he didn't want to be in it now. At least last night his mother and Elya had been there and their combined presence made him feel safe. After Elya left, another feeling had begun to build up, pressure rising up his toes through his kneecaps and into his stomach, flooding upwards into his chest until it burst forth into the outburst he'd made earlier when Elya was leaving. Even as it happened he was ashamed of himself, even as the tears flowed he was furious at them for showing. He hadn't meant to cry, but he really didn't want Elya to leave and he'd only realized it when he woke up and the pilot wasn't in the tent anymore.

Eventually his mother stopped badgering him and he felt the grim satisfaction that he'd outlasted her and all the others by keeping his stubborn watch. His mother went about helping with the chores, always keeping him firmly in sight like he was a skittish dog she feared would run off at the first opportunity.

He hated when people treated him like he was so fragile he would break at the slightest touch.

He wasn't gonna run off. After reason returned, he'd realized that Elya had been right. He couldn't leave his mother here by herself. Before the Kryl, he wouldn't have given leaving her alone a second thought. He used to be out of the house early to play with the other kids in the village, sneaking away at sunrise and not coming back until long after sunset.

But those days were gone now. The pace of change made him dizzy.

Hedrick brushed the hair out of his eyes with his fingers and glanced furtively up at the sky, his body tensing at the sight of every strangely shaped cloud, every swooping bird he mistook for another egg plummeting down from space, pregnant with death and destruction.

He cast his eyes down in shame, the crease in the land and

the bright green forests blurring as the memories of his actions returned to haunt him.

It was my fault, Hedrick thought. *They saw us first because we were out in the field.*

The egg had come down hard and fast. It bounced and tumbled like a giant ball. They had watched, naively fascinated, as it settled and then ruptured. They had stood frozen, fixated, as the egg's walls petaled open like a flower in the springtime, revealing leggy creatures in yellowish liquid-filled sacs, until one broke through with a clawed hind foot.

The first week after they moved to Robichar, Hedrick had seen a mama cow give birth to a calf. It was an event because, before they got approved for colonization on Robichar, he and his mom had always lived on space stations or in eco-domes, where meat was grown in vats. So to see this majestic creature up close—so much more real than the holovids—giving birth to a calf both fascinated and grossed him out.

The Kryl emerging from its egg was kind of like that, but with giant insects instead of a cow—and far more alien.

Like when he'd seen the calf emerge from its mother's hind end, he'd stood, transfixed, watching the Kryl. His friends all stood next to him, saying "Ewwww!" and "Gross!" as the creatures tore apart the sack and then began to eat it. It was disgusting and compelling at the same time, so unlike any experience he'd ever had before. He felt nauseated but was unable to tear his eyes away.

Some of the girls got scared and ran back to the village but, like a fool, Hedrick had stayed to watch.

And then the creatures had noticed them.

"What are you doing?" Amy's mother said. She had walked up behind them. "Kids, get over here! Inside. Quickly now. To the nearest house."

"I've got to get back to my mom," Hedrick replied.

"There's no time! Oh, Earth's last lights, they're coming. Run. Run!"

Amy went with her mom. Ignoring her instructions, Hedrick sprinted back toward his house. Clifton ran alongside him for a minute, but the chubby kid was slow and wheezy and Hedrick rapidly outpaced him.

He searched for the new door his mom was supposed to be putting on the house today. It was colorfully painted and hard to miss. The new door had been leaning up against the house when he left that morning. *There it is*. As he approached he saw the new painted door had been hung and the old one was off its hinges, leaning up against the side of the house.

His mom had shouted at him to get inside, just like Amy's mom had, to hide, to get out of sight. Hedrick panicked and dove behind the old door that was leaning against the house, thankful for the shelter, for any shelter.

And then the slaughter started.

Hoarse screams. Heavy thuds. The sound of rending flesh—

Hedrick staggered to his feet as the forest and rolling hills ran together in his vision. He sniffed, wiping snot away with the back of his hand, and blinked his eyes free of the memory.

He forgot why he was waiting here, watching the forest. He probably looked like some moon-eyed sissy, crying by himself. It wasn't like Elya was just going to walk up that path and smile and bring his friends back from the dead.

Nothing could bring them back.

Hedrick's stomach growled and he was ashamed to be grieving and hungry at the same time. Clifton didn't have the luxury of being hungry anymore. Dead people didn't get hunger pangs.

Hedrick looked around. His mother was up to her elbows

in soapy water, scrubbing their dirty shirts from yesterday— someone had provided baggy hand-me-downs to them both —and handing each item off to the gold-skinned servant bot, who rung the shirts out with his rotating mechanical arms and hung them on a line in the sun. She was smiling and laughing at a story another woman was telling, but Hedrick couldn't help but feel sad watching her. They had machines for washing clothes in the village. Was this kind of daily drudgery their whole future?

He forced himself not to look skyward as he hurried into the shelter of the cave. Once inside, safe in the covered half-light, Hedrick let out a sigh of relief. At least in here the sky didn't glare ominously down at him. At least in here it was cool and quiet and nothing would rain death and destruction from outer space.

Except for one or two old folks napping in their tents, the cave was empty of people.

Hedrick found leftover stew in a covered container, set aside away from the fire. They'd used last night's leftovers for breakfast this morning and this was all that was left.

He snuck a few bites, looking around to see if anybody had seen him. They hadn't. And when he'd eaten as much as he dared, enough to sate his hunger but not enough to make them think he'd stolen it, he replaced the lid on the container.

Hedrick's throat was parched now and he wanted a drink of water but didn't see any nearby, so he walked around the perimeter of the cavern, searching. They'd been hauling water earlier, but maybe that was for laundry or bathing. He didn't know where they kept the drinking water. Probably somewhere cool and dark and dry. They may have been weird, but these people, these followers of Animus, were no fools. Hedrick recognized some of them. Several had come to his village along with the priest, helped him set up Solstice services—arranging chairs, gathering folks for the sermon that Father Pohl gave, and distributing offerings afterwards. On the one hand, that made these people all seem a bit more trustworthy. They weren't *total* strangers to him. But on the other hand, if they'd been hiding in this cave, he wondered what else they'd been hiding. They must have been socking supplies away for months and months, long before the Fleet arrived to evacuate the colony.

Though he found no water, the food began to reach his stomach and the satisfied feeling of being full calmed him. Hedrick always felt better after he ate. His mom said it ran in the family. Hedrick just thought it was that he liked food. He'd eat anything. Apart from salad, but that wasn't really food, in his opinion.

He didn't find any water. He did, however, find the cloth-covered stash of weapons the man, Charlie, had pulled a gun out of the night before when he heard the planes flying overhead. The pile was noticeably slimmer but it still looked like there were plenty of weapons. More than enough to spare.

Hedrick replaced the tarp and walked farther back into the cave. It was dark and shaded here and none of the electric lights or bots were positioned behind the last tent, the biggest one, which belonged to Father Pohl. Hedrick glanced in and saw a single bare cot with a rumpled blanket and a plain wooden desk. A leather-bound book on the desk. Its spine read, *Scriptures of Animus: The Great Migration, Volume III*. The rest of the set of books lined a small shelf on the floor in the corner.

Hedrick lost interest and moved back behind the tents. As his eyes adjusted to the darkness, he saw that his assumption had been right. Dozens of crates were stacked here, ostensibly with supplies. Weirdly, one was filled with dirt and stank to the high heavens. He supposed that was some kind of fertilizer to help grow food. They'd had plots of planted vegetables in the village that smelled the same way.

Hedrick found another couple of boxes that had little plastic vials, each filled with a handful of seeds. That was odd. Or was it? He supposed not. These people really were hoping to outlast the Kryl. *How long would we have to stay here?* Hendrick wondered.

He moved on and eventually found what he was looking for. Water barrels. It didn't occur to him until now that perhaps this kind of water wasn't even drinkable, but one of the barrels had a spigot and he was too thirsty by this point to care. If it was good enough for the plants, it was good enough for him. The water had a strong sulfur taste with metallic undertones, but it was cool and refreshing and he didn't mind the mineral flavor. As he was tilting his head to catch the water falling out of the spigot Hedrick noticed something—a faint sparkle shimmering down the hall. Rocks speckled with what looked like gold shone at the very back of the cavern, fifty meters or so beyond where the stash of supplies ended.

Is that why the priest and his followers were risking their lives to stay in this cave? They were hiding some kind of treasure?

Back on *Erythro*, the cramped and decaying space station where they lived before they immigrated to Robichar, he'd known a bald old geezer named Yujene with a missing front tooth who collected gems and geodes. The stones looked like plain rocks on the outside but, when split open, revealed a miniature garden of colorful crystals on the inside. Hedrick spent hours with the old man tilting the geodes in the light and rolling their names over his tongue—quartz and amethyst, agate and gypsum, black calcite, lapis lazuli.

In outer space, where a pound of water was the most valuable material, geodes were expensive luxury items.

Yujene told him they were an indulgence even for the ultra rich. But the geezer collected them anyways and always said that if you polished them smooth and worked the crystals into decorative lamps or the base of a holoscreen, people paid enough for them to make it worth his while.

Yujene also had a few samples of a rock called pyrite. Practically worthless, pyrite is the same color as gold and can even seem to exhibit the same characteristics. As Hedrick approached the back of the cavern, he thought of this impersonator metal—commonly called "Fool's Gold" because people mistook it for actual gold. That's what the flakes on the far wall looked like to him, Fool's Gold. Except he'd forgotten what Yujene taught him about how to tell the difference.

Still, the flakes drew his curiosity and knowing what little he did know made him *more* interested, not less, about the glittering among the darker vein of granite.

As he followed the pattern in the rock, the gold flakes gathered and twisted around each other in an undulating wave pattern, braiding up and down in a startling dance. Something about it didn't seem natural. Hedrick followed the twisting pattern around the corner and, though he expected the cave to get darker, he began to notice a faint green glow up ahead.

Hedrick looked back in the direction of the supply crates and, beyond them, the tents. It would be easy to find his way back. The hallway branched two ways. He'd just take his next right, then the next right after that and he'd be back where he started.

His mother would probably start worrying soon, if she noticed he was missing. Maybe Hedrick could just peek around this corner and see what that green glow was coming from. He wanted to know so he could maybe send a message back to Yujene, share what he discovered. Who knows?

Maybe it would pique the man's interest, and anyway, it gave Hedrick a reason to send him a message. The old geezer would be delighted to hear news of geodes on Robichar.

So Hedrick followed the glow around the corner and was pleasantly surprised to see that the rocks here *did* emit an ambient light that seemed to come from no source in particular. It wasn't green, necessarily, so much as white light reflecting an undertone in the walls of the cave, which had narrowed to a passage only big enough for three people to walk abreast.

Now there was no doubt in his mind. This was not a natural occurrence, but a man-made formation. Excited, Hedrick picked up his pace and continued to follow the twisting, wavy lines of gold flakes, like an unbroken chain. He soon came to a dead end, where the gold chain twisted into an arched frame about the size of a doorway. Atop the arch sat a golden pattern of flakes that reminded him of a crown, like something the Emperor might wear.

Hedrick ran his fingers along the frame—smooth gold spots bordered by rough granite ridges—he could tell that there had once been intricate carvings here, but the ridges had been worn smooth by time.

Up close, the pattern made no sense. Only when he stepped back and took in the whole design did the impression of objects solidify. He saw now how the crown was made of five round points, like gems set into the rock itself.

The same five-pointed pattern had been repeated in the center of the frame. Hedrick reached out and tried to place his fingertips in the five indentations, but his hands weren't big enough. Whoever's hand this pattern fit was much larger than his.

Using three fingers from his left hand, plus a thumb and pinky from his right, Hedrick finally fit his fingers into each of the five indentations, imitating the crown shape. As he held the shape, Hedrick felt resistance, a spongy softness, and finally the stone gave way to mist, revealing a chamber beyond.

Hedrick stumbled forward and fell to his knees. When he raised his eyes, they bulged from his head at the same moment his breath hitched in his chest.

That hadn't been natural. No way, no how. The stone had just vanished! And this…

Any concern he'd felt, however brief, at falling through the gilded doorway vanished as he took in the glittering chamber.

The walls here glowed brighter than the hallway he'd just come through. And here, glowing green orbs were set into each of the three corners of the room, a triangular hall that slowly tapered to a point at the far end, directly opposite the doorway Hedrick had come through.

Bordering the room at the highest point were intricate engravings. People with the heads of animals, animals in the shape of ships, and ships in shapes he couldn't be sure weren't animals *or* people.

He saw giant gates orbiting stars and a great, powerfully built warrior armed with a staff. One mural that drew his eye was carved of ebony and opal, and depicted a procession of planets culminating in a star, and around the star gathered some kind of fleet. *The Kryl!* Panic gripped Hedrick's throat. There was another fleet—or maybe an army was a more accurate term—on a similar mural in opposite colors, black-on-white. Only not black or white at all, but shifting colors that changed depending on the angle, like quartz crystals.

Dozens more carvings lined the floor and middle sections —mathematical equations, fantastical creations, ritual sacrifices, anatomical drawings of trees… of all things, trees?

"What is this place?" His voice echoed loudly enough to make him flinch.

At the far end of the room, near the tip of the spear that this chamber formed, there was a dais. And atop this dais, remarkably, a geode.

"Yujene is going to be so jealous when I tell him about this."

It took twice as many paces to reach the geode as he expected. Some kind of optical illusion? But soon he did reach it, a perfectly round stone riddled with cracks that turned at right angles, almost like the circuit board for a robot he'd seen once. The same glow that lit the chamber shone through the cracks in the stone, but brighter, making it seem like a giant glowing puzzle ball.

Propping up the strange geode was one of two pairs of massive hands—the biggest hands he'd ever seen. They dwarfed his hands and would probably make even Elya's hands look like they belonged to a child. Both pairs of hands —one holding the geode, the other empty—were cupped as if they were meant to hold something, like you might cup your hands under a spout of water to catch it, as Hedrick had done earlier. Perhaps the empty set was meant to hold an object of some kind, too? Another one of these glowing geode puzzles?

He was dying to locate the source of that green light. Yujene had taught him how these rocks often hid such beauty inside. Hedrick reached out to touch the geode and hesitated. He almost didn't want to. He was worried it was booby-trapped. That's what always happened to the starship wreck divers in his favorite holovids. But it was just a geode...

Or was it? Every kid in the Solaran Empire grew up hearing stories of ancient myth and legend. Most of those stories took place during the Great Migration. The one his mother liked to tell best was of men meeting The Spirit of Old Earth at the edge of a black hole, and being guided to

Ariadne, which became the first colony world the Solarans settled and the seat of the new Solaran Empire. Other stories told of magical healings, of technological feats of wonder, of encounters with mysterious, super-advanced xenos known as the Telos.

Something about this room and the geode made him think of those stories. And of legends from Old Earth, too— the ancient Egyptians and their pyramids, the Americans and their great cities filled with skyscrapers. The Americans, in particular, were said to have created some particularly grue-some and horrific machines, bots that came to life and turned on their slave driving masters…

But how could any of those ancient powers be respon-sible for this artifact? How would they have gotten to Robichar when this was supposed to be the first colonization effort this small forest moon had ever undergone?

So many questions without answers.

The glowing green light within the orb seemed to pulse, calling him. It reminded him of Hedgebot, the way it seemed to brighten and dim, although the two were nothing alike otherwise. Before his fear crept back in, Hedrick reached out his hand and lifted the geode from the gigantic cupped hands.

He tensed, waiting for the whole cave to shake and fall in on top of him, or for some kind of spirit to wake in anger. Animus was known to be vengeful, to punish misbehaving children… his mother liked to tell him those stories, too.

But nothing happened. Then the orb's weight shifted—*up*, lifting from his hands into the air.

The orb exploded in slow motion, separating into its constituent pieces along the lines of its cracks. It expanded over his head and spread throughout the long, triangular room. As Hedrick studied the pieces, he realized with a sudden intuition that each piece of the orb must represent a planet. The source of the glow at the orb's center was a star—no, *several* stars. The "planets" rotated around the stars, forming several star systems. A quick count revealed at least ten before the whole arrangement began to spin slowly around the room.

Hedrick had seen a starmap in a hologram before he came to Robichar. He didn't recognize any planet or star system from that map. Whatever this map depicted, it wasn't the Imperial galaxy he was used to seeing.

He gaped open-mouthed at the starmap above him as it danced through the air. He wished Elya were here. He'd only known the pilot for a day but he just *knew* Elya would have loved this, would have marveled and wowed along with him. And he'd bet Elya knew more about star systems and maps of the galaxy than he did.

For the first time in his life, Hedrick truly grasped the gargantuan scale of the universe and all knowledge in it, compared to his relatively tiny understanding. It nearly sent him to his knees. Tears sprang to his eyes when he contrasted this wondrous experience with yesterday's slaughter and their nightmarish flight into the mountains.

Humbled, Hedrick watched the starmap dance overhead. He began to wonder how he was supposed to get it to stop. As the idea sprang to mind, the map began to spin ever tighter, pulling inward and fitting pieces together, repacking itself and finally coming to rest in the cupped hands where it had started.

Did I do that? Was it his thought that triggered the starry dance to begin with?

Hedrick glanced over at the cupped pairs of hands once more. Something had rested in the other pair of hands, he felt sure of it. Something was missing. Set into the wall above each hand was a kind of shield. Round and webbed with fissures, like the orb below it, as if it, too, had once been powered by a thousand tiny stars.

The hands themselves were shaped like human hands, only they weren't human. They couldn't be. He counted the joints on his fingers. One, two, three. One, two, three. One, two, three.

Then he counted the joints on these hands. One, two, three, *four.* One, two, three, four—*five?*

Fragments of ancient legends swam in his head, but no story he'd ever heard told of aliens with five-jointed fingers.

"Boy, what are you doing?"

Hedrick whirled around, his heart racing, sweat pouring down his back. A man in robes of rough brown homespun stood in the doorway. His cowl was pulled up over his head, but Hedrick recognized his voice.

"I'm, uh, sorry, uh. I didn't—I mean, I—"

The man held up his hands placatingly. Hedrick jammed his mouth closed. "It's okay. I see you found our place of worship."

"Worship?"

"Yes. That's why we chose this cave, so that we can worship here."

Hedrick pursed his lips. "Services for the solstice always take place outdoors, under the open sky. The Book of Animus says—"

"The Spirit of Old Earth resides in every atom of our being, outdoors or indoors. Wait a minute… Didn't you help us set up the chairs at the last solstice?"

Hedrick nodded.

"That's right! I love those services, don't you? Which is your favorite part? The psalms, the sermons?"

"The music." Hedrick quietly hummed a bar.

"Ah yes. Good memory! Tell me your name again?"

"Hedrick."

"That's right. Your mother's looking for you, kiddo. Why don't you come with me?"

Hedrick glanced back at the orb and the cupped hands. Did the man see the orb expand into a starmap? Did he know those hands had too many joints to be human? Was Hedrick not supposed to see the orb or know that? He was afraid that saying something would get him in even more trouble, so he kept his mouth shut.

The man beckoned. "Come on, before she gets too worried."

"Sure, sorry. I um, I just got lost—"

"It's all right, you didn't do anything wrong. Come on, now."

The man led the way out with a strident step. When he glanced back, Hedrick saw that the rock had re-materialized and the braid of golden flakes in the rock had disappeared. He didn't remember hearing a door close, or any stones slide aside.

They took the next left.

"Isn't the cave that way?" Hedrick asked.

"Not to worry, I know a shortcut."

SEVENTEEN

"Ten minutes until the original evacuation deadline," Harmony said.

The destruction of the shuttle had caused more delays on Robichar than Kira had anticipated. Debris had to be cleared off the launch pad while extra starfighters were sent in to deliver a replacement shuttle, then patrol to protect the spaceport from additional harm. The Kryl went to ground until nightfall, when they began to drop additional packages on the planet. Then it took longer than she liked for the last few thousand residents to be coaxed onto the new shuttle. Kira reluctantly admitted that it was rational, people's reluctance to board a shuttle the day after one had been destroyed over the same launchpad, but Earth be damned if it didn't just gut her every time mission-critical timelines got blown, no matter how often it happened through the years.

And each casualty added to the total body count made her more and more anxious. This was supposed to be a simple mission, undertaken out of an abundance of caution. And now she'd lost pilots *and* civilians. The Colonization Board would certainly hear about this and harangue her for it. She hoped they felt guilty as hell. It was their fault this evacuation took so long to get approved. They could have had it done months ago if they'd heeded her warnings when she first brought them to the Board.

Kira was known for doing the impossible. Putting down rebellions, capturing Kryl recon vehicles whole for Imperial scientists to study, delivering First Class escort missions without a hiccup.

And now this. It wasn't even close to a full failure, and yet the losses smarted.

"The shuttle has left the atmosphere and is on course for the final Mammoth."

"Where's the hive?"

Her navigations officer, Captain Freelt Garand, had been personally observing the Kryl. Harmony was also monitoring them, of course—one of many systems she was operating simultaneously—but Garand had been the one responsible for helping coordinate the distribution of the floating mines, and they each needed something to keep their minds occupied right now. Waiting and watching the Mammoth fleet, who waited and watched for the shuttle, was more agonizing than raking nails slowly across an aluminite surface.

"Still seeking out and disabling floating mines, sir," Garand reported. "That should keep them occupied for a while."

"Keep both eyes on them. I want to know *before* they make a move."

"Yes, sir."

"Major Loris."

The weapons officer turned toward her. "Sir?"

"Get those nukes primed and ready to deploy at the first sign of movement."

"Yes, Admiral."

The door to the bridge irised open and Kira forced down a sense of irritation. Colonel Volk entered, looking a little haggard, and walked directly over to her. "Sir, Captain Osprey has something you'll want to see."

"Can it wait?"

"I'm afraid not."

"What's the situation in the medical wing with the sick pilot?"

"Catastrophe averted. This is something… else."

She took a deep breath. It was a relief not to lose another pilot. Keep that casualty count down. But if the colonel was sending her to see Osprey, it meant he didn't want the officers on the bridge to see what she'd discovered. At least they were being discreet. It still annoyed her to be pulled away.

"Take over for me, Colonel. Make sure that shuttle docks safely."

"Aye, sir."

She found Captain Osprey in the war room sipping coffee. The pilot was reviewing footage in three separate frames— the hangar in one, the sick bay in another, and the dashboard footage from her Sabre in a third. The captain also sported several new scratches and scrapes along her face, and dark circles under her eyes. Kira nodded approvingly. She liked to see her young officers give their best to any assignment she gave them, and the lack of sleep meant Casey was taking this one seriously.

Kira's role here was to rein the captain in, like a jockey keeping a racehorse in its lane. Even if the horse bucked, the jockey only did it out of love—and a driven desire to win.

The only other addition to the room was a small, relatively inconspicuous aluminute jar, the kind you might see a doctor use for collecting samples from a patient—set on the octagonal table as far away from the captain as possible. What looked like a worm was curled in a bloody puddle at the bottom of the jar.

"What on Earth is that thing?"

Osprey paused her footage, stood, saluted sharply. "That came out of Lieutenant Park, Admiral."

"I see."

"He was one of ours, sir. One of the Fightin' Furies."

Kira knew very well the nickname of the 137th. She knew the names of every squadron under her command, but this one held special significance. It was her former squadron, the posting where she had met Captain Ruidiaz all those years ago.

"And how is your Lieutenant Park?"

"He's recovering, sir. He'll have a scar, right here." She drew her middle finger along the line of her right clavicle. "But they tell me he'll make a full recovery. We owe his life to the shipboard AI. She extracted the parasite. I think it's Kryl in origin."

The captain's back was to the hologram, so the captain didn't see Harmony whirl Casey's form around in an elaborate dance and dip.

Cut it out, Kira thought furiously, even as she allowed a genuine smile to form on her mouth. "I'm glad to hear that. We've lost enough good soldiers for one mission."

"I agree, Admiral. Which is why I was reviewing footage again. If that thing is what caused Lieutenant Park to go mad, it stands to reason that it—or another like it—is also responsible for what happened to Petty Officer Mick Perry."

"Who else knows about this?"

Captain Osprey paled. "Colonel Volk. Lieutenant Olara Yorra with the Furies. A few others who happened to be in the sick bay at the time. Admiral, you have to understand, I—"

"It's not a criticism, Captain, we just need to get ahead of the response. Unanswered questions lead to panic. Harmony, please draft a shipwide memo."

"Draft has been sent to your inbox," she said without a moment's pause.

"Thank you."

Captain Osprey opened her mouth, then closed it. Apparently she'd never seen the shipmind being used as a secretary. Kira considered it a fair trade. If she had to put up with Harmony's eccentricities, the least the AI could do was draft boring memos.

Kira approached the jar and bent down to examine it. It wasn't a worm, as she had first assumed, but a miniature xeno of some kind. She recognized the blackish-purple coloring of the exoskeleton, the wickedly curved, if miniaturized, talons. But apart from some vague relational similarity to the Kryl, she'd never seen anything like it. And certainly not anything like it *inside* one of her pilots. "What in all the hells is this thing?"

"I don't know, sir. I've just been calling it 'the parasite.' The more important question, in my opinion, Admiral, is how did it get aboard the ship?"

Kira looked up. *How, indeed?* She raised her eyebrows at the captain. "I assume you have a theory? Don't be shy."

Captain Osprey turned back to her footage. First, she showed the sick bay. A man woke groggily and clutched his head.

"That's Park?"

"Yes, sir. He was unconscious after the gas canister ruptured in the hangar. Lieutenant Yorra took him to the sick bay to recover, and when he woke up he had a headache."

"He was concussed," Harmony chimed in. "A headache is a natural reaction to such an event."

"She has a point," Kira said.

"That's what I thought. Except then I realized that Petty Officer Mick Perry exhibited exactly the same reaction after my Sabre docked in the hangar."

Now it made sense why she had multiple feeds open. She was comparing Lieutenant Park's reaction with Petty Officer Perry's. When Osprey pulled that frame forward, she saw a small mousey-looking man flash a smile at Captain Osprey, and then clutch his head as a sudden pain caused him to wince.

"I see they both had some kind of head pain, but what makes you think it was caused by this parasite?"

"Well it's hard to see, but—" A control board appeared on the desktop. Casey hunched over the table as she attempted to wind back the film. "There! Did you see that?"

"Not exactly... Harmony," Kira said, "zoom in and sharpen the image."

The control board was pulled away from Osprey as the AI adjusted the frame, zooming in and sharpening on the speck of dust the captain had pointed to in the frame.

The enhanced image showed an oversized mechanic in grease-stained coveralls ducking under the wing and plugging in a diagnostic cable as a thin, web-like strand dripped down from the starfighter. The parasite itself curled in the aluminite jar was barely the size of her thumbnail. If that was the parasite in the holovid—and it could be, about the size and worm-like shape of it—it fell onto Petty Officer Mick Perry's hair near his ear.

Seconds later, he gripped his head.

"How many more of these things are on our ship?"

Captain Osprey winced. "I expected you'd ask that, and I'm sorry, sir, but the answer is I just don't know."

Kira heaved a great sigh.

"Admiral," Harmony said. "The last shuttle has reached the Mammoth."

"Thank you. Tell Colonel Volk I'm on my way back."

"There's one more thing, sir. The question of how it hitched a ride back on my ship in the first place."

"And what's your theory on this one?"

Now it was time for the third frame. This was the same footage from Osprey's Sabre they'd reviewed before, she could tell by the timestamp and the tail number on Captain Never's ship, not to mention the drone he was pursuing.

She fast-forwarded through the phasing maneuver that had caught Kira's eye, only stopping when Osprey herself fired upon the Kryl drone, raking its underbelly and rupturing a fuel sac.

"See that?"

Kira crossed her muscular arms. Osprey had turned the tables on her in an unexpected way. The roles of student and teacher had been momentarily reversed. "Fuel? Or some kind of bodily fluid? It's common knowledge that the drones are not machines, but living organisms. When they're hit, they bleed."

"Yes, sir, but I think this is a trick. Not only does the drone enter the atmosphere after I shot it—Harmony's lidar readings have it landing on the moon under power—but I flew right *through* that liquid. Whatever it is, I think that's where I picked up the parasite. It must have clung to the outside of my starfighter and when I got back into the hangar, infected the first host it could find." She swallowed and fought off an involuntary shiver. "It could have been me, but it got Mick instead, sir."

"How would that little thing survive the vacuum?" It looked so insubstantial and weak, curled up at the bottom of the jar.

"Maybe the liquid protected it somehow. You said your-self, the Kryl aren't machines, they're organisms, and if their drones and ships can survive the vacuum, then it's not a big leap to assume the parasite can, too."

Kira cursed. The captain had a point, a damn good one that she didn't have time to deal with right now. But she was in command. It was her job to take problems like this in stride.

"Harmony, I want you to sweep the ship for signs of similar lifeforms. Contact Major Obin Seklor in Engi-neering and tell him to search every ship in that hangar with a microscope. Also, make sure every starfighter and shuttle gets scanned as it comes back into port. Advise him to section off a part of the hangar for quarantine. Also, alert the Chief Medical Officer. I need her to come up with some kind of screening protocol in case anyone else shows up with another one of these little vermin lodged in their nose."

When she was done giving orders, she looked over at Captain Osprey, who had melted in her chair as the stress of the investigation fell away. Harmony leaped into action, scanning the parasite with a laser and delivering missives to various parts of the ship.

"Captain, you report back to the sick bay and make sure you haven't been infected yourself."

"But Admiral, I haven't—"

"I don't want to hear any excuses. You're not flying until I make sure you're clean and healthy."

She straightened and gave a sharp salute. "Yes, sir!'"

"Admiral, there is one more thing," Harmony said. She had taken the form of Captain Osprey again. The captain blinked at the AI's hologram as she recognized the resemblance.

"What did I forget?" Kira asked.

"Nothing, Admiral. It is simply that we've located Captain Nevers."

"What!" Osprey jumped out of her seat. "Where? When?"

"On Robichar, in the foothills thirty kilometers northwest of the spaceport."

"Is he alive?"

"I cannot tell, Captain. Only that the cube from his starfighter has finally connected via tightbeam. I am once again picking up radio communications from the moon's surface as well, so perhaps Captain Nevers cleared whatever was jamming the airwaves."

Captain Osprey's face was flushed, her eyes wide, and even the bags under her eyes seemed to vanish in the sudden rush of elation. She turned to Kira, longing plainly evident in her face.

"Fine, you can join the Search and Rescue team—but only *after* you report to the sickbay and are cleared by the Chief Medical Officer herself."

"Thank you, sir! I won't let you down."

"Admiral!" Another voice spoke through Harmony's facial interface. The face morphed from Osprey's feminine features into those of a gruff man with a shining hairless pate. "The Kryl just finished clearing the mines. We need you up here."

"On my way, Colonel. Is the shuttle unloaded yet?"

"Nearly."

"Good. Contact the captains of each longhauler and tell them to plot a hyperspace course back to Ariadne and prepare to jump."

EIGHTEEN

S*tupid, stupid, stupid.*

Elya ground his palm into his forehead. Dirt got into everything down here—his eyes, his mouth, under his fingernails. He spat in disgust.

How could I have been so naive?

All the signs had been there. The priest's kind offer of help. Charlie's sudden cooperation in planning the infiltration. The whole crew's ever-so-reasonable request to leave Hedgebot behind. Even Thom's irrepressible nervousness should have been a dead giveaway. Of all the men he'd traveled with since that morning, he had gotten to know Thom the best. And *still* he hadn't seen it.

Elya should have trusted his instincts. His whole being had screamed out not to trust the priest. Escorting Heidi and Hedrick up into the mountains had seemed like the best option at the time, but he should have returned to his plan after delivering the woman and her son to that nutty cult of fools. He should have struck out on his own and focused on getting back to the Fleet. There's *always* another option. If he'd stuck to his plan—to his training—he'd never have been betrayed, let alone stuck in this dank hole in the ground.

You can only be betrayed if you allow yourself to trust people in the first place. That was a painful lesson, one it seemed Elya kept having to relearn.

They'd taken his pack and his water and left him Hedgebot, disabled and powerless. He had no weapon, not that the blaster had any juice left after the fight with the sentinels. Without water, he wouldn't last more than a couple miserable days down here. Without his bot, he wouldn't be able to signal for help.

The hole itself was small and cramped, barely wider than both arms outstretched, with walls made of soft dirt. The grate over top of the makeshift prison cell was fashioned to a metal frame and held fast with a chain. The soil was soft enough that if he managed to get up there and gain enough leverage, he might be able to dig the soil out around the frame with his hands, making the hole wide enough to drop the grate inside the hole, then haul himself out.

But when he tried climbing the walls, all Elya did was pull dirt down on top of himself. When his arms were filthy and the dirt began to burn in his eyes, he gave up and stopped wasting his energy. He hadn't even come within arm's reach of the grate.

They'd chosen well. The hole was deep, the soil too loose to climb. He was going to die down here.

Elya jerked out of a restless slumber to the sound of engines roaring overhead. He would recognize the noise of a Sabre in flight anywhere. Their hybrid engines were designed to work in space as well as in atmosphere, where they made a noise that had always reminded him of a yzir, a predatory cat species native to Yuzosix, purring happily—right before it pounced on a field mouse.

They're still looking for me! Hope flared in his chest.

"Hey. Down here! I'm alive. Hey! *Come back!!*"

His mouth was so dry and parched that his upper lip split from being stretched too wide. *Who's the fool now?* They couldn't hear him. Screaming was a fruitless endeavor. They weren't even really looking for him—they were looking for the tightbeam connection with the cube, not an idiot pilot who got himself trapped in a hole in the ground.

Still, he shouted. What else could he do? Elya screamed himself hoarse for what must have been a solid hour after the roar of the jets had faded from hearing range.

It was all he could do. And even that wasn't enough.

Feeling useless, he removed a folding screwdriver from a hidden compartment on Hedgebot's mechanical body and used it to take the bot apart. It was a lost cause. The contact plates had been mangled, as he'd already seen. He was pretty sure the battery still had some juice, but it wasn't something he could fix without new brackets.

The rage he'd felt while yelling for help seeped out of him, then. Like Hedgebot, Elya too had lost his power source. He lay there, lips throbbing, back aching, full of raw emotion, a condensed cloud of anger and shame. He eventually went numb. The red soil sapped him of his strength and fed it to Robichar. Robichar, in turn, would feed it to the Kryl.

The circle of life always ended in death. If he was lucky, he would die of thirst and exposure long before the xenos found his body.

At first Elya mistook the faint whine for a ringing in his ears. *Eeeeeeee.* He'd been here for hours and, since the starfighters passed overhead, he'd imagined many such noises. The lack of water and the heat of the jungle, even in the relative cool of the dank hole, had begun to make him dizzy and light-headed. He didn't trust his own mind. When the whining noise paused, there was a faint rustling of footsteps, and Elya's throat seized. Was it a Kryl groundling? Or had Charlie returned to finish him off? Or maybe it was the priest come to gloat about his foolish plan to stay on Robichar.

Hah.

"Elya?"

A face appeared over the grate. Elya felt certain he was hallucinating. "Heidi?"

"Finally." She exhaled deeply. "Thank Animus I found you."

Wait a second, he thought. *Is this another trick? Fool me once, et cetera.* He was so tired and dehydrated that even finishing his thoughts seemed like an extraordinary effort.

Elya gathered enough spit to swallow, then croaked, "How did you find me?"

"Heard you yelling. Even then it took me a while."

Elya struggled to his feet, his sore body protesting. The power of reason seeped through the mist of despair. "But... you... what are you doing out *here*? Where's Hedrick?"

Her lips pressed into a thin line and though her face was cast in shadows, Elya recognized the way her face pinched as her jaw hardened. His mother got that look when someone threatened one of her boys. "Hedrick went missing this afternoon."

Elya's jaw fell open. "Oh, no."

"When you didn't show up with the rest of the men and the priest, I knew something was wrong. They told me you got killed by the Kryl, but I didn't believe them, not with Hedrick still missing. They almost had me *convinced* Hedrick had wandered off. We searched these narrow tunnels in the back of the cave all morning, it feels like. When the priest came back without you, I knew they had been lying to placate me." She twisted her lips and hung her head. "He would never run away without me. Not at a time like this. So I snuck away, stole one of the skimmer bikes they had hidden near the ravine and came looking for you."

So it *had* been a skimmer he'd heard! Not the auto they'd left on the mountain pass, but a hoverbike. Elya couldn't help but laugh. *Heidi sure showed them!* It felt good to laugh.

"I'm glad you find this amusing, but Hedrick is still out there! He could be in danger! I need to find him. Please." Her voice cracked on the last word and Heidi choked back a sob.

She was as desperate as he was. She was also his ticket out of this death-trap. Elya gestured around him. "Can't do anything from down here."

Heidi yanked on the grate. "It's stuck. Hold on, there's some stuff in the bike's storage compartment."

She brought back a couple pieces of linen—rags or towels —and tried to wrap them around the grate to haul it out, but it wasn't enough fabric to reach the bike. She disappeared and returned a few minutes later with a big rock, which she dropped on the chain a few times in a vain effort to break it.

"Forget that, just dig around the outside of the grate."

She found a smaller stone shaped like a trowel that she was able to use to dig out the edge of the grate. From his limited vantage point, Elya saw dirt fly and then heard a *clunk* as the stone struck another piece of rock.

"Uh, Elya. This is cemented in."

He cursed. "Damn it. Try digging farther out in front of me."

It took several more agonizing attempts, working the problem from both sides, before they found a solution. Elya bruised his leg muscles and bled from his fingernails clawing dirt out of the wall, while Heidi began to excavate the cement, digging out at its edge with the stone spade and her fingers. Fortunately, whoever had installed this makeshift prison cell hadn't built it to last forever. Heidi reported excitedly when she found that the cement was only about 15 centimeters thick. She got under it pretty quickly. Then Elya, elbow deep in the dirt wall, located a tree root and was able to haul himself up higher in the shaft to kick out big chunks of earth.

"I see it!" Heidi cried. Seconds later, the dirt Elya was clawing at with his filthy hands shifted and light shone through. They brushed fingertips.

This breakthrough reinvigorated their efforts. They quickly widened the hole enough for Elya to pass Hedgebot gingerly through. They widened the opening considerably more, until it was large enough to fit Elya's head and shoulders. He had to wriggle and worm his body back and forth, kicking more soil downward, but it was chopped and loose now.

"Come on!" Heidi cried. "You're so heavy, you have to push with your legs."

Elya spat dirt out of his mouth. "I'm—*pffttt pfftt*—trying!"

She yanked on his flight suit. A fabric seam tore at his shoulder. Elya finally got his dirt-filled boots on top of that tree root and *kicked*. His shoulder popped loose and he and Heidi fell, together, back onto the damp forest undergrowth.

Elya had never been so happy to see a canopy of trees in his life. It must have been late afternoon, approaching nightfall. The skimmer bike lay against a tree nearby, its storage compartment flipped open with Hedgebot lying on its back atop a pile of rags. The temporary foot Thom had given him stuck out at a weird angle compared to the others.

The sight popped an airy sense of relief at having escaped

certain death and replaced it with a hard fist of anger. Elya came up on his elbows, then rose shakily to his feet.

"If we don't know where your son went, how are we going to find him?"

"I was really hoping you'd have some idea where they took him."

Elya's brow furrowed as he thought furiously. *What do they want with the boy? Why would they kidnap him?*

He didn't know. Unless Hedrick saw something he wasn't supposed to and they just wanted to get rid of him... but why take him and not his mother? What did he do to deserve such treatment?

A high-pitched whine cut through the forest, silencing the background music of chirping birds.

Elya hurriedly kicked some dirt back toward the hole they'd dug, then scrambled for the skimmer bike. In the distance, in flashes seen between thick tree trunks, another skimmer bike zoomed by. A brown robe fluttered about the driver's frame. The hood was pulled down over the man's head, so Elya couldn't see the face, but he recognized the priest's luxurious yet worn homespun robe. He clutched something to his front. A small figure.

A small boy-shaped figure.

They were gone in a flash.

Elya pushed Hedgebot into the storage compartment, snapped it closed, and jumped onto the bike. It hummed to life as Heidi hopped on behind him, holding tight to his waist as they pursued the priest and the boy.

NINETEEN

"Alpha one zero niner, prepare for take-off."

Two mechanics darted under Casey's Sabre. The wheel chocks were removed and diagnostic cables unplugged. She felt the encumbrances being shed as if the starfighter was her second skin.

"Raptor out, throttle's coming up. Checking cabin pressure…" Casey rattled off her checklist, confirming fuel reserves, controls, weapons and emergency systems. "Ready?"

"You're a go," said flight control.

She rested her helmet back against the seat and took a deep breath. Her heartbeat quickened in her chest, as it always did on the runway. The Sabre rocketed forward, pressing her into the seat as her starfighter launched from the hangar. "Whoo!" She guided the plane through the blue-tinted atmospheric shield and into space at speed. "Yeah!"

Flight control chuckled.

It felt damn good to be back in the cockpit. Especially after the invasive medical examination that left her feeling filthy and violated. They had found no sign of parasitic infection in her, or in Yorra, who cleared the hangar behind her. Park was still recovering in the sick bay. He briefly returned to consciousness before they left, but he didn't have his wits about him. The medics said his condition was still touch-and-go, and she was glad to leave him in capable hands. Casey, herself, felt less than useless sitting bedside vigil. That sort of job wasn't for her.

This was.

She banked left and soared over the Mammoth fleet, which had begun to spread apart as they prepared to jump into hyperspace. A welcome crew would be waiting for them on Ariadne, ready to transfer the civilians into the refugee camps, and begin the process of relocating them to other, safer colony worlds.

Yorra's starfighter came abreast of her. They did a quick run around the Mammoth fleet together. Finding no threats in their visual field or on lidar, they veered toward Robichar.

In the distance between Robichar and the unnamed gas giant it orbited, small pops and flashes of light could be seen. It reminded Casey of a far-away fireworks show, or maybe a fraught press hearing where the reporters were clamoring forward with rapidly firing cameras. In reality, she knew that starfighter squadrons had begun to engage the Kryl hive in battle. The floating mines had delayed their progress, but that had merely been a diversion, a way to buy the admiral time to get any remaining civilians off planet and into the Mammoths. *The best defense is a good offense*, as her father used to say. He and Admiral Miyaru would have gotten along swimmingly.

Casey fought down the urge to redirect her flight path and join the battle. She wondered, briefly, if her father and the admiral had known each other during the Kryl War. Had they fought together? He'd never mentioned anyone named Kira or Miyaru, and the Empire was a vast place, with many fronts of the war being waged against the Kryl. It's possible they had never met. But Casey sensed that he would have approved of her approach.

Whether Inquisitor Osprey would have approved of his daughter's actions…. Well. He would certainly have something to say about foolish emotional attachments and risking your neck for no damn reason. But he wasn't here now, and she could do without the guilt trip. Her mind was made up and the admiral had approved it. Nothing to do now but get the job done. And fast, before the Kryl broke through and started landing more than advance forces on Robichar.

"Gears, listen up. We're to rendezvous with the Search and Rescue team, retrieve our missing pilot and then get back into the fight as fast as we can."

"Roger that."

She knew the plan, of course. And it was just the two of them. But old habits dug deep grooves, and the briefing gave Casey something to hold onto.

"Captain." Yorra hesitated. "What if we don't find him, sir?"

Casey glanced one more time at the distant fireworks. The flashes of light seemed so harmless from here, but she knew that up close, her comrades were dying in blazes of superheated fury. They had hundreds of starfighters, yet every precious life lost was a tragedy.

She brushed a finger over the trigger on her control stick.

There would be time to use that later. She lifted her itching finger and began the descent to Robichar.

"We'll cross that bridge if we come to it. Let's go."

They came down over a mountain range and linked up with the Search and Rescue team. Three Sabres had been flying a grid pattern in search of Nevers.

"Match frequencies." Seconds later, she and Yorra were on the same broadbeam channel as the SAR pilots.

"Hail, Furies," the leader of the SAR team said as he rocked his jet from side to side, waving at her with his wings. "This is Major Antonin speaking."

"Any luck finding our missing pilot, sir?"

"Negative, Captain. We found his scuttled Sabre quickly, and it seems like he got away safe, but there hasn't been any sign of him since. We traced his tightbeam signal when it appeared, but have not yet received visual confirmation of the target or the cube."

Casey frowned. That was worrisome. Anything that separated Nevers from his cube—his lifeline—had to have been not just important, but life threatening.

"Take us to it."

"Roger. Follow us."

They reached the end of the mountain range and turned sharply to come back. They flew out over a luscious valley carpeted with trees and passed the spaceport. The launch pad still showed blast marks, but debris had been cleared from the runway and piled to both sides.

"This must be where the shuttle exploded," Casey said to Yorra on a private channel.

"Freaky, Cap."

Casey had to agree. There were no people left now, giving the scarred, barren landscape an apocalyptic countenance.

Major Antonin's voice cut back into their conversation. "Signal's coming from that ridgeline."

"Copy that," Casey said. "Have you conducted a search on foot?"

"Negative. We were just getting to that when you arrived."

"We'll take the lead on the ground if you want to continue aerial recon?"

"Copy. Can do."

Sabres were uniquely designed to alight in hostile territory without need of a runway, for emergency landings on small space stations or remote asteroids. You had to be a fine hand with the balance, but Casey and Yorra had lots of practice. It was, after all, how Yorra had gotten her call sign, "Gears." The memory of the lieutenant destroying three sets of landing gears made her smile. She had no such issues this time. They set their Sabres down on top of the ridgeline near the reported source of the tightbeam signal without incident.

The cube could be anywhere within a couple hundred meters. It was strange how bare the ridgeline was. There were no people in sight, certainly no sign of Nevers and no sign of a cube either. Casey popped the canopy of her cockpit and hopped down onto the grass. After checking her suit's parameters—standard operating procedure; she knew this planet's atmosphere to be breathable but her training went deep—she unsealed her helmet with a soft hiss and shook her chin-length bangs out of her eyes.

Yorra jumped down from her craft and removed her helmet as well. Her glistening black hair had been tied up in a bun.

"Where the hell is the cube?"

"Signal's coming from around here somewhere. Let's split up. You search that way, I'll go this way."

Anxiety formed a knot at the pit of Casey's stomach as they scoured the rocky ridgeline. After pacing the area for several minutes, neither Yorra nor Casey had managed to locate it. She radioed back to the Major using the comm in her Sabre. "Major Antonin, is it possible that you got the location wrong?"

"Negative," he said "The signal is coming from your location."

"Could it be a false reading? Interference from one of the communications arrays at that spaceport?"

"Unlikely, Captain. Signal's definitely coming from your area."

Casey frowned and cast her eyes out across the ridgeline.

Yorra was still searching. She cocked her head as she stared at a pile of stones. There was a lot of loose rock up here. Lieutenant Yorra kicked a couple aside then bent down and lifted a stained and battered cube out of the pile. "Found it."

Her voice didn't sound excited. The hard knot in Casey's stomach fell out into a pit of dread.

She joined Yorra at the pile of stones and picked through it, expecting to find Captain Nevers' body. They found no body—to her relief.

If his cube is here and Nevers isn't, where did he go?

Together, they examined the cube. It was battered and dented, but these things were made out of aluminite, the strongest man-made metal alloy in the known universe. It obviously had been damaged, and not merely by Nevers' crash landing. Some of the tiny dents looked like they might even have come from gunshots. She recognized the burn scar from a blaster rifle, and even a couple dents that looked like they came from high-powered projectiles, maybe one of the gauss rifles favored by drop troopers and special forces? Those scars alone told her more about what Nevers had been through in the past day than anything they'd heard so far.

"This got ugly," Yorra said.

"Someone didn't want us to find it, either. They must have hidden the cube up here after they realized they couldn't destroy it."

"So what do we do now? How do we find Nevers if he doesn't have the cube? He could be anywhere."

Casey slowly shook her head. *If he doesn't have the cube, he's as good as dead.* But she wasn't ready to give up on him yet. "We take the cube and we keep looking."

"Are you thinking what I'm thinking?"

"If someone stashed the cube up here, that means Nevers isn't the only person left on Robichar."

And if Nevers wasn't alone, that meant—in spite of the apocalyptic landscape around the spaceport—there were still people here. People who would be slaughtered when the Kryl hive landed.

Admiral Miyaru considered the evacuation complete. And yet, here was evidence that people had been left behind. Why had they refused to evacuate? Or had they simply not been able to get to the spaceport in time? The latter seemed unlikely, considering how much advance notice the Empire had given the colony.

Casey took the cube to her Sabre and locked it safely inside, then used her comms to report what they'd found back to Major Antonin.

"Smells fishy," he said.

Yorra made a thoughtful sound. "If I'm Captain Nevers and I crash-land just a few klicks from the spaceport, that's where I would go first. It's the most logical destination."

"But if he made it there," Casey said, "he would have been able to make contact with the Fleet. Maybe even fly up with the last shuttle. As far as we know, he didn't." She remembered the apocalyptic landscape littered with debris from the shuttle that exploded. Had he been on it? "When did that shuttle go down?"

"Around the same time as Nevers arrived."

"Okay… let's assume he wasn't on the shuttle. If he lands

near the spaceport, he probably saw the shuttle get shot down. Then what does he do?"

"I don't know, Captain," Major Antonin said."It took almost a full day before we got any reading on his cube's tightbeam signal. We were also having comms problems with our broadbeam systems. We kept having to fly back up to ten thousand feet to talk to each other."

"So he can't go to the spaceport and his cube won't connect. The first thing he'd do is try to make contact, surely."

"You'd think."

"Major, are there any other spaceports nearby?"

"Not on this side of the moon. You'd have to fly due south for an hour to reach the nearest one."

Casey did some mental math. That was about a third of the way around the small moon's surface. On foot, Nevers never would have risked a journey of that distance, if he even knew where it was.

"Major, where else can you find a comms system on Robichar? Did you see anything in your search?"

"There are a couple old bases built by the original colonists. Prefab buildings and such. There's probably a comms array there."

Casey and Yorra got back into their Sabres and zoomed skyward. It didn't take long to find the compound.

"That's new," Major Antonin said. "The comms array wasn't damaged like that last time we flew over."

Casey glanced down. Blast marks scarred the land here the same way they had at the spaceport. The only difference was, this base was occupied by Kryl. The place crawled with groundlings. More than she'd ever seen in one place, except in old war footage on the holovids her father kept on a shelf near his medals and memento displays.

Using her Sabre's cameras, she zoomed in on the communications array—no longer operational. It had been slagged and then partially grown over with Kryl membrane.

"It must be Nevers. He figured out what was jamming the signal and destroyed it." Hope rekindled in her chest, a small guttering flame. "Couldn't have gone far. Keep searching."

"The admiral said to return to Fleet once we had the cube."

Ignoring him, Casey streaked out over the valley, using the Sabre's infrared capabilities to search below the thick canopy for any sign of life.

"You can go if you want, Major. I'm not leaving the planet without my pilot."

Silence on the line.

"Are you going to help me or not?"

"Hold, Captain."

More silence.

The background tone of the comms changed as Major Antonin's line was replaced with another. Only one vessel had the ability to take over a channel. "Captain, this is your admiral speaking."

Casey clenched her teeth so hard her jaw shook. She forced herself to take a deep, calming breath and braced for the worst as she attempted to keep her tone neutral and purely professional. "Yes, sir?"

"Send Major Antonin with the cube. I'll allow you to continue searching for Captain Nevers, but mark my words: if you're not back in the *Paladin* with him before the last Mammoth jumps into hyperspace, you're on your own until the cleanup crew gets here, and even then, it's unlikely they'll risk lives to rescue you from occupied territory."

Casey scrunched up her face in puzzlement. Osprey had been ready to argue for her course of action. Words had been forming themselves into statements and justifications in her brain, lining up like good little soldiers on the tip of her tongue. Nevermind. Forget it. Who was she to question an admiral when she was prepared to give Casey exactly what she wanted?

"Understood, Admiral."

"Stand by, Captain. Harmony wants to speak to you."

Harmony? The shipboard AI wanted to talk to *her*?

"Uh, yes, sir?"

A smooth female voice came on the line, like the ideal of a broadbeam news anchor. "Hello, Captain. I admire your bravery and commend your persistence."

"Th-Thank you? I think?"

Usually Casey basked in her compliments, drawing them out to make them last. But everyone knew the AI only talked to the admiral, so it felt weird to hear such a thing. Maybe she *shouldn't* have drawn so much attention to herself. Everyone said the shipboard AIs had as much influence advising the Emperor as Fleet Command, or even the High Priest of Animus himself. It made her nervous to be put under that kind of microscope. Beads of sweat trickled down her neck under her helmet.

"Be mindful that the Kryl horde is making its way toward Robichar. If my models are accurate, they're likely to touch down near your location."

She gulped. "Thanks for the heads-up."

"You're very welcome. Bring your pilot home safely. Here's Admiral Miyaru again."

"Thanks... Admiral?"

"Yes, Captain?"

"How long do I have, exactly?"

"Until approximately..." There was quiet on the channel as calculations were run and discussions were had—away from the microphone. A rustling as the admiral returned. "1830 GST."

Casey checked her heads-up display. Galactic Standard

Time… if she accounted for the flight back to the destroyer on maximum burn, that gave her just over two hours to find Nevers.

"Copy that, Admiral. Raptor out."

Casey gritted her teeth and refocused on the windshield. The HUD overlaid topographical heatscans on the forest beneath her.

Where did you go, Nevers? What could possibly be more important than getting home alive?

TWENTY

H armony danced and flashed like some airborne laser show. Kira swiped a hand through the hologram and the AI's floating motes of light danced aside, swimming around her hand like a weightless liquid.

"That girl's head is harder than a piece of star metal."

"Yes, Admiral," Harmony said, the tone of her voice almost mocking. The back of Kira's neck warmed as the image of a younger woman with a haughty upraised chin and a familiar crop of bleach-white hair was projected into her mind. Harmony spoke the next lines clearly but silently through the control chip in Kira's neck. Though the bridge hummed with activity and people as the XO directed the battle with the Kryl hive, only Kira heard these words: "I remember another captain with a stubborn streak. She was young and talented and full of a righteous fury."

The image of her younger self combined with Harmony's words cast Kira backward in memory. Had it been nearly twenty years since she was first stationed on this ship? The missions go slow but the years rush past...

She'd been deployed on the *Paladin* with a wing of Scimitars—the older model of starfighters that Sabres evolved from. The destroyer had been sent to the front, to the outer curve of the fifth spiral arm, where they were holding the line against Kryl encroachment. She'd gotten her first bogey on that deployment—her first dozen, in fact. She'd also lost friends, defied her admiral and spent time in the brig for insubordination.

Oh, how the tide had turned.

It was her third night of isolation in the brig when Harmony first revealed herself to Kira. Her squadron had been called out on several back-to-back offensive bombing maneuvers. She was sick with anger and a feeling of being left out, unable to sleep and worried for the squad. Particularly, the man she'd fallen in love with—Omar Ruidiaz, a pilot like her. Harmony reported the fight to her, maneuver by maneuver, tracking the captain and her other comrades. This calmed her enough that she had finally been able to fall asleep.

Harmony had also been there on Captain Ruidiaz's last mission. The AI had charted the jump course that carried them behind enemy lines. They landed on the Kryl home-world—no one knew the Kryl word for it and Solarans were loath to name it, so most people just called it Planet K—where their intelligence operatives said the Queen Mother was located. Their objective had been to drop an antimatter bomb on the Queen Mother's lair, then jump back to Impe-rial space before they were spotted.

The mission did not go according to plan.

On the *Paladin*, Kira shut her eyes and pinched her temples between her thumb and middle finger as she fought back the tears of anger that threatened to rise up. Even more than a decade later, the memory stung. Intelligence had only given them a partial picture of the landscape. The lair had an extra layer of protection they hadn't anticipated, a giant shield of Kryl carapace that had been grown over the top of it like a buffer against the sky. They were forced to drop into Planet K's oxygen-rich atmosphere. Against Kira's recommendation, Ruidiaz dove low to deliver the payload. The Kryl, of course, defended their Queen Mother vigorously. Ruidiaz ejected, saving himself while his Scimitar plowed into the Kryl's defenses—but the anti-matter failed to detonate.

Kira refused to leave him behind, for she knew Ruidiaz had survived the ejection. Against orders, she touched down and went searching for him, nearly being overrun by an avenging clutch of Kryl sentinels.

Though she found him, Ruidiaz refused to retreat until the objective had been attained. He took the payload from his downed Scimitar and insisted on delivering it himself. She waited for him and—Earth damn him—she actually believed he would come back.

But he didn't. The detonation lit the night sky and she knew in that moment that he was beyond saving. And though she felt this horrible knowledge in her heart of hearts, Kira didn't want to leave. Survival instinct took over as the sentinels closed in, going berserk with rage. To save her own life, Kira had been forced to leave him behind.

She knew that was why she really gave Captain Osprey permission to go after Captain Nevers. The captain had been surprised. But if there was even the slightest chance the young pilot was still alive on Robichar, she had to let Osprey do everything she could to find him. It's what she would have wanted, were she in the captain's position. Kira would forever regret not trying harder, not risking more, to bring Ruidiaz home. Even after every sign pointed to his demise. Wounds made by regrets and what-ifs had a tendency to rot and fester. Kira hadn't left a soldier behind since Ruidiaz, and she didn't intend to change that now, not so long as there was a chance.

All Captain Nevers needed was a chance.

Kira took a deep breath and blew it out. "Young and talented I may have been. I was also a naive fool."

"Yet you have not lost hope."

"Depends on the day, Harmony. Depends on the day."

Kira turned her eyes back to the viewscreen, which showed the Mammoth fleet and the battle with the Kryl hive beyond. Though perhaps battle was the wrong word. The starfighter squadrons had been ordered to use fly-by, hit-and-run tactics to harry the enemy while reducing the risk of a direct conflict. It was working well enough to buy them some time, while also delaying the Kryl's descent to the planet, which gave the captain more time to find her missing pilot.

But Kira noticed now that the hive had begun to try to land some of their larger ships. They were taking enormous losses to their drone numbers to do so, even sustaining damage to make it down to Robichar.

She didn't understand it. She didn't know why they were so bullish to set down on this moon. She had almost fooled herself into believing they weren't interested in destroying the Mammoths when a swarm of drones separated from the bulk of their force and came screaming in their direction.

"Incoming bogeys!" Colonel Volk shouted. "Deploy defensive perimeter. Ready anti-ordnance laser defense array!"

"Harmony, connect me to the first two Mammoths in the jump sequence."

"Yes, sir. Channel open."

"This is Admiral Kira Miyaru of the *Paladin of Abniss*. Have you finished charting your courses?" *They damn well better have*, she thought.

"Yes, Admiral." The voice of the female captain on the other end of the line breathed a sigh of relief. "Should we initiate the jump?"

"Do it."

This was the Mammoth that had been hit with a torpedo before. She wanted to get them to safety first, to avoid any risk of them getting hit again. They'd made hasty repairs, and a second torpedo would effectively obliterate any chance of escape. The possibility that a damaged craft would be ripped to shreds in hyperspace was too high to take the risk. So they went first.

Half the starfighter squadrons that had been flying defensive patrols around the two dozen Mammoth longhaulers arced toward the incoming cloud of drones. Harmony identified two dozen torpedos that the drones had already released, drawing red boxes around them in the main viewscreen. Kira couldn't help but clench her jaw as the Sabre pilots chased the torpedoes, taking them out one by one with their blasters and targeted missiles. The drones kept coming.

"See you on the other side, Admiral," the Mammoth captain said. "Jumping in 5... 4... 3... 2..."

Two Mammoths at the apex of the fleet, which had drifted hundreds of kilometers apart as they plotted their individual hyperspace jump courses, blurred in the viewscreen, seeming to drag and speed up at the same time, elongating and then streaking into a series of white lines, like stars in stasis.

In a blink, they were gone.

Two down, twenty-two to go.

"Two Mammoths clear," Harmony reported.

She contacted the next set of longhaulers and repeated her orders.

"Take out the rest of that incoming ordnance!" Colonel

Volk shouted into a microphone that connected with the Sabre squadrons as he paced across the bridge before the viewscreen. "If a single piece of shrapnel scars one of my Mammoths, you dogs will be running recon missions at the edge of unknown space until the Fleet forces me to retire or I die of the heart attack I've been expecting for years."

Kira fought down a smirk as the other officers on the bridge turned away and covered their mouths with hands. A little humor was good at a time like this. So was a little punishment-inspired fear.

The laughter died when one of the Sabre pilots miscalculated, veering into the path of a torpedo. His shot was good and the torpedo he'd been going for blew up halfway to the Mammoth fleet, but he was too slow to avoid the one coming behind him, which locked onto his heat signature and blasted the pilot and his Sabre into dust.

"Earth end you, I did *not* give you flyboys permission to turn this into a kamikaze mission!"

She let Colonel Volk rave and rant at the pilots as they chased the torpedoes and eliminated them one by one. No more pilots were lost, thankfully, and Kira was keeping a tally in her head. They'd already suffered more casualties on this mission than even Harmony had predicted, and she would be grilled on why that was when she got back to Ariadne.

Two more Mammoths jumped into hyperspace.

Twenty left, Kira thought. *Hurry up, Captain Osprey. We've lost too many good pilots. Don't you dare make me leave another one behind.*

TWENTY-ONE

E lya had never wished so badly to have Hedgebot by his
side. As he banked the skimmer bike around a massive
tree with sprawling branches, thicker than most of the trees
that made up this tall forest, he spied movement in the
underbrush. With his heart in his throat, Elya pulled up
short, spun around and drove back the way they had come.

"Where are you going? He went that way." Heidi gripped
his waist with a ferocious strength that bruised his ribs.

Elya ignored her. He may not have Hedgebot, but by this
point he knew where the other bike was headed.

"Groundlings," he said.

Elya parked the bike, grabbed Hedgebot's lifeless frame,
then dragged Heidi off the bike and over to the thick tree
they'd passed a moment ago.

She seemed exasperated with this unexpected setback,
but followed his instructions anyway, climbing the tree and
sitting herself in the first branch.

"Up," Elya whispered. "Go higher."

She climbed up three more thick branches until she was

hidden in the canopy, her face shielded by leaves. Elya perched next to her with a finger to his lips.

Heidi opened her mouth to protest, but clamped her mouth shut over top of the words.

He pointed ahead and mouthed, "Watch."

They didn't have to wait long. In a few minutes, a groundling prowled into view. They watched it through a break in the leaf cover as it lifted its head and sniffed around.

If there was one thing he'd learned about these creatures over the last maddening day of fight and flight, it was that they seemed to navigate mostly by smell. The groundling sniffed the air and looked around.

Though it obviously had some idea that they'd been there, it couldn't locate them. It looked up at the tree but didn't see them. The groundling sniffed toward their tree, then around the skimmer bike.

They waited, tense, until the groundling lost interest and loped away. Elya expelled his breath.

"How did you know it was there? Did Hedgebot tell you?"

Elya hefted the bot's dead weight in his palm. "No, he's still off. But maybe some of his behavior has rubbed off on me over the years."

She snorted. "Oh sure, you can smell danger."

"Actually," Elya said, "I just recognized where the other bike was headed."

He'd been turned around, disoriented, at first. This had just been another pathless part of the forest, but as they followed the other bike, he came to the conclusion that there was only one place the priest could be taking Hedrick. He didn't know why or what Father Pohl's plan was, but it was the only thing that made sense.

"Come on, let's see if we can get a little bit closer."

Heidi took a deep breath and exhaled. "Okay."

They scurried down the tree and made their way carefully forward, tiptoeing softly and trying to make as little sound as possible. They were poorly armed for such a situation. Elya's blaster had been taken when Charlie hit him over the head and pushed him into that hole in the ground. And Heidi had stolen the bike in such a rush that she hadn't taken any weapons of her own. So here they were, two unarmed people sneaking up on a compound controlled by the Kryl.

Whenever they saw movement ahead, they stopped and waited quietly for the groundlings to scurry by. There were dozens of them patrolling this forest.

"We need another distraction," Elya said, "Or some way to get through."

"Where did the other bike go?" Heidi asked. Elya didn't know. What he did know, however, was that the Kryl were patrolling the encampment much the same way a squadron of starfighters would patrol around the Mammoth fleet. Therefore, it was logical, even for a Kryl, that they would be patrolling inside a certain radius from the encampment.

So Elya took his bearings and ranged out, trying to stay the same distance from the encampment as that tree had been, and circled around the place.

"Finally, a little luck," Elya said when he spotted the other skimmer bike. It had been abandoned and leaned up against a tree trunk.

Elya popped the lid of the storage compartment and it was all he could do not to whoop in victory. He found a set of power tools inside, the kind that would be used to repair the skimmer bike if it somehow got damaged or disabled on a ride.

"I'll give the priest and his followers credit for one thing," Elya whispered to Heidi, keeping his voice low, so as not to attract unwanted attention. "They know how to be prepared. They're all alone on Robichar now—or at least that's what they think—and if anything happens, they can't rely on somebody else to come get them. So it's sensible to carry a repair kit in the skimmer bike."

"Why wasn't there one in my bike?"

"Probably because the one you stole hadn't been prepped for travel. I'm sure they only have a certain number of these kits and they probably don't just keep them in the bikes all the time. Whoever took this one came prepared."

Elya lifted the repair kit. Beneath it, they found an extra water skin, rations, and a rough brown blanket. While Heidi ransacked the supplies, Elya took the repair kit several feet away to a clear spot on the ground. He laid out the blanket, set Hedgebot down and dumped out the repair kit to get a better look at the tools.

It's got to be around here somewhere, he thought. *Ah! Here we go.*

He found a little plastic bag with spare contact plates— little metal discs for mounting a battery onto a computer— and brackets. Also, a handheld welding torch.

"Thank Animus for standardized parts." These brackets were larger than the ones installed on Hedgebot, but if he could get them to fit they should work the same.

He examined Hedgebot, placing the little guy's battery beside him. As he'd seen before when he examined it, there were deep grooves on the bot's underside, as if somebody had taken a screwdriver and jammed them into the metal plates, damaging the connection between the battery and Hedgebot's central processing unit. All he really needed to do was get that power flowing again.

Thankfully, the battery hadn't been damaged, just the contact plates and brackets. If he were still stuck in that hole in the ground, Elya wouldn't have been able to do anything about it. But with the repair kit there was a chance that he could bring the bot back to life.

Elya carefully removed the damaged hardware. Then he

took new contact plates from Hedgebot's hidden stash of spare parts and fitted them on. After that, he took the oversized brackets from the skimmer bike's kit and welded them to the bot's underside. It was bulky, and the brackets stuck out too far, but it was workable.

Elya reconnected the battery, took a deep breath and glanced at Heidi. "Here goes nothing."

He held in the two buttons that would reset Hedgebot. For a moment, there was no reaction and Elya thought he had done something wrong. But then Hedgebot wriggled in his hand, beeped in a very sleepy, confused sort of way and peered around. Elya hoped that the bot's memory hadn't been damaged. Would he recognize Elya? Would he obey his commands? Would all the programming he'd added for Sabre repair and maneuvering, all the custom code he'd spent so many hours writing, be lost?

"Aww," Heidi cooed. "Hi little guy. Welcome back."

Hedgebot chortled in digital tones, spun, tripped over the power unit which bulged out from its belly because of the oversized brackets. It beeped a questioning tone at Elya

"Sorry, bud. You'll have to make do with it for now."

Hedgebot's reply came across as sarcastic and slightly annoyed, yet somehow still thankful. That was the Hedgebot he knew and loved.

Then the bot reared up on his hind legs—or rather one leg and one peg—and peered about. Its glow returned then, a faint shimmer at first and then a blue nimbus that could barely be seen in the afternoon sunlight.

"All right, bud. Here's the thing," Elya said. "We've got to sneak back to that Kryl encampment and find Hedrick."

Hedgebot cocked his head as if to say, *Are you out of your Earth-blasted mind?*

Maybe he was.

But if the priest had left this bike here, there was only one place they could be going on foot. Elya and Heidi needed to see whether the boy-shaped figure he'd spotted on the bike was, indeed, Hedrick. And if so, try to scheme some way to get him back.

"I know. You're right. This is crazy. But what choice do we have? We need your help. Lead us through the forest and keep us away from the groundlings."

Hedgebot shook himself, fiber-optic bristles flaring out. Then it scurried ahead in the direction Elya had indicated. Its programming was good, it seemed. It was still listening to him. And it still had its personality, which was, after all, a mirror of his own.

"Be as quiet as you can," Elya said, "and stay close. We may have to backtrack quickly."

Together, they made their way forward, padding softly through the forest, setting their feet down on soft loam and roots wherever possible. Each time he or Heidi accidentally snapped a twig or stepped on brittle leaves, Elya tensed and his body broke out in a cold sweat. They made their way forward a hundred yards before Hedgebot glowed red and they had to run back the way they had come.

They waited with their backs pressed against a tree as a groundling appeared and sniffed where they had been a moment before. They waited until Hedgebot's orange-red glow had faded to yellow and finally blue again. When the bot indicated that the path was clear, they continued to pick their way forward, moving east and then west to avoid the layers of patrolling groundlings, but inching ever forward.

They had a couple more close calls, but Hedgebot never led them astray. At one point, when a groundling came close enough to smell them, Hedgebot darted twenty meters in the opposite direction and scurried up a tree. They took advantage of the distraction and crawled forward, leaving the bot to fend for itself.

The fence finally came into view. Hedgebot rejoined them a few minutes later, having evaded the groundling.

Elya looked around. The priest must have been out of his mind to come here. Elya knew he possessed some kind of protection from the Kryl, so maybe it wasn't as crazy an idea as it may have been otherwise.

They didn't see the priest at first. Elya did spot two sentinels in front of the prefab building that they had identified as being guarded earlier that day. The damage to the fence that they had caused was nearby. Elya saw now that it had been patched with more of that sticky webbing. The Kryl did quick work.

But where was the priest?

"Elya," Heidi whispered, "Look."

Elya padded back toward her and peered through a gap in the prefab buildings to the front gate.

A man in brown robes stood there, hood still up. Hedrick sat on the ground, his knees clutched to his chest, rocking back and forth nervously.

Heidi got up as if to run to him. Elya grabbed her and forced her back into a crouch. "What are you doing?" she hissed.

"Wait," said Elya. "If you go to him now, groundlings will be on you in seconds. Then you'll both be captured—or dead. Is that what you want? Both of you as Kryl food?"

She huffed and looked down.

Elya tried to peer at the priest's face, but he kept his cowl low and his back to the sun, so his face was cast in shadows.

Elya should have known better than to trust that bastard. Using the name of Animus to fool people into trusting him, and now here he was making some kind of pact with the Kryl, some kind of deal. What was he using Hedrick *for*? Better protection? Elya racked his brain. It didn't make any sense. If the priest had come to parlay, what made Hedrick so valuable?

The only thing Elya could think of was that Hedrick would make a tasty Kryl snack. But what would that buy the priest and his followers? And who would Father Pohl even negotiate with to make such a deal? The groundlings and the sentinels seemed to have binary modes—guard or kill. They couldn't be reasoned with. They didn't possess rational thought or a language since they were controlled by the Overmind. Unless…

The sound of a door latching in one of the prefab buildings floated on the wind. The man in the robes straightened. Two sentinels flanking a third figure walked toward the front gate where the priest was waiting.

A sentinel hauled the gate open, one of the posts dragging a curved line through the dirt. Father Pohl grabbed Hedrick's wrist and hauled him to his feet.

The boy resisted, but the man was too strong. He dragged Hedrick forward, throwing him to the ground in front of the Kryl. Heidi gasped, throwing her hand over her mouth, and then let loose a string of creative cussing that would impress even a drunken loadmaster.

His view of the two sentinels and the third figure was cut off by the prefab building as they walked back the way they had come. The sentinels were hulking figures. One of them, he saw happily, was missing an arm. That must have been from the explosion Thom triggered. The creature's carapace had grown over the wound, sealing it. It reminded Elya how inhuman these xenos were, with abilities that were beyond human comprehension. They could heal quickly, absorb more damage than any person could take. They were dangerous. If he and Heidi wanted to save Hedrick's life, they would have to be very smart and very, *very* careful.

Elya crawled to his left until the group came into view

again. He could see the third person who was, unlike the sentinels, smaller, almost man-shaped. Tall, yes, taller than Elya, perhaps even as tall as Admiral Miyaru. And though it, too, was covered in purple-black carapace, like organic armor, its body shape was basically human.

Unlike the sentinels, whose weapons were ingrown talons and teeth, this creature carried a rifle slung over its shoulder. An older model, like the blaster rifles used in the Kryl War, with smaller battery packs and less range than the newer models. Perhaps this creature had stolen the gun from a Fleet soldier or one of the colonists.

The xeno gestured. The priest dragged Hedrick forward and the sentinels closed the gates behind them.

"Now what?" Heidi demanded.

"Now, we sneak in and try to get Hedrick out before they notice us."

"Why the hell didn't we do that before, when we had the chance and they were outside the damn gates?"

Elya glanced up at the sky. Even if they did rescue the boy, would they have time to get back to the Fleet? He sighed heavily as the notion that he may never make it back to the Fleet sank in. Up to this point, he had held out hope that there was still a chance that the Search and Rescue team would connect to his cube and then come find him, somehow, even though the cube had been taken from him.

Now he finally resigned himself to the fact that the rescue he'd pictured wasn't going to happen. No one was coming for him. No one even knew where to look.

Elya was on his own.

A certain part of him felt that this situation was inevitable. He had always been on his own. The only person he had ever truly been able to rely on was himself. And Hedgebot, of course.

Only, now it was different. Heidi and Hedrick were also

relying on him. No Search and Rescue team was coming for *them*. They weren't his family, weren't even his squadmates... but he was all they had. He and Heidi were Hedrick's only chance to get out of the Kryl encampment alive. And even though Elya couldn't get back to the Fleet, if he could save this boy's life, if he could get Hedrick and Heidi to safety, if he could help them survive just a little bit longer, that was a good thing, a noble thing, and worth the risk.

In a flash of insight, Elya understood why Osprey had been giving him such a hard time about not acting like a team player. When things got ugly, they only had each other to rely upon.

Well, here he was. Elya may not ever be able to make it up to Osprey. But this new team he'd inadvertently joined needed him now.

That would have to be good enough. He could make it up to Osprey and the Furies later... assuming he made it out of this alive.

"All right," Elya said. "Here's what we're gonna do."

TWENTY-TWO

Hedrick clutched his bruised upper arm as they passed through the gate into the compound.

By the time he realized that Father Pohl wasn't taking him back to his mother, it was too late. He hadn't been lying about the shortcut through the caves. It spit them out into a shaded grove where a pair of skimmer bikes were chained up. Father Pohl asked him if he wanted to take one for a ride.

"You bet I do!" he'd crowed.

When Father Pohl insisted on riding with him, for safety, how could he refuse? Hedrick didn't know how to operate the unwieldy vehicle. It hummed like a plasma cannon between his legs, the weight of it sending jolts of excitement through his body. He didn't even get suspicious when Father Pohl turned the nose of the bike downhill. The wind whipped through Hedrick's hair. But as they descended through switchbacks and came to the base of the valley, zipping along tree-lined trails and then along packed dirt paths, a shivery, distrusting dread had settled itself in the pit of his belly.

Hedrick tried to ditch Father Pohl in the woods when they finally stopped. The bald, hawkish priest had been busy shoving side-satchels into the bike's storage compartment when he slipped behind a tree trunk, quiet as a mouse. But Hedrick hadn't gone thirty meters when the priest's bony fingers seized his arm and yanked him off his feet. Hedrick kicked and clawed but the old man was way stronger than he looked—or Hedrick was way weaker than he'd realized. Either way, after this escape attempt, the priest refused to remove his hand from Hedrick's arm until the groundlings closed in behind them. A few minutes later, they paused on the blackened ground at the foot of the chain-link gate. The dirt looked as if something evil had been struck down by the righteous hand of Animus himself.

Ten or fifteen of the foul, hunch-backed spider-dogs Captain Nevers called groundlings made a half circle around them, cutting off their retreat. Oily strands of saliva dripped from their hinged, hanging jaws. When Hedrick closed his eyes, he remembered how they had pounced on a small girl, opening her throat with their teeth.

He knew very well that if he tried to run now, the groundlings would gut him in a similar fashion. Counterintuitively, the only person who could protect him was Father Pohl. He was the reason the groundlings kept a certain distance. The priest held that glowing green geode. It must have been the same one Hedrick had seen last night in the canyon, when Father Pohl had rescued them from the groundlings. As long as he held it, the Kryl kept their distance.

Hedrick hadn't been able to tell what it was last night. They'd been too far away and Hedrick had still been in shock, totally preoccupied with his own survival to worry about anything else. Now, as Father Pohl led him around a puddle of black liquid that had pooled in the soot-stained soil, he recognized the orb as a sibling of the geode he'd discovered in the glowing chamber deep in the caves. Only, rather than blow into pieces and float over his head, this orb was mounted with a marble handle, and all of its green light came from three triangular apertures spaced evenly around its face. The amount of light each opening emitted could be adjusted by twisting the handle, like a lantern. The object was only about the size of a grown man's fist, and it was currently inactive. Father Pohl gripped it tight as they followed the two hulking Kryl and the other one, who seemed to be their leader, a disfigured man-shaped creature armored in Kryl carapace.

Their escorts led them down a row of prefab buildings and stopped before the second-to-last one.

Father Pohl hesitated, holding up the lantern like a shield. "That's far enough. We can make the trade here."

Trade? Hedrick's mind flitted about, like a panicked bird in a cage. *What trade? Is he planning to give the Kryl that geode?*

"After inspection." The disfigured Kryl spoke as if it had marbles in its mouth. Hedrick snuck a peek up at the Kryl's face and was startled to see that it had one glossy, multi-faceted bug eye—and one human eye, brown flecked with spots of neon yellow that reminded him of radioactivity warning signs on space stations.

"We had an agreement," Father Pohl said.

Hedrick's skin crawled. *Who would make an agreement with these monsters?* That's when he knew Father Pohl had to be insane.

"We did," the Kryl rumbled. "And we shall uphold our end of the bargain, provided you are not attempting to deceive us."

Father Pohl clenched his jaw and stepped toward the Kryl, bearing the lantern and twisting the handle ever so slightly. The xeno hunched its shoulders and took half a step back.

The green glow pained the xeno, but the effect on this pitiful disfigured monster seemed muted. The groundlings kept their distance as if a physical force was pushing them back. This Kryl was more intelligent, if uglier, and seemed not only to understand what was causing the effect but was able to resist it to some extent.

What Hedrick had seen in that chamber had been nothing short of miraculous—an advanced artifact crafted by an ancient intelligence, or so he believed. This Kryl's ability to resist such a power frightened him more than the groundlings, more even than the hulking security guard Kryl who had stepped back to take up posts on either side of the doorway the xeno wanted them to enter.

Father Pohl worked his tongue around the inside of his mouth as he considered this dilemma.

"Please don't!" Hedrick blurted out. Only after he spoke did he realize he'd said it out loud. By then Hedrick was too scared not to finish. "Give them what they want and let's get out of here. Please!"

The xeno who spoke opened the door to the building and gestured them inside magnanimously. It was such a human gesture, delivered in such a halting, half-hunched, stilted way that it gave him the total creeps.

Father Pohl's face clouded over. Finally, he nodded and pushed Hedrick ahead of him.

Hedrick flicked his head rapidly from side to side. "No, no," he said, "I don't want to go in there."

Father Pohl grabbed his bruised arm and dragged him forward.

Hedrick had half a mind to fall to the floor and throw a tantrum. It used to drive his mother crazy when he did that, but when he saw the humanoid xeno had followed them through the doorway, suddenly moving forward seemed like a safer option.

He was beyond relieved to see that the hulking Kryl—one of whom he saw was missing an arm—remained outside.

The room they had entered seemed to be a kind of foyer or entryway. Double doors ahead of them led to the rest of the building. The door behind clicked shut.

The humanoid Kryl limped around them and pushed open the double doors, gesturing them forward. Father Pohl edged through the door, being careful. Not wanting to be stuck with the xeno alone in this tiny room, Hedrick scurried past, keeping close to Father Pohl, and gave a shout of fright when he walked face-first into a bunch of cobwebs. He batted at the sticky strands, which wadded up between his fingers. These were like spiderwebs times a thousand. Hedrick had to rub his hands together to get the strands to ball up and then flick them to the floor. The stickiest boogers you ever saw.

"Ugh, gross," Hedrick blurted. "What is this stuff?"

Father Pohl, too, had run into cobwebs but was dealing with them better than Hedrick was. He held the lantern up and the green glow seemed to burn the goo away.

"Give me your hands, boy," Father Pohl said. Hedrick held out his trembling hands. Father Pohl shined the green light on them from the triangular aperture, directing it with a twist of the handle, and they melted away from his hands too.

Only now did Hedrick lift his head and look around. He'd never been in one of these prefab buildings before. Walls which separated the building into several rooms had been knocked down to make a single large room. He could still make out the edges of door frames, the grooves where the walls would fit. The walls had been ripped away by a terrible force, leaving thin material behind—sharp, twisted metal shards sticking up out of the floor and ceiling. Perhaps those hulking Kryl outside had done the demolition.

The room seemed to glow, but not like the caves that had led up to the golden chamber. That had been a natural radiance, while this was a sickly yellow gleam, the same color which flecked the Kryl's all-too-human eye. It was as if the disfigured Kryl and the growth coating the floors and walls of this building had each been injected with poison.

When Hedrick walked forward, his feet came down on something sticky. More Kryl goo, soft and squishy. Each time he lifted a foot, the glowing yellow imprint where his shoe had been glowed and dissipated. Every light fixture in the building had been covered over by the same fungus. Cobwebs hung along the perimeter, remaking the space into a series of pods with a hollow in the center where they stood.

"This way," said the Kryl, stepping around them and leading them toward one of the pods at the back of the building.

To Hedrick, it felt like he was in some kind of spider's nest. The whole place had an arachnid feel. He realized now that those hadn't been cobwebs, but some kind of fibrous Kryl goop they had slung from the ceiling.

Many-legged bugs, about the size of toy bots, scurried away from the glow of Father Pohl's lantern, hiding themselves in the cracks in the floor and in dark corners. Though he didn't trust the man, Hedrick stuck tight to Father Pohl's side, sheltering in the glowing green bubble of safety cast by the artifact. Whatever he did, Hedrick knew he had to stay in that ring of green light.

His eyes searched the walls, looking for an exit. There had to be a back door out of this place, didn't there? Or a window. A window would be fine, he was small. He hadn't been able to search the side of the building, but there had to be some way out.

Each webbed pod they passed was lined with veined, spidery-looking eggs. The smaller ones had translucent skin, so he could see the contents inside. Tiny Kryl, like the spiders on the floor or the groundlings outside, were growing in each. They were strapped to the wall with the cobwebs to keep them upright.

They were growing more Kryl.

"Bring the boy here," the humanoid xeno said.

Father Pohl nudged Hedrick forward. "Do as he says."

"No," Hedrick said. "You do it!"

"It's okay, boy," the Kryl said, "I'm not going to hurt you."

Father Pohl pushed Hedrick forward. He scrabbled backward as he struggled to stay in the safe ring of green light cast by Father Pohl's artifact.

"Take off your shoes," the Kryl said. "And stand here."

Hedrick saw there was a slightly upraised platform where the Kryl was pointing. It formed the base of some kind of machine set against the back wall. Some of the equipment looked familiar, manufactured by Imperial printers like the building they were in. However, there were several Kryl growths on the equipment, large bulging fistulas that pulsed and squirmed unnaturally. Across the monitors, beneath the layer of Kryl cancer suspended in a clear liquid, text flashed across a screen and computer towers hummed as the cooling fans worked overtime.

When Hedrick didn't move, the Kryl bent down and, with veiny hands bearing several purple-black splotches, he removed Hedrick's shoes. Hedrick counted the creature's fingers and knuckles. One of his hands was very human. The fingers each had three joints, same as Hedrick. It served to reinforce the contrast; whoever had built that glowing chamber in the caves was neither human nor Kryl, but something else entirely.

When his shoes had been removed, the xeno dragged

Hedrick onto the platform. Immediately, the sticky goop seeped over his toes. Hedrick's gorge rose and he vomited on the ground. The Kryl didn't seem to care, he just stepped over the puke and pulled some kind of cords from the wall. They were long strands with a mucous texture that shone in the yellow light. The Kryl creature set them against Hedrick's temples.

He tried to struggle then but something about the touch of those strands at his temples paralyzed his muscles. Hedrick's breath began to come in quick panicky gasps. *I can't move,* he thought. *Why can't I move? Oh, please, Animus, don't let this be the end.*

"What are you doing to him?" Father Pohl said. There was a tremor in the man's voice that Hedrick hadn't heard before. Not when the priest had scared off the groundlings in the canyon, not when they'd approached the gate. Only now did the priest seem frightened of what was about to happen.

And if the priest was afraid, Hedrick was terrified.

"It is none of your concern," the Kryl said.

A warm stream of urine began to seep down his leg, pooling at his feet. Still, Hedrick was unable to move except to breathe. His eyes darted over as he saw the humanoid Kryl manipulate some of the computer equipment by touching the pulsing, liquid-filled sacs.

After a minute of this, the Kryl gave a kind of satisfied moan that was half bug and half human. Then he reached into a cocoon-like growth and lifted out a many-legged worm no thicker around than a piece of string.

Father Pohl's tongue darted out to wet his lips. "Don't forget what you promised me."

The Kryl inclined his head ever so politely. "You have my word. Your followers will not be harmed."

"Nor will you come to our territory or poison our water supply, or attack any of our people."

"I know the terms of the agreement," the Kryl growled. "Do you dare question the Overmind?"

"I'm just being clear," Father Pohl said. "That was the deal: I bring you a human child, and you let us live in peace."

"Yes," the Kryl said, "that was the deal."

The xeno lowered the worm toward Hedrick's head. The tiny creature began to squirm the closer it was brought to his face. It reached out toward him.

Hedrick began to hyperventilate then. Apparently he wasn't completely paralyzed because the panic set in and his chest heaved as he gasped for breath.

There was a flash of blue at the corner of his vision. Was this the last thing he would see before he died?

Sparks flashed from the corner above and behind the computer monitor. Something electronic popped in the computers, and the machine released a plume of smoke that smelled like burning hair.

The strands at his temples went limp and fell away. The goop that had climbed over his feet lost its shape and spilled away like water. The xeno, still holding the worm, turned, growling angrily.

The building went black. Hedrick lurched forward, throwing himself to his knees and landing with a splash.

A small creature pulsed red and blue between his hands. Hope flared in his heart as Hedgebot scurried forward several feet, then paused and looked back at him. The bot went dark.

He crawled forward toward where it had been a moment ago. Something strong grabbed his arm—the priest, most likely—but with all the gooey crap on his hands, he was able to squirm out of the man's grasp.

Hedrick stumbled to his feet, slashed at the sticky strands that glommed onto his face, and ran for his life.

TWENTY-THREE

When Elya first encountered the requirements for astrobots in the Fleet manual, they seemed like complete overkill. Why would any unit need that many capabilities? He came to learn that astrobots were essential for completing minor repairs on long missions. They were even helpful as a second set of eyes. The high tech ones could be used to aid in navigation or take aerial photographs on recon missions or even fly a Sabre as a backup to the autopilot system—although Hedgebot was too small for that skill and didn't have the memory needed for such software.

But never in a million years did Elya imagine Hedgebot's abilities would be used in a situation like *this*.

Hedgebot painstakingly sliced through the Kryl excretions which had been used to patch the hole in the fence made by Thom earlier, although it took a lot longer to accomplish the same task due to the stickiness of the substance. Elya kept having to scrape the bot's underside with a stick to get the gunk off. They had to make sure the hole was big enough for all of them. It would do no good to squeeze the bot through if they couldn't get the *boy* out.

Heidi kept a vigilant lookout while the bot worked. All of the groundlings had gathered on the opposite side of the compound near the gate, to observe the priest and Hedrick's arrival, so none stumbled upon them as Hedgebot worked. A minor stroke of luck.

Hedgebot's miniature laser cutter had been a particularly difficult piece of equipment to install. According to the Fleet manual, all astrobots were required to have one, in order to carve the pilot out of a cockpit that had been damaged in a bad landing. This had crossed his mind as Elya fell to the surface of Robichar yesterday—it was, in fact, an aspect of the same tool that Hedgebot had used to repair the Sabre during the fall, rerouting power back to his control column.

"Come on, buddy," Elya muttered. He felt exposed without his sidearm. If one of the groundlings did happen upon them, what would he do? Strangle it to death?

Hedgebot finished his work and Heidi and Elya slipped through the fence, wiping stray strands of webbing from their faces as they hurried to the back of the building the sentinels were guarding, and into which Hedrick, the priest, and the other Kryl had disappeared.

They hid themselves in between the two buildings, sticking to the shadows cast by the setting sun. They were still weaponless, but perhaps they wouldn't need weapons if they could just grab the boy and run. That wild hope didn't keep Elya from picking up a dusty piece of metal piping from a pile of unused materials stacked behind the building. It chimed softly as he lifted it. Heidi chewed her lower lip and peered around nervously while Hedgebot went to work on the back corner of the prefab.

While they waited for the bot to cut through the 3D-printed siding, a dread curiosity filled him. What was in this building that was worth guarding so closely? The Kryl must be protecting something… but what? And then to force the boy and the priest inside?

Whatever was in there was valuable to them. Valuable and, in all likelihood, exceedingly dangerous.

It made him mad enough that the priest would betray Elya and kidnap the boy, but to drag Hedrick like some kind of prize to the Kryl's doorstep? What an absolute betrayal of his humanity. Before, Elya had been keen to help the priest and his followers, if he could. It was lower down on his priority list—after "connect with the Fleet" and "don't get gutted by a groundling"—but he wouldn't wish on anyone the experience of those poor, lost souls who had been left behind on his homeworld. After all, the priest and his followers just wanted to live their lives in peace, without interference from the Empire. He couldn't blame them for that. But to give a child to the Kryl to achieve it?

That crossed the line.

Holding the pipe, Elya examined a few other pieces of machinery at the back of the building: a condenser and fan for an air conditioning unit, and a standalone battery wired up to solar panels on the roof. While Hedgebot cut the hole in the back wall of the prefab, Elya palmed a wire cutter he'd taken from the toolkit in the skimmer bike and searched for the main power line.

The fan from the A/C unit was whining loudly, which was probably the main reason the groundlings and sentinels hadn't noticed them yet. The small hiss of Hedgebot's laser cutter was drowned in the noise of the fan. Whatever was drawing electricity in the building, it took a lot of power. As he searched the tangle of wires, Elya noticed that the panels from several of the other prefab buildings had had their power rerouted to this one. It didn't take a genius to figure out that cutting the power would piss the Kryl off. It would also cast the inside of the building in darkness and, while it was a risk to Hedrick, he thought the darkness would give the boy a chance to slip out of his captor's grasp.

It was the best plan he'd been able to devise. The only plan. He had to try it.

Hedgebot finished cutting a small square in the bottom corner of the prefab. "Okay, pal," Elya said to his bot. "You go in and find the boy, but stay out of sight and keep your light off. I'll count to thirty then cut the power. And when I do, you find Hedrick and lead him back out to us."

The bot beeped an affirmative tone and crawled inside.

"Counting down from thirty, twenty-nine, twenty-eight…"

Elya hadn't reached the teens before Heidi gasped and clutched her mouth. She reached out with her other hand and hauled Elya behind the air conditioning unit.

"What?"

She clamped her hand over *his* mouth.

"Groundlings," she whispered.

Elya's breath caught in his throat when he spotted the pair. Two groundlings were sniffing the ragged strands of Kryl webbing hanging from the fence where they'd come through.

Elya adjusted his grip on the metal pipe.

The lead groundling hopped nimbly through the hole and raised its face in the air. The three slits of its nose contracted minutely. It cocked its head, the slope of its body showing like a hunchback in silhouette.

Elya handed Heidi the pipe and lifted the wire cutters, very quietly fitting the first of the power cables—one of the small extension cords—into the cutter's sharpened nose.

He severed the line with a *snip.*

The Kryl jerked its head. Elya snipped the second line.

The second creature mimicked the movements of the first.

Ka chowm, ka chowm. Vvvooooott. Ka-CHOWM!

Elya recognized the telltale percussion of an unsilenced gauss rifle firing in the distance. Two shots, reload, two more shots. A real pro on the trigger.

Charlie.

Did he realize Elya had escaped his underground prison? Or was he coming after Heidi, once he realized she stole the skimmer bike?

One of the groundlings snapped its head in the direction of the new noise, then slunk back through the fence, trotting away as it gained speed. The other stayed put in the compound, its body held frozen like an ambush hunter afraid of startling its prey.

Two on one, Elya thought. *Better odds.*

He severed the last of the smaller power lines then gripped the rubber handles of the wire cutter in one hand. Wrapping his other hand over his closed fist for support, he jammed the cutters down into the rubber housing protecting the central line which fed into the prefab building.

The fan next to him slowed, clicking as it came to a stop. The groundling nearby finally spotted them and chortled an aggressive warning. As the creature sprinted in their direction, Heidi stepped out from behind the air conditioning unit wielding the pipe and swung it underhand. *Bullseye*, Elya thought as the pipe connected with the groundling's jaw.

Instead of sweeping it clean off its feet like he'd hoped, it stumbled back and then recovered. But Heidi was there again with another clean strike, this time from overhead. Elya cringed at the sound of the xeno's skull cracking as its legs gave out. Normally he wouldn't have thought the woman capable of such force, but fear for her son and survival-induced desperation had momentarily imbued this mother with a hideous strength.

And Elya helped, too. He jumped on the struggling creature's back and used his weight to hold it down. The xeno scrabbled at the ground, mewling and whining as the pipe rained down on its head.

"Die you… twisted… monster!" she snarled in time with her blows.

When the xeno was still, Heidi stepped out of the slanted shadow cast by the roof and into the sunlight, breathing heavily. Yellow blood and pale bits of brain splattered her shirt and face.

Elya looked up as a sentinel stepped into the mouth of the alley, blocking the sun. It hinged open its massive, slavering jaw and waved its tongues in the air, as if by doing so it could taste their location.

Elya felt its roar deep in his belly. A wet sensation of fear sprang from the seat of his stomach and spread through his body.

A skimmer bike zipped by along the fence, kicking up a cloud of leaves and dirt as the driver hit the reverse thrusters and spun about.

"Heidi! Elya!" It was Thom, yelling at them from the skimmer. Not the one they had left in the woods, but a different bike. The priest's?

"This way, hurry, while they're distracted!"

Elya blinked. "Hedrick's in there. We can't leave him!"

Thom went pale—even in the sunlight—the blood draining from his face. His eyes focused over Elya's head to the sentinel as it lumbered into the alley.

A groundling leaped out from behind a tree trunk and knocked Thom to the ground. The machinist gave a strangled, breathless shout. A blaster discharged, and the sound was followed by the clatter of metal as the groundling kicked the gun out of Thom's hands. Elya and Heidi looked at the sentinel, then at Thom, then back at each other.

"You help Thom," Elya said. "I'll lead this big bastard away."

"What about Hendrick?"

"Hedgebot's got him."

"Are you sure?"

"We don't have a choice!"

The sentinel fell to all fours—or rather, to all threes, since this was the sentinel that had lost an arm earlier. It shook the ground as it landed.

"Go!" Elya shouted, shoving Heidi toward Thom. "Get the gun."

Heidi sprinted around the corner without another word, heading straight for the opening in the fence. Elya followed her to the corner, but turned the opposite direction. He paused just long enough to pick up another metal pipe and toss it at the sentinel.

The creature let the pipe bounce off its head and roared, enraged. The ruse worked almost too well. He stumbled into the fence as he fled.

The sentinel gave chase.

Elya passed the last alley and turned down the outside of the prefab building at the end of the row. There was more ground here between the building and the fence. He sprinted across the clearing.

Behind him, on three legs, the sentinel ran with an awkward, loping gait. As Elya moved away from the building, he realized the xeno didn't really mean to catch him, but rather to force him into the open.

The other sentinel had left its post at the door and was already charging, bearing down on him at a frightening pace. Their psychic link allowed them to coordinate without speaking or even seeing each other.

Elya veered out away from them both, trying to use the angle to his advantage. The talons of the second sentinel caught his flight suit and ripped the fabric, scraping across his ribs, as he twisted by. He ground his teeth against the pain and made a beeline for the relative safety of the pre-fab buildings again, this time aiming for the front.

As he sucked air and stretched his legs, a familiar robed man stumbled out of the doorway clutching his left eye. Blood streamed between his fingers.

Father Pohl looked up, something about the view causing his face to drop. Perhaps it was the sight of Elya. Perhaps it was the two massive xenos closing in behind him. Who could really be sure?

Elya had such a fierce hatred of the priest by now that he was able to reach down into some deep well of energy inside himself and haul out an extra burst of speed. He sprinted at the priest. Instead of running, as Elya would have expected any sane person to do, Father Pohl stood his ground while using his free hand to fumble inside his robe.

Out came a geometric stone large enough to hold in two hands. It had a U-shaped handle for gripping on one side, like a handheld lantern. Clutching the object between his elbow and his body, the priest turned the handle, exposing three triangular apertures that emitted a bright green light.

"Back," he shouted, holding the object aloft.

Panicked screeches from the sentinels behind him were followed by the scrape and scrabble of clawed feet in dirt.

Elya didn't slow down, just lowered his shoulder and drove it into the priest's solar plexus, nailing him to the wall of the prefab beside the half-open door.

He fumbled for the geode and managed to tear it out of Father Pohl's weakened grasp.

"No!" the priest cried, gasping for air. "You can't! That's mine. *Mine,* I tell you."

But the priest was injured. The wounded eye was obviously causing the man a great deal of pain. Elya slipped his fingers through the sphere's handle and used it to shove the priest to the ground.

To his shock, the sentinels remained at a distance of about thirty meters, puffing and panting. Their heads were strangely tiny compared to their bodies, with those deeply inset, beady eyes. From here, he could see that the carapace of the one which had had its arm blown off in the raid earlier was patchy and bubbly around the missing limb, like it had been dipped in a vat of boiling grease.

But they didn't come any closer.

Father Pohl scratched at Elya's ankle with his free hand. "Please," he said, "you don't understand what you're dealing with."

Elya stepped out of the priest's reach and watched the man struggle to his feet.

As he did so, Elya took two steps towards the sentinels. Their faces changed in what he could only suspect was fright. The slits of their nose and eyes closed over with semi-transparent flaps and they squealed and scurried back.

What he'd mistaken for a flashlight in the canyon was no such thing. This incandescent artifact was what the priest had used to scare off those groundlings. It seemed to be made of stone, but it had a kind of thin, metallic quality. It was surprisingly light and airy. The mechanics around the lid where it spun were finely crafted, if somewhat stiff. The stone resembled marble, but truly, it was like no material Elya had ever seen. The green glow seemed to come not from a power cell or battery, as he'd expected, but from the hollow center of the stone itself. And no matter how he angled it, he couldn't see into the bright core, which shone forth like a tireless emerald star—without giving off any heat.

"Well, isn't that interesting," Elya said. "This is why you think the Kryl can't hurt you? This... what is this thing?"

"A blessing from Animus himself," the priest growled.

Elya blinked dumbly at the man. The situation was so improbable, so unlikely, that Elya no longer registered belief or disbelief. He felt as if his awareness had separated from his body, like he was watching himself in some kind of bizarre holovid. Scene: Brown-skinned Solaran male, breathing heavily, bearing an object of alien design, facing off against a one-eyed priest of Animus and two cowering Kryl sentinels.

"Turn off the relic."

Elya turned to look down the barrel of an Imperial blaster. It was an older model, the barrel wider than he was used to, the sight thicker, the handle longer. However, the hand holding the sidearm didn't belong to Charlie or Thom, as he would have expected. His eyes tracked down the arm to a mutated torso and patchwork face straight out of his worst nightmare.

The disfigured creature who had met Father Pohl at the gate.

"I'm impressed, kid. Didn't think you'd survive the landing, let alone the surprise I sent after you."

Elya felt his body tremble and his grip on the object go slack. He clutched it to his stomach and staggered back half a step as dozens of groundlings swarmed into the compound and spread out around them. They remained at the same distance as the two sentinels, pacing. The xeno holding the blaster, though, didn't seem as affected as the others were. A bead of sweat tracked down the human portion of its forehead, alongside a seam that sealed the rest of its skull with a carapace-like growth. The arm pointing the blaster at Elya was rock steady.

And for some reason, not pulling the trigger.

Elya took the opportunity to study the mutant. Two claw-like feet covered with chitinous membrane that climbed up its legs and armored thighs. A utility belt around the waist bore what must have been thirty kilos of gear—a holster for the pistol and half a dozen charge packs, a small knife, a large knife, a heavy duty waterskin, and more. It wore no clothing and its torso was covered in thick Kryl hide that was scaly and purplish-black. While the right arm, holding the blaster, was human, the second arm was a gift of its Kryl DNA, far too big for its body, muscular and monstrous. Probably male, judging by the voice, but who could say, now?

As for its face, Elya shuddered to take it in. Part human, part Kryl, with a clicking mandible where the mouth should be. No ears, just orifices in its head, studded with thick veins that pulsed. One human eye, discolored and bloodshot, yellowish neon, as if the fluid within the sclera had been tinted with radioactive dye. A patch of brown hair cascading down to obscure the human part of its face—jawbone, forehead, eye, temple, cheekbone, even an eyebrow.

Whatever this mad patchwork monster was, it was partially human. And unlike the sentinels and the groundlings and every other variation of Kryl xenoform he'd studied in training, this one spoke galactic standard.

"Didn't think you'd survive the landing…"

Recognition finally dawned. "It was you flying that drone," Elya whispered.

The mutant gave a hideously sinister chuckle, then stared into a middle distance as some silent communication passed between it and the other Kryl. A pack of the groundlings sprinted behind the buildings and returned escorting Hedrick. The boy held a screwdriver in his hand, bearing it like a sword. It was covered in blood and Elya knew what had happened to the priest's eye.

Heidi shuffled in behind him, followed by Thom clutching his shoulder, which had been dislocated. He moaned. Heidi seemed more or less unharmed but the fear that pinched her face pierced Elya's heart.

"I won't ask again. Turn the ancient relic off."

Where was Hedgebot? Had he somehow managed to evade capture? A bot was supposed to be harder for a Kryl to track since it didn't have an organic scent like a person or animal.

The mutant shifted its blaster a few degrees and pulled the trigger. Elya blinked and jerked backward as a bolt of plasma took Thom in the throat, venting his windpipe.

"No!" Elya's breath came heavy and fast. Whatever anger he'd harbored against Thom for his betrayal, he didn't wish the man dead. "What did you do that for?"

A horrible sucking noise came from Thom's throat as he tried and failed to fill his lungs with air.

"You weren't listening." The mutant turned the blaster to point at Heidi. "She's next. Then you."

Hedrick was no longer wailing, scared, at the slavering groundlings slowly circling them. His eyes brimmed with tears and he stared straight at Elya, his face open, pleading. Heidi wrapped her arms around her son and pulled him to her. She closed her eyes and her lower lip trembled.

Elya gripped the handle and rotated the geode. Its green light flickered out.

He dashed forward, fell to his knees, and gripped Thom's shoulders where he lay. The man's mouth worked, making words without sound. At first, Elya couldn't understand him. He looked like a landed fish gulping for water in the alien air. Then Elya made out the words his lips were forming over and over again.

"I'm sorry, I didn't know. I'm sorry, I didn't know. I'm sorry…"

"Didn't know? Didn't know what, Thom?"

Thom thrashed. Elya pressed the man's body to the ground, trying to hold him still. Thom hauled one last breath through the ragged hole in his throat, and made several awful, strangled gurgles before he finally went still.

What didn't he know?

Elya could have sworn, from Thom's behavior just prior to Elya getting beaten and thrown into a hole in the ground, that Thom had known *precisely* how Charlie and the others were planning to trap him in the forest and leave him for dead.

So what didn't he know, then? And why had Thom changed his mind and come back to help? And how the hell did he know they were headed back here in the first place? Unless…

Unless the thing he didn't know was that Father Pohl had been planning to hand Hedrick over to the Kryl. Thom must have found out and come to stop him.

Any anger Elya had been feeling at Thom evaporated. He'd been too late, but the man had come back to try to make things right.

And lost his life for his efforts.

Elya gripped the relic, which had been resting between his knees, and stood.

As he spun, something struck his jaw with the force of a sledgehammer, sending Elya reeling and the ground rushing up to meet him.

The Kryl mutant bent down and picked up the geode. The priest protested, but the monster beat him down with a powerful Kryl fist. Father Pohl fell to his knees beside Elya, begging and pleading for his life.

Sentinels and groundlings rushed forward. The mutant

smiled as the humans were all prodded to their feet and ushered into the prefab.

Elya was the first to step into the darkness.

———

Hedrick whimpered as the groundlings clawed the screwdriver from his shaking hands. He'd swiped it from the floor when the lights went out. Then hands grabbed at him. Hedrick spun around, stabbing the priest in the eye. He hadn't meant to. He just wanted to get away.

He'd followed Hedgebot into one of the woven pods and out through a hole cut in the back corner of the building. When he emerged, his mother was there. "Mom!" he'd cried as he fell into her arms. But then the groundlings had surrounded them and led them around to the front of the building where he'd seen the monster pointing a blaster at Elya's head.

Standing helpless while the Kryl threatened his mother had been excruciating, scarier even than the "inspection" they'd been performing on him before. His hopes for escape were dashed again when they were all led back into the darkened building. Hedrick couldn't help the fearful sobs that came out of his mouth. He dug his heels in, resisting entering the darkened building. It was so much worse this time, knowing what was coming. His mother tried to keep the Kryl off of him, but there were so many of them and they were so strong. What choice did they have?

There was a few minutes of awkward waiting in the dark foyer of the building as the monster man gave unintelligible orders. Several Kryl went around the back and after a short wait, the lights came back on.

Whatever had been done to cut the power had just been undone by the awful Kryl. Hedrick looked around for

Hedgebot, hopeful that the bot might still be waiting to lead them to safety.

He didn't want to die like this.

Elya groaned when the power came back on.

Of course they repaired the damage he had caused. And they did it fast. In addition to being internally wired into a psychic network with the other Kryl, they had a facility with technology and an ability to manipulate electronics through organic means. That gooey webbing the Kryl poured over everything and the sentient fungus, must be another interface for their psionic abilities.

If the mutant was a nightmare, what he saw when the lights came on was a nightmare factory. A vast amount of the webbing had been spun around the room, creating smaller pods out of the large space. They were led past the first couple, where several embryonic xenos were cocooned in large chrysalises, perhaps baby sentinels or groundlings.

As they moved past the woven pods, they finally entered one on their right hand side. This one, too, had a set of chrysalises, but they were taller, coming up to the level of Elya's chest. And unlike the others he'd seen, these didn't have any creatures in them, which was worrisome. He studied the mutant, who had its back to Elya as it explored the chrysalises with its hands. What kinds of monstrous experiments were these Kryl planning on performing?

This was like nothing he'd ever been trained on, nothing he'd ever seen. Not the inside of this building and especially not the Kryl-human mutant who seemed to be in charge. It had been strange enough to see a flying drone occupied by a Kryl pilot. Now, it made a scary kind of sense. This creature, whatever it was, had been sent here on a specific mission.

Historians and xenoanthropology experts had always assumed that the Kryl invaded planets to drain them of natural resources. They assumed the Kryl were coming to Robichar for the same reason—to mine the metals, to steal the fresh water, to dig up the radioactive isotopes they relied on to power their ships and hives. To expand to another world and spread like the galactic disease they were.

But the inside of this building spoke of a more nefarious purpose.

"What do you want?" Elya asked.

"Why, power, of course."

The creature's mandibles once again spread into a ghastly imitation of a grin. The xeno hefted the "ancient relic" and set it on the counter next to a holoscreen covered by the Kryl fungus. The membrane, which was a living, breathing thing, seemed to pull away from the artifact, as if it posed some kind of danger.

If Elya could just grab the geode and turn it back on, maybe they would have a chance of escaping.

"And knowledge," the mutant Kryl continued. "Like the Ancients before us, we will do whatever is necessary."

Ancients? Everyone knew the legends. The Ancients, or the Telos, were an ancient species of super-intelligent beings who had been old when humanity was still painting cave walls back on Old Earth. No one had ever met a living Telos, but xenoarchaeologists had discovered remnants of their great civilization scattered across a dozen different worlds— rotted tombs, abandoned temples, ancient cities half-sunk in the sand.

Some legends told of these Ancients sharing technology with Solarans during the Great Migration. Some people— conspiracy theorist types, mostly—believed that the hyperspace drive was a hand-me-down from the Telos. That was nonsense, of course. A figment of the Empire's collective imagination. It was easier to believe that a race of god-like beings far older and far more advanced than humanity helped lift us up into a spacefaring civilization, since most records of those eras had been lost to space and time. Easier, somehow, to believe in uplifted celestial beings than to accept that humanity had left the shores of paradise because their world was dying.

Elya had always supposed these were just stories. Myths. It was more interesting to imagine that the Ancients had chosen humanity. That they had blessed us, like the priest believed Animus had blessed him. But Elya knew how stories got warped by the passing of time. Half the ones people told of the invasion of Yuzosix weren't true, and that tragic event had only occurred twelve years ago.

And yet…

Some part of him had always wanted to believe in the Telos. And the Kryl *had* been repelled by that geode and its green glow. There was power in that. And perhaps, if it were studied, knowledge, too.

"This is both necessary *and* inevitable," the mutant went on. "The Ancients left very specific instructions. We are simply following in their footsteps."

"You're crazy," Elya said. What the mutant was saying made no sense.

Elya formed a new objective. If he ever did make it out of here, he needed to take that relic with him. Deliver it to Admiral Miyaru, get it into the hands of Imperial scientists to study. He didn't know what the mutant was babbling about, but anything that could repel the Kryl was worth studying.

The mutant grabbed Hedrick's arm and dragged him away from his mother and onto a raised platform. "Now, where were we?"

Elya had noticed before that the boy was barefoot. Now,

he realized why. The gelatinous Kryl excretions glommed over his ankles, stabilizing and trapping Hedrick in place. The mutant picked up thick white tendrils of webbing, which were pulled out from the computer console, and attached them to Hedrick's temples. The boy's jaw went slack and Hedrick's eyes rolled into the back of his head as he moaned.

Heidi screamed and threw herself at the boy. Groundlings forced her back.

"Stop it! Leave him out of this," Elya demanded.

The Kryl didn't acknowledge him.

Hoping that if he kept the mutant talking, he could figure out a way to stop whatever it was planning to do to Hedrick, Elya said, "You expect me to believe anything you just said? Necessary *and* inevitable? Don't give me that high-minded crap. Not when you're torturing a helpless little boy."

The groundlings hemmed him in on every side. A sentinel had even compressed its bulk to fit through the door and stood blocking the main entrance. The only other exit was the hole Hedgebot had cut in the back wall. No way he'd make it there. Not unless he left Hedrick and Heidi here to fend for themselves, and he wasn't willing to do that.

The boy arched his back and cried out as the platform on which he stood came to life. The gelatinous goop seethed with electricity, dimming the lights in the building. Energy coursed through the fungus covering Hedrick's legs, little lightning arcs that crawled and sparked like a miniature storm.

Heidi collapsed in a sobbing heap. Elya watched helplessly as the goop on Hedrick's feet began to harden, fading from translucent to opaque before his eyes, and then hardening into a shell and forming the first layer of carapace that marked all Kryl.

Elya's mouth twisted in horror as he glanced from the

suffering boy's feet to the leering mutant, who produced a writhing worm pinched between a thumb and forefinger. It lifted the worm out and held it over Hedrick's head.

In a flash of understanding, Elya realized the xeno was turning Hedrick into a Kryl-human hybrid—just like the mutant.

Heidi must have come to the same conclusion Elya had. Before he could think to move, she launched herself at her son, screeching and sobbing as she scrabbled to reach him. Spittle flew from her mouth as several groundlings restrained her with their bodies and claws. She struggled against their grip and continued to cry hoarsely. Though these Kryl were all born killers, they didn't harm her. Apparently the mutant in charge got a thrill out of having them all watch.

Or, it had other plans for them.

Elya moved toward Hedrick, but a single blow from the mutant xeno's monstrous Kryl arm knocked him to the floor.

As he staggered to his feet, Elya caught sight of the priest. Father Pohl's remaining eye had gone impossibly wide as he stared in horror at the scene. "You!" Elya stabbed a finger at the priest. "This is all your fault! Do you see what you've done?"

Father Pohl's mouth worked soundlessly.

"Did you know he was planning on turning the boy into a xeno?"

He shook his head. *No.*

"And you thought Animus was protecting you? Well, you were wrong. You're a liar and a fraud. The only thing you're leading people to is their destruction. Do you see now? *Do you see?*"

The priest's eye darted toward the relic then hardened into orbs of agate. "Animus protect me."

Not a statement. A prayer.

Father Pohl took one step and lunged for the relic.

The mutant xeno had just finished planting the worm on Hedrick's head. The tiny parasite disappeared up the boy's nose. As the mutant turned, it brought its bulky Kryl arm heavily across the back of Father Pohl's neck.

Remarkably, the priest didn't go down right away. He stumbled into the counter and managed to claw the artifact into his hands.

Elya watched, dumbstruck, as a sentinel charged across the room, bellowed into the priest's face, and seized him by the neck. It lifted the priest into the air by one arm, his feet kicking beneath the hem of his robe as the creature strangled him.

The geode slipped out of Father Pohl's fingers and bounced off a hardened part of the Kryl fungus covering the floor.

It rolled forward and came to rest almost exactly halfway between Elya and the mutant.

Time slowed, the way it sometimes did in the cockpit of a Sabre. He became simultaneously aware of everything around him—Hedrick's whimpering cries, Heidi's sniffles and sobs as she shoved uselessly against the groundlings holding her, the priest's choked gasps as he struggled to avoid getting his windpipe crushed in the sentinel's massive paw—

The mutant Kryl staring Elya down—

Even the small Kryl creature with sickly yellow spikes in its back, which glowed softly as it climbed across the ceiling above him, hanging by a single claw over the mutant's head.

Wait, he thought. *That's no Kryl!*

Elya locked eyes with the mutant as Hedgebot released its hold on the ceiling and landed on the mutant's face, brightening like a sunflare, blinding orange-white. The mutant cried out and clawed at Hedgebot, ripping the bot off its face and dashing it against the wall.

Elya darted forward two strides and then dropped to the ground, his momentum carrying him forward.

The ancient relic slid right into his hands.

He gripped the round base of the geode and rotated the handle clockwise, hoping for the best while preparing himself for the worst.

TWENTY-FOUR

Casey lowered her Sabre until she was a few hundred meters over the treetops of the endless, lush forest crowding up against the foothills. Lieutenant Yorra mirrored her movements, angling about a hundred meters off her left wing. They flew north, paralleling the mountain range, in thirty kilometer strips. On each pass, they ranged farther out from where they'd discovered Nevers' battered cube. Minutes ticked by at an aggravatingly quick pace, yet they found no sign of their missing compatriot.

"Earth damn him!" Casey punched the dashboard. "Where could he have gone?"

She pictured the damaged cube they'd passed off to Major Antonin and the others as they rotated back to the *Paladin*. Her worst fears crowded her thoughts. "This is all my fault."

"What?" Yorra's voice sounded high and tinny in her helmet. "If it weren't for you, we wouldn't still be down here looking for him."

Casey just shook her head. "I should have stopped him from chasing that drone."

"You tried, Raptor. He ignored you. And then Admiral

Miyaru RemOp'd your starfighter when you tried to go after him."

"There's more. I didn't tell you before because the admiral didn't want me to, but I need you to know so you don't try to stop me from taking the blame. It's my fault that parasite got into the hangar—it rode piggyback on my Sabre." The words kept spilling out. Casey couldn't stop the flood. "Which means it's my fault Perry and Colonel Walcott are dead. Not to mention hurting you, and Park. He…" She choked on the words, but forced them out anyway. Her voice cracked. "He may have permanent internal damage, all because of me."

"Naab is tough and our medics are the best in the Fleet. He'll make a full recovery, just you wait and see."

"And now we can't locate Nevers. It's all my fault."

"Respectfully, Captain, shut the hell up. It is *not* your fault."

Her anger rose up. "Excuse me? Is that any way to speak to your captain?"

"I'll speak to her any way I deem necessary, sir, when she's got her head this far up her own ass."

Casey blinked. Coming from anyone else, that would have summoned forth a fiery retort. Coming from a close friend like Yorra, the insult somehow shocked her and cleared the fog of blame and self-hatred. She finally stopped rambling.

Casey blinked tears out of her eyes. Yorra was right. As much as Casey looked outside of herself for approval, she also had a tendency to take on the burdens of those she cared about most. Some of this was her fault, certainly. Maybe if she hadn't berated Nevers so hard before the mission, he would have listened to her when she told him not to pursue the Kryl drone.

But wishing wouldn't change the past.

After a minute of awkward silence, Casey said, chagrined, "Sorry, Gears."

"Apology accepted. Now let's keep searching for Fancypants, huh? I'm looking forward to giving him hell for being shot down by a Kryl drone when he's safely back on the *Paladin*."

Casey frowned, but decided to keep the *other* secret—about the drone's ability to phase through solid objects—to herself.

"It doesn't make sense," Yorra added. "Someone had to have put that cube up on the ridgeline. Other people passed by there."

"If there are still other people on Robichar, they're... I don't know, underground or something. Some place our scanners can't reach. The only sign of life we've found was the encampment the Kryl took over."

"What if...?" Yorra paused. "Never mind."

"What is it?" Casey demanded.

"It was a dumb idea."

"Tell me."

"Nothing."

"Gears, we only have half an hour left to locate Nevers. Spit it out."

She waited while Yorra cleared her throat. "What if... the Kryl captured him and it was them who put his cube up on the ridgeline?"

Casey felt her blood run cold. She'd be lying if she said the thought hadn't crossed her mind. She just hadn't been willing to voice it.

"There's one thing that doesn't make sense about that theory. The Kryl have their own weapons. They *are* weapons. So if it was Kryl who hid that cube on the ridgeline, why did it have blaster and bullet marks on it?"

The protocol to scuttle downed starfighters existed

because of the warp drives that were in some high-speed stealth reconnaissance ships, the broadbeam and tightbeam transmitters, and their radioisotope cores. Fleet intelligence certainly didn't want the Kryl to get their hands on those. But as far as guns, the xenos had never been interested. They ignored any carbines or sidearms they came across.

"I don't know," Yorra said, "maybe that happened before the Kryl took him."

"Hell, we haven't got any better ideas. Let's make one more pass over that encampment, see if we can find any sign of him."

Assuming the Kryl did have Nevers there, it seemed a grim prospect. The odds they would find him alive were slim. And if they did, they'd only have thirty minutes to plan and execute a rescue mission. It would take five just to get back to the old compound…

As they made their way south, the heat detection software overlaid on the landscape below her finally picked up signs of life that were larger than the small forest creatures they'd been picking up so far. As she studied the forms overlaid on her HUD, she picked out a group of four people—humans, undoubtedly—working their way at a rapid march through the forest, headed toward the Kryl compound.

"Yorra, do you see that?"

"Affirmative. These people could be the ones who left the cube up on that ridgeline."

"Maybe." *But why the hell are they running* towards *the Kryl encampment?*

Casey's shields pinged as a projectile ricocheted off her left wing. Her heart hammered in her chest as she swerved away. "Aaaaaand they're shooting at us."

"Who, the men or the Kryl?"

"The men!"

"Why would they do that?"

"I don't know."

As the compound rushed beneath them—a brief wound in the forest canopy, gaping wide—Casey studied the heat signatures of the four people in the forest, now well behind them, pressing a button to order the software in her starfighter to track them as she continued to focus on flying. The group of four were moving faster now, running and mowing down groundlings as they approached the compound.

"Be careful, they're armed *and* trained. Based on the way they're moving, I don't think they're carrying any ground-to-air missiles, but Animus knows those things get easier to hide every time I see a new model."

She wondered if Admiral Miyaru's orders would change given this new situation. Procedure dictated that she should provide an immediate status report, now that an enemy had fired upon them. She didn't want to, for fear that the admiral would tell her to abandon the rescue mission and return to the *Paladin*.

She hung her head. "Earth damn it all." She could only hope that Admiral Miyaru was still feeling generous.

She dialed her tightbeam into the *Paladin's* signal. To her surprise, Harmony answered immediately.

"Any luck locating the missing pilot, Captain?"

"Maybe, sir." It seemed wise to prevaricate so the AI didn't jump to any conclusions. She and Admiral Miyaru were a symbiotic unit and Casey needed this to go smoothly.

"You don't need to sir me, Captain. Harmony will do."

"Harmony, I'm afraid I have some bad news. We found more people down here. Four of them. Soldiers. They're armed and hostile." The thought riled her up enough that she rattled off the rest of the report with crisp efficiency as, with subconscious ease, Casey pulled the Sabre around and veered back toward the occupied compound. "One of them may even have a high-powered gauss rifle. They shot at my Sabre and then slaughtered a handful of Kryl. The only good bug is a dead bug, so I can't be mad about that, but I don't see why they would shoot at *us*. Are there any other forces on Robichar?"

"Negative, Captain. Yourself, Lieutenant Yorra and Captain Nevers are the only ones left on Robichar, according to my tracking system."

That meant that whoever those four men were, they weren't SDF. At least, they weren't *anymore*. "Civilians, then?"

If they were here to kill Kryl, who was she to stop them?

Yorra chimed in: "Don't they know the Kryl are coming?"

"Of course they know, they just mowed down a dozen groundlings."

"What I mean is, do they know the rest of the hive is coming? Otherwise, why haven't they evacuated?"

"It's possible they do not, if they lived somewhere remote and did not receive the Imperial missive," Harmony said. "We've already met our quota of civilians for the evacuation based on the Empire's colonial census data and calculations for mission-acceptable losses."

It was chilling to hear the AI talk so cold and statistically like that, but Casey supposed even the most advanced emotive functions couldn't make an AI truly empathetic to human loss of life. Casey frowned. She also couldn't summon much sympathy. If an armed militia wanted to stay here and fight off the Kryl hive, let them. All she cared about was getting Nevers back to the *Paladin* in one piece.

"Captain," Yorra said with a rising inflection. "I think you'll want to see this."

Casey's eyes roved across the ground toward a commotion in the compound. A ragged hole had been torn in the side of a prefab building. A dozen Kryl stumbled out in what her father would have called a rout. They moved in a disorderly, panicked way, climbing over and around each other in a desperate attempt to gain some distance from the building. The creature who had made it the farthest was a massive, bulky sentinel. It clutched its comically small head, which looked like a baseball on top of a giant slug from her bird's-eye view.

In the shadows cast by the late afternoon sun, a vibrant green light pulsed out of the hole in the prefab.

"What in the hell?"

She turned her scanner on the damaged building in question. It was placed second from the end in a row of identical prefabs. The scanner showed it lit up like a small star, emitting light and low-level radiation to the area around it, so much that she could barely make out the forms inside.

She counted four, maybe five—hard to tell—life forms remaining inside. Every Kryl that stumbled out seemed to be suffering in some way. Once the creatures made it far enough away from the building, they shook their bodies and hissed in anger, but didn't attempt to retrace their steps. It was like some kind of invisible barrier was holding them back. The radiation? The light? By the Spirit of Old Earth, what was going on inside that building?

As she was circling in the sky watching the chaos below and thinking these thoughts, her mind trying to puzzle out what would be an appropriate course of action in this situation, two more life forms made their way to the exit—Solarans, not Kryl.

She expected them to be suffering as well, but when they emerged, they seemed unaffected by the radiation.

"Is that a kid?"

Unless her eyes had gone bad, it was a mother and a child. They were frightened and obviously in quite a hurry, but otherwise unaffected by what was happening to the Kryl.

Something else darted out of the ragged hole in the side

of the building and into the green-tinted shadows. A tiny creature, maybe a Kryl. The woman and child followed it. They moved in the opposite direction from the rest of the Kryl, toward the fence. She noticed that a skimmer bike lay on the other side.

Yorra gasped. "Is that... Hedgebot?"

Casey's eyes widened as the pilot's words kickstarted her awareness. Once she said it, Casey, too, recognized Nevers' bot.

"Harmony!" Casey shouted. "We've got a sign of Nevers. His astrobot is on the ground."

"Do you have visual confirmation of the pilot?" Admiral Miyaru's voice came on the line suddenly, causing Casey to jump.

"No, sir, not yet." Casey flicked the safety on her weapons to the *Off* position. "But I'm not gonna wait around to find out. Nevers doesn't go anywhere without that bot."

"What's your plan, Captain?"

"Increase his odds of survival," Casey said. She laid her finger into the trigger, aiming at the big, heavily armored Kryl clutching his tiny head just outside the edge of the glowing circle of green twenty meters from the prefab building. She pressed the button down as she yelled, "Get some!"

TWENTY-FIVE

When Elya twisted the handle of the geode, revealing three triangular apertures in the round part of the stone, a wave of bright green light washed out from his position like a shockwave, deafening him.

It took Elya several seconds to realize that it wasn't the artifact making the noise, but rather horrible, keening cries coming from the throat of every Kryl in the building, and probably some outside. Even the sticky lichen coating the floor seemed to be writhing in agony.

The sentinel dropped the priest, clutched its massive arm against one side of its gumball head, and charged into the nearest wall, sending computer equipment crashing to the floor and squashing half a dozen chrysalises under foot as it scrambled to escape the light's reach. Its enormous thrashing arms ripped a hole in the prefab building, peeling it back like a metal can and slicing itself on the sharpened edges as it wriggled outside.

The groundlings also went mad, abandoning their hold on Heidi to clutch their forelimbs over their earholes as they screamed. They staggered around like they were drunk or half paralyzed, their back limbs wobbling and unable to support their weight, until they, too, reached the open air.

That left Heidi, Hedrick, Father Pohl, Elya and Hedgebot with the Kryl mutant, who also seemed to be in pain, but wasn't nearly as incapacitated as the others. The only thing Elya could figure is that since he was partially human, he had a partial immunity to the relic's effects.

And that was worrisome. Because he seemed to be the most dangerous of all.

"Hedgebot, get the woman and the boy out of here!" Elya shouted.

The boy squinted, clutched his head and moaned in pain. Was the relic's power affecting him too, now that the parasite had crawled up his nose? Hedrick reared up and sneezed, once, twice. On the third go, snot shot out of his nose onto the floor and in the yellowish-clear liquid, a parasite writhed.

Elya thrust the geode down at it. The parasite squirmed in the puddle of mucus, affected by the power of the emerald light. Elya brought his boot down on the worm and ground it into paste. As the worm died, so too did the xeno exoskeleton that had formed around the boy's feet. It began to melt, dripping strands of loose mucus to the floor as it liquified.

Elya lifted Hedrick from the platform where he cowered and thrust him into Heidi's arms. "Go! Take Thom's skimmer bike. Don't look back."

Heidi nodded as she took her dazed son and hurried away.

As she went, the Kryl mutant staggered to his feet, its faceted xeno eye squinting in pain.

"No," it said, mandibles clacking around its very human tongue. "No, he belongs to us now. Overmind X needs him."

Elya raised the glowing artifact and thrust it toward the mutant xeno, who raised its arms and fell back, giving Heidi room to slip out of the opening.

"You stupid Imperial pawn," Father Pohl spat as he, too, limped upright, using both hands to steady himself against the slimy webbed wall. "You've just killed my people. As good as murdered us in our sleep."

"You did that, you traitor," Elya said. "How could you steal the boy from his mother and bring him here? How could you?"

Elya felt rage rising within him. Now that he had the artifact in his hand, he was in control. The Kryl couldn't harm him. Father Pohl was too weakened by his injuries to do much damage. But now he understood the priest's previous attitude. No wonder the man hadn't been afraid of the Kryl. With something as powerful as this Telos relic in his possession, of course he'd deluded himself into believing he could keep his people safe.

"You brought me the boy!" Father Pohl said. "We didn't have any children with us. But then you brought him to me, and I didn't have a choice! That was the agreement."

What could the Overmind possibly want with Hedrick, or any other human child for that matter? The Kryl had murdered countless millions since the conflict between the two races began fifty years ago, during invasions just like this one. They could have taken a child from Yuzosix. They could have taken Elya himself twelve years ago, if they had wanted to.

What was so different about this time? What had changed?

Elya sneered at Father Pohl. The old priest had gone off the deep end if he thought Elya was to blame for what he did. "The only one responsible for your suffering is yourself. You could have chosen to evacuate along with everyone else."

"I had a plan to keep my people safe! Until you lot showed up."

"Any plan that involves sacrificing the life of a young boy

to keep yourself safe is no plan at all. You're as bad as the Kryl if you're willing to trade the life of an innocent child for your own protection."

"This is my home! I refuse to be driven off by these god-forsaken xenos. Disgusting, godless creatures. And I found that relic. It's mine. Give it back!"

The priest lunged at Elya, who sidestepped the fumbling charge and brought his free elbow down on the back of the man's neck. Father Pohl tried to get up, but his arms trembled and he collapsed. He moaned as his face struck the ground.

Elya turned to the mutant Kryl, who was still twitching with the effort of staying in the same room as the ghostly green ambience emitted by the ancient relic. "And you. What did you try to do to the boy? What was that thing you put up his nose?"

The Kryl just smiled at him and gestured to its own face. "We've had some time to perfect the technique." It glanced toward an empty chrysalis which, Elya realized as he turned his head, was perfectly boy-sized. "I was subject zero. The first patient in her grand experiment. It nearly killed me, you know. The pain of that relic is nothing like what I lived through during the conversion. But I nearly killed her, too, so it was only fair."

Elya took a step back out of involuntary revulsion. Subject Zero kept staring at him, and though he wanted to turn away, Elya found he couldn't.

"Grand experiment? What are you talking about?"

"They kept my vital organs alive by putting me in one of those." Subject Zero nodded toward the chrysalis. "Most of my body perished, but after some adjustments they managed to find the right balance of proteins and chemicals needed to sustain me."

This seemed to confirm his theory of why the power of

the ancient relic was dampened for the mutant. He was part-human, and the relic only seemed to affect Kryl, not Solarans. Elya studied the human half of his face, the brown eye. Something about that eye seemed so familiar, but he couldn't place it. Perhaps Elya merely saw his own humanity reflected back in the mutant's twisted visage and didn't want to believe it was possible.

"So what, you were going to put the boy through the same hell? Turn him into some kind of deformed monstrosity like you?"

Subject Zero spread its mandible mouth. The grin revealed a few scattered human teeth. The left side of the jaw was missing entirely.

A cold fear tingled through Elya's chest and into his extremities.

"You knew about this, priest?" Elya couldn't bring himself to call the old man "Father" anymore.

The priest had rolled into a seated position. He used the wall to lift himself back to his feet. He limped toward Elya. His missing eye was a gory black hole in his head. His face twisted and he clasped his hands before him in supplication.

"She came to me. I had no choice. Once she knew I had it, she'd never stop coming after me no matter where I was in the galaxy. You have to believe me. It was the best I could make of a terrible situation. I prayed on it. Animus said he would protect me. He told me to gather a flock and lead them into the mountains, but *no* children. The Overmind wants the children. She told me so."

"Animus," Elya scoffed and spat at the priest's feet. "That wasn't Animus talking. It was your own cowardice you heard."

"NO!" the priest said. "No. No, you don't understand. They would have killed us all. Who do you think alerted the Empire that the Kryl were becoming a nuisance on

Robichar? If it weren't for me, *nobody* would have gotten out in time. How do you think they knew the hive was on the move in the first place?"

"The Empire is always keeping tabs on roving Kryl hives," Elya said. But he was no longer sure.

The mutant was grinning again. Drool hung from its lower mandible, its pincers trembling with the pain the relic was causing.

"I was trying to save Robichar," the priest went on. "Once the Kryl came and took what they wanted, they would leave. Then we could rebuild. Robichar would recover!"

'There's no recovering a planet invaded by the Kryl," Elya said, disgusted. "They sucked the oceans dry on Yuzosix."

"She would have left Robichar whole! That was the agreement."

Elya looked back at the mutant. "Would your Overmind X have upheld her end of the bargain? Once you got what you wanted, would you have left?"

An inky darkness spread through the mutant's eyes. Its wide grin faltered and its shoulders jerked forward with a cracking sound of ligaments sliding over bones. Attenuated legs unfolded from the creature's back and Subject Zero fell forward onto hairy, clawed feet. The head with half a human face lifted and twisted at an unnatural angle.

"We would have sucked this world dry." The voice that came out of the mutant's mouth was not its own. It had a distant, echoey quality as if coming from a different room. Elya noted the look of pure fear that came over Father Pohl's face. As the voice resounded, he began to tremble and inch back toward the tear in the wall. "And we still shall if we do not obtain the weapons of the Ancient Ones. Their relics are our... *Inheritance.*"

Something about the way the human side of the monster's face gleamed with pleasure when it uttered this absurd statement triggered an old memory in Elya—bizarrely, one of his fondest memories.

He had been sitting in a holoscreen booth in the library on Yuzosix, one of the nice ones you had to book a week in advance in one-hour time slots. Elya used to go there to explore archival footage from the Kryl War. After sorting through countless press conferences, news stories, theories, and lectures given by xenobiologists, Elya had finally landed on a set of recordings of the Fleet's finest. His hands had shaken with excitement when he realized he was holding actual battle footage. From a relatively minor offworld skirmish, granted, but *actual* footage of *actual* pilots flying *actual* starfighters was, in itself, exhilarating.

Later, Elya had come to know the cockpit-cam perspective very well, but back then it had all been new. The way it jerked and twirled with the pilot nauseated him at first. But Elya stuck with it, watching from beginning to end, over and over again.

The final moment of the footage was his favorite. After the drones were all destroyed and the Scimitars returned to the destroyer to dock, there was a moment when the pilot hopped out of his seat and squatted down to grin into the camera lens, a mad twinkle in the man's eye.

It was the first time Elya had seen candid footage of his childhood hero—Captain Ruidiaz, the man who attacked the Queen Mother and drove the Kryl horde back to their home planet, ushering in the end of an era, the end of the war, and over a decade of peace.

The human half of the mutant Kryl's face… it belonged to Captain Ruidiaz.

Elya lifted his knee to his chest and drove a combat boot into the Kryl's face, then brought the geode down next to the mutant's skin. The green light was thickest where it emerged from the triangular apertures in the artifact. As the emerald glow poured over the Kryl, it melted the creature's carapace like acid.

The half-Kryl, half-human mandible mouth opened as the creature began to scream. Though his whole body cringed in disgust, Elya forced himself to move forward.

Subject Zero scrambled backward on its spiderlegs. The darkness faded from its eyes, and the sharp intelligence of Ruidiaz's brown eye returned, along with the shiny faceted nature of the Kryl eye. As Elya advanced and brought the lantern close, it lunged at Elya.

He raised the geode up to defend himself and gasped when the creature passed right through him.

In a singular, flowing motion, the mutant kicked itself upright, folded the spider-like arms into its back, and phased through the wall.

Just like the drone had phased through his Sabre.

The priest gawked at the wall in stunned silence, then turned to stare hungrily at the relic, eyes darting up to Elya. The man bared his teeth, covered his injured eye with one hand, and stepped outside through the ragged opening opposite the wall through which Ruidiaz had disappeared.

Elya cursed. He hurried outside after the priest.

Father Pohl was just stepping out of the alley and onto the blood-encrusted parade ground, the soil of which had been torn up by the scraping of hundreds of Kryl claws as the creatures ran from the power of the ancient relic. Elya closed the distance.

"Elya!" Heidi called from behind him. "Watch out!"

He heeded her warning and pulled up short. Father Pohl also heard her, and he turned in time to face a mad sentinel bearing down on him. The priest was struck by the thousand-kilo creature running full speed. He went flying backward and struck the ground hard, his body rolling limply across the dirt.

Elya felt a moment's satisfaction that quickly turned to sickening pity for the priest. The sentinel carried onward, past the priest's body. The groundlings began to run in that direction as well, the direction he assumed Subject Zero—Captain Ruidiaz—had gone.

A new noise intruded through the chaos of retreating Kryl—the soft roar of starfighter engines. Their sound increased in pitch until they were straight overhead. Guns blazed as the lead Sabre mowed down the panicking groundlings and remaining sentinel, still retreating. A second Sabre joined the fight.

Elya whooped loudly. He turned back to Heidi and Hedrick, who stood, mouth hanging open next to her, staring up at the starfighters and watching the carnage. Whatever innocence that boy had possessed, it was gone now.

But he was alive. And that was a win.

"I guess now we're even," Elya said to Heidi. "I saved your life, and you saved mine. Now, let's find some cover until they can land!"

Elya waved with both arms, one hand still gripping the relic.

The Sabres rocked their wings back and forth as if to say, *Acknowledged. We see you, Nevers. We're here to take you home.*

TWENTY-SIX

The swarm of drones was so close now that they colored the backdrop of space a mottled purple and off-black. And when the gas giant around which Robichar orbited, with its swirling yellow storms and streaks of brown and blue moved behind the swarm, it seemed as if Admiral Kira Miyaru's view of the planet was partially blocked by another cloud.

Only the swarm was no cloud. It was a suffocating army of mindless killers.

The trembling voice of a Mammoth captain came online. "Admiral, permission to jump?"

"Granted," Kira replied without hesitation.

The Mammoth nearest the *Paladin* in the viewscreen stretched, elongating, and then snapped forward as it made the transition into hyperspace.

That left two Mammoths. Just two.

Captain Osprey better hurry the hell up, she thought.

"The array is in position and locked, Admiral," Colonel Volk said. "Permission to engage?"

"Fire at will," Kira said.

Colonel Volk nodded at Major Loris, the weapons officer, who referenced a time-stamped code as she punched a sequence into the concave holoscreen. Once the sequence was authorized by Harmony, there was a faint humming noise, a vibration Kira felt through the soles of her boots, and then lasers raked over the swarm of Kryl drones.

The lasers were invisible to the naked eye, but Harmony overlaid a reddish light on the viewscreen so that the bridge could see where their weapons were hitting. Visible explosions—not modified by the AI—sprang up across hundreds of drones at once. Debris scattered as the nearest wave of drones began to combust. They popped and sputtered, like a cosmic being had thrown a handful of salt into a gas burner.

A counter Harmony placed in a corner of the main viewscreen began to tick up from seventy, to two hundred, higher and higher. It finally settled on four hundred and fifty eight.

The cloud of drones barely seemed diminished by the losses. They didn't slow their advance or even flinch. Kira wondered—not for the first time—if the Kryl had any compassion for their own kind. Did they feel loss, or fear? Did the Overmind controlling this swarm force them forward against their will, or did they fly happily to their deaths?

"Again," she ordered.

Colonel Volk relayed her orders. They began to warm up the laser array for a second pass. It took several minutes for the lasers to charge enough to do the damage they needed them to do. In the meantime, projectiles and missiles were fired, taking out handfuls of drones at a time. The XO paced across the bridge with long, anxious strides. Kira forced herself to sink into the command couch and be still. Her officers needed to see a calm, level head in charge, despite the anxiety she felt churning in her gut.

"Admiral, you have an incoming transmission from Captain Osprey."

She checked the time. The pilots should be on their way back by now. Kira hoped this was good news.

"Open the line." The level of background noise changed to the familiar sound of engines dampened by the sound-proofing material lining the Sabre's cockpit. "Captain. Any issues getting off the ground?"

"No, sir. We just cleared Robichar's atmosphere."

Kira closed her eyes and took a deep breath. "I'm glad to hear that, Captain Osprey. Avoid the swarm of drones on your way back to the *Paladin*."

"Yes, sir, I see that on my lidar. We charted a route around them."

If she didn't have any other news, she would have simply contacted flight control. She was obviously holding something back. "Is there something else, Captain?"

"Nevers wasn't alone when we found him, sir. We're bringing two civilian refugees up with us."

She frowned. "There's no time to transfer them to a Mammoth. We'll carry them on the *Paladin* until we get back to Ariadne."

"Admiral, this is Captain Nevers on the search and rescue shuttle. Osprey thought you'd want to hear this personally. I'm pretty sure I met the Overmind down there... through a sort of proxy. A hybrid mutant, half Kryl and half human."

Kira inhaled sharply and gripped the arms of the command couch so hard her hands shook. *That's impossible*, she thought.

But was it? This evacuation had been full of strange occurrences. First, the phasing ability of the manned Kryl drone. Then the parasites that had driven two men mad. Why not a Kryl-human hybrid, too?

The xenos were evolving, all right. Evolving more inventive—and possibly more effective—ways to kill Solarans.

Her heart pounded in her chest as these thoughts flitted through her mind. Taken together, all of this evidence should be more than enough to convince the Colonization Board to finally halt their eager expansion into distant, indefensible areas of space, like they'd done with Robichar; maybe even enough to convince the Emperor himself to come out of his pleasure palace and take an interest in the affairs of his people for a change.

If the Kryl were back on the offensive, the Solaran Empire needed to prepare for war.

TWENTY-SEVEN

Quarantine in the hangar was a new thing. Both Elya and Captain Osprey were quickly cleared. Hedrick went through next. When the boy entered the scanner, Heidi met Elya's eyes through the clear plastic walls of the quarantine bay. There was a tense moment where the AI hesitated... then the green light went on and the boy was allowed through.

Heidi and Hedrick were escorted to the hospital to get checked out by the medics. Elya delivered the geode into Admiral Miyaru's hands personally for safe-keeping, then talked to flight control and got himself assigned to a new Sabre.

On his way to the starfighter, Elya stopped by the bot machinist's station and checked out a replacement power source for Hedgebot. When the new battery was inserted, Hedgebot rolled onto his feet, made his body very small and compact with upturned bristles, and cycled through a rainbow of colors. It took the bot a few moments to recalibrate before it beeped questioningly.

"We're back on the *Paladin*, buddy," Elya said. "Now, come on. We've still got work to do."

BEEP beep. Hedgebot shook his body like a wet dog. Translation: *Really, man?*

"Afraid so. Can't let the squad down."

The Sabre that was standing by for him had been preflighted, so all he had to do was put on his helmet, seal the cockpit and get comfortable. Elya looked around and took a headcount. "Where's Naab?"

Osprey and Yorra were in their Sabres beside him, but Park was nowhere to be found.

"He's still in the sick bay, recovering," Yorra said darkly.

"Recovering? What happened?"

"Bit of a long story," Osprey said. "Would have told you on the flight up but we were distracted talking about other things." Most of their conversation had revolved around Elya's encounters with the Kryl, Heidi and Hedrick, Father Pohl and his followers. And then, of course, relaying the most important news—about the Overmind's desire to collect the Telos artifacts and turn children into mutants, not necessarily in that order—to Admiral Miyaru.

"Don't worry, Fancypants," Yorra chimed in, "he's tougher than some Kryl parasite. Naab will be back cracking jokes and rolling spliffs before you know it."

Elya's stomach dropped out, a feeling reminiscent of high-speed maneuvers in his starfighter but caused by a terrible recognition. He'd kept the bit about the parasite to himself. He'd figured there was no reason to make trouble where there wasn't any, and was vindicated when Hedrick cleared quarantine. Now, he knew why the quarantine procedure had been put into place initially. "Did you say parasite?"

"Some xeno parasites hitched a ride on my Sabre and got loose on the *Paladin* while you were gone," Osprey said. "Two of them wormed their way into the heads of a couple crew and made them go crazy. We thought it was space madness at first, but as it turned out…"

Elya closed his eyes and let himself feel waves of helpless sorrow roll through him as Osprey told the story of how Petty Officer Mick Perry had been infected and blown himself up, causing the death of Lieutenant Colonel Walcott and injuring several others, including Park, in the process. This explained the caution tape around a repair in the corner of the hangar he'd noticed on the way to his starfighter.

Osprey was ordered to pull her Sabre into position for launch, so Yorra picked up the thread and told Elya how Park had woken up in the sick bay and started acting the same way the mechanic had.

"But we recognized the pattern and managed to corner him. Raptor forced him into the surgical bot, and the thing extracted this tiny Kryl parasite."

"Extracted? You didn't destroy it?"

"No," Yorra said, "From what I understand, Admiral Miyaru is keeping it locked up somewhere so that Imperial scientists can study it when we get back to Ariadne."

"Can I see it?" Elya told them he thought it was the same kind of worm Subject Zero had tried to put up Hedrick's nose. He asked if there were any more, but they told him that Harmony scanned the entire destroyer and had found no other xenoforms aboard.

"That's messed up," Yorra said. "No wonder the boy looked so traumatized. Not to mention exhausted. The search and rescue pilots said he slept most of the flight up."

"Admiral Miyaru is going to want to hear this herself," Osprey added.

"We've got a lot to catch up on," Elya said. He'd glossed over the part about the relic's abilities. He was waiting to show that to Admiral Miyaru personally, when there was more time, and now it sounded like he might even have a subject for a live demonstration. "But the mission's not over yet."

"Right you are. Furies one-eight, check?"

"Two," Elya said.

"Three," said Lt. Yorra. "Let's frag some Kryl."

Most of the wing was already deployed, so they didn't have to wait long. A few ships ahead of them had come back for minor repairs or refuels. In a handful of minutes they were rocketing out of the hangar and into space.

They switched over to the Fleet comms with attentive mic discipline. When they had received their orders, Captain Osprey repeated them to her flight—a team Elya was glad to be a part of, knowing their squadron's numbers had been depleted in the short time he'd been gone—and even more so knowing that he almost didn't make it back.

Never before had he felt such camaraderie with the other pilots.

"There's just one Mammoth left. We're flying patrol. Keep the drones from getting within firing range and be on the lookout for torpedoes."

"Wilco, Raptor," Elya said as he pressed a button in front of him. Wing-mounted blasters unfolded from their internal bays. He couldn't see them from where he sat in the pilot's seat, but he heard the metallic clacking sound as they extended. Hedgebot, too, clicked his claws along the edges of the cockpit as he climbed overhead, clinging to the tiny seams between the frame and the transparent aluminite panels of the cockpit shell and pulsing a soft blue-green.

"I'm glad to be back too, pal," Elya muttered. "Believe me."

Elya took a deep breath and exhaled a great sigh of satisfaction. Another pilot might have been scared to climb back into the cockpit after a crash landing like he'd experienced.

But for him, there was no place he'd rather be. It felt good to have his hands back on the stick again.

Elya closed his eyes and cast a prayer out into the great deep dark—to the universe, to Animus, to the spirit of Old Earth itself—a prayer of gratitude.

Thank you for letting me get back on the horse.

He'd never seen a horse except in Old Earth paintings, but the ancient maxim was clear.

Elya flicked his broadbeam channel to squad-only comms. "Time to ride!"

"Yeah!" Yorra's grin practically seethed through the channel. "It's a bug roast."

"Stay alert, Flight 18," Captain Osprey cautioned.

In a moment, he understood why. As they came around the destroyer, Elya saw them, a seemingly endless swarm of insectoid drones dotting the black expanse of space as far as the eye could see, filling every inch of emptiness and bearing down on the last Mammoth. The vast mass of Kryl hadn't been this close on the ride up. They had made progress while his flight was re-deploying.

Now, they were so numerous they blotted out his view of Robichar.

"Earth's last light!" Elya said. "There are so many of them…" Squadrons of Sabres were already engaged in battle. "We must be outnumbered a hundred to one."

"All we need to do," Osprey responded, "is keep them away long enough for the Mammoth to jump to hyperspace."

Elya knew that only one or two ships at a time could initiate jumps from the same region without destabilizing the fabric of space-time. This last Mammoth had to wait and, while they waited, the Kryl drew near… the admiral was cutting it awfully close.

Elya gazed through a gap in the drone cloud toward the Kryl mothership. She was too far away to see more than a bright speck, but he could tell she had parked in geosynchronous orbit and had begun to send landing vessels burning through the atmosphere of Robichar.

"They're landing on the moon. Shouldn't we be trying to stop them?"

"Those aren't our orders," Captain Osprey said.

"Roger that," Elya responded. Though he wanted to drop nukes on the larger ships and save Robichar from the invasion they were about to endure—even if the vast majority of citizens had already been evacuated—he knew from experience what disobeying orders could lead to, so he bit his tongue and did as Captain Osprey said.

They joined the melee. Elya directed his anger and fear toward smoking bogeys—he got two before a torpedo launched toward the Mammoth.

"Not this time," Elya muttered as he fired one of his auto-targeted seeking missiles and eliminated the threat before it even got close enough to scare the Mammoth.

No matter how many bugs they squashed, the swarm kept coming. There seemed to be a limitless supply of drones. Unlike the manned drone that had shot him down on Robichar, these didn't seem to be very talented pilots.

"Where do they get all these damned drones?"

A countdown began across the Fleet-wide broadbeam.

"Ten, nine, eight…"

Elya fired his guns, shooting another drone.

"Seven, six, five…"

Lieutenant Yorra and Captain Osprey took out a drone apiece.

"Four, three, two…"

Elya narrowly ducked a drone that had been beaming straight toward him. He sped up, laid on his thrusters and came around upside down relative to Robichar, so that the tail number on the Mammoth appeared inverted from his point of view.

"One."

The Mammoth streaked forward as it jumped into hyperspace.

A great cheer poured through his comms.

"Well done, starfighters," said Admiral Miyaru over the broadbeam. "All Mammoths have jumped to safety. The evacuation is complete. All units return to the *Paladin* ASAP so we can join them."

More cheering. The frequency of the commander's message changed as she piped into their flight's private channel.

"Captain Osprey, Captain Nevers," she said. "Report to War Room Two for debrief." And she signed off.

"And that's our cue," Captain Osprey said. "Head back to the destroyer, Furies. Feel free to deal with stragglers on the way, but no major detours."

Elya leaned back in his seat and closed his eyes, breathing deeply, satisfied. Although he'd been training with the Fleet for years, for the first time, Elya felt clearly that whatever good they'd done here, none of it would have been possible without his team. Because they refused to leave him on Robichar, Elya was given the opportunity to once again be part of something bigger than himself.

Elya opened the broadbeam channel as they were coming back around to the *Paladin of Abniss*. "Hey, Raptor. I gotta say something."

She paused. "You know you're on the broadbeam, right, Fancypants?"

Earth, how he hated that nickname. Elya fired his last missile and took out a drone that had veered into their path. It had separated from the bulk of the swarm, ventured off alone, and wham, space dust. He refused to let himself walk that road any longer.

"I do," he said in his calmest voice.

"All right. Go ahead."

"I owe you an apology, Captain. I'm sorry. I should have listened to you. The truth is, some part of me will *always* be a refugee. Being down there on Robichar gave me a chance to relive that—to remember what it feels like to be trapped. Hunted. To have your exits cut off from you." He took a deep breath. "To feel completely powerless. If I'm being honest, that's why I spend so much extra time in the sim. But more training time won't make a lick of difference if we don't stick together. In fact, it puts us all in danger. I see that now and I'm sorry."

"You don't have to go it alone," she replied.

"And I'm grateful for it. For not giving up. For coming to get me. I owe you."

"This one's on us, Nevers," Yorra chimed in. "The Fightin' Furies watch each other's backs!"

"That's right," Osprey replied, her smile brightening her voice. Though he couldn't see her face at the moment, Elya could picture her jutting her chin forward, fierce and proud. "You're stuck with us now, whether you like it or not."

TWENTY-EIGHT

Captain Osprey and Captain Nevers stood and saluted
sharply when Kira stepped into the war room.

This was a different room than she and the young captain
had spoken in previously, but it was identical in layout. An
octagonal table took up most of the floor space in the middle
of the room, with a desk-mounted holoprojector that,
instead of Robichar, now showed Harmony's glittering
female avatar of choice. Captain Osprey's eyes slid sideways
as she recognized her own form in the AI's hologram, and
one of her eyebrows lifted slightly. If she thought Harmony's
obsession with her odd, she didn't comment on it.

Kira nodded at the two young officers before resting her
gaze on Nevers. He had dark circles under his eyes and bore
several cuts and bruises along his face and jawline, but for
the most part seemed healthy and unharmed.

"Glad to see you made it back in one piece, Captain."

"Thank you, sir. It's good to be back."

"How are you holding up?"

"Well, sir, all things considered, I think Hedgebot took
more damage than I did."

300

The round form that had been perched unmoving on his shoulder elongated its body. "Is one of his legs different than the others?"

"Yes, sir. Emergency field operation."

Kira smiled. "Smart thinking."

"He saved my life more than once, sir. Don't know what I'd have done without him."

"You're going to have plenty of time to reflect on it. I want you to report for mess hall cleaning duty after dinner, tonight and every other night for the next month."

Elya stiffened and lifted his chin. A normal person might have let their head droop, but not a Fleet pilot. "Yes, sir."

"And you're running extra training drills. No pilot under my command disobeys the orders of their superior officers and goes unpunished."

"Yes, sir. Very wise, sir."

"Did I ask for your opinion, Captain?"

"No, Admiral."

She let his words die and the following silence hang in the air. It felt good to see the young officers sweat and squirm.

"Captain Osprey, you're to join him for the first two weeks. The only reason you get a break is that you were able to locate and trap the Kryl parasite. I appreciate how you took the initiative there."

"Understood, sir. Thank you."

Captain Nevers opened his mouth, thought better of it, and closed his mouth again.

"What is it, Captain Nevers?"

"Sir, is the Kryl parasite still in your possession?"

"It's under guard in a sealed airlock. It was the only way I could be sure it wouldn't sneak back onto the ship or infect another one of my officers."

Captain Osprey visibly relaxed at this news.

"I need to show you both something," Captain Nevers said.

"What is it?"

"You'll have to see it to believe it, sir."

You'd be surprised what I've seen, boy, Kira thought. What she said was, "Very well. Lead the way."

A short walk across the *Paladin* brought the three—plus Harmony, who traveled invisibly through the halls and in Kira's mind, like a distant thought—to an unused airlock in a remote quadrant of the ship. If Fleet mechanics needed to send out bots, or sometimes even people, to make external repairs, they'd use one of these smaller airlocks.

The door had a rectangular window at the top and was flanked by four Fleet security guards. Each of the stoic soldiers bore a rifle slung over one shoulder. They also each had standard-issue SB-44 blasters holstered on their hips, and several stun grenades on their belts. One of them was almost as tall as Kira.

She hadn't needed to tell the guards to take precautions— the idea of a Kryl parasite scared the tar out of most SDF soldiers. But she did tell them to keep their assignment quiet. She preferred to keep the information under wraps. The last thing she needed was the Colonization Board catching wind of the parasite and pre-empting her efforts before she had a chance to present her case to the Executive Council or—best case scenario—to the Emperor himself.

The four guards came to attention as they approached.

"At ease, men. All right, Captain. What is it you wanted to show me?"

His eyes darted between her and the guards.

"Give us a little privacy, but keep us in your sights."

"Yes, sir."

A pair of guards moved down the hall in each direction.

"This is what I wanted to show you." He held up the artifact—the geode, he called it—by its handle. They'd retrieved it from a lockbox in the bridge on the way here. "A weapon made by the ancient Telos, I think. It has the power to harm the Kryl."

Kira blinked. "Really?"

She cast her memory back over her decades in the war against the Kryl. Of course, there had been rumors of advanced weaponry that could kill a hundred bugs with the push of a button, or do other fanciful things, but as far as she had been able to tell, those were war stories invented by bored or desperate soldiers. As an admiral, she had access to many classified documents on such subjects, and just as with incidents of so-called "space madness," there had always been a simpler and more rational explanation.

So far.

"Skepticism is a perfectly reasonable reaction, sir. If I hadn't seen it for myself, I'd have thought the same thing. Hedrick—the boy we brought back—tells me he found a golden cave where another object like this one had been kept, in the cave where the priest and his followers were hiding. Whether anyone else knew about the relic is unclear to me. What I do know is that when I turn this handle—" He mimed the action with his hand over the geode. "—it emits some kind of forcefield that causes excruciating pain to any Kryl within about thirty meters. I'm pretty good with machines, sir, and although I've examined it, I have no idea how it works. The best I can figure is that it emits radiation that is uniquely attuned to Kryl DNA."

As a veteran of many ugly battles with the Kryl, this idea immediately appealed to her. She imagined the special operations they could conduct with this tool. If it really did have the power to repel Kryl, it would give them a huge tactical advantage.

"Show me."

Elya nodded. "I'm not sure if it will work through the airlock door… but let's find out."

He turned around and walked toward the airlock. Captain Osprey stepped up to the window with Kira so they could both see the parasite in its tiny, sealed jar on the floor inside.

"How will we know if it's working?"

"You'll know."

Elya lifted the relic and rotated the handle one hundred and eighty degrees by applying just a hint of twisting pressure.

Kira didn't see anything at first. Then an emerald-tinted wave that distorted her vision, like a heat shimmer rising off the tarmac on a hot summer day, radiated outward from Elya's position. Even the guards down the halls flinched.

The Kryl parasite didn't just flinch. It blew itself up to five or six times its size, easily filling the container, and then used its inflated bulk to smash itself repeatedly against the side of the jar as it struggled to escape. It moved with such force that it knocked the jar onto its side and rattled around until Kira reached out and turned Elya's hands, deactivating the relic.

She kept her hands on top of his as Elya stared into her face with the whites of his eyes wide and glimmering. "Wouldn't want to let that thing loose, would you?"

"No, sir! I'm so sorry. I've seen this thing in use and even I didn't expect that strong a reaction, sir."

She took the geode back from him. He seemed only too happy to let it go. "How did you come by this artifact, Captain?"

He filled her in on how the colonists he'd taken shelter with had double crossed him, then tried to give the boy,

Hedrick, to the Kryl to be turned. The boy's life was a bargaining chip they intended to trade in exchange for protection from the Kryl.

Obviously, it didn't work out how they'd planned. And now she was angry knowing that someone had given a child to the xenos. Such an act was tantamount to murder.

With the practice of deep experience, Kira noticed the anger, thanked it for doing its job, and then let it go. It still took a second for the emotion to pass.

Into the silence, Nevers spoke again. "There's something else, sir."

Kira inhaled and refocused on the pilot.

"Subject Zero, the half-human, half-Kryl mutant I told you about... When I asked about this Overmind X, *she* took over and spoke to me through it. She said they would suck Robichar dry. She also said that she was after more relics. At least that's what it sounded like. She called them 'the weapons of the Ancient Ones.'"

Captain Osprey, who had been quietly stewing while Elya told his story, snapped her head up. "That can't be good."

"She said the relics were their 'Inheritance,' whatever that means."

Kira pursed her lips. *Are some of those war stories more true than even SDF intelligence realizes? No wonder the Kryl want the weapons for themselves. In the hands of the Solaran Empire, weapons that powerful could truly end the conflict with the Kryl once and for all.*

"It means we've just painted a big target on the side of our ship. Relics here, come and take 'em!" Captain Osprey spread her hands in the air as if hanging a marquee banner, then cleared her throat and clasped her hands behind her back. "Sir."

"You're not wrong, Captain," Kira said. "But at least if we

know what's coming, we can prepare. Did you get any sense that they'll come after this relic?"

"Maybe? Probably not while they're busy with Robichar. If what the boy says is true, there's at least one more relic there. Plus whatever the Kryl normally do to strip a habitable planet of its resources."

She nodded and fell into thought. There was much to do. Kira now had all the evidence she needed to make the Executive Council understand that a second wave of the Kryl War was coming, but if she meant to be *heard*, she'd need to get an audience with the Colonization Board and lay out the case in a way that could not be ignored.

She surfaced from her planning to see Osprey and Nevers arguing under their breath about something. "What is it?"

"Tell her," Captain Osprey said.

Nevers hesitated before gathering his courage to speak again. "I've loved watching footage of starfighter pilots flying since I was a kid. I'd recognize his face anywhere." He glanced at Osprey, whose eyes were hard as aluminite. "I believe that Subject Zero is—or was, at least—the legendary starfighter pilot, Captain Ruidiaz."

The hairs on the back of Kira's neck and arms stood on end at the same time as the chip in her neck heated up. She noticed Harmony's lights materialize in the hallway as the AI asked, "Are you certain?"

Nevers blinked at the AI. "I can't be a hundred percent sure, but yes, I'd bet on it. Whatever's happened has changed him, but... I know that face. It's Captain Ruidiaz. He's not dead after all."

The hallway suddenly tilted and Kira found herself on the floor, the geode rolling between her knees. She brushed a hand across her smooth crop of white hair. Her palm came away slicked with a cold sheen of sweat. Security guards rushed in.

"Sir!"

"Admiral! Are you okay?"

"Stop crowding her!" Captain Osprey barked. "Give her some space to breathe."

Kira swatted away the hands that didn't immediately jerk back. Her anger gave her strength. After a moment, she rose to her feet. Captain Osprey, Captain Nevers and the guards were all watching her with concern wrinkling their brows… She hated that look, hated seeing the pity in their eyes. It made her feel weak and small. It made her feel like she did when she'd lost him. Since his death, her every waking moment had been dedicated to doing everything in her power to never feel like this again.

Kira squared her shoulders. "I was there when Captain Ruidiaz sacrificed himself to save us all. I attended his funeral. I grieved him—for *years*. I've visited his grave, for Earth's sake. Whoever Subject Zero is, it's not Omar Ruidiaz." Her voice cracked when she spoke his full name. She took several deep breaths, waiting for someone to challenge her. No one did. "Omar is dead."

Kira turned sharply on her heel and marched away. She didn't want her officers to see her tears.

TWENTY-NINE

While he was shaken by Admiral Miyaru's reaction to the mere mention of Omar Ruidiaz, Elya gave the geode over to the security guards willingly enough. They let him tag along as they brought the artifact not back to the bridge, but to a secure vault located behind the bridge, itself situated within a detachable lifeboat known as the Ripcord.

The Ripcord had the ability to separate from the *Paladin* and transform into an autonomous stealth spacecraft, should the need arise. No captain worth her salt would abandon her ship, which was why this detachable unit was not part and parcel of the ship's bridge. The units had only needed to be used a handful of times in the Fleet's history. Each story of precious lives saved, of cargo delivered, was attached to a medal of valor or aluminite-plated memorial on Ariadne.

Once the relic was safely stowed and the door sealed, Elya realized he'd come to a decision. He had no interest in making history. He didn't want a plaque engraved with his name. The events of the past two days had helped him realize just how much he wanted to keep on living. It felt good to frag some Kryl drones along the way—any of his squadmates would heartily agree—but he wanted to live long enough to see the difference his efforts made in the galaxy. Not be turned into some mad science experiment for the Kryl and their insatiable hunger. He shuddered to imagine what would have happened to him had Osprey not found him. Or what might have happened to Hedrick, had Subject Zero been able to finish the transformation.

Or what was going to happen to those who had been left behind.

As for Father Pohl, somehow the priest had survived getting tackled by a sentinel. Elya had seen the priest stagger away from the violence clutching his gory eye socket. Charlie and his buddies had shot their way out over the bodies of dozens of dead groundlings. He hoped they'd brought enough ammo and power cores to last them a while. Without the artifact, they were screwed.

With these heavy thoughts for company, Elya paced through the halls of the *Paladin*, Hedgebot tailing him quietly. He was exhausted and, at the same time, still too wired up to sleep. The gunmetal gray corridors, curved slightly inward, seemed not to choke him, like they had before, but to unfurl before him, an endless path. He meandered aimlessly for a while, criss-crossing the ship as he took in the familiar sights and noises. He bobbed to music that drifted out of berths, inhaled the faint smell of soy and grease in the mess hall.

Until finally, he paused, looked up, and felt a huge grin spread across his face.

Elya rapped on the metal with his knuckles. The noise echoed in the corridor, then the round door split into petals and slid into the wall, revealing the inside of the berth. A private room in the otherwise empty guest quarters.

"You're back." Heidi stood there with a quizzical half smile on her face.

"I come bearing gifts."

The boy gasped and practically rocketed out of the bunk he'd been relaxing in.

"What's this for?" Heidi asked.

Elya stepped over the threshold and threw his hand into the air, releasing a small object that glinted metallically. It buzzed with a faint *whirrrr* and hovered in place.

Hedrick, whose brown hair was mussed from sleeping, stared wide-eyed at the bot's engines—miniaturized but functional.

"It looks just like your starfighter!" he shouted, hopping and pointing.

"That's because it *is* just like my starfighter. It's a scale model of the Sabre. And you control it with this." Elya handed a tablet over to the boy. Its corners were sharp, the quartz surface polished and shining. Hedrick accepted the device like it was an ancient treasure—cautiously, with a wide, awe-filled smile. "It's yours."

"Don't you need it?" Heidi asked.

"Nah, don't worry, I've got a backup."

This was his backup, but he could buy a new one when they got back to base at Ariadne. It would mean he'd send a bit less money home next month, but that was okay. It was for a good cause, one his mom would be proud to support. *Yeah,* he thought, *that feels right.*

"You didn't have to do that," Heidi whispered. He could tell she was barely holding back the tears.

"I wanted to."

"Thank you."

Elya met Hedrick's eyes, which took a moment as the boy was now circling beneath the miniature starfighter and staring up at it with his mouth hanging open. Elya thumbed over his shoulder toward Hedgebot, who hung upside down from one of the load-bearing struts in the hall behind him. "One more thing. I loaded some tutorials and games on there for you. If you want to learn how to build a bot like Hedgebot, or fly a skimmer, or anything else. There's thousands of holovids, hundreds of thousands of books. I copied over most of my library. Well. All the stuff you have clearance for."

The boy's eyes glistened, and he threw his arms around Elya's waist, gripping the back of his uniform tightly with his free hand while the other held the tab.

"Thank you, thank you, *thank you*," Hedrick whispered.

Elya knelt down to return the hug. He'd been just as grateful as Hedrick, once, to someone who had shown him a similar kindness. And now he knew that the ultimate reward was truly to be found in the giving.

THIRTY

Captain Casey Osprey walked into the rec and was greeted by salutes and rough claps on the back. Word had gotten around about how she'd found Nevers on Robichar, and also that she'd been working directly with Admiral Miyaru on some kind of security breach. Though many asked her for details, she declined to comment, following the wishes of her commander that such information be kept private.

At least for now.

She basked in the admiration of her colleagues and made small talk with several of them, exchanging stories of the fight, reliving the thrill of it as she recounted her experiences. Casey felt the joy as a low fire in her chest, warm and welcoming. And, for a change, that was more than enough.

After mingling, she searched again for the rest of her squad. They had promised to meet her here, but she didn't see them yet. She found an empty table with four chairs. Casey loved being in the rec, surrounded by the noises of revelry and celebration on the heels of a successful (if strange) mission. She decided there was nowhere she'd rather be. She watched the crowd, letting her mind drift peacefully.

Suddenly, the whole rec rose to their feet as a unit and began to clap.

Casey stood on her chair to see over the crowd and felt gooseflesh prickle her arms as a smile spread on her face. She whistled loudly and joined the applause as the rest of her squadmates stepped through the doorway.

Ever the showboat, Park raised a bandaged hand and then took an exaggerated bow. Naab had another bandage wrapped around his neck under his flight suit, and there were dark circles under his eyes, making them look bigger, and his face gaunter, than usual. Otherwise, he looked pretty good. Healthy. Alive. With a flourish, he reached into a jacket pocket and took out a hand-rolled spliff. Someone stepped out of the crowd of applauding pilots and sparked a lighter. He inhaled deeply and blew out a cloud of smoke. "I'm back. Now let's get this party started!"

Nevers and Yorra, flanking Park, made their way into the crowd behind him.

Yorra got plenty of congratulations, both for helping save Park's life (despite the commander's request they not talk about the parasite, it was impossible to keep stories of Naab's hospitalization from spreading), and for playing a key role in Nevers' rescue.

Captain Nevers, however, didn't make it two steps into the rec before he was thronged by curious pilots. He ran his hands through his thick, dark hair as he answered their questions and blushed. He patted the Hedgebot's metal head, who perched on his customary place on Nevers' shoulder and emitted a pulsing blue nimbus.

It was twenty minutes before Nevers finally peeled away from the questioners and came to join them at the table. He sighed as he sat down.

"You're a celebrity now, Fancypants!" Park said. He held an empty fist out, as if pointing a microphone at Nevers. "How's it feel?"

"Weird. Getting shot down is a dumb thing to be known for."

"They're not proud of you for getting shot down," Yorra said, "They're proud of you for surviving."

"I have you two to thank for that. I almost didn't get rescued, if you'll recall."

Nice to hear him acknowledge he didn't do it alone, Casey thought.

But Nevers' face was flushed and Casey could tell that while he was uncomfortable with all the attention, something about the experience had given him a renewed sense of confidence. He slouched in his chair and set Hedgebot carefully on the floor. The bot circled up next to his chair and laid his little head on Nevers' boot to rest. Casey noticed that he'd found a moment to replace the bot's missing leg with one that matched. His robot companion was whole again.

"Maybe we should change your call sign to Crash," Park joked. "Oh, wait! I've got a better one: Skid—for how you put that Sabre down belly first, skidding across the ground, and because you probably crapped your pants when you did it."

"I did not!"

"Easy for you to say. There weren't any witnesses."

"SKID," Gears mused, ticking off each word on a different finger. "Survived Kryl In Denial… of pooping his pants."

The three of them threw their heads back and laughed until tears streaked down their faces. Nevers rolled his eyes and smiled, but didn't object to being the source of their amusement. He waited for them to catch their breath.

"If it's all right with you guys, I think I'll stick with Fancypants."

"Yeah?"

"What can I say? It's grown on me."

"You know, those two refugees must be super thankful," Yorra said, wiping her eyes, "If it weren't for you, they'd be goners now. That's worth something, Fancy."

"Tell that to the rest of the people who got left behind on Robichar." Nevers' eyes focused on a middle distance.

"That's not your fault," Osprey insisted. "The priest's followers had the opportunity to evacuate with the rest of the population. They chose not to."

Nevers shook his head. "They still think Animus is going to protect them."

"Maybe. But you can't worry about that. That's not on you. If they hadn't double crossed you and left you for dead, you would have tried to rescue them, too."

Nevers bobbed his head back and forth. "Yeah, I would have. I wanted to." He nodded once, firmly. "You're right. I did everything I could, and a boy and his mother are alive because of us. That counts for something."

Naab produced four shot glasses from a hidden pocket in his flight suit. He set them down on the table. Gears pulled out a flask and filled each glass up with a rich amber liquid.

"To Fancy," Park said, raising his glass, "for living to fight another day."

"To the squad," Nevers added, "for refusing to give up on me."

"To Lieutenant Colonel Walcott," Yorra said, "who gave his life to protect us."

"To the Fleet," Casey said, "who keep Solarans everywhere safe from the xeno scourge."

They tossed back their shots and slammed the glasses, face down, on the table.

Nevers got up and grabbed a cup from the shelves that held all the games. "So," he said, rattling the dice in the cup, "Who's up for a game of aleacc?"

THIRTY-ONE

The stone door dissolved into its constituent particles, revealing a golden chamber beyond.

Omar Ruidiaz clicked his mandibles, the Kryl equivalent of rubbing your hands together with excitement. The habit had disgusted him when he'd first realized he was doing it, but by now he had grown used to some of the tics and habits imparted by the Kryl half of his altered genes. It still gave him the shivers when his extra legs extended from his back, and even thinking about it now made them twitch where they were folded, hidden, beneath a layer of armored carapace. Fortunately, they only insisted on coming out when he was truly angry or frightened, and that was not the emotion driving him forward now.

Omar shoved the priest into the chamber ahead and looked around for traps. The frail man stumbled forward, favoring his bad leg as he staggered to the angled side-wall, as far away from Omar as the narrowing room would allow. "Here it is. This is what you wanted, right?"

No lasers or spikes sprang from the walls. The room remained quiet.

Omar smiled, which made the priest grimace, so Omar smiled even wider. He enjoyed watching people squirm. He didn't spend a lot of time among full bred humans these days, and it was one of the things he most enjoyed when he did get the opportunity. He used to do the same when he was hazing rookie pilots in the Fleet. Not all his memories from his life before had stuck with him through his long and painful transformation. The memories that did stick tended to be of people at their most vulnerable—wounded, hurt, or at least deeply uncomfortable.

Father Pohl glared at him. His gaping eye socket had been covered over with a bandage. "I gave you what you asked for, now let my people go."

Omar shoved down a strong instinct to rip off the gauze and explore the inside of the man's skull with his tongue. *Patience.* "I need to confirm the artifact is what you say it is, first."

The priest scowled, then turned and limped to the dais at the far end of the room.

Omar observed the glyphs carved into the walls, the golden sheen over the stones, the way everything in here seemed to glow, as if the very rock itself gave off light—as if it was made not of sand and stone, but of stardust. He set each foot carefully down in front of the other, tense, expecting a trap. The ancient race of beings known as the Telos had a reputation for being very clever. The other chambers Overmind X had shown him, memories glimpsed through their shared consciousness, had been rigged with explosives, or designed to self-destruct at the first hint of Kryl. Although the Telos vanished from the universe over ten thousand years ago, the booby traps they left behind were as destructive as the day they were planted.

That was, after all, why she had expended so much time and energy on his transformation. Omar's genetic sequence,

Solaran mixed with Kryl, confused the Telos technology enough to let him simply step through most of their defenses.

It seemed to be having the intended effect here. Of course, it probably helped that the defensive artifact which used to be kept here had been taken by the Solarans to their ships. Overmind X had been furious that such a valuable piece of Telos technology had fallen into Solaran hands. They could use it to cause real damage, if they woke up to the reality of its true potential. The upside, however, was that the relic's removal seemed to have left this chamber unprotected.

Omar had the idea that his fate would have been different, had he possessed such a powerful relic. He didn't know exactly why, or how, he would have used such a weapon to change things, but the thought tugged at the back of his mind, on the tattered fringe of a distant memory...

His thoughts scurried back into the dark hole they emerged from when the priest plucked a stone orb from the carving of a giant pair of hands with too many knuckles, and shoved it at him.

"See for yourself," he snarled.

Omar was careful to grab the smooth stone with his human—as opposed to his Kryl—hand. He felt it reach its tendrils into his flesh, probing, seeking, verifying...

The orb shuddered. *Come on!* he thought furiously, trying to get the thing under control. Overmind X would be extremely displeased if this didn't work. It would have been so much easier if he'd managed to convert the human child. Such a child wouldn't be encumbered by the Kryl parts Overmind X had been forced to include in Omar's haphazard transformation. The evolved parasite she'd created afterward was designed to work on children who were still early enough in their development that the parasite could take root and work itself into the genome over time without causing them lasting physical harm.

Just when he was wondering if any of the priest's other surviving followers were young enough to produce such a child, and how Overmind X might help accelerate the process, the ancient relic in his hand quit trembling and opened for him, its petals unfurling like a flower.

Pieces of rock and specks of light separated themselves as they rose into the air over his head. They moved apart until they resembled a map of the galaxy—but he didn't recognize any of the systems, despite his years of experience reading such starmaps.

Lifting his hand, Omar extended one finger and made slow, clockwise circles in the air. The specks of rock that represented planets began to churn around their respective stars. Slowly, at first, and then faster, until the whole array of objects and light were swirling like a storm. After several minutes, the storm slowed, then stopped. He rewound it slightly until he found the point in time he was searching for.

The present.

He searched until he found Robichar, checked it against Overmind X's collective memory of the system. They matched. His mandibles rubbed against each other.

Well done, my child, a voice whispered in his mind. *Very well done. We finally have a starmap to guide our search.*

Omar made another gesture Overmind X had taught him. Bright beacons of light shot up from four different planetary bodies. Of the seven major relics they knew about, three had already been retrieved. There was the one Omar wore sewn into his belt, which gave him and anything he touched the ability to phase through solid objects; the one Overmind X carried, the source of her knowledge of the Telos; and the one the Solarans had taken from Father Pohl, reputed to be the last of the artifacts, the one that resonated on a destructive frequency with the Kryl genome. That left four major relics in their original resting places, their powers waiting to be discovered.

He turned to Father Pohl, who had grown pale and very quiet.

"Your people are free to go," Omar said.

"Thank Animus." The man closed his eyes. His Adam's apple bobbed as he swallowed. "You'll let us live in peace?"

Omar nodded slowly, trying to keep his mandibles from rubbing together. "Your people are safe."

"May the Spirit of Old Earth protect us. Thank you. Thank you."

As Father Pohl spun on his heel, Omar's mandibles began to clack a rapid staccato. In a single fluid motion, he reached out and drew a sharpened talon across the exposed front of the priest's neck. Blood sprayed across the walls of the golden chamber. The man's limp body crumpled to the floor.

Omar fell on him, drinking greedily, lapping at the blood that poured down the priest's neck.

Like the priest, it was too late for all of the Solaran Empire. They just didn't know it yet.

Next in the Series

Grab the next book, *Hidden Relics*, and read on to find out what Overmind X and Subject Zero's next gambit will be…

How Kira breaks the bad news to the Colonization Board…

Why Casey erupts over the arrival of her new squadron commander…

And what new trouble Elya lands himself in while digging for the truth about Telos relics.

Get it now: *Hidden Relics*

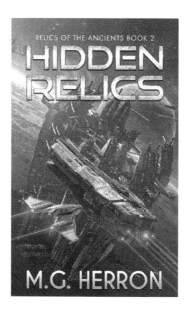

THANK YOU

I have a lot of people to thank for helping to bring this project to life.

My wife, Shelly, whose unwavering support and belief in me has lifted me up more times than I can count. Without her, none of this would be possible.

All the freelancers who have contributed to this project deserve to be mentioned by name: the artist Elias Stern, Vivid Covers for typography, and my editors Amy Teegan and Steve Statham.

Let's not forget the military veterans and pilots who read early versions of *Starfighter Down* and corrected my many mistakes and goof-ups: my father, Colonel James Herron (US Air Force); Lt. Colonel Tim Hebel (US Air Force); combat journalist Sullivan Laramie (US Army); Chief Warrant Officer Jerry Leake (US Army); and commercial pilot Jenny Avery. These people taught me a lot, and any mistakes with flight mechanics that might have snuck through the rigorous editing process are my own!

Beta readers, including those above, helped me improve

the story and they deserve a special mention, too. Specifically, Bob Truman, Wayne Key, and Paula Adler.

And the following readers jumped in to help with proofreading and catching flubs and errors in the first novel: H Chesno, Jenny Avery, James Green, Wayne Key and Maureen Henn.

Special Thanks to Kickstarter Heroes

This series was first launched on Kickstarter! The campaign raised $12k in 4 weeks, and it wouldn't have been possible without the support of these heroes. A special shoutout to:

Tim Hebel, Jennifer Whitesell, Jacob Moyer, Gregory Clawson, Jerry Leake, James Herron, Tim Cross, Leigh, Lawrence Tate, Sebastián, Tyler Prince, Adam Knuth, MJ Caan, Jacen Spector, Jerome, Chad Anthony Randell, Linda Schattauer, Peyton, Marouane Jerraf, Mette Lundsgaard, Destin Floyd, Pierino Gattei, Rhett and Kathy Leonard, Dietrich Thompson, Becky Herron, Missy Burrows, Cindy Lorion, Chris Wooster, Lauren Appa, Nikhil Daftary, and Joe Bunting.

ALSO BY M.G. HERRON

Translocator Trilogy

The Auriga Project

The Alien Element

The Ares Initiative

The Translocator (Books 1-3)

The Gunn Files

Culture Shock

Overdose

Quantum Flare

The Gunn Files (Books 1-3)

Other Books

The Republic

Boys & Their Monsters

Get science fiction and fantasy reading recommendations from MG
Herron delivered straight to your inbox. Join here:
mgherron.com/bookclub

ABOUT THE AUTHOR

M.G. Herron writes science fiction and fantasy for adrenaline junkies.

His books explore new worlds, futuristic technologies, ancient mysteries, various apocalypses, and the vagaries of the human experience.

His characters have a sense of humor (except for the ones who don't). They stand up to strange alien monsters from other worlds... unless they slept through their alarm again.

Like ordinary people, Herron's heroes sometimes make mistakes, but they're always trying to make the universe a better place.

Find all his books and news about upcoming releases at mgherron.com.

f 🐦

Made in the USA
Columbia, SC
24 October 2021

47653853R10200